Praise for *High Cotton*

"This is a beautifully written book. Its young-man-speaking-from-memory quality is powerful, original, fresh, and funny."
—Jamaica Kincaid

"Pinckney has upped the ante on depiction of black America. In a book rife with irony, fantasy, humor, and historical detail, Pinckney has created a gallery of characters whose quirks and passions ring with a truth previously forgotten or ignored."
—*San Francisco Chronicle*

"*High Cotton* is witty, powerful, intriguing, and insightful. But more than this, it's honest—sometimes painfully honest—in its portrayal of black life in America."
—*The Washington Times*

"*High Cotton* is tight and elliptical. . . . One is richly rewarded. . . . This writer's debut as a novelist is an auspicious one."
—*Chicago Tribune*

"An extraordinary accomplishment . . . This tender, often droll portrait of one young life is also an arrestingly mature, original account of the condition of being black through several generations and of America in the sixties—a major part of our history. It is also beautifully written, exhilaratingly intelligent, and a joy to read."
—Susan Sontag

"Powerful and important . . . Pinckney is showing us what it is to be a part of a transitional generation, living neither in the present nor in the past."
—*New York Newsday*

"Stunningly brilliant . . . *High Cotton* has sharp prose, witty insights, scholarly asides and quotations, and progressive narrative techniques that make it a strong work."
—*The Philadelphia Inquirer*

"Pinckney's wit can be both cutting and generous. He is fluent in the joys of the absurd. But *High Cotton* is more than picaresque. It raises fundamental questions about what it means to be black in America."
—*Mirabella*

CONTEMPORARY AMERICAN FICTION

HIGH COTTON

Educated at Columbia, Darryl Pinckney has been a Hod-
der Fellow at Princeton and a recipient of grants from
the Ingram-Merrill, the Mrs. Giles Whiting, and the
Guggenheim Foundations. His work has appeared in
many publications, including *Granta* and *The New York
Review of Books*. He now lives in Berlin, where he is completing a critical book on Afro-American literature.

HIGH

COTTON

Darryl

Pinckney

PENGUIN BOOKS

PENGUIN BOOKS
Published by the Penguin Group
Penguin Books USA Inc.,
375 Hudson Street, New York, New York 10014, U.S.A.
Penguin Books Ltd, 27 Wrights Lane, London W8 5TZ, England
Penguin Books Australia Ltd, Ringwood, Victoria, Australia
Penguin Books Canada Ltd, 10 Alcorn Avenue,
Toronto, Ontario, Canada M4V 3B2
Penguin Books (N.Z.) Ltd, 182–190 Wairau Road,
Auckland 10 New Zealand

Penguin Books Ltd., Registered Offices:
Harmondsworth, Middlesex, England
First published in the United States of America by
Farrar Straus Giroux, 1992
Published in Penguin Books 1993

1 3 5 7 9 10 8 6 4 2

Illustration on title page: detail from *Dawn in Harlem* by
Winold Reiss from the collection of Beth and James DeWoody.

PUBLISHER'S NOTE:
This is a work of fiction. Names, characters, places and incidents either are the product of the author's imagination or are used fictitiously, and any resemblance to actual
persons, living or dead, events, or locales is entirely coincidental.

THE LIBRARY OF CONGRESS HAS CATALOGUED THE HARDCOVER AS FOLLOWS:
Pinckney, Darryl.
High cotton / Darryl Pinckney.
I. Title.
PS3566.I516H5 1992
813´.54–dc20 91–23158
ISBN 0-374-16998-5 (hc.)
ISBN 0 14 01.7503 2 (pbk.)
Printed in the United States of America

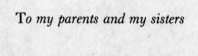

To my parents and my sisters

In the negro countenance you will often meet with strong traits of benignity. I have felt yearnings of tenderness toward some of these faces—or rather masks—that have looked out kindly upon one in casual encounters in the streets and highways. I love what Fuller calls these "images of God cut in ebony." But I should not like to associate with them, to share my meals and my good nights with them—because they are black.

C h a r l e s   L a m b

HIGH COTTON

1 / *The New Negro*

No one sat me down and told me I was a Negro. That was something I figured out on the sly, late in my childhood career as a snoop, like discovering that babies didn't come from an exchange of spinach during a kiss. The great thing about finding out I was a Negro was that I could look forward to going places in the by and by that I would not have been asked to as a white boy.

There was nothing to be afraid of as long as we were polite and made good grades. After all, the future, back then, assembled as we were on the glossy edge of the New Frontier, belonged to us, the Also Chosen. The future was something my parents were either earning or keeping for my two sisters and me, like the token checks that came on birthdays from grandparents, great-uncles, great-aunts.

The future was put away for us, the way dark blue blazers were put away until we could grow into them, the way meatloaf was wrapped up for the next nervous quiz meal and answers to our stormy looks were stored up for that tremendous tomorrow. Every scrap of the future mattered, but I didn't have to worry my breezy head about it because someone was seeing to things and had been ever since my great-grandfather's grandmother stepped on the auction block.

All men were created equal, but even so, lots of mixed messages with sharp teeth waited under my Roy Rogers pillow. You were just as good as anyone else out there, but they—whoever "they" were—had rigged things so that you had to be close to perfect just to break even. You had nothing to fear, though every time you left the house for a Spelling Bee or a Music Memory Contest the future of the future hung in the balance. You were not an immigrant, there were no foreign accents, weird holidays, or funny foods to live down, but still you did not belong to the great beyond out there; yet though you did not belong it was your duty as the Also Chosen to get up and act as though you belonged, especially when no one wanted you to.

You had nothing to be ashamed of, though some of the Also Chosen talked in public at the top of their lungs, said "Can I get" instead of "May I have," and didn't say "please" ever. United we stood, which did not include everyone on the block. It wasn't right to think you were better than your neighbor, but it also wasn't smart to want to be like the kids who ran up and down the alley all day and were going to end up on a bad corner in front of a record shop dancing under the phonograph speaker strapped above the door.

Forgiveness was divine, but people who moved away from you at the movies, tried to short-change you at the new shopping mall, or didn't want you to have a table at the Indianapolis Airport restaurant would get what was coming to them, though they acted that way because they didn't know any better. All you had to do was ignore them, pretend you hadn't heard. Those who dwelled in the great beyond out there could not stop His truth from marching on, but until His truth made it as far as restricted Broadripple Park, you did not go swimming, because even the wading pool at Douglas Park had something floating in it that put your mother off. Douglas Park was not much fun. There were no train engines to climb over, no hand-carved carousels. The YMCA that met there let its beginning swimmers splash naked. Your father could step around whatever turned up in the water as often as he liked, but if you and your sisters got sick from swallowing something other than chlorine your mother was going to go back to her mother in Atlanta and never speak to your father again.

To know where you were going, you had to know where you'd come from, though the claims that the past had on you were like cold hands in the dark. Those elderly relatives, old-timers in charcoal-gray suits and spinsters in musty fox tails, who went out of their way to come to Indianapolis to have a look at you, those wizards licking gold fillings and widows coughing on their bifocals whom you didn't want to travel miles and miles or eat ice cream with—they were among the many pearly reasons you had to hold your Vaselined head high, though you were never to mention in company your father's Uncle Ralph Waldo, who had lived the blues so well that he wound up in a nuthouse without the sense he was born with because of a disease. Grand-father Eustace spelled its name so fast not even your sisters were able to catch the letters.

Above all, you had to remember that no one not family was ever going to love you really. The Also Chosen were one big happy family, though the elderly relatives who hung over holi-days like giant helium balloons couldn't stand the sight of one another, which gave fuel to the blue flame of confidences and bitter fine points that burned until the stars folded up. Sometimes the old-timers seemed to be all there was. They far outnumbered their younger relatives. The family tapered off, depopulated itself from shelf to shelf, but the ranks of the old-timers promised never to thin. They enlisted the departed in their number, on their side, which added to their collective power to dominate those of you who would never know what they knew.

The old-timers boasted of their ability to bug you from the grave, saying one day you'd want to talk to them and they wouldn't be there anymore. They'd hint that they'd be watching you closely from wherever they went when they passed on. Your dearest reminded you every morning of the problem that you would never, never get away from. However, escape I did, the burden of consciousness was lifted from my round little shoulders, and for a while there I was gorgeously out of it.

Grandfather Eustace was the emperor of out-of-it, yet he was also a distinguished man who tried, in his way, to answer all the questions. Even before I was old enough to listen he was crouched in the prompter's box, anxious to pass on that record of alienated majesty. I spent much of my life running from him, centripetal fashion, because he was, to me, just a poor old darky. I did not return his phone calls, I cashed in his train tickets, I went to the movies when he came to visit, but he was forever rising through the waves of my denial, sustained by the knowledge that he, his father and mother before him, his brothers and sisters, his sons and daughters, were a sort of dusky peerage with their degrees, professions, and good marriages among their own kind.

"Your grandfather," my father once said, "suffered from being black at a time when everyone was white." Grandfather Eustace never let us forget that he had been educated in the Holy Land: at Brown and Harvard. He was a terrible snob, his pride somehow outrageous and shaky at the same time. He had a finely developed idea of his own worth and enjoyed, like ill health, the suspicion that no one else shared it. He took the high road, but because he made the journey in a black body he lived with the chronic dread that maybe he wasn't good enough.

Grandfather acted out his contradictions in high-handed style. One of his brothers with whom he carried on a lifelong feud pointed out that before Grandfather became a minister he failed to hold on to the simplest clerk's job because he could never get along with his superiors or co-workers. Even after he became a man of the cloth more than one quiet church went to extraordinary lengths to rid itself of the "dicty spade" who wore his learning on his sleeve and pitched his sermons over the heads of the supplicants.

Yet it was for their sakes that he was called to God. He loved to be among what he called the honest folk and preferred to be the only emissary from the Talented Tenth—Du Bois's elect, whose education was to be like a beacon to the unwashed. Believing that they looked up to him, Grandfather was consumed by a passion for the poor, the forgotten. His vocation revealed itself one twilight during the Depression when he found himself wandering through Yamacraw, the red-light district that clung by its fingernails to the rib cage of railroad in Savannah, Georgia. Yamacraw was so violent that the police never crossed the tracks.

Surrounded by fired-up types, Grandfather began to bother their heads with visions of his own. The sons of Belial calmed down, and in a delirium of relief Grandfather talked on and sang and lamented. Hardly anyone followed what he said, but it sounded like the gospel truth because the theatrical, sorrowful young crackpot who stood before them with his arms stretched toward the rain clouds was touched with such a command of the language of the other side. He wasn't drunk and he didn't pass the hat, which proved that he was a cut above the usual jackleg Bible thumpers who cried out every Saturday night. Yamacraw carried him, the man they themselves might have been, into tin-roof shacks and fed him turnip greens. When they grew restless with his hootch-free eloquence, the messenger accepted an escort back to the fringes of decent Savannah. They left him serene in the flivver dust, in the middle of a digression on Pascal's wager.

Grandfather never got over the admiration in those faces, the rapt attention, the melancholy shadows thrown by the dented kerosene lamps. He also never again preached like that, but the Word meanwhile had become flesh.

Grandfather couldn't help himself. Whenever he opened the door he was on a mission to prove that the world didn't know whom it was dealing with. He came from the Old Country. Not Lithuania, not Silesia. The Old Country, to us, meant Virginia, Georgia, the Carolinas, spectral mileposts of cane swamp and pine, remote tidewater counties swollen with menacing lore. He was born in 1898, in "the quarters" on a farm near Dublin, Georgia. Sherman's march to the sea had left former slaves and masters together, ruined and forlorn. Decades later, devastation lingered over the region like a corrosive fume.

Grandfather considered it good form not to talk to us about the hardships he had witnessed, just as his grandfather had thought it wise not to speak too truthfully about his years in bondage. Instead, Grandfather told of stealing melons as a boy. He remembered, for me, the sweetness of the dropping peaches, walking behind the plowmen and their mules, fishing in the silvery creeks, the scent of scrub oak, of turpentine stills, the thrill of hearing at night the consoling songs of toil and deliverance. No more auction block for me.

Grandfather's real story, the one he never told, began, as they say, earlier than he. Perhaps his ancestors lived on the savannahs of Benin; no one knows. They were lost to us in the aorta of history. Certainly his forebears endured the voyage known as the Middle Passage. They were dragged from Africa to Charleston, South Carolina, to the potentates of mercantilism, in coffles aboard ships with names gratifying to their captains—*Swan, Hannibal, Temperance, Desire.* Grandfather liked to say that his family had arrived before the Pilgrims, but after that he gave no more thought to them than he did to stuffed mammals in a children's museum. He, too, knew the famous paradox that a slave could be punished for a crime, but an ox could not commit one.

"Is it possible that any of my slaves could go to heaven and I must meet them there?"

Grandfather's grandfather Limus remembered Crescent Plantation and the legendary occult practices of the pagan, Old Bess, who was his grandmother—maybe. "Old Bess pretends to be mad and works not." Limus was something of a blacksmith, more of a farmer, and every inch of the way a true believer. Limus, born a slave and buried "free," belonged, in Grandfather's mind, to that strange, unsalvageable land of smallpox and murder, of hot hours over slow-burning kilns, palmetto brooms, bunched guinea corn, rice fields. Grandfather had Limus saying at the age of eighty in 1905, "The family was always kind and considerate of its slaves."

Grandfather's father, born in a new black town, Promised Land, South Carolina, the year the freedmen were enfranchised, was called Esau or "Free," the most common nickname of the period. Limus was against Esau's leaving the land. "You have no need that anyone should teach you." But a bush said his name and, spreading the Word like chicken feed, Esau set off for the Atlanta Baptist Seminary, an enthusiastic college for black men that began in a church basement. Esau took with him little but the name of the English planter family, those Carolinians—what were they to him?—who'd signed the Constitution, made speeches on the desertion of slaves, negotiated with Talleyrand, twice failed to win the Presidency, and boasted of not using nets as protection against malaria-carrying mosquitoes, because to these failed Presidents nets were effeminate.

It was said that Esau sold berries to raise money, and if not berries something for nickels and dimes. The Atlanta Baptist Seminary was embraced, he fretted over the character of his namesake in the Bible, and when he was ordained who was there? Hannah Lloyd, a student at the Atlanta Baptist Female Seminary across the road, one of the little earnest pioneers cloistered and finished for the future of the race. With Esau their future of rectitude was not far from home.

They were married outdoors, on what had been a drill ground for Union troops, and then assigned to the missionary field in southern Georgia, a large territory that included part of the nasty tarheel of Florida. Grandfather's mother, "Pass Me Not Hannah," they called her, daughter of the Atlanta Baptist Female Seminary, was something of an heiress, so they said, so Grandfather liked to say—a thousand acres and silver spoons to ladle the gravy even after the price of cotton fell.

Hannah's Seminole blood made her quick-tempered, they said, and she was strict with her five boys and merciless with her three daughters. She called on the saints to strengthen her paddle, "the household persuader," against sass and shiftlessness. Grandfather and his brothers were good swimmers, but the local hole was declared off-limits because Hannah feared that the boys who went there, black and white, would expose her sons to disease and bad grammar. They learned to keep to themselves on their paved street, or to play in abandoned "big houses" overgrown with Maréchal Niel roses.

Esau settled down as pastor of the Thankful Baptist Church in Augusta, Georgia, in 1912. The poetry of Paul Laurence Dunbar went on Hannah's Index, as did tunes like "Under the Bamboo Tree," and to dance was to taste the apple, though she was pleased to claim W. C. Handy as her husband's friend. Instead of these pleasures, there were the glories of George Lofton's

Biblical Thoughts and Themes for Young Men and Women, many histories of Jesus, illustrated Scripture galleries, Tennyson, and W.E.B. Du Bois, whose every utterance was taken as an addition to the King James Version.

Nothing unpleasant ever broke through the narcotic of Grandfather's nostalgia, though the traditional horrors actually happened. What now seems tired was then fresh. Esau came home wet with whiskey after some provincials, the parlor word for crackers, ordered him to drink and shuffle, and backed up their threats by shooting at his feet. One night Esau hid under the floorboards of a forsaken country church while the necktie party that had elected him honored guest of the hickory tree raged over the benches. Grandfather hoarded these memories. Those that he handed out freely, the gentle yarns improvised during sermons and radio talks, gave him a satisfaction not unlike watching someone who has power of attorney sift through a shoebox of Confederate dollars.

One by one Esau commended his sons to the high school attached to his alma mater, renamed Morehouse College, from which rock Grandfather and his brothers were catapulted North. Hannah in her collar and the three dazed daughters in their pegged skirts watched the caboose for a sign. This was the eve of the Great War and the Great Migration, when thousands upon thousands of black people got up and quit the South. Grandfather said that the emptying of a town like Augusta was so sudden it was like the lancing of a wound.

> *We have enough, but not too much*
> *To long for more.*

Grandfather enrolled in Brown University in 1917 and failed his first English essay assignment, "How to Carve a Turkey." Everyone on College Hill wanted to be an officer. Grandfather surrendered to the Army Training Corps. He sat in chilly alphabetical order with every other nervous freshman, but army rules did not permit the six black students to eat or sleep among whites. During exercises they were set up as a separate squad at the foot of the column, with space left for imaginary soldiers. But no amount of serge could help him to pass muster at Sigma Phi Delta.

"Don't go where you're not wanted," a handbook of etiquette published before the thaw advised black youth. Grandfather was enchanted with the Harvard Summer School before President Lowell swore to preserve the dormitories as God had intended them. He found it hard to stay away. *Ulmus procera, Ulmus hollandica, Ulmus hollandica belgica* in the Yard, the winged fruit cascading to the ground before the oval leaves opened, just as Du Bois might have seen them.

"I was desperately afraid of intruding where I was not wanted; appearing without invitation; of showing a desire for the company of those who had no desire for me," Du Bois said. To spare the dignity of his classmates, he read with Santayana in an attic and the only teacher he could recall who asked him home was William James.

"School was joy unconfined," Grandfather said. The shock of hearing the wireless for the first time; the falling thunder of the Army-Navy game; the stillness of the heavy Providence snowfalls; tea in Boston with the poet William Braithwaite and his wife; Roland Hayes, the great gentleman tenor, at Symphony Hall; the surprise of the college president, Dr. Faunce, offering his hand at chapel; the obscure lodgings that had the "goody" who came to sweep, the fireplace he filled with soft coals, rooms in his memory animated with cordial struggles over the Dyer

Anti-Lynching Bill and the merits of the football genius Coach
Robinson.

He rushed back, in 1921, with a Bachelor of Philosophy degree, to Harvard and Thomas Nixon Carver, his gruff professor
of economics. He would have remained forever in the Indian
summer of graduate school had he not, between lectures on so-
cialism and single taxism, fetched his bride from the Lucy Lane
School and Hampton College, an Augusta girl with misleading
Pre-Raphaelite hair, and embarked on the first of his several
calamitous meditations as a businessman. "Teach us, O Lord, to
know the value of money. So many of us are spending what we
do not earn," Du Bois said.

Long before white people began to jump from windows,
Grandfather was broke, beating a retreat from South Station. It
was the custom, back then, for black passengers to carry food;
once over the Mason-Dixon line they were not invited to the
dining car. Grandfather trained his young family in knee pants
to ride hungry rather than see his wife tote a basket.

When the price of bread had fallen, when the breadlines were
segregated, when his children were deposited at the table of his
mother-in-law, the black people of Savannah asked Grandfather
why he kept a box of day-old bread by his steps and received
the white hobos who hated him. He said, "Christ said feed the
poor." Blacks did not take to the boxcars and roads, for fear of
being picked up and sent to the chain gangs. "If someone reported
you, you were gone." But tramps walked down Route 17, the
coastal highway, all night long on their way to hunt for winter
work in Florida.

Grandfather reinvented himself as a gentleman farmer purified
by error. Mistake number one: in 1926 he resigned after six
months as principal of Booker T. Washington, the new high

school in Atlanta, to become one of the millionaire strivers fawned over in the upbeat Negro press. After speculations in steamship cargo, livestock futures, mechanical washer wringers, and asphyxiated baby chicks not a foot of top soil from what his mother and father had left him—if they had—remained to be put up as collateral. "The poor die differently from everyone else," he said.

Grandfather resigned as superintendent of schools for a county that, in deference to his Yankee education, had paid fifteen instead of twelve dollars a week. He pushed off on a bicycle to sell life insurance for a dime. When that didn't work, he traded in his trouser clamps for a Model T and sold policies for a quarter. They said he had just enough charm to snare quail. Then he walked out of Thunderbolt because his colleagues at Georgia State College were "teaching some ignorance." Success didn't like him, his brothers said.

"What is more aromatic than a pig roasting on a cold, clear morning?" Grandfather learned to farm from catalogues and almanacs. He wouldn't say who made the down payment on the six sandy acres outside Savannah where he studied the Depression, the "siege of misery and want." To pay for fertilizer, he taught algebra and English at Dorchester Academy, a vague Congregational church school in the sticks that was nevertheless better than the county schools.

Wanting his respect for nature to be of the transcendental variety, he suppressed the truth of how hard he worked his land. As it turned out, it took more than philosophy for a black man to dig brass out of the hills.

Figs and pomegranates, unsuitable to the climate, wilted. His brothers said that Grandfather could grow or breed everything, he just couldn't sell anything. Vandals destroyed the plum, the pecan, the umbrella china trees, and Grandfather played, with delicate outrage, the hand he was dealt. He heard the screech owls in the persimmon and obeyed: Arise and go to the city.

The Holy Spirit, his heritage, had been waiting, like medicine on the shelf, and never mind that he pretended he had accepted a position with the family concern, much like his classmates back on Beacon or Chestnut Hill whom he could not afford to dream about. Never mind that he went into the church because, in the end, he had no place else to go.

Old Esau had been a kind of down-home *Misnagid*, but Grandfather signed on with the Congregational Church, the smallest denomination in the black South, in remembrance of what he thought of as the hale New England character and the abolitionists who had swarmed out of the North to plant schools in the red clay. The faithful beat their cardboard fans of lurid funeral-home advertisements like wings, waiting for the zeal of His house to eat up Grandfather even a little bit. "If you can't whoop and holler you might as well do something else," an experienced preacher with a hip flask told him. Perhaps in some cupboard of Grandfather's mind the Congregational Church was an extension of Boston's Somerset Club.

Back then, to belong to the Congregational Church, a black had to pass the "paper-bag test"—"bright and damn near white." Grandfather was the darkest bag they'd ever let in. His constant worry was not that he was a black man but that he was a dark black man. Of his brothers and sisters the ones he liked least also happened to be the lightest. The condescension of high yellows hurt. He was easily riled around his wife's family. Their almond complexions told the old Dixie story. His mother-in-law was the daughter of a governor's son. She had seen her father only once, when he slapped her mother. She married a boy who also sprang from mustard and cracker seeds. They wore their fair skin lightly, as a trick on governor's mansions. They could have crossed over, and that, combined with their shrewd business sense, provoked Grandfather.

He told his wife that because her mother was a bastard her

mother was no good. "Don't ever become an educated fool," my grandmother's mother once told me, her blue eyes slitted with contempt for the Big Dipper pilots she had known, chief among them Grandfather, the king of spades.

She said the smartest man she ever knew, her mother's father, could read only a little. He was also the meanest man who ever lived. He worked for the railroads. Because of the Indian in him, she said, he had a girlfriend at every stop. The whites couldn't take away his job until they stopped using wood to fuel the engines. He never forgot that his life was a living battle and had never tried to dress it up as anything else. Great-grandmother sucked her dental bridge and said that Grandfather's revelation, his maiden sermon ventilated before the sinners of Yamacraw, had about it, like everything else he did in those mongrel years, a touch of the psychotic.

He once gave a sermon fifty miles south of Savannah. The church in the little clearing was so rustic you could see between the slats. He told the turned-up heads that if they wanted to believe in God, they had to walk the last mile and accept those who hated them. "Write me as one that loves his fellow man." The black people, some in overalls, said it was the most wonderful sermon they'd ever heard. Even so, the church did not ask Grandfather to hurry back. They were used to hell-raising preaching. They wanted to be told that they couldn't be thieves, that they couldn't be fornicators.

The schoolteacher among them had never heard of "Abou Ben Adhem." He didn't doubt that Grandfather loved the poem, but he suspected that Grandfather also loved his love of it, and how much this love had impressed the whites who had come just to hear him, taking it for granted that the front pews had been reserved for them. Unsuspecting, Grandfather climbed into his used Touring Hudson with the canvas top that rode like a tractor, thinking he'd introduced them to one of the higher things in life.

Grandfather needed his history with him at all times, like an inhaler. He ran over a hunting dog in a colony of peckerwood cabins. "Come quick, this nigger done killed our dog." In his secondhand suit from Millsby Lane & Son, Grandfather brazened an apology. A white man in yellow galoshes squinted. "You that nigger preacher? That dog wasn't worth a damn. Let him go on."

But Grandfather wasn't that easy to get rid of. Drive the nail where the wood is thickest—in the hollow, motor idling, quoting Longfellow to the rednecks of Brunswick, Georgia, a pastor who would be free all his life of the moans and groans and writhings of the evangelical, appalled by the gold, by the grasping glitter of the modern usurpers of the old faith.

For all I knew as a child Grandfather Eustace came from an Oldsmobile. He rarely made the trip to see us, because we lived on the wrong side of Indianapolis, "right there with the hoi polloi." Ours was the ugliest house on the block, Grandfather Eustace said, and for once my father didn't hand him any back-talk. In the spring it submitted to new coats of paint, and after the wood had absorbed enough labor, the house looked even more like a wrecked boat tossed on a hill. The hawthorn bushes declined to grow, but dandelions flourished, which meant that the taciturn handyman had to come twice a week with his rotary blade mower.

The retired Baptist minister and his deaconess looked out at our patchwork yard from their apprehensive, gingerbread perfection, and who knew if the neighbor we called the Last of the Mohicans on the other side could see what we saw, that the boat's insides were beyond hope.

When his Oldsmobile pulled up in front of our seventeen steps, the squirrels ran, unwanted presents and my mother's interrupted doctoral dissertation were resurrected from under our beds. Time went out the window when he came and the skies seemed to gloat and sing "We are holding back the night." I knew from the first that I had to be on my guard, had to get my face ready for the next humiliating test, to plan on my way to the basement how to skip by him without inciting too much fuss because, like the unchained boxers on the block, Grandfather bit hard.

Imposing in manner, conditioned by an order in which the shortest distance between two points was a zigzag, Grandfather sucked up the air, left behind that carbon-dioxide feeling. He had his specialties, one of which was to remind people that if they had heeded his advice they wouldn't have gotten into trouble. For instance, Savannah's trade in naval stores had collapsed by 1941. The federal government wanted to build a huge troop camp. Blacks who had only scraps of paper as titles of ownership from Reconstruction days were going to have their land bought or condemned or confiscated. Grandfather out with his grub hoe spotted the planes mapping boundaries. He suggested to neighbors to take options and sell: war was war. They ignored him, because he was always telling them what to do, and were displaced. Years later he was still saying they should have listened.

The most Grandfather's second wife dared to say was that he talked like a man who was born knowing. Grandfather sometimes turned on us like a rigged trap, and of course the benevolent gaze of the sage became the glare of the patriarch. He was not an accomplished minister for nothing. If an adversary was innocent of one crime, some other transgression lay hidden in the shrinking heart. Grandfather invoked the Book, sent out the verses on guilt patrol. An avalanche of wisdom from Deuteronomy, Kings, or Wendell Willkie shook the bulbs in the ceiling.

His accusing looks were as coercive as his ability to summon

Scripture. His mahogany skin may have lost its burnish, but his cider-brown eyes were still almost too expressive for his own good—in his day it was often dangerous for a black man to reveal too much intelligence. Grandfather was a consummate actor. Assured of his lines, his script, when my father got him on the ropes Grandfather would leap over him with something like "Grieve not thy father when thou art too full." His eyes would relax and he seemed on the verge of laughter, as if to ask, How about that? Like the ring of it? We always gave up. Reason was easily stoned by Old Testament wrath.

Grandfather's performances were seldom concluded without the handkerchief for the sorely tried brow. He had strong, elegant hands and was meticulous about his appearance, his granite-colored hair, custom-made shirts, and pliable, hand-sewn leathers. His communicants demanded their money's worth, especially the sick and the shut-in, who swooned, he thought, at his neat creases and metaphors, and all those women who waited for the lilt of his prayers.

We endured long pauses before he accepted the flags of truce. He ignored conciliatory conversation, which was a trial for him. Grandfather concentrated on newspaper headlines upside down under plants, on my sisters' fried braids, on the screams of our playmates in the alley, until he couldn't bear to see us deprived of his talk. All smiles, he'd rub my stupefied head for luck, signaling that these sparrings were a form of family fun.

It was 1960 and Jesus wasn't waiting at home plate anymore. My parents went to church only when they wanted to be seen. Grandfather had baptized my sisters and me over his very own font, down in Louisville, Kentucky, for the time being, and the New Testaments he'd given us were requisitioned by our Sunday-school staff. My parents pulled us out after they heard some of the pre-Scopes notions we were fed, including the axiom that children who placed their hands in mailboxes were snatched up by Satan.

My sisters had gone into the Sunday business of selling automobile brochures from car lots that wouldn't give my father a loan. They also did a fast trade in civil defense pamphlets: get shielded, drop flat, bury your face, don't rush outside after bombings, don't drink water from open containers, do not listen to or repeat rumors. They hid the contraband in *Mad* magazines, in *Tom Brown's School Days*, one of those out-of-place, out-of-time things Grandfather liked to read from, more for his pleasure than ours, and worked nearby out-of-bounds streets, because customers who didn't know us could be relied on not to make troublesome phone calls. I was paid to stay behind.

The engine of Grandfather's old shoe surprised us counting up the day's take of quarters. "Say 'Howdy' to your Old Moon." He swatted his way through the pattern of gnats that danced over our steps and nowhere else on the block. We packed quarters in our socks. He said we looked as if we were facing the dentist's chair.

Grandfather's beige second wife brought up the rear, limping, the mark of her childhood trial, polio. He used her, a woman, to express things he could not. He was always saying that she was dying to see us, but we knew better. She was not my grandmother, not like my mother's mother. Grandfather's real wife was gone, dead from cancer in 1941. She and her intriguing curls had eternal rest upstairs in the hall closet, in a department-store box of photographs. My aunts said that before they were sentenced to hard time in a shoofly boarding school in South Carolina their stepmother had worked them like chars. We got back at the second wife by not calling her by any name.

Grandfather said it was a good day to duck out on his assistant pastor, because the National Baptist Convention was meeting in Louisville. The offices of that brotherhood inspired the worst sort of contention among the members. The battles were known to upset Dr. King's stomach. Factions came to blows in elevators and in hotel lounges. "Please, Lord, hold steady this hand while I cut this man."

The reader of faces waited in his what-have-we-here pose: hands on his hips. Secrecy is the overprotected child's dissent, but Grandfather already knew what was up. We didn't have to throw our parents to the lions that day. Tornado Watch, when my sisters piled blankets and cans in the southeast crevices of the basement, had been overthrown by Freedom Watch. I didn't know what protest was, but my sisters said that the clothes laid out for us showed that protest was up there on the charts with Easter.

The movement that had not waited for Grandfather's consent infused everyday life with a longing that made intercessors unnecessary. A multitude discovered that it had immediate, unimpeded access to the burning truth, and maybe for that reason Grandfather didn't think much of it. He wasn't quoting "Abou Ben Adhem" anymore. Talk of love as the "ultimate creative weapon" made him cringe. His God was not personal, open; He was formidable and avenging.

Suffering was redemptive, but some things, after so many years, were buried too deep and might lose their spell if brandished in the streets. Not by might, nor by power, but by my spirit alone, saith the Lord, which clearly did not include "running locofoco with every who-shot-john." Parading around and eating at Woolworth's were, to Grandfather, neither sane nor courteous. "That Bond boy ought to know better," he once said. "He didn't come from just any home." Grandfather thought his sudden appearance would force my father to give up his plans.

We had to hear about the time Grandfather went to a symposium at Talledega College in Alabama. Trains didn't run from Birmingham to the little black college. The teller at the bus station window wouldn't let him buy a ticket and sent him to the other side. The same teller appeared at the other window. She sent him back to the first one. Eventually, she tired of his passivity and sold him a ticket. He spent the night outside rather than stand in the crowded Jim Crow waiting room. On returning home, he wrote to the officials of the bus line demanding that they correct the inequities of segregated travel.

Once, he continued, he was en route to a budget meeting of the General Synod. He and another minister stopped at a restaurant where they could buy food but not sit. "It was my personal privilege to get an appointment with the owner of the firm. In the closeness of his private office, the three of us—God, he, and I—had a quiet talk together."

We went downtown anyway, without the mandate of heaven. My sisters were made to leave their genuine U.S. Army sergeant's helmets behind. My father had to grip the steering wheel with paper towels, his palms were sweating so much.

A buffalo would have been less out of place than a skyscraper in the downtown Indianapolis scenery of faded brick department stores and mock Prussian monuments. The two movie houses were chaste, but Union Station had a reputation for estuaries of piss and men in the terra-cotta archways with aluminum foil wads full of stolen wristwatches.

The vast War Memorial Plaza spread out toward the state legislature. The Depression had tabled indefinitely plans for a brilliant reflecting pool. Instead, asphalt extended five blocks from the national headquarters of the American Legion to the entrance of a colossal chunk of limestone that featured a pyramid

lid. Replicas of gaslights alternated with ailing trees to commemorate the natural resource that, after railroads and slaugh-
terhouses, was responsible for the boom-town designs of the
"Crossroads of America." A stately obelisk pulled the blank pavement together, and tanks along the perimeter were a popular
attraction.

I'd never seen so many black people whom my parents didn't
know. Of course I didn't have that word yet. I'd not even heard
"black" used as a term of abuse. The Dozens, as winos called
insult rumbles among pre-teens under netless basketball hoops,
were still on the list of things to look forward to. Grandfather,
the son of a race man, said "Negro" in public, and the way he
said it left no doubt that the N was capitalized. But when Grandfather said "Negro" he described an abstraction.

Synaptic delay prevented my making the connection between
Grandfather's parishioners and the offhand "we" of my parents'
front-seat talk, talk that concerned the way "we" were treated at
lunch counters on the off-ramps to hell. In my heart I believed
my mother's story that she was the real Shirley Temple. My
nerve endings finally passed on the news when I found myself
walled in on all sides by Negroes about to define themselves.

We accumulated like pennies near the military mall, between
a statue of a grim Abe and a fountain. A sculpture of a wood
nymph had been stolen and everyone said that the caravans of
police cars were to discourage further theft. Compared to the
storms to come, some half-dozen assassinations later, our march
around the huge patriotic parking lot was like the haphazard,
casual milling around on the lawn after church—patent-leather
huddles of busy men canceling dates, aviaries of women in pink
hats and white gloves. "Give me some sugar," they said when
they bore down on children to pass out kisses. The most med-
dlesome among the ladies removed their gloves to straighten bow

ties or smooth down hair. The nastiest moment came when they licked their fingers to rub dry skin from my cheeks.

We walked through a gauntlet of spectators, sunburnt men with toothpicks and milkshake straws rotating like cranks in front of their thin lips and women who looked as if they did their hair with egg beaters. More goblins came to stare from the tops of coupes and from the carved doors of the Scottish Rite Cathedral. My sisters and I, with our acute myopia, our bottle-bottom lenses, kept a fix on my father's jacket, on my mother's jacket, vanished with them and bounced back behind the ear-nose-and-throat man and the pediatrician.

Even the judge who had won a grand slam and gone into cardiac arrest at the last bridge tournament rose from his sickbed to fall in step. They came, though this was before the chance of getting on television had begun to be "factored in." It was strange to see people who would have died rather than be accused of having flowers that "showed off" call undue attention to themselves smack in the middle of town, in front of so many others who were keeping quiet, arms folded, not about to join in.

Up one side of the plaza and down the other grownups were loud in public. How long? Not long. They made noise and the songs were almost like church, only faster. In church the hymns were dragged out. On the street people sneaked through verses, and then bore down hard on the end, as if they were stomping out a fire. I saw something nervous and steely in the excitement, expressions like that on my sister's face when she made up her mind to go without training wheels even if it meant hitting the telephone pole.

We didn't know what to do with our hands. One section wanted to lock arms, another wanted to clap. There were no stars at the head of our procession to show us what to do. My parents said the city fathers and the quislings among us had

scared them off by saying outsiders would get what was coming
to them. My parents and their friends agreed that they hadn't
needed speeches after all. It didn't matter how long an audience
had been sweating, nobody ever willingly cut short a speech.
Leaders, especially, were driven by the code that said, "I've written this out and you're going to hear every word."

The march had started well enough, but without speeches and
banners there was no point to come to. The protest broke up,
people left abruptly, rolled away like beads of mercury. My new
shoes were covered with dust as fine as powdered ginger and I
wanted to hurry home, to sink back into that state where good
news for modern Negroes couldn't find me.

Grandfather said he'd never met a rich white lady he didn't
like, which was more than he could say about the Negro movers
and doers he'd dealt with in his time. Old Eleanor was worth
more than the whole WPA. What the country needed was another aristocrat in the White House, a Puritan to scorch confusion, a man with a name as solid as Thorndike or Augustus.

He thought back to the Depression, when the Rockefellers on
holiday in the Sand Hills were moved to donate copies of *Collier's*
to the churches. My father said we didn't want charity anymore.
Grandfather had his theories about good whites and bad whites.
My father said some of us needed whites more than others.
Grandfather said we would not catch the whites he needed by
trying to stretch "Congo" lines from our front porch all the way
to Money, Mississippi.

We could never tell what would set Grandfather off. He said
my father knew precious little about discrimination in the army,
since he'd spent most of the last war trying to dodge the draft.
My father said Grandfather hadn't exactly crossed the Rhine
either. Grandfather said He would have mercy on whom He

would have mercy. The beige stepgrandmother switched channels to *National Velvet*. She was annoyed that our old set didn't pick up ABC.

Grandfather said that if my father had wanted to keep studying and not die peeling potatoes for white second lieutenants he should have gone to a good school like his. My father said that Dr. Mays had been more of a father to him than Grandfather had. Grandfather said my father would not have been at second-rate Morehouse in the first place had he not been expelled from second-rate Fisk for calling the French teacher queer. We were sent to bed.

"See you in the funny papers," my mother said. I turned away. I had come down with something that couldn't be cured by three cheap words and a squeeze.

The next morning Grandfather and I were alone in the kitchen. We both wore "flesh-colored" nylon stocking caps. His was knotted in back. I had on two stocking caps. The feet drooped over my ears. I was in a Cleo the Talking Dog phase. I got up with the earliest light, lapped chocolate milk from a bowl on the floor, lay down by the back door, panted, and tucked my paws up under me.

Grandfather looked at me, a severe expression I was to see again years later when I had to confess in person that I'd flunked a course, which meant my chances of getting into his alma mater were dwindling, and at a time, he said, when blacks were wanted so desperately that any park ape who could manage long division was admitted. Grandfather's look said he knew my brain was damaged but not in any way he could pin down.

"Come here, and on two feet, if you please," *Plessy vs. Ferguson* contemplated *Brown vs. Board of Education*. "I want to tell you something and you remember it, you hear? You might not see me again."

"Where are you going?"

"Never you mind. I'm not coming back and that's a fact. Your daddy has no right to make you live here. He has no right to turn you into a dog."

Grandfather, as ever, was true to his word. He didn't come to see us again until we invaded the white suburbs.

2 / *Old Yellow*

My friend the television set had begun to send awful pictures from the Old Country. Nice Negroes, in 1962, before mothers and children went to war over "naturals," looked like disciples of Father Divine—austere hair, correct clothes. "Put it in the bank, not on your back." But being or looking like someone who came from a decent home wasn't protecting anyone down there.

I worried that when the plane landed in Atlanta we'd be put in jail; that when I was stung by a bee in my grandmother's garden the hospital would not allow my mother to visit. Maybe there were signs over the raised marble water fountains, maybe my mother pretended not to see them, maybe the old woman with Parkinson's disease who sat two seats in front of me was white, I couldn't tell, but even if there had been a law against Jim Crow trains, blacks were so scared we would have sat in the colored car. Going to visit Aunt Clara in Opelika, Alabama, demanded, like taking a vow, that a part of the self must die.

I liked my mother's Aunt Clara because in her photographs she had an organ and looked like Miss Havisham in the film

Great Expectations. When her driver, G.C., came to fetch us from the dinky colored waiting room in a powder-blue Cadillac, I liked her even more.

Opelika slept in a liverish tranquillity, and it was clear to my sisters and me that we would have nothing to do with the town proper and had better not ask why. My mother didn't know the name of the movie house because nice people did not let themselves be foisted upstairs to the buzzards' roost. That summer of surreptitious feeling even strolls for a Sun Drop soda at the drugstore with the tin FROZEN-RITE signs that Aunt Clara owned were in doubt. G.C. said that cracker youth, "Kluckers," sometimes rode around in darkened cars, just to frighten people, but everybody knew that Opelika had no facilities worth integrating. "I guess folks go to school."

Exhausted camellias sagged over lawns. Those were the fine houses of Mr. Charlie and Miss Ann, G.C. said. Yes, my mother said, every house was owned by the same people and she hoped I would never meet them. Then came an intersection, and immediately after it the scent of spearmint from either side of Aunt Clara's blue drive.

Her house, a respectable structure of glazed brick fronted by four sleek columns, peeked at the road—Avenue A, the battered pink post said—through a regiment of willows and wretched dogwoods. Avenue A continued downhill, unpaved as it entered the Bottom. We didn't have to be told who lived there.

Aunt Clara waited inside the front door. She had never been a beauty but passed for one because of her light, almost transparent skin—green veins were visible in her face. There was something girlish in her step, in the way she arranged her pleats and hands when she sat, handed around questions, cups, and crystal tumblers of Nehi. Small, with a high forehead and a little colorless hole for a mouth, swabbed by many years of liking herself, Aunt Clara was accustomed to being, if not admired, at least talked about, and if not for her looks or heart, then for the strand of pearls that lay like a pet against the folds of her neck and the sea pearls that dangled below her unconvincingly dyed black hair.

Uncle Eugene had been dead for some time, but Aunt Clara did not lack for company. Arnez, Muriel, and Nida Lee busied themselves around her. Childless, Aunt Clara had sort of adopted Nida Lee. She sent her to school and Nida Lee worked at a small college in Holly Springs, Mississippi, when she was not living across the road from Aunt Clara's drive, ready with talk like a wet mop while "Miss Clara" opened magazines.

Nida Lee came out of her corner gushing, extremely tall, fat and alarming. She got me alone in a window seat and said we were going to get better acquainted. She announced and won a contest to see who could identify what tree in the pampered forest that deluded me was Aunt Clara's foxwood, her laurel and cherry. I was not to overlook the peach trees, the fledging Cedar of Lebanon, and was clearly old enough to appreciate skyrocket juniper. Her voice rising, she made me approve patches of parsley and thyme, and cluck over what should have been marigolds.

We weren't used to a nice elderly black lady telling anyone to shut up, but then we also weren't used to Nida Lee's maddening tidbits of news—"Negro socialites" had tried to crash the opera at the Fox Theater in Atlanta. She said the next thing you knew they'd be dining in the Magnolia Room at Rich's Department Store. Aunt Clara said she would not frequent establishments where they stroked the dog with one hand and fed customers with the other.

Nida Lee had a savory item up her sleeve. Marilyn Monroe had committed suicide. I'd never heard the word before. My mother acted as though Nida Lee carried a dead mouse in her mouth.

"What is it, Nida Lee? We're not paying you any mind," Aunt Clara said.

Arnez said after lunch she would show me the little house in the back yard where they once had peacocks and still kept chickens if I promised not to get dirty. "They don't do nothing but poot all night, but it's good for the flowers."

"Cousin Arnez, aren't you hungry?"

"I ate."

"She's not your cousin," Nida Lee said behind a door.

"Who is she?"

"The maid."

Arnez lived quietly in one of Aunt Clara's shotgun cabins across the creek with her old mother and her sister, Muriel, who was paid to fidget with scissors. I was to hear them on the footbridge as they came to and left work, the weight of Arnez's slow, even tread, the staccato of her sister's high-strung steps, running ahead, turning back, and catching up. Muriel's head had destroyed her life. Her hair was shorter than mine. It wouldn't grow and she'd tried everything.

Most of the elderly people I visited kept their living rooms separate from real life as I knew it. Plants and slipcovers and an undemocratic fastidiousness around the obligatory bowl of stuck-together rock candy I took to be a natural part of getting on in years. Aunt Clara's house had no hierarchy of dishes, no child-free zones, hostile borders, or speed limits, but the rooms themselves slowed me down. Her house was a zoo of things, dewdrop prism lamps and fire screens, a wild preserve for the pedestal sideboard, the painted sofa with potpourri sewn into the cushions.

I was perfectly free to study the living habits of lyre-backs in the vestibule, rockers, tables, mirrors, walls, secret doors, and gilt settees maybe because Aunt Clara counted on my not daring to. A sign on my mother's face said, "Don't feed the rugs." Around the ancient Steinway was a deep ditch; another moat protected the famous organ in its nook of flocked paper. Even Aunt Clara seemed like an exhibit, part of the uncontrolled decor, a specimen in the menagerie of ceramic dog figurines.

She grew up in a family that thought of itself as inhabiting a middle kingdom. Back in the days when white scholars argued that high yellows were the tares among the wheat, that were it not for frustrated mulattoes blacks would not agitate, it was consoling to think that the majority of whites lived and died under the curse of being "poor white trash." Her mother believed that the Also Chosen should give to Jim Crow the subversive inflection that the custom of segregation shielded nice Negroes from the contamination of whites. But Aunt Clara was as obsessed as Thomas Jefferson with the "algebraical notation" of blood mixture.

Aunt Clara's grandfather was a "boss mechanic," a carpenter, blacksmith, and wheelwright known by his nickname, "Handy." Family memoirs said what a black family back then would want them to say: that he was "seven-eighths Caucasian and possibly one-eighth Negro," would never consent to be whipped, and didn't know who his parents were.

Aunt Clara's Uncle Sterling claimed that when he worked as a "shaver," an errand boy, after the Civil War he overheard a Union colonel who considered himself an expert on nigger trading say, "The mother of that boy's father was a beautiful white girl from one of our best families. It seemed to be a case of real love for a young mulatto, a trusted man, a servant. The child was taken away and sold as a slave and to this day the secret has been kept." Maybe Uncle Sterling trusted his memory when his white colleagues were hoodwinked by the story and urged him, a professor of religion, to write it down.

Aunt Clara's father, also called Handy, was born around 1856 in Roane County, east Tennessee. His mother had the "personal care" of the food repository, but after slavery, Uncle Sterling, the author of the memoir, was capable of saying, "their best years were behind them." Three of thirteen children survived. They went the folkloric seventy-five miles on foot for the chance to go to college. Walk, believer, walk.

After Clark University and the Gammon Theological Seminary in Atlanta, Handy settled in Opelika, as presiding elder of the Methodist Church and friend of day laborers and sharecroppers who had driven their herds from the border states at night, which meant that the cows were probably stolen. He published inspirational allegories about necromancers, "Mr. Truth" and "Mr. Lie," and was the bane of many a minister. His reports had the power to deprive them of their churches, to transfer them into oblivion. It was said he made even his bishop nervous.

Aunt Clara was born in Opelika—in 1896 perhaps and at home certainly. She was always "molting her years," trimming her age, my grandmother said. Her cards were already on the table, one of which foretold clouds of muslin, colored subdebs, and Clark University. "A lot of important people fell through chapel."

When Uncle Eugene began to court her, he'd walk her home to Avenue A. Finally, her mother sailed from the house and down the lawn: "You may call on her if you wish, young man, but you may not talk to her on the street." When they married he was a shadow surgeon called in by white hospitals, strictly off the record, and had a lucrative side business in secretive cases: performing abortions on whites.

The newlyweds orbited around her parents, and after the old folks were gone they demolished the house and took their time putting up an expanded version of the original. She and Uncle Eugene used their light skin to get what they wanted, which was mostly to enjoy the theater up North. Then Uncle Eugene died, and as they say, some of her went with him. More of her kept leaving; eventually Aunt Clara stopped going out to places where she'd meet people, even church, and had her hair done at an undisclosed location. She was sensitive about being hard-of-hearing.

The recluse on the hill, she lived, in the Southern phrase, on the inherited capital of family responsibilities, which had dwindled to reading the obituaries and keeping up a strong correspondence with cousins in Philadelphia, Washington, Jersey City, with her sister in Atlanta, and her brother who, after the Great War, sold his Packard, married a French-Canadian girl from Winnipeg, took a job with the railroad at the Manitoba end of nowhere, and never set foot in Opelika again.

She had been educated to be a teacher, like her mother before her, like all her female relations. It was a "holding pattern" profession. "Ariel was your mother's favorite." Aunt Clara was disappointed by my response to *Tales from Shakespeare*. Our personalities, insofar as they existed under the detention-center conditions of good behavior, were colors for her to squeeze out, assets or liabilities that somehow reflected on her. "Why, you're the darkest one in the family."

Aunt Clara's activities, dictated by the privacy of her setting, were unchangeable, a routine that absorbed everyone into the perpetual shade of the house. She seemed to know by magic where a light had been left on, as far as the bathroom on the third floor. The telephone never rang, but it was a feminine way of life, one designed for waiting—waiting for the mail, for the uncomfortable man from the Farmers' National Bank, for the husband to come in from house calls, the father to return from travels around the state, shaking the outside world from his coat.

There was a limit to my enthusiasm for exploration among crocheted covers and bizarre vesper chairs, though Aunt Clara's things became interesting as they moved up from the first floor. They evolved to higher levels in forgotten rooms until they attained pack-rat nirvana in the attic. Tinted pictures of bayou picnics, of bearded faces that looked past me; men's hats; thick phonograph records, radios, phonographs; chests I could not unlock; microscopes from Uncle Eugene's studies at Meharry; camphor ice, oxide of zinc ointment, and quinine pomade for the relief of gathered breasts, nasal catarrh, and pleurisy, medicines that dated back to the scandal of Theodore Roosevelt breaking bread with Booker T. Washington. I couldn't trace the scents of fir and formaldehyde to their sources.

Aunt Clara preferred that I not ransack the memories of her mother and Uncle Eugene. I was welcome to sit with the grown-ups, to help her wrap dust jackets that she decorated herself around _His Eye Is on the Sparrow_ by Ethel Waters, _The Makers of Venice_ and _The Makers of Florence_ by Mrs. Oliphant. She read for the same reason that she tolerated Nida Lee's prayers: both induced sleep.

Aunt Clara's favorite book for the last eight years had been the autobiography of Marian Anderson. It was a great inspiration to her because it read like one long thank-you note to the churches of Philadelphia, as if her career had been the desk tidy she'd always wanted. The great singer traveled with an iron to press her own dresses. Aunt Clara did not, however, approve of Miss Anderson revealing how much she paid for her gowns.

Like the swan that strove only to keep its feathers brilliant,

Aunt Clara enjoyed the company of family when she knew in
advance what the talk was going to be about and to make certain
that she didn't miss anything she did the talking. Aunt Clara
remembered the 1939 World's Fair in New York; the exact time
of night a cousin died of gangrene up in Chicago; the name of
the German professor the FBI arrested after it was discovered
that he was transmitting right from the Spelman campus; the
Northern Lights pattern of her sister's silver at meetings of their
club, the What Good Are We; the sheriff who received a Ford
Foundation grant because he hadn't killed anyone.

Details reassured her, like an oil and tire check. She could
remember the number of beaux she had before she met Uncle
Eugene. The most impressive was a boy haunted by the memory
of his grandmother throwing him from a second-story window
when she thought whites were breaking down the door during
the Atlanta riot of 1906. She wondered what had become of him.
Most likely he had gone North. He'd often said that if he'd stayed
in Georgia he'd have been lynched. She was in favor of hotheads:
it was a masculine prerogative. She liked my father ever since
he overcame "Fear Thought" in school and joined the rallies in
support of Henry Wallace's right of free speech.

Aunt Clara talked like someone who had made up her mind
not to leave any footprints. The lotus hum of her intermittent
conversation, like the current from the electric fans in opposite
corners of the sun porch, subdued hours. Her odd singsong
pursued the smell of butane from my mother's lighter. "Gene
never could make up his mind, don't you know. Picayunes.
Wings. Hit Parade in the can. Dominoes. Lucky Strike in the
green package. Philip Morris. Cavalier. Coffee Time. That was
the war."

She remembered very well how upset a cousin was when
E. E. Just punched him at Howard University. I thought she

meant the famous Negro biologist had knocked her cousin down. But no, Dr. Just never spoke above a whisper. To get punched, back then, meant to receive a failing grade. Aunt Clara's cousin had worked too hard on his laboratory manual, copying bacteria from books when he wasn't sure what he saw under the microscope. Dr. Just had included blank slides, in order to teach his students not to draw anything if they didn't see anything.

Some women were house-proud, some were husband-proud, and still others were pleased with their connections. Aunt Clara was all three. She was proud that Mattiwilda Dobbs had sung at my mother's wedding, that a Washington cousin's collection of poems had been reviewed in the *New York Evening Post* before the Depression silenced him, proud even of his parting remark that Jefferson must have had her in mind when he said he had yet to find a black who uttered a thought above the level of plain narration.

Aunt Clara liked to "go places," but she hadn't been anywhere in years and evidently her opinion of wherever she had been had solidified around the issue of service. Holidays at Dobbs Ferry began promisingly enough, but things went quickly downhill to the poor Melba sauce in yet another lackluster Rhode Island Plaza restaurant in Washington, D.C., before "they" finally let "us" in elsewhere. Aunt Clara had probably never had the chance to grade hotels. Her traveling had been done in the days when you depended on "kissing cousins" for a bed.

It was an indoors life, even a long ride in the powder-blue Cadillac was an indoor event. The trouble was that we all wanted to ride in the back seat. The automatic windows were more rewarding to me than the remnants of cotton fields or the dignified remains of Tuskegee Institute. Aunt Clara looked disturbed when someone wanted to stop. She was hardly aware of what the car passed. If we were heading toward Goat Rock Lake, she was twenty years behind, back with my mother on Auburn Avenue in Atlanta, going into Yates's Drugstore for Dr. Palmer's Lotion.

Uncle Eugene's early death had intensified some of her human instincts. Ebony cabinets bore a clutter of condolence letters, birthday cards, photograph albums. She collected funeral programs like signed menus, though she no longer attended funerals.

She liked to plan her funeral, what music she would have and which preacher she would not. Her dilemma was that she couldn't bear the thought of worms and bacteria eating away at her, of taking up room. She wanted to be compact, but cremation was, if not illegal in Alabama, not done. Aunt Clara was pleased with the idea; with another something that no one else had. It was newfangled, like an item in a catalogue she was the first in town to receive. She said my mother could put her ashes in one of Nida Lee's hollowed-out flamingos or discreetly scatter them in the aisles at Rich's Department Store. What she wasn't sure about was what Uncle Eugene would think. She wanted to be with him, but he was buried on the wrong side of town.

G.C. rolled us in the direction of the segregated cemetery. My mother and sisters got out to go to Uncle Eugene through the brambles. Aunt Clara and I were to have a friendly talk about the unmanliness of being afraid of graves. Her tears were so refined they were abstract. She wished I had known Uncle Eugene. "He was sharp."

G.C., facing the wheel, said that what he was was the sun that shone in many a back door. "Turned them every which way but loose."

Aunt Clara couldn't hear him. Nobody here but us coloreds in a Biedermeier mood, her smile said.

The hours were as confining as chapel must have been in Aunt Clara's schooldays, beginning with breakfast, which owed something to the threat of roll call. The legendary lazy South, if it had ever existed, was gone, preserved in the movies Aunt Clara claimed never to have heard of. We knew nothing about the failed march in Albany, Georgia, that summer and the celebrations on the other side of town of what they were calling Martin Luther King's Waterloo. The NAACP was an underground organization in Alabama, but we didn't know that. All we knew was that we were stuck. My sisters referred to Opelika as Alcatraz.

My sisters could stand it. They read. They tried on clothes, raided trunks of brittle silk, damaged satin, inspected the paper dolls from my mother's girlhood, poured their afternoons into past and future recital pieces. I had not yet recovered from the shame of having failed to perform "Turkey in the Straw" in public after thirteen attempts and hated the sight of Aunt Clara's sheet music strewn across loo tables and ottomans. Carrie Jacobs Bond, *Japanese Love Songs* by Clayton Thomas, *At Dawning* by Charles Wakefield Cadman, *Kate Smith's Folio of Heart Songs*. My mother said the organ was not a toy.

Music helped to seal up Aunt Clara's house. For some reason, she wouldn't play the love songs she really liked. In front of company, even family, she limited herself to halting performances of classical music. With her rheumatic complaints, she pedaled away the days—" . . . qua . . . re . . . sur . . . get . . . ex . . . fa . . . vil . . . la." Her chin went rigid and her amused eyes crossed behind misty glasses as she faced down the truculent notes. My grandmother used to say her sister sounded like a dying cat in a thunderstorm.

From a back room came the rhythmic chorus of answering motors: the Wilcox & Gibbs for chain stitching, one machine for straight, slant, and swing-needle, another for quilting. The room smelled of cloves and mint, old-fashioned weapons against moths.

Muriel traced and stitched her way through continents of velvet, flowered orlon, checkered nylon, lowly cotton, and raised to a high level the iron she used to spare herself the trouble of basting.

She thought of herself as saved, tucked away in the same room as Aunt Clara's garage of sewing-machine classics, among them a Pfaff and Necchi no longer in working order. Muriel kept it by the window and stroked the machine's intricate parts with a rag from time to time. It was a shrine in the middle of door pouches of thread, bolts of rayon, broadcloth, linen faded in spots from having been left so long on a window seat, and a dressing dummy I was not sure Muriel didn't talk to.

I was forbidden to play king-emperor on the balcony. My mother did not trust my balance. Not only would Aunt Clara not allow ball playing on the closed-in sun porch, she appealed to my mother to enforce her ban on having balls themselves in the house, as if toys were as dirty as pets.

Killjoy Nida Lee wondered how one child could make so much noise in a driveway. When Nida Lee brought a message from "Miss Clara," she smirked as though she had once again one-upped Arnez by leaving her to bring the platters. My sisters retaliated by shrinking ever so slightly from her pinches and pats. We were supposed to feel sorry for her because she was once on a regimen of cortisone injections and had never been able to lose the weight. I was warned not to ask Nida Lee to play the second piano in the back room.

"Touch me, Lord." Her inner spark had been ignited again.

"What is it, Nida Lee?"

"No harm in praise."

"I don't want that foolishness today," Aunt Clara said.

Nida Lee was driven to the piano in the back room whenever Aunt Clara seemed in the mood to pass remarks about ugly black women with pierced ears, or when she couldn't participate in Aunt Clara's grilling of my mother for news about nice Negro women's clubs, those groups that met and raised scholarship money between discussions about how the salad spinners that had just come on the market could be used to dry stockings when the machine was broken.

"How is the Links Club?"

"It's getting browner."

When Nida Lee let herself expand at the upright, she tried to coax me into prayer. "Until my hands are new, aw, I'll be clean when You get through." Religious emotion was funny to me. Added to the way Southern blacks talked, it was difficult for me to control myself.

I looked down the road into the Bottom. Flat trucks raised a sultry dust in the mornings. Women went by with baskets of laundry for white people on their heads. Two women, their faces protected from the sun by black rain umbrellas, with big pocket books crooked in their arms, feet spread out in shoes that slapped against their heels, nodded my way as they ambled by.

"Where are you going?"

"A good piece up the road."

I was about to double up for a good laugh. "Better not," Arnez said. "Better not."

Nida Lee enjoyed the highest opinion of herself as Aunt Clara's eyes and ears around town, down in the Bottom. She was often on the lookout to see who was coming 'from down under the hill.' If Aunt Clara needed anything, Nida Lee would hurry to volunteer. "Now, you know how you get from exposure."

"You are a saint."

"Go on, Miss Clara."

She enjoyed getting out of the house, especially when it meant that she could wake G.C. and make him back out the Cadillac. Nida Lee returned with tea, tumid pound cakes—Arnez's baking was not what it used to be, she said confidentially—and a whole lot extra.

"Now tell me," Aunt Clara said, "what has that woman done now?"

I got the impression from the names of the miscreants who featured in Nida Lee's daily reports that the black South was filled with "bigs" and "littles"—Big Johnny, Little Johnny. "Big Mary said to this white lawyer when he called that Mrs. Harris was having her teeth made and after this week she will talk to her and see what she can get her to do. Big Mary is like they say. Underworld people play a profit game. That woman is doing this on Mrs. Harris. It hurts me to see people deceive an aged person for their own profit." She practically screamed her report, not caring that little pitchers were present, because she wanted to get it out before she forgot something, like model students who deliberately left their notecards behind when they recited Mother's Day speeches.

"Mrs. Harris is failing fast and Big Mary is with her night and day." Nida Lee put on her solemnly satisfied expression, that of the cat with the dead mouse, when she insinuated herself onto the sofa near Aunt Clara's ear.

"It is very hard for Mrs. Harris to get up out of the large chair in the dining room and when she does she's out of breath and some days she does not feel like getting up at all. Big Mary was told that for Mrs. Harris to gain weight will cause her death. The doctor said this, but that woman is still serving the same fat food."

"Isn't that pitiful." Aunt Clara liked to keep up, but without the muss of too much contact. Anyone Arnez defended as just being friendly, Aunt Clara condemned for taking liberties, showing bad manners. Familiarity, on her part, was also Pandora's Box. If Nida Lee reported that a reverend's wife had asked after Aunt Clara and thought she might pay a call one of these old days, Aunt Clara looked ready to bar the doors. I pictured Aunt Clara fleeing acquaintances, in case they approached with ticking packages.

"I told her you were feeling poorly."

"I can't have that woman in my house. Not until I can get Arnez to get a honey dripper to do something about those drainpipes." Aunt Clara called any man who did yard work a "honey dripper," though the term hadn't been current since World War II, and referred specifically to army privates on latrine duty.

"She's not coming."

"Say what? That woman is a horror story. I don't know how some people can live so long and not know you're not supposed to wear hats at night."

"She's not coming. She fell down last week."

"She did what?"

"She hurt herself. She fell down."

"She *fell*. You know I don't like it when you talk like a linthead."

Aunt Clara also liked to hear Arnez's news: who had been taken away to the nursing home in Columbus, Georgia; whose husband had gone to the store for cigarettes and not been seen for three days; which family had been left property by a branch that passed for white but was too dark to try to claim it; whose daughter had ended up in jail out in Texas.

"Isn't that pitiful?"

"That's pitiful."

"I seen little Johnny and don't you know his wife is going to lose that kidney."

"Say what?"

Nida Lee didn't like it when Arnez had some news that particularly interested Aunt Clara. Not to be undone, she pulled
terrifically huge rabbits out of her hat. My sisters called them
Pitiful Contests. Nida Lee reminded Aunt Clara that it was
almost four years to the day that some poor widow's three grand-
sons were killed on the same day, two in Tulsa, one on the
highway. "Now that was pitiful."

By the end of the first week my stomach was a muddle of
cream, lime sherbert, butternut squash, and grits. "Child, you
don't know what's good," Arnez said. My palms began to stink
of violets, furniture polish, ammonia, and a varnish that seemed
to coat Aunt Clara's whole life and protect her from the effects
of time.

I heard, at night, the windows fall on their rope pulleys; someone on the catwalk; my sisters' accounts of haints in the woods,
of Nida Lee's voodoo potions, her nine lumps of starch moistened
with Jockey cologne; and Aunt Clara playing scratched Angel
recordings alone in her room, tallying up the pieces of a Scrabble
game to determine which letters she should order.

"Why you want to go and tell a lie on my sister." I heard
Arnez with Nida Lee in the kitchen. Muriel was in disgrace.
Nida Lee had told Aunt Clara that Muriel was stealing. Muriel
admitted with copious tears that she took things, food mostly,
down to the men working on the other side of the creek. Otherwise, she just wanted to show them things. She always brought
them back.

I'd followed her and her covered dishes by the shotgun cabins
with TV antennas. Her courage expressed itself in her not hiding
her head under a hat or a scarf. She sewed extra ribbons on her
dress when she went "out to the road" or "down under the hill"
and picked at the thread until they dropped off one by one.

The men hadn't seemed very interested in Muriel's show-and-tell. They politely took the food and went back to joking among themselves. She waited around, her face taut, looking for a way into their afternoon break.

"They been saying it forever. How we can't live without them. How much understanding there is. Son, when I was in Georgia I could have lived real good without crackers, I can tell you. There was this long line of paterolls."

"What?" Muriel interrupted.

"Where you from, girl. Who whipped the slaves. They were called paterolls. The no-account trash that did the whipping."

Muriel's face said that you can, after all, get blood from a turnip. But she wouldn't leave them alone. I wasn't sure what the men did. I knew there was a cotton mill that made sheets and bed linen in some mysterious part of town. They seemed to be part of a road crew.

"If your wife heard you talking like that, she'd roll over in her grave."

"If she's rolling over, it's with her legs wide open."

I ran when Muriel ran, terrified of being left alone in the trees and not finding my way back.

Aunt Clara said that if she ever caught Muriel taking Uncle Eugene's silver engraved case to offer a honey dripper a cigarette again she'd give her something to cry about. It was only because Arnez was crazy about her that she put up with her, anyway. She remembered how Arnez used to carry Muriel around when she was a baby. They trailed behind their mother, whose job it had been to walk with an umbrella when my mother wanted to go into town and look at the Rexall window.

The heat fell like an edict. The creek shriveled, exposed dry, cracked banks, like my skin was back home, my skin being why

I wouldn't explain why I refused to take off my shirt in gym.
Hornets circled nests, yellowhammers dived at stunted tomatoes;
I was playing Pip meets his long-lost father on the marshes and
also looking out for the boy from the back line. Mine enemies
are lively and they are strong. I believed in the world's Mani-
chaean division into bad boys without shoes and victims with
glasses.

He also lived in one of Aunt Clara's shotgun places, evidently
that's how bountiful and given to multiplying was her father's
land. He could climb trees. He said he was going to come back
for me with a BB gun and dared me to leave the back yard. I
took the path of least resistance and went on saying "What larks"
to myself as if he hadn't been there.

He returned with something like a slingshot. Little missiles
whizzed by my shoulders. To get it over with, I sat cross-legged
in the dirt. Some of them hurt, but I didn't say anything. If
things got out of hand I could always run and tell, though that
boulevard of appeal wasn't as trustworthy as it used to be, after
a cloakroom conference with a teacher on the perils of growing
up a crybaby and a tattler. It taught me that the rule of squeal-
to-a-woman-never-to-a-man had its disastrous exceptions.

A coward is a man who does not know how much he can get
away with. Nonviolence carried the day. My assailant ordered
me to get up and come on over the fence. Ezell smelled of lemon
that his mother rubbed on him to keep off mosquitoes. He had
a younger brother called Brother. Before I knew it, I was AWOL
again, sneaking down the road to look at two goats that Ezell
said were special. They were "nervous" goats with sad pink eyes.
When I clapped my hands or screamed in front of their noses,
they fainted.

Ezell had to go home and make lunch for Brother. They had
two rooms, a kitchen, and an outhouse sprinkled with lime.

There were square and triangular newspaper panes in the windows; newspaper made scabs on the walls. Ezell drained catfish on newspaper when he took it from the frying pan. He fixed a plate for me. The head was still attached. Brother turned slices of white bread into grease balls and popped them in his mouth. I couldn't move, didn't know where to look.

"Your grandmother is a witch. Everybody says so."

"So what, you're a black nigger and you don't have a television."

"We all will be called on in to Judgment," Nida Lee said. "Father, we know that you know all about us. If you find anything contrary, remove it, cover us in Your blood. Stir up some boy before it's everlastingly too late."

She just wanted to get back at me because Aunt Clara said in front of everyone that Nida Lee had once thought of wearing sequins before five o'clock. "They would have thought you didn't know any better."

I would have told on Nida Lee, but I didn't want to worsen my punishment for having gone over the fence. Arnez brought lemonade and a selection from Aunt Clara's collection of benign picture books. I haunted the third floor, counted the days until G.C. could huff and sweat to show my mother how heavy our luggage was.

After Opelika was once again where it belonged, down there somewhere in the Old Country, where they boiled clothes in big, black smoking pots, it got harder to get away, to winnow back into my sack. Television added tear gas, gasoline bombs, University of Mississippi at Oxford—I thought James Meredith had tried to register at Oxford University—to my vocabulary.

And the South, as a landscape, would be, for me, always, a

48

series of interiors, living rooms where I braced myself when I heard something crash in another room. An aging mother would explain that her daughter was sick and hurry off to see what had been broken. Before the visit was over, the daughter would appear—not as the popular, pretty thing her mother couldn't stop talking about, but as a woman toothless as a turtle who had been drinking all day, teetering to the kitchen, which was why she kept herself hidden, covered like a mirror after a death in the old days.

The Old Country became a sort of generalized stuffy room, no matter how many reunions of old-timers I attended. It wasn't safe to explore the South. The old-timers themselves discouraged too much curiosity about what lay beyond the gate. It was a place of secrets, of what black people knew and what white people didn't. No old-timer said openly that Rosa Parks had been secretary of her NAACP branch and a student of interstate commerce rulings and the Equal Accommodations Law of 1948 before she decided she was too tired to move.

The old-timers fell silent whenever I entered the room, paused like someone in a hurry but too polite not to give directions, and then went back to the possibility that Roy Wilkins of the NAACP hated Martin Luther King of the SCLC because there was not enough real estate in the social-studies textbooks to house them both. Meanwhile, television passed on its pictures, the connecting tissue. The representations survived the subject and eventually overtook my own images, which were less durable than waxwork figures in an exhibition of Black Life at the Smithsonian.

Aunt Clara hushed up and died in the middle of one of those undreamed-of summers, when Birmingham turned out to be like Johannesburg, the mental concertina wire between her and all manner of neighbor unmolested. That was the end of her careful packages, her many parcels of *Little Women*, *Little Men*, Nancy Drew mysteries, P. L. Travers, Hans Christian Andersen, puzzles, painted-tongue seeds, stoles, suits with the wrong lapels, chafing dishes, Uncle Eugene's pajamas, and lavender cards that said, "I wanted you to have these ere I go."

Moving-van loads of things were set free by her own fingers, which had turned orange-ish from sickness and had never voted. She deeded their cabin over to Arnez and her sister until their deaths, at which time it would revert to her estate, and told Nida Lee from her colored-only hospital bed that if she came to her homegoing services not to wear any shouting shoes. An undertaker bought the house.

3 / Black and Blue

The Great Society seemed to blossom with Voting Rights acts, but dread of the meantime mixed with the pollen. John Birch Society billboards attested to an allergic reaction and for several days I thought my parents knew the lady named Selma who'd been killed on a highway in Alabama. The minister who presided over the grape-juice Second Presbyterianism of certain social Sundays began to stammer like the widower who lived on the corner, next to the filling station's soda machine, when he harangued his steps and spilled his cup of suspiciously dark tea.

All along I had been receiving tidings of great joy from the transistor radio I held to my ear under the covers. Runs with my allowance to the drugstore on the bad corner meant a haul of fan magazines and crossing the Mersey with Gerry and the Pacemakers and the Beatles. *A Hard Day's Night* begat, for me, *The Loneliness of the Long Distance Runner*, *The L-Shaped Room*, and *The Boys*. I violated curfew and slipped downstairs to soak up *Saturday Night, Sunday Morning*. A spokesman for the local station warned that Albert Finney might shock us.

My bicycle became a motorcycle and anyone whose feet

dragged from the back seat was Rita Tushingham. I was a bloke, like those who dangled cigarettes at the proper angle in grainy black-and-white films, though I wasn't sure what a quid was. I was a Ted, though my parents wouldn't hear of pointed shoes. I hoped to become a Rocker, but my parents vetoed denims under any circumstances. They were also adamant against my Mod ambitions. London, my father said, would have to swing without me.

We weren't Jamaican or Barbadian. We were just black, but I leapt upstream in a single afternoon from Edward Eggleston's *The Hoosier Schoolmaster* to Josephine Tey's *Daughter of Time*. I was a working-class hero one day, the dead body surrounded by candles at Churchill's state funeral the next; kidnapped and framed for pickpocketing in the morning, then imprisoned at night like the princes in the painting by Sir John Everett Millais on display in Chicago. In exquisite solitude I scooped out a valley by the side of the house and filled it with water for Trafalgar, which raged loud and long, until the hose caused the sunless sea to overflow into a neighbor's basement.

The wire mesh of our sceen porch was as black as Ray Charles's sunglasses. I could watch the world go by, but the known world could not see me in my robes of state, scepter and orb in hand. I appeared in full regalia on the ramparts of the Tower only when my parents and sisters were not at home and the sitter was on the telephone, at which time two burgundy comforters became available, as well as a cummerbund, assorted buttons and brooches, a black lacquer cane that a bridge player had forgotten and would never find again, and a puffy black velvet hat from that region of the upstairs hall closet where my mother consigned clothing she would no longer be caught dead in.

The steep hill of our yard became the cliffs of Dover. The street, Capitol Avenue, which I was forbidden to step into under pain of never being allowed outside again, sleepy Capitol Avenue with its regulation elms, was the English Channel. Classmates who threw rocks from their doors across the street lived in France. The school crossing up the sidewalk was Hadrian's Wall. Then came Scotland and, farther north, the terra incognita of houses with driveways. The corner filling station down the sidewalk I cast as the Atlantic. There the game ended. Beyond the filling station were many bad corners, crumbling limestone bridges, and the serious business of "downtown."

The role of traitor went to Buzzy. His crimes included calling me a liar when I said I saw the Beatles at the state fair and saying that the Beatles said they would never let a nigger like me kiss their boots. Buzzy was a certifiable hoodlum: he wore sleek Stacy Adams shoes without socks. It was only a matter of time before he had his hair konked and rolled up in one of those damp scarves favored by thugs on bad corners. On a field trip to Monticello he managed to get the class so worked up that people at rest stops asked our shame-faced chaperones if we were orphans.

Buzzy lived on Hadrian's Wall, on the corner above the school crossing, in a house that was half painted and almost as dilapidated as our wrecked boat. Buzzy's hill had mange. A Ford had averted another Ford and careened almost up to his porch. The grass wouldn't grow back. He often stayed home to take care of his mother, a woman whose hair had a *National Geographic* wildness.

He was allowed to stay up and drink 7-Up when his mother had company. She sometimes went through party moods. Cars parked all the way down to our house. The whole block tried not to hear the music. Buzzy wasn't sent to bed when the adults began to talk like adults. His mother's friends didn't coo, pinch his cheeks, and wait for him to go upstairs in pajamas he was too old for. They came in shooting from the hip, as I saw it. He'd already tasted beer.

He was twelve, a bulldog with fists like the muscle men's in the back-page ads of comics. His osprey eyes gave him a clean shot at prey tromping home with pressed maple leaves, paper Halloween pumpkins, irregular Christmas stars, and Easter baskets caked with Elmer's glue. The safety patrol was too scared to blow the whistle on him. The white principal agreed with parents that Buzzy was a candidate for reform school, until Buzzy's mother flew out of her *National Geographic* remoteness and made a scene in his office and all over the hall, after which the principal took the line that no Negro boy was too young to learn to defend himself.

Buzzy made being good look like a sort of fatalism. At most, "behaving" meant that you were sometimes left alone, left to make what you wanted of the *Illustrated London News*. Mostly, your waking hours were a tight schedule of obligations and activities to be gotten through quickly, like the magical checklist of your prayers. The teachers said Buzzy was being selfish when he disrupted class. But he wasn't. He was sacrificing himself. He was the Dessalines of the fourth grade, the deep seeker who, wanting things to be different, could only hammer away at the way things were.

Buzzy had positioned himself on our steps. "That's my car," he promised himself when one he liked went by. He was known to drop stolen baseball bats or to let go of my neck to stand in rapture as a Stingray roared by carrying a demon who held the thread of life in his hands. Traffic had a sedative effect on Buzzy, like a fire or a tank of fish.

Cars were sacred anyway in Indianapolis, the "All-American City." The miracle of speed brought out the pioneer fervor. The new dealerships behind the state house and the used lots on the fringes of the airport, decorated with placards, chattering flags, and strings of dancing bulbs, possessed the healing power of

revivalist sects. Come forward, brethren, and accept this Coupe
de Ville. The Memorial Day race—"White Trash Day," Grandfather called it—was a tradition of beer cans thrown from passing
cars, white Pat Boone shoes, checkered trousers, white belts,
increased highway fatalities, and condoms peeking up in the
reservoirs like water moccasins. Buzzy was at his least belligerent
when one of his mother's friends said he'd take him to the Speed-
way for the time trials.

Sweat weakened the brim of my crown and smudged my lenses
as the traitor studied the English Channel and crushed a praying
mantis between his fingers. I would have mounted an honorable
attack with my cane had the shushing of my robes not given me
away. I stood under the August sun covered in bedspreads and
ornamented like a Christmas tree.

"Make me faint," Buzzy said.

He was careful with me ever since my sisters had sold their
stock of car brochures to him. He'd gone into his mother's purse
while she slept it off on top of her stereo cabinet with the bass
thumping through her. But I thought my appearance provocative
enough for Buzzy to send my scepter like a javelin through one
of the pinned-together curtains of our hermit neighbor, the Last
of the Mohicans. He showed so little interest in the chance to
pick on me that I decided he was sick.

A Rolls, the first ever sighted on Capitol Avenue, purred down
the street. I jumped out of my garb. "Don't act like you never
had nothing," Buzzy said. I put my hand in my pocket too late.
The old woman in the back seat must have seen me wave to her
chrome. I told Buzzy that the tangerine hidden in my hat had
come all the way from California.

"Them niggers out in California crazy. My daddy saw them."

I tried not to interrupt, but it irritated me when Buzzy got
out of his depth. Wat Tyler led the Peasant Rebellion, I had to

tell him, way back in history. They burned manor houses and tax collectors, but that was in my England.

"Is not. Watts in California," Buzzy insisted. I gave up, collected the symbols of my authority, and withdrew.

Unless my parents admitted that Wat Tyler's riot happened in 1381 and the Magna Carta in 1215, I was going to stuff my ears with Brussels sprouts. I was given the opportunity to reconsider my tone in my room, where I sat folding my collars under to make my jackets like the Beatles'.

I heard the whole neighborhood at play in the diffuse after-dinner light. My sisters had invented a new game for my friends, a combination of Go Fish and Bread and Butter Come and Get Your Supper. They christened it Call Out the National Guard. Buzzy used the switch on stragglers and screamed, "Kill, kill, kill, burn, burn, burn," with such realism that my parents sent him home.

"Go home, Buckwheat," Buzzy said the next day when I walked below his hill. He waited until his mother took her nap before he hurled non-returnable bottles at motorists from behind a dead tree. I turned at Hadrian's Wall, keeping an eye on the bottle Buzzy aimed at me, and crept through the alley where the tumble-down garages also served as clubhouses for older boys who raced tires with sticks and spoke to one another in a code as mysterious as Masonic ritual. "If you're black step back."

A monster once stalked Capitol Avenue, at the end of summer or in the first days of school, whenever our small world needed him. The alarm would go up that "Chuddatabacca" was coming and fifty children stampeded down Capitol Avenue, dropping books and new paints. We crashed into the safety patrol and even went up Buzzy's hill on our hands and knees. The screaming would go on all afternoon. Far into homework hours I could hear posses crying "Chuddatabacca" and pounding the earth.

Unfortunately, I once turned back with Buzzy on a dare and saw the monster: an old black man, his jaw working under a straw hat, rigidly sitting on a buckboard driven by a gigantic brown mule. Lizards of saliva dripped from its mouth. Its shoes were on backward, preventing the beast from getting a proper footing. It moved in sections. The wet neck bobbed down and up, its front hooves scraped the pavement, hind legs caught up, flanks quivered, and the dumb cycle began again. The wheels of the empty buckboard turned with a wrenching, iron noise.

My sisters offered water, then yelled that our parents were calling the police. The old man was sitting so low his hat made a bridge between his shoulder blades. Cars came up, tiptoed around the mule, and sped away. Where the rural apparition had come from, how he'd gotten his name, and where he was heading we were never able to figure out. He never passed my way again, though I heard the alarm from time to time, when the big kids from the alley clubhouses wanted to amuse themselves.

Capitol Avenue was the emotional equivalent of a child's depthless, one-dimensional drawing: a swatch of blue at the top, a strip of green at the bottom, brown stick figures in the blank space of the middle. A little sadism crept into the smallest pleasures, like capturing red and black ants in jars and watching the two armies bite to the death. When the ground froze we stole rice and listened to the robins feud with bigger birds over who was entitled to it, until much larger crows entered the picture and that was that.

I had information Buzzy would be sorry he missed. Something was up with the Last of the Mohicans. Two men in plaid shirts had been sniffing around the doors of our seldom-seen neighbor all morning. Their faces were red and looked undefrosted. From my porch I could spy unseen as they banged on the side door, the back door, and pleaded with the three diamond-shaped windows of the front door. "Ma?" They left and returned several times. Finally, they came back with a box-shaped woman in white shoes with thick soles. She gave one of the men a key and dabbed at her hairnet.

I forgot about them until the ambulance arrived. My mother wouldn't let me cross the yard to watch, but I could hear the Last of the Mohicans when they carried her out. The attendants and the two men talked into the stretcher. Sheets poured over its sides like Kleenex sticking up after too much has been yanked too fast. The boxcar woman tested the front door and waddled with a suitcase and a grocery bag under her chin. The bag split, a can of Ajax poked out.

They tilted the stretcher to get it down the steps, and the Last of the Mohicans whimpered, very much like the dachshund I'd once found in our back yard. It whined when I tried to touch it. The handyman called the pound. He said the dog had worn its halter too long and it was cutting into its skin. The ambulance was down the street when Buzzy arrived with his dummy Molotov. He chucked it anyway. "Go home, Whitey."

Things always finished in the same place. Trips that began with loading the car under the cover of darkness ended in the middle of the night at familiar steps worn smooth like headstones or soap. In the mornings, surveying Capitol Avenue, swaying like a cobra, I tried to capture the sensation of being in between places. I was a passenger on a plane or a bus who doesn't worry about what he has abandoned or what will greet him when he arrives.

One day an eyesore pulled alongside the cliffs of Dover. The driver's door of the ailing Studebaker was broken. Uncle Castor climbed from the passenger's side, without presents, a confiding, appealing expression all over his face. To look at him was to

think that Buzzy had been right about black people never showing their age. He was thin as a celery stalk and not much taller
than I was, but his clothes were vintage and weird. Before I
learned he was a musician, I thought he was a gangster. Grandfather said Uncle Castor played the horses.

"What's your story, Morning Glory?"

Sometimes they "passed away," the old-timers, but still more
appeared on the porch of our wrecked hull like arguments for
the spontaneous regeneration of barnacles. They emerged from
the grime of highway travel—"Swing low, sweet Cadillac," the
Dizzy Gillespie song goes—from bright, dry hours, trailing ribbons of exposition about absent kinfolk. They brought plants
overwhelmed by the cellophane around the pots, heavy suitcases
with empty secret compartments, boxes of chocolate, and were
themselves like nut-filled morsels in a Whitman Sampler.

We weren't ready for Uncle Castor. He'd been scheduling and
canceling his trip all summer in a series of urgent communications
that worked my mother's nerves. Telegrams were Uncle Castor's
little secretaries. He adored to be on the telephone to Western
Union, crusading against lawyers, shady music publishers, former colleagues, and Grandfather. Wires not only demonstrated
Uncle Castor's importance, they were proof of his sincerity. Once,
when he was really hard up, friends at the Tuskegee Institute
arranged for him to teach there. At the last minute he got cold
feet and sent a telegram of apology to practically every member
of the student body.

Uncle Castor said he'd driven from Saratoga without stopping.
From what we could make out, he was watering his herbaceous
bed, thinking of where he last saw his car keys, and the next
thing he knew he was on the Pennsylvania Turnpike, hoping
his car had one last long trip in her. For a snap decision, he had
quite a few suitcases and satchels.

I got to help him take his things to the "extra room," which was little more than an extension of the attic, a graveyard for lamps, chests of drawers dotted with woodworm holes, and corner tables with wounded knees. There were three mattresses on the bed alone. He asked if I remembered him. I did and I didn't. That was the way it was with the passing clouds of old-timers. I remembered the story that back in the Depression he played with Noble Sissle's orchestra and had been loved by "café society." One night in London he was busy with last-minute changes in the program. He felt someone tug at his tails and slapped the hand away. He felt another tug and saw the Duke of Windsor, then Prince of Wales, smiling. Uncle Castor's surprise visit almost made up for Buzzy's announcement that he was going to live with his father in Watts.

I woke Uncle Castor at the crack of dawn. Yes, he had also seen the Duke of Kent before he was killed in the war.

"Are you famous?"

He tried his hands around my neck. "I will be by the time I get up."

Uncle Castor had brought his own sugar. He drank coffee with a cube between his teeth, wiped his hands with a soft handkerchief that he tucked up his left sleeve, and asked for toothpowder or dentifrice instead of toothpaste, all of which seemed to fit a man who dressed as flamboyantly and spoke as primly as George Washington Carver. Uncle Castor had sailed on the *Ile de France*, traveled on the *Flying Scotsman*, and been on friendly terms with the head porter of the North British Hotel. He had seen gigolos in Nice and Cannes with a suggestion of rickets in their legs do the Buzzard Lope and the Walk the Dog. He had made the Dolly sisters laugh. He promised to send me some of his clips.

His life had been a travelogue, but around us his favorite topic was Grandfather. "To this day it is impossible to get through his head without an executive order." Grandfather frequently said that his younger brother was a bum because (a) he had dropped out of the New England Conservatory, (b) he didn't have two nickels to rub together, his savings would not fill the tip of his shoe, and (c) he never paid the phone bills he left behind.

For his part, Uncle Castor answered that the only Latin Grandfather had ever had was "agricultural Latin." In the program of a church conference of which he was moderator, Grandfather had added the University of Chicago to his education. "Those were correspondence classes," Uncle Castor confided to my parents.

The bad blood went back to the 1920s, when Uncle Castor arrived in Boston and Grandfather told him that he didn't know enough Latin for the conservatory, that music students were expected to have mastered several languages. Uncle Castor took a job in a second-class hotel in order to pay for evening classes. The night school wanted to know why a colored boy needed to learn Italian. He also saved up for violin lessons. That's when he found out that languages were only for voice students. His teacher took back his practice violin and recommended that Uncle Castor study the piano.

I told him what Grandfather had said about our house. Uncle Castor remembered that the Klan so resented his mother's parents they threatened to burn down their house if they painted it. Grandfather once told me that the family also came from Norfolk, that our name had Norman roots. Uncle Castor said his father and grandfather had been dark as tar. Uncle Castor was much lighter than Grandfather.

I held to our Norman heritage all the way to and back from

the drugstore on the bad corner where Uncle Castor hadn't been able to find his brand of cigars. He wrote down the serial number of every five-, ten-, and twenty-dollar bill in his possession because in his time more than one storekeeper had tried to cheat him.

We stopped at Buzzy's corner. As usual, no one was on the street. Nevertheless, Uncle Castor looked over his shoulder, the way boys at school checked behind them in the bathroom before they invited a select few into the stall to view a stolen *Playboy*. He kept a small tin of snuff in his pocket, just for show, he admitted. Uncle Castor faked a sneeze and said that Grandfather never did have good sense.

Across Capitol Avenue the girl no one played with because her father was said to be a numbers runner galloped around her yard, which had been rubbed down by the passage of children from school. She inserted hairpieces, "falls," into her own nest, neighed, and tried to watch the synthetic tails fly behind her. Uncle Castor said that the masters of Sweetwater Creek and Crescent Plantation weren't interested in female slaves. I waited. Where there is most light, the shades are deepest. He said that his grandfather and probably his grandfather's father were dark because the men whose names sounded like those of Booth Tarkington characters had not been as interested in the female slaves as they had been in the males.

Grandfather always said that Uncle Castor had a mean tongue, that he did a pretty good job on the dead, but he never got the living right. Uncle Castor was glad that Grandfather hadn't found out he was in town. He said his brother was capable of dropping everything to come up and put rubber bands on his sleeves just because he himself had to wear them. He said Grandfather's favorite meal was Drowned Scout.

———

What I didn't know about Uncle Castor he would one day put into a book. Born in 1905, he once brought home a bandleader who wanted to hire the precocious child as a novelty act for a tour of seaboard cities. One night he slipped out to keep an appointment playing for a social club. He was paid $9.60 in the traditional quarters, nickels, and dimes. The jingling in his pockets betrayed him.

Uncle Castor never entertained any doubt that he was above the pentatonic eccentricities of the Tuskegee Institute Singers. He dreamed of going to the Royal Academy, like the black composer Samuel Coleridge-Taylor. Instead, he was sent for safekeeping to Morehouse's valiant, no-fuss preparatory school, which did its best to cram into black students what they hadn't been offered in the schools they'd survived. Uncle Castor won his seat on the Louisiana Lackawanna, his ticket out of Georgia, by invoking the doctrine of the Talented Tenth, reminding his father that Booker T. Washington had entrusted his only daughter to the Hochschule in Berlin.

As a result of his entrance examinations at the New England Conservatory, Uncle Castor was placed in the intermediate division. He who is perfect shall be a master. Dexterity passages and daily devotions: a book on each shoulder, a half-dollar piece on the back of each hand as he played through major and minor scales up to a certain metronomic speed for at least four octaves. The exercise was repeated with a quarter on each hand, then nickels, then dimes. If the coins fell, he had to start over.

Students did not speak to each other without an introduction. They drank coffee side by side without an incline of the head. The six or seven other black students looked through him, but behind his back called him a "high hat" because his instructors thought well of him. Students were not required to wear formal dress at the opera and he sat alone with his half-price ticket in the Metropolitan Theater, hoping that he had not overreached himself.

The conservatory said that he was very good and that it was unfortunate a black boy could not hope for a concert career. He thought of signing up with the Pullman porters and running on the road, shipping out with the *Twentieth-Century Limited* on a dead run, but he discovered the blue notes of a fast set, the children of Ham and Japheth elbow to elbow over giggle water. They had parties every Saturday where he met piano plunkers who made money though they could not play a complete diatonic scale. Hearing Fletcher Henderson's band was, for him, the killer.

The white men at the musicians' union to which Uncle Castor applied didn't believe he was a student, and when they saw his card they sent him to the black union, where the secretary, hung over, pocketed his ten dollars. He met James P. Johnson, once the most sought after recorder in the player-piano industry, from whom he learned about um pah, fill in, and the Jim Crow that would confine him to the roadhouses on the outskirts of town.

But Uncle Castor was lucky. He was chosen to wear the red fez of the Black and White Orchestra, a six-piece, racially mixed ensemble much in demand in Franconia, Crawford's Notch, Mt. Washington, and Keene, New Hampshire. The "big" union accused them of booking engagements without its permission, held an inquiry, exonerated the white members of the crew, and fined the black ones. Uncle Castor didn't want to go back to the Friday nights where it didn't matter what a band played as long as it was loud or the fraternity parties where the bass sitting at the top of the steps used the collars of the drummers below as music stands. He caught the excursion train to New York in the company of Johnny Hodges, then a teenager too brilliant for the local scene.

Hodges took him to the Hoofers' Club, a basement on Seventh

Avenue, where he entered the big leagues. He started a Boston that brought an answer from the sidelines: Louis Armstrong in cutaways. "Pops" or "Smack" Henderson took his band downtown, solemn as pallbearers. Uncle Castor went upstairs with the men from the theater pits who had no work on Sundays. He marveled at the stretch of Fats Waller's hands at the organ, but cringed at the mugging and bouncing he did for the audience. Uncomfortable with the barrelhouse style, Uncle Castor auditioned for Noble Sissle, the ace of syncopation, who preferred a layered, flowing sound.

Noble Sissle and His International Orchestra topped the bill at Les Ambassadeurs in Paris. An Argentine orchestra played at tea, a French group serenaded the dinner guests, followed by supposedly limpid waltzes from the Viennese. Spackled into the cracks was a band of morose Hungarians who complained when no one trod their way through the gloomy folk tunes. The piano was mounted on a platform so that Uncle Castor sat high above the quota of Polignacs, Twysdens, and Goulds. Detectives tried to blend in without losing sight of the necklaces they guarded. Electricians once drenched the assembly in a rainbow of light, but the effect was so tempting the police begged them to stop.

In the 1930s Uncle Castor, first pianist and assistant arranger, working from 5 p.m. to 5 a.m., was too busy to notice as the "Spectac" began to list in the waters of fashion. The number of newsmaking engagements from Madrid to Stockholm declined. The jive-happy jumped ship. Meanwhile, Europe headed back to war. Sissle's "noted aggregation" returned home to unlatch its horns, but something had been broken in the transplanting. And the miles dried up. Audiences at the Biltmore had even stopped singing "Farewell, Harlem!" Uncle Castor knocked around as a relief pianist, "ghosted" for Fred Waring, wrote and published songs no one recorded, and couldn't recall precisely when he felt himself pushed aside by the new, aggressive sounds of 18th and Vine and 29th and Dearborn. He came to rest as the "featured nightly attraction" at a hotel in Saratoga.

All of this Uncle Castor would one day type up in bold capital letters. He secreted over four hundred pages about the beauty of minor thirds, his triumphs over rivals and inadequate scores, the hectic life of numbers that had to be learned in an hour and princely sums that slipped through his hands in even less time. What Uncle Castor did not know was that his gladdened tribute to his own talent and times would fall into Grandfather's possession. Grandfather stuffed the huge single-spaced manuscript inside the dustbag of a vacuum cleaner, where it remained hidden until both he and his brother were dead.

Uncle Castor liked to quote Edith Piaf when he backed me into a piano lesson: Remember where you came from and send the elevator back down. But I was lost the minute he began to get misty about contrapuntal devices, the rotary movement of his forearm, the special meaning of wrists thrown upward and high finger positions. The impromptu sessions were mostly a matter of his wiping my oily fingerprints from the keys. Uncle Castor relented and capped the tedium with stories: how his teacher dozed like a shrink until he felt the weight of the silence and snapped awake to tell him that his Czerny was unacceptable.

The tutorials he offered me and my sisters were a form of singing for his supper. A week had gone by and Uncle Castor showed no sign of moving on. He sensed that there was a limit to the entertainment my parents and their friends derived from his demonstrations of how the open fourths and fifths of Nathaniel Dett's "Juba Dance" could be grafted onto another song, how the left-hand accompaniment gave it an open harmony and a foot-tapping beat. A rubato passage—he liked to lay on the lingo—of a Chopin prelude could also be taken uptown. "My improvisation is weak" came across as an apology and a need to be reassured that he was not overstaying his welcome.

In his embarrassment that he was still with us, Uncle Castor became timid and elderly. Though he made himself scarce, we could tell when he was out and when he was holed up in the extra room trying not to breathe, pretending that even his ego was dormant. He had learned the tactic of being unobtrusive from his life on the road. Upstairs, he was back in Ostend or Sheffield, in the seedy rooming houses where he'd been given a bed with the utmost reluctance and had to practice by silently running his fingers over any flat surface at hand.

He let himself out in the afternoons, dressed in a vaguely zoot-suitish mode. "Man and nature scorn the shocking hat," Grand-father always said. Uncle Castor came back after we had eaten, also a legacy from the time when band dates had lost their glam-our. He occasionally accepted what was urged on him in the kitchen. He must have been surviving on pizza at the new place on the bad corner. It was the only place nearby and he never used his Studebaker. He once told me he had lived for years on brandied peaches.

"Buster Brown came to town with his big old britches hanging down," Buzzy whispered very close to my ear.

Late at night Uncle Castor drifted along the walls like a daddy longlegs. I heard the bath fill very discreetly. The creak of the back stairs told me that Uncle Castor was on his way to the living room. I watched him from the front stairs, through the banister. He unpacked score paper and books. He'd shown me the choice calligraphy on several title pages that read "Paul at Samothrace." An oratorio based on Shango cult themes, it was to be his apotheosis. Anyone could have guessed that he was touchy about having played "Sweet Georgia Brown" instead of Debussy on stage all those years.

He moved his hands, but didn't depress the keys. Perhaps he

was afraid to wake us. He made a stray mark or two with his pencil, one from a bundle that looked like the Italian Fascist emblem. He removed his shoes and stretched out on the sofa, one sheer sock hitting the other, making a sound like someone trying to strike a match, as if to say this was what the paralysis of being both too afraid and too superior to compete looked like. Then he saw his address book. The number he dialed was a long one. "I haven't seen a thing," I heard him say softly. "There was an enormous tree. Today I looked and it was gone. They chopped it down. But it's a lovely view." Perhaps the person on the other end of the line was like me and believed everything everyone said.

Soon it would be time again for school, for gray Sundays of "Izler Solomon Conducts the Indianapolis Symphony Orchestra," for cold Mondays of new math, new threats to the cliffs of Dover, stapled mimeographed sheets of paper crowded with "Thoughts for the Day" and rhymed couplets in praise of the War on Poverty.

Sometimes, after school, these sheets dropped from linty pockets and sailed ahead of me in the wind. Once, when the rain was falling quickly, smoothly, like grain from a silo, I watched a sheet get away from me into a locked yard formerly known for its peonies. The blue-green ink dissolved and made a map of some far country, of roads into the open.

Buzzy made racing-engine sounds behind the wheel of Uncle Castor's Studebaker, and the dandy who reversed charges in the middle of the night leaned through the passenger window and struggled to calm the windshield wipers and lights. I arrived as he finished his story.

"I spent the first twenty years of my life assuming that my feelings would be hurt. The people coming toward me on the street I thought were going to beat me up. Like they did Roland Hayes in Georgia. You may think I exaggerate, and I do, but it was like that."

I watched Uncle Castor in his outlandish suit with the Chaplinesque seat head toward the filling station to begin his daily look around the neighborhood. Buzzy stroked the corroded edges of the car's body and said that Uncle Castor had been, like him, a janitor's helper. The big boys from the alley had teased Buzzy about the pickup truck he rode around in when he worked one Memorial Day weekend helping one of his mother's friends to spear and bag litter in the city parks.

I was sure Buzzy had gotten it wrong or was just being evil, but when I later asked Uncle Castor to set Buzzy straight he said that he had been a shoeshine boy as well. One summer when he was still a student, he bumped into a nice little ragpicker who had the 25-cents-per-hour practice room across from his. The Italian boy worked as a barber's apprentice and talked his boss into giving Uncle Castor a job. The boss didn't like the way they got on. He gave them breaks at different times and then ordered the ragpicker to keep his distance from the shoeshine boy because their friendship was bad for business. Eventually, he found fault with Uncle Castor's buffing and fired him.

Buzzy continued to position himself on our steps, but he wasn't waiting for me. I suspected that Uncle Castor bought him pizza. He could go to the bad corner anytime he wanted. He shared with me his versions of Uncle Castor's stories, who in turn was delighted to confirm that he had once earned $19.80 a week in a railroad yard replenishing the linen supply on the sleeper cars and worried about his hands, the bags were so heavy. When Uncle Castor was not much older than we were he had worked at a steel mill in Youngstown, Ohio. He hurt himself making bands for cotton bales and was reassigned to a more strenuous position at stacking until a friend told the foreman that Uncle Castor had lied about his age.

"It usually means your ears are not working when you prefer slow pieces to fast pieces. You should be glad to have them both." I'd intercepted Uncle Castor and played the new Beatles album twice in an effort to detain him. He was itchy, as though his Stutz were waiting so machine and man could flash together down the Avenue Gabriel. Uncle Castor said the houses on our block were close together, but there was more neighborliness in the beagles' pen behind the filling station and the helicopters overhead returning to the army base.

My friends were divided into those whose houses I could enter and those I couldn't. On our block it was advisable to play only in yards when I went visiting. If I wanted water, I had to come home. From the outside, on Capitol Avenue, the upstairs rooms of Buzzy's house looked as though the walls were covered with a plush material, like the inside of a Lincoln Continental. I couldn't put into words for Uncle Castor the trouble I thought I would be in if my parents found out that he had fallen into conversation with Buzzy's mother and I had followed him into her living room.

"Young lady, I was top cream." Uncle Castor counted off the names again: Coleman Hawkins, Benny Carter, Will Vorderley, Willie "the Lion" Smith, Buster Bailey, Bub Miley, Tommy Ladnier, Don Redman, Wilbur and Sidney Deparis. He wiggled his fingers, as if he had inserted a large, sparkling emerald on each. Buzzy's mother nodded from the bucket-seat position of an easy chair from which the legs had been removed. She wore a thug's scarf and "pedal pushers," stretch pants with stirrups under her soles. She looked naughty, like Eartha Kitt.

The living room appeared as though it had been furnished with car seats. Except for the stereo cabinet, nothing had legs. I sat Indian-fashion on the low sofa next to Uncle Castor. A tonic-and-something stood on the sawed log that acted as a coffee table. Buzzy's mother said she herself had painted the skyline that went around the walls. There were many Empire State buildings in it. She had had to experiment before she got one that satisfied her. Uncle Castor said that when he was in London he missed his chance to sit for a painter named Philpot because of the Palladium's schedule.

Buzzy's mother said that before Buzzy was born, when his father was stationed overseas, she had sat in Hitler's seat at the Olympic stadium. Her dream had been to compete in the Olympics in Rome. In an unofficial race she beat the official world's record in the women's mile.

Uncle Castor said that once Sissle and the boys were flown over to play at the Cole Porter party at the Ritz in London. They held back on the open brass and outshone Jack Hylton's band, then the toast of England.

Buzzy's mother said she once danced for a living on a pyramid. Her solo was to build to a crescendo as the spotlight fanned open. A stagehand missed his cue and instead of a pinpoint light he turned on the full spot. The glare frightened her so much she lost her balance.

Uncle Castor said every nothing town with a depot now had a Ritz Hotel. At the Ritz in Paris the American clientele managed to keep out coloreds, no matter how famous they were. It did his heart good to see waiters and tradespeople spit on the tips white Americans left, though they were pocketed on second thought.

Buzzy's mother said that she opened a dance school when she came to Indianapolis, but she had to give that up, too.

Uncle Castor said that a white woman on the *Ile de France* insisted that he vacate the chair that was too close to hers; an Indian on B deck accosted him with the insults he had learned on A deck.

Buzzy's mother said she let herself dry naturally when she got out of the tub. She didn't use towels.

Uncle Castor said whites in Paris cut in front of him at American Express and a woman from Virginia protested that she would not have been forced to share an elevator with him back home. Experts in "muleology" were forever approaching his table and saying to his guests that nice girls didn't drink with tack heads. The Americans asked, "What do you boys want over here?" or "What do you boys have against the flag?" and the British said, "You, face-ache."

Buzzy's mother said that what she liked most about the musicians who came out of Kansas City was that they were all so big and black. I said we had to go.

Buzzy walked us down Capitol Avenue. He jumped on my back. Buzzy had his moments. Once, when I caught a high fly, he got me in a hammerlock and said, "Finally did something for the team."

I tried to keep an eye on Uncle Castor, in the way you worry that a relative might be giving away money to total strangers. When he wasn't on the telephone, I knew he was flapping toward Hadrian's Wall for another discussion with Buzzy's mother about the times he came back dead tired from the steel mill and played a little Zeg Comfrey or Irving Berlin anyway to please his friends or the kind of music that used to fit a three-minute recording and what sort followed in the era of long-playing records.

I walked back and forth below Buzzy's hill, just as he used to stake out ours. Buzzy's mother emerged from the house with a tonic-and-something to cool her forehead. Uncle Castor followed, still counting on his slender, knotty fingers: Small's Paradise with Sparky Bearden and the gang in the Dawn Patrol; Jean Patou and linebackers "beating up the watch" in the Buttes. Buzzy brought up the rear, doing the shilly-shally.

One night Buzzy's mother knocked on our door just before my bedtime. She said she was hunting for Buzzy and then said she had invited Uncle Castor over for an evening of chitterlings but he must have forgotten. The babysitter said she would pass on the message. The sitter came from one of those oviferous families of religious girls who weren't even allowed radio. She studied Buzzy's mother, particularly her hair, and never took her hand from the doorknob.

Uncle Castor's suitcases were packed and he'd gone out with my parents. He'd asked me that afternoon to slip up the street with a note for Buzzy's mother. I waited to ask permission to go out until the hour I was certain the sitter would refuse me. Buzzy's mother said she would have called, but she didn't know our number. She said she was glad Uncle Castor wasn't sick. I didn't hear the screen door slam right away and knew I still had a chance to give her the note and say that I was sorry for having forgotten to deliver it, but something held me back.

Later that night I surprised Uncle Castor at his post by the telephone. He quickly picked up a copy of *Ebony* when he heard someone coming. It was the centenary issue of the Emancipation Proclamation that had been carefully preserved under the telephone book. I'd taken a crayon to the face of Frederick Douglass on the cover.

"Bless my soul, you winged me good. I nearly flew." He uncrossed his legs. "I used to talk like that. I had to. It's fine not to be one of them. You just can't let it show." He turned back to the business in his address book. "Ninety-nine and a half percent won't do."

I meant to confess about the note, but something again held me back. He thought I had gone back to bed and dialed one of his long numbers. I watched him squeeze the sash of his bathrobe as he murmured wearily into the receiver, "In God we trust. Everyone else trusts in cash." The person on the other end of the line was hearing, probably not for the first time, how Uncle Castor had been robbed.

Every popular composer was, in his books, an "alligator," one who stole the melodies and arrangements of others. He had a mental dossier of examples. Hadn't John Powell plundered the songs of Virginia Tarheel plantations? More than anything, he wanted to frighten some Hollywood types with lawsuits. He said in 1947 one no-talent radio star actually sent an agent to climb his hotel fire escape, pry open his window, and take the music right off his desk. Uncle Castor believed he had been defrauded of fees and royalties, of all sorts of money, including the inadequate, paranoid kind, "black folks' money."

As if he had used up his allotment of visits at one throw, Uncle Castor never passed through town again, but the beanstalk he planted in our back yard threatened to grow forever into the region of the clouds. While the widower who lived next door to the filling station cursed and worked to start the Studebaker, Uncle Castor said he was fourteen when he first informed his mother that he was going to Paris. He held out an atlas and she called the doctor.

Buzzy and his mother never got to read about the lindy and tango lessons Uncle Castor would give them if they ever came up to Saratoga. "Hey, face-ache." A week after Uncle Castor's departure Buzzy waved a bag of potato chips over my head. "My mama said not to give you none." He said he had something else for me. He said it as if he were citing an unusual but generally known fact of nature, such as that the Nile flows northward. My sisters said they didn't realize how big Indianapolis was until they tried to run away from home.

The Vienna Choir Boys came to Indianapolis. I badgered my parents, those suckers, until they secured tickets. I slept with mine under the pillow so that it came out looking like one of those unlucky stubs swept from warped planks at the racetracks in Ohio, where betting was legal. Curled up to hide from the garage light outside, I switched from the dream channel on which I appeared as a waif bedding down in the hay far from his dying father, the king, to the channel on which I lifted the pillow high to reveal in place of the ticket an embossed invitation from the Augarten Palace in the way I once found that a grubby lateral incisor had been transformed into a silver dollar.

My fantasy had me in some celestial tabernacle, aglow with such intensity that the conductor begged me, the sad, innocent soprano vulnerable with worthiness, to lead the brotherhood on stage. I assumed that the uniform of the Vienna Choir Boys had rating badges and that after a succession of standing ovations, joined in by my heretofore skeptical sisters, I would be elevated to an officer of the line. In my mind's eye I saw the sailor uniform with the wide collar fussed over by my godmother and a bevy of classmates who fought back tears of contrition for having persecuted a nightingale.

The disturbing sign was that in my dream the uniform was visible, but I wasn't. Even when I pictured myself eating European style, with the knife in my right hand, the camera cut from the sailor's sleeve to the plate to get around the thorny problem of there having been no brown wrists in my prophetic film of the moment, *Almost Angels*. But I wouldn't be "Four Eyes" or "Chicken Chest" anymore. I'd be beautiful and in front of the Mozart Fountain. I didn't know the difference between

Schubert's *Twenty-third Psalm* and "Ezekiel Saw the Wheel," but scared money will get you no money, as Grandfather liked to say.

The night of the performance I brushed my teeth until the gums bled, applied coconut goo to my legs and elbows and such a quantity of dressing to straighten my hair that we were late. There was nothing I could do about the Chinese-lantern shape of my face or my father's decision that he had to work late or my mother's firmness that even if the choir had come from Timbuckthree she was not going to wear gloves.

The program's phrase "world-famous" flitted around in my brain like a captured starling; the choristers, shedding radiance, wafting soft fragrance, looked and sounded alike; and an inner voice said, "Sleep." My mother declined to nudge me, to win her point about the gravity of my desire to be a part of the Hurok audience. I wanted to meet the "singing ambassadors," Fritz and Kasper, Master Zink, Peter the young overseer, and his pretty cousin Liese anyway.

I knocked on heaven's door and approached the nearest halo wearer, who every day was up at 6:15, never ill, never bad, stupid, or ugly in the opinion of his sisters. He received my program and produced a pen with the heavy sigh of one explaining for the last time the theory of relativity to the village idiot. I thought I had nothing more perplexing in my memory bank than the day numbers were added to zip codes, but backstage where, justified by grace, the dimples had been turned in with the sailor suits, I suddenly remembered the untouchable horses of Indianapolis's Timberview Stables.

It was my sister's birthday and we had an appointment. A storm had passed through and dark branches on the roads reached up to snag axles. Timberview stood in what I thought of as country. Healthy steeds ate up grass and compliments unknown to the swaybacks that walked in a circle of flies at the state fair or dropped green mud on the trail at Fox Lake. Timberview's horses cantered out of the 1957 *World Book Encyclopedia* that a salesman had agreed was the steal of 1958. But inside they said the stable wasn't open and no horses were available. They insisted that the storm, the lightning, thunder, and other acts of God had left their horses in no condition for us to ride. I recognized the fence around the palomino in the glance of the Vienna Choir Boy.

"They own the fields, but not the horizon," Grandfather once declaimed in the aisle at 7-Eleven.

4 / *The Color Line*

Sounds were different in the suburbs. Because there were, to my ear, fewer noises, I imagined that they were bigger, clearer, and more meaningful than the medley of Capitol Avenue and its tributary, the alley. Our new neighbors were remote, hidden by trees, winding fences, ivy, and double doors. Raccoons and boogymen shook the woods; cardinals banged into the picture windows and boomeranged from view; crows kept watch from telephone wires, disappeared behind chimneys, and popped up with kernels of dry dog food in their beaks. Golden retrievers scampered ahead of half-naked boys on bicycles shouting themselves home from a swim. They moved into the weeds when a car went by. I, too, could tell from a long way off if a car was going too fast around the smooth curves.

In the distance I could hear the rip of a hand-held buzz saw, the smack of a basketball hitting a garage, the swish of sprinklers making lawns soft and shiny, the slap of the evening newspaper landing on driveways the color of the lead in No. 2 pencils and, from the country club across the road, the whine of canopied golf carts, the exclamation of someone watching his ball fly over the barbed wire into the ditch. What we, the new black family, couldn't hear our first day in the suburbs were the sounds that went with the slashing of our tires and the decapitation of our mailbox.

But there was no going back. Freedom had come on in and real life was beginning. I turned a page and started over. Capitol Avenue was wiped out. It had never existed. I forgot to ask to be taken into town to visit the bad corners and my playmates from whom I had parted so tearfully. It was like getting a second childhood, there was so much room for make-believe in the suburbs. Once I determined that the neighbors couldn't hear what went on in our kitchen, even the arguments between my parents ceased to worry me. I used to lie awake at night on Capitol Avenue, like a civilian in a bomb shelter, hearing against my will whose father had said who was no good, whose aunt had predicted disaster, but suddenly these battles had nothing to do with me, like the peasants who merely looked up when horsemen galloped across the fields described in the mildewy book about the Wars of the Roses that Grandfather Eustace had let me keep.

The undulating stretch of the segregated country club, which doubled as the voting precinct, gave the impression of open scenery, in spite of the barbed wire, but that was something like a conceit. The area had been farmland. German immigrants had perhaps chosen Indiana because parts of it reminded them of home, of Thuringia. In some small southern Indiana towns the street signs still bore High German script. But in our neighborhood nothing remained of those days before the Irish arrived with the railroad and their priests except a narrow black-green canal and a clapboard tollhouse with a plaque.

The old toll road that led into the city was still called the Michigan Road. We called it the highway. Burger King hadn't been thought of yet. NO SHIRT, NO SHOES—NO SERVICE, signs in the pancake restaurants said. Somewhere along the line the descendants of the German plowmen had become hicks, and the farms and apple orchards disappeared.

The country club was part of the ruse, the optical illusion. Just as there were dude ranches, there was such a thing as dude country. It looked like my sisters' summer camp: rustic approaches that twisted toward dwellings with all the conveniences. The roads of the township themselves had summer-camp names: Mohawk Lane, Deer Run Circle. Some neighborhoods in the sprawling township that made a horseshoe around the top of Indianapolis had formed "private communities," hired private police patrols, and dubbed themselves with village names that faintly recalled the Northwest Territory: Fallen Timbers Park, New Marietta, Harrison's Creek. Mostly there was an English ring to everything.

We moved into the one house that had too much window for what had been cleared and built up around it. If we weren't careful we'd strut our Negro ways in a fishbowl. A jazzy woman, my mother called her, a divorcée, sold us the house. Its look, 1950s futuristic, went with the woman's gold go-go boots: too much redwood, too many acute angles, deep purple in the master bedroom. The jazzed-up divorcée was spoken of as the only person in the world who had had the guts to defy the invisible line, which seemed to strengthen itself with every new law passed against its fortification, and the *I Love Lucy*—era modernism of the house itself was not only a planet away from our wrecked boat on Capitol Avenue, I thought, but also a break with everything old-fashioned, everything on which Grandfather and the Negro Section of the Keep Smiling Union had had to put the best face.

"We" constituted 10.1 percent of the nation's population, had six guys in the House of Representatives, one man in the Cabinet, a woman on the federal bench, a posthumous Congressional

Medal of Honor winner, and I didn't care. In giving myself up to what I thought of as the landscape of freedom, I detached from myself and from those responsible for me, as if a white neighborhood were the end of all struggle. The Lady Leontyne had gone the distance for us all. *Ritorna vincitor!* I was, once again, out of it, until I discovered, a few years later, the social satisfactions of being a Black Power advocate in a suburban high school.

My isolation was difficult to maintain, not because of the urgency of the news, but because my mother would not act the part of mistress of the robes and my father had no intention of being master of the horse. My parents' idea of their duty toward me went far beyond the custodial chores to which I tried to confine them. But in what was for me the dramatically uncharted meanwhile, I was alone, in my head at least, and even now I don't know whether the lie owed its unfolding to the universal derangements of puberty or to my being a new black student in what I described to Grandfather, with furtive pride, as an overwhelmingly white school.

Someone was always trying to interrupt, to get between me and the paradise of integration. Grandfather Eustace took a renewed interest in me because of Westfield Junior High School. An expert on white classrooms, he told me to call if I experienced any difficulty of adjustment or was graded unfairly—and he told me to call collect, to circumvent my father's complaint that not only would he have to put up with Grandfather's interference, he would also have to pay for it.

Once my mother stopped dropping me off in the school parking lot and turned me over to the skills of the uncommunicative and unbelievably overweight bus driver, I suffered no traumas of any kind, much to Grandfather's disappointment. He worried that I did not have the stuff to speak up when mistreated. It wasn't like him to hunt for that kind of thing, but then his problems, like those of the rest of the minority of 10.1 percent in 1966—remember them that are in bonds, as bound with them—were not mine.

The yellow school bus was on time on mornings that got darker and darker, mornings of rain, frost, untrammeled snow; and it was there, mud free, on mornings when the sun's running yolk caught the moon in the ether. My new school was miles away —these were the days before court-ordered busing, before long rides were considered harmful to white students—and the bus meandered by drained swimming pools, clay tennis courts, collapsed barns, abandoned greenhouses, a colonial-style fire station, an unsuccessful-looking Catholic church with matching grammar school, and a complex called the Jewish Community Center.

Like everywhere else, the suburbs had good, bad, and middling addresses. The school bus picked up cheerleaders with bouncy hair; sulky white trash who smoked in front of hot rods on cinder blocks in scrappy yards; nerds from the chess and visual-aid clubs who howled when the bus passed dogs in the act of doing it in the nettles; and the show-offs from the Golden Ghetto, that strip that had gone fabulously Negro professional in the early 1960s.

With their never-wear-white-after-Labor-Day clothes-consciousness, their coordinated outfits that did homage to the seasons, clothes so new that in some cases the packing cardboard had not been removed from the collars, the black kids made a screaming tribe in the back of the bus. I sat in front with the nerds, directly behind the melting Buddha driver.

I lost the show-offs from the Golden Ghetto at the doors to Westfield. I saw them again during gym period, when their voices reached full fire and the coach applauded the towel-snapping in the showers. But even in gym I was at a safe distance from the

show-offs, having been assigned to the squad for nerds and tub-
bies, guys who, in a game of "burn ball," when one team tried
to murder the other with a basketball, either immediately ran
into the line of fire so that they could sit for the remainder of the
class period or hung back by the bleachers until they were picked
off like plastic ducks in a shooting gallery.

I came upon two or three of my fellow black students whom
I had known in the banished, forgotten days of Capitol Avenue.
One boy had been a playmate and then disappeared. I saw him
infrequently, when our parents went to the same picnics. We
picked up at these picnics where we had left off in his or my
back yard, hammered at badminton birdies, and then he was
gone again, waving from the back of a new Buick Electra.

People vanished that way from my Capitol Avenue life. They
simply didn't live nearby anymore and the sledding parties on
their hills came to an end. Families moved, mothers became
Catholics, fathers went over to the Republicans. I didn't pick up
much in those days, like a radio with a broken antenna that has
to be moved from corner to corner before it can adequately receive
a signal, but in the hallway at Westfield, unable to remember
the combination to my locker, I understood where many of them
had been disappearing to.

I scarcely acknowledged my former playmate and soon he
failed to notice me in the halls. It was harder to deny two popular
girls from my former life. They were older, "cool" in Westfield
terms, because they were loud at the black table in the cafeteria
about the Tighten Up, the latest dance step, and yet their names
appeared on the straight-A list of the honor roll published in the
school newspaper. I never saw them on the bus.

In Capitol Avenue terms they were real "upper shadies," because they had never lived anywhere near Capitol Avenue and
were often on their way to Cape Cod or coming back from Hilton

Head. Boarded-up theaters in the "inner city" were named after their grandparents. Their hair almost bounced, their braces flashed in the fluorescent light, and they had my sisters' permission to make comments about my "high-water" trousers. They said my cuffs fell so high above my shoes I wouldn't have to roll them up in a flood.

But their laughter couldn't follow me far: the rules of Capitol Avenue no longer applied. My sisters had stuck by their school in town and that had not been easy. It was an old high school with many sentimental graduates who wept at community meetings and devised through their tears a plan to save the school from the black neighborhood that had grown up around it and was closing in. To preserve its racial harmony, the school had been allowed to go private, to give entrance exams and charge tuition. I was on my own at Westfield. My sisters' grades didn't hang over me, the teachers didn't show up at NAACP meetings. No one knew who I was, and what I was I set aside every morning at 7:45.

My new classmates were ready with batting averages, won-lost records, and the history of shutouts. The names of Queen Victoria's nine children, nineteen grandchildren, and thirty-seven great-grandchildren did not fall into the category of anything anyone but me wanted to know. Westfield was like a stocked fish pond, brimming with opportunities. I had only to cast down my bucket where I stood. But I was like the tourist who doesn't want to look as though it is his first trip in business class or his first attempt to buy aspirin in a foreign drugstore. I behaved as though I had been among the Westfielders all the while and was finally shedding the protective coloration that had kept me completely unseen.

I wanted to copy the manner of the coolest boy in my grade —his shiny brown penny loafers with slightly worn-down heels;

the way he spun the calculus ruler of the advanced mathematics student; the noncommittal way he let himself be detained for a moment by admirers, like the terribly rich who must always be on guard against that someone who affects social ease; the way his letter sweater tapped his hips as he made his graceful escape; and the way—never mind that my hair couldn't "fall," that my glasses had thickened—he swept his Beatle hair out of his eyes, moiré-gray agates that accepted the devotion of all and gave nothing back.

Grandfather mounted a new high horse—the advantages I was about to receive, which raced too near his perfunctory "blessings we are about to receive" over the congealed canned ham and pineapple. It upset him that I was not moved to compare what he conceived of as the elaborate equipment in the chemistry and language labs of Westfield to the inadequate "learning tools" I might have had, had I gone on in the schools that served the world according to Capitol Avenue.

The pleasure of my circumstance depended not only on my perverse wish not to comprehend Grandfather's point, to show that I was not one of his underprivileged youth group members sweating under an obligation to be thankful, but also on superstition, on a Lot-like contract of deliverance. I couldn't allow myself to look back, having presented myself to myself as one who had never been anywhere but where I was.

I lived entirely at my surface, passing without reflection from class to class, like someone out for a walk noting when the clouds either darkened or dissipated. The school facilities and high property taxes of which the township was so proud that its citizens voted in referendums against absorption into the city were, for me, so intent on approval, only decoration. My appreciation was like the relief of someone who has crashed a party but isn't asked to leave, in gratitude for which, and also from misplaced pride, he doesn't touch a bite.

Scene 1. The English teacher who believes the harassment of having a large family has taught him all he needs to know about being understanding calls out the scores on the Dickens multiple-choice test. He holds back the new student's test paper for an after-class conference. "I want you to be honest with me. I can't help you if you don't let me know when the material is too hard for you. Now be honest with me. Did you cheat?" The hands of the surprised Negro student—"I was so conscious of having passed through scenes of which they could have no knowledge"—fly to cheeks that Clearasil hasn't helped.

Scene 2. The dwarfish American-history teacher begins to recite, but is drowned out by the Negro student in the second row who, in the shock of recognition, gets carried away. "Unheard beyond the ocean tide their English Mother made her moan." The teacher squints, the way the peckerwoods must have regarded the abashed Negro student's grandfather when he ran over that hunting dog in Brunswick, Georgia, back in the Depression. He says, "You're going to be President of the United States one day," which he also says to humor restless children at his moonlighting job as a shoe salesman. It sounds like "You that nigger preacher?" Fortunately, the teacher doesn't ask the Negro student to finish the poem. The Negro knows only the first stanza, because once on a visit to Concord, Massachusetts, his uncle bought him a miniature plaster replica of the "Grave of the British Soldiers."

Scene 3. The coolest kid in the eighth grade says hello "first" to the Negro student in brand-new penny loafers.

My happiness was a sin, of that I had no doubt, but even so I was not prepared to endure the punishment of following the oil stains down to Louisville to hear one of Grandfather's chilling sermons. That faculty the adolescent has of tuning out didn't work with Grandfather. His voice I could not ignore or daydream against. One Sunday my objections were answered with the unusual, frightening argument that Grandfather needed us. I would rather have lived with the Murdstones than be needed by anyone.

Louisville was as quiet as a back lot. We thought the service had been canceled, the church on Chestnut Street was so still. Grandfather was deeply attached to its stained-glass windows, which were, he liked to say, much older and sturdier than he and would be around long after he had joined his crowd in heaven. I knew that the little Congregational church represented the niche Grandfather had found late in life. He had never been anywhere else in my knowing him, but the family said they couldn't believe he had managed to stay in one place for so long. It was getting on to twenty years. "They'll put him out," Great-grandmother said every year when we called her on her birthday. "They'll get to know him and put him out quick."

But he went on, more interested in fighting the urban renewal that had brought an interstate highway too near his church and reduced the houses around it to rubble than in saving souls. "For our wrestling is not against flesh and blood; but against principalities and powers, against the rulers of the world of this darkness, against the spirit of wickedness in high places." He was often on local radio in those days, warning against "eminent domain" and the hotbeds of corruption that low-income housing projects inevitably became.

The dreaded stepgrandmother, clutching her cane like a throttle, pretended she didn't see us and took her seat directly under the pulpit. She hated it that Grandfather had a family, connections she couldn't do anything about, those extraneous mouths around the soup of the evening, beautiful soup. Old-fashioned hats with feathers moved around her in the semi-darkness. My mother, who hated to cover her head, pulled a bow from her purse and stuck it on. The gesture announced that we were officially not ourselves, that we belonged to an entity that over-rode our regrets for the phone calls, television shows, and Sunday boredom back home.

The reds and greens of the windows were bright as lollipops; strands of light touched the floor and dyed the wood yellow. Otherwise the interior of dusty, painted brick was lost in an electric bill—conscious gloom. The small number of parishioners, my father said, was a bad sign, as if a friend's show were having a troubled run when he'd been saying how much the public loved his act. Some old-timers settled to doze conspicuously in the rear; a great gap opened between them and the fervent ladies in front. We, Grandfather's family, couldn't fill up the middle sufficiently.

I could make out the shine of hair, the glint of spectacles, and the white collars of the choir. A reedy organ began the prelude, a side door admitted a small herd of stragglers. They had the air of having "conferred upon a weighty matter," as Grandfather would say. One jaunty man noticed us and was so indecisive about how wide to make his smile of welcome that I heard his jaw crack.

A woman with a two-toned face, like a pinto's hide, spoke to the stepgrandmother, who barely inclined her head before she swiveled it around. She was inelastic with complaints from the neck down, but what she could do with her head never failed to make me think there was a tank gunner operating the gears behind her sour eyes. Her steel-girder look shot right by me. Then she grinned, as if at the approach of a bride.

Grandfather entered from the rear, alone—except for his black robe. I had the impression he wasn't wearing it; the black robe was accompanying him, surrounding him, attending him, filling up the aisle as he came briskly forward with his hands clasped in front. The sleeves billowed and I pictured arresting officers on either side of him. If he could have gotten away with having a crucifix precede him, he would have had his congregation bowing and dipping. One could almost smell the incense as he passed.

His people, as they had once called themselves, were at a turning point that Sunday morning, as I was to understand later, when I thought back to the way those in the front pews snorted and rolled their eyes as Grandfather sailed up the steps. Purges were inaugurated in a similar fashion in Westfield's cafeteria: an ultra-cool kid would eye the kid whose membership in the set was probationary, make the yin-yang, up-down face that signaled "dork at twelve o'clock," and the others at the lunch table, afraid of losing their status, would also make the happy-crying face, tell the victim who was cool yesterday but today just another dork who had gotten above himself that all the seats were saved, and snicker as the outcast carried his tray to a lonely spot, too wounded to seek refuge with the nerds he had dumped.

The flame-like bulbs in the candle-like lamps along the walls must have been cued by this solemn arrival. More of Grandfather's theater: I am the light. I imagined his people inflamed with resentment, like Protestants back in the days of Jacobite mumbo-jumbo. Grandfather's demeanor suggested that God would show His face only at his personal request. It was plain that he was up there at the rostrum and we weren't. They mistrusted his scrutiny of Scripture for that reason. I'd been slow to hang up one day and heard him tell my father that his board had refused to vote him traveling expenses to a Bible seminar. They said he had studied long enough to know what he was talking about.

The choir tiptoed to hold a note, but Grandfather couldn't wait. He intoned, "I command thee in the name of Jesus" several times, at arbitrary points during the hymn, random interjections, I knew, from the reaction of the organist, who jiggled on his bench as he attempted to control the choir at the same time. Grandfather looked the part of the clergyman, consumed by the image of some wonder across town, over the river, far away. Whenever he barked, "I command thee in the name of Jesus," the organist struck harder, waved more vigorously, and snapped a look at the madman who'd spoiled his arrangement.

It didn't help that the good sisters and brothers in the precious choir placed more confidence in the instincts of the soloist than in the discipline of the ensemble. Grandfather's call, "I command thee in the name of Jesus," threw them off even further than their tendency to upstage one another. By the time they reached the last hill of "Keep Working for Jesus," the altos were in a struggle to hold the tempo and the tenors babbled to catch up with the sopranos, one of whom glared at her neighbor and inched forward to keep herself on key. "I command thee in the name of Jesus," Grandfather said again. Command thee to do what?—to pay attention, I gathered, but he abruptly took his throne and played with the folds of his robe.

Perhaps Grandfather had a motive in allowing the uneasy silence that ensued, a simple demonstration to the combative women in the front pews that within their spheres, the Naomi Circle, the Eve Circle, or the Eunice Circle—groups meant to review the business of the congregation and to discuss questions of faith which in reality functioned as grievance committees and conspirators' dens—they may have been movers and shakers, but when it came down to Sunday they were lost without him, sitting around without the least idea of how to glorify His name.

No assistant pastor dashed in from the wings; the humbler

chairs on either side of Grandfather remained empty. He was in sole command of his stage and studied his robe for some time. Then he gazed into his congregation, but not at any one of us. His look fell behind us, like someone on a porch roused by the familiar greeting of a neighbor coming for a visit. He watched his invisible friend draw near a melodramatic amount of time. The organist dared a patient background chord. I distinctly heard the woman with the pinto-hide face hiss and say, "Crazy as a Betsy bug." A brilliant, white smile of the purest malice seeped into Grandfather's coffee face.

As a child I knew that Grandfather was not Moses because the illustrations in my Sunday-school book depicted a heavyset, thin-lipped beggar with snarled hair. When I saw a drawing of the young, winged Satan among muscular cherubim I didn't know who Grandfather really was. "Let us pray," he finally said, and threw open his arms.

The service had something of the start and stop of Grandfather's old shoe parked in what he called, in the interest of historical accuracy, "the carriage house." He could have scared a Marine with his stern messages from St. Paul, but that morning he read as if talking to himself, his voice barely audible above the scraping. The congregation mumbled the Lord's Prayer and the Apostle's Creed like a schoolroom aware of collective guilt. "Offertory pans" that resembled deep-fry baskets on long poles went around with much change-making and pantomime of alms-giving. The two ushers sidled away with the cash and never came back.

The choir warped a few more hymns of adoration, sometimes in collusion with the audience, and always with an experimental, piercing wail from one of the sopranos. No babies were brought to Grandfather's church and that was as odd as traffic without horns blaring. Through it all Grandfather loomed above us, composed, even during the insulting settling-down hubbub before his sermon. The congregation made a fuss about getting comfortable, as if to say it had been through his walks with Jesus before. I fancied that I heard a newspaper back in the old-timers' section.

Walk Grandfather did, back and forth, four steps to one side of the pulpit, then four steps in the opposite direction. Not once did he pause or speed up or slow down. He walked, swung around, walked back, and swung around again. His words seemed to depend on his being in motion, in the way a shark can breathe only if it keeps moving.

"First of all, their religion got both of them into trouble. Daniel in one way, Elijah in another. That is the perennial fate of the serious religionist, whether his religiousness expresses itself essentially in conduct or articulates itself specifically in worship." He was in his element, and as he pivoted, he moved his reading glasses from one hand to the other. His robe flared at these turns. Had I ever asked him to join in my old game of king-emperor and tear through my mother's closets in search of memorial hats and bedspreads I suspected he would have done so with alacrity.

There was an aspect of the school theatrical to his style. A winning innocence went into his gliding to and fro, and also into the vainglory of his rattling on with such easy authority. Grandfather was two years away from his seventieth birthday, the granite hair had thinned, the crown of his head was beginning to show like an island in the mist, but I had a glimpse of the lithe boy he must have been, committing to memory a speech condemning the slave trade from the set of Pitt's orations that his father had given him and that he still kept by his bed.

"Trouble is logically the lot of both types. Daniel got into trouble in the same manner that the first-century Christians did.

Publicly, like theirs, his religion expressed itself essentially in conduct. Like theirs, his conduct was open to all but his worship was private. Even as they were, he was ostracized, persecuted, and subjected to martyrdom."

He was positively shining. Either his head or his glasses reflected the lights. A white dot followed him along the back wall, like the ball that bounced from word to word on the television screen so that the audience at home could "Sing along with Mitch."

"Of Daniel the narrative relates that he was distinguished above the satraps because an excellent spirit was in him, for as much as he was faithful, neither was there any error or fault found in him. Like ours, Elijah's religious genius went largely into public worship, and conduct was decidedly a secondary matter. Even as we are, he was beset on all sides by denominational antagonists, harassed by sectarian opposition and driven from the field of power. Of him it was said that he was very jealous for Jehovah, that he ran for his life and that he requested for himself that he might die while on his way to Sinai, where pathetically he claimed to be the only real one of his kind left. Of us it can be likewise said that we cling desperately to institutional self-preservation and that we run home to God with our particular excellencies."

Grandfather, the step migrant, walked on. The congregation of retired drugstore owners and schoolteachers lifted their heads at words like "bloodshed," thinking they recognized something of the apocalyptic vocabulary from the battlefield states. They had decided that they wanted "heart religion," like everyone else, but Grandfather could not imitate storefront showmanship. He lectured his congregation on the vanity of piety, his posture announcing that he was as strict as his model, the old Harvard dean, Willard Sperry.

Ears rolled up among the front pews' hat flora of taupe, burnt orange, and canary yellow. Molars went on insolent display. One old-timer made a lot of noise getting his watch from his pocket; a woman appeared to be balancing her checkbook. I wished he'd stop for a minute, lean on the rostrum, and tell the story about the women in France who wore such high, elaborate wigs that mice made nests in them. I found myself moving in my seat. My parents gave me a keep-still look. My sisters played tic-tac-toe on a program. We used to play a game when we went to church. We'd each select a word beforehand, "God" and "Lord" were excluded, and count how many times it came up during the sermon. The winner got a share of the losers' dessert.

The sheer flow of Grandfather's words suggested that it was dangerous for me even to pretend that I had fallen asleep. The white dot on the brick wall returned and followed Grandfather in his revolutions. It occurred to me that this was not a reflection from his glasses or his crown, no matter how much they shined. The dot was, in fact, pursuing Grandfather, trying to alight on his head. I turned around: nothing back there but the lolling heads of the old-timers. They were too far away anyway.

Grandfather also must have finally noticed the moving dot. Any evidence of concentration fled his face. The little spot disappeared, as if someone had clicked off a flashlight attached to a key ring. I couldn't possibly get blamed for the practical joke, but I felt guilty. Old-timers simply did not pull that sort of schoolboy prank. The beige stepgrandmother ground her metal cane into the floor. I coughed—"germ," my sisters said—because Grandfather looked, quite suddenly, like a senior citizen on a bus, adrift and in danger of missing his stop. Maybe he was at a crossroads of sorts, trying to decide in what style he should proceed, up or down. His eyes roamed slowly over the hard hearts in the front pews, like searchlights from a guard tower.

I'd seen that look before: at Westfield Junior High School. The two cool girls, the upper shadies, had written a play, "Twenty Negroes Land at Jamestown, Virginia." The cast included most of the black table in the cafeteria. For some reason, every word struck me and the other blacks who weren't performing as hilarious. After the all-school assembly, the two girls confronted us one by one.

They said if we weren't part of the solution, then we were part of the problem. Whenever a black tried to do something, they said, other blacks came along and tried to tear them down by acting worse than white people. Black people hated to see another black person get anywhere. Black people hated to see another black person get attention. Black people thought they could do better whatever a black person in the spotlight was doing, just because they were black, too. Then they went home and told their parents, who called my parents.

"The Daniels and the Elijahs of all time and any time have always gotten into trouble." Grandfather, the day's poet of metaphysical need, recovered. "The Daniels will get into trouble with the forces and principalities of wickedness and the Elijahs with other religionists. When Daniel learned of the plot against him he simply went home to his house, where the windows were regularly open toward Jerusalem, and thanked God as before time. When Elijah heard from Queen Jezebel he went for his life across the border and wailed to God on the subject of religion's futility. The religion which rises to visibility in terms of unassailable conduct is automatically possessed of the potential stuff it takes to face life's crises in scorn of consequence. The religion which manifests itself solely at the point of correct worship or proper belief possesses no inherent resources against the day of trouble."

Even I thought it was small of Grandfather's people not to

throw out an encouraging word, not to part with a single token cry of "Teach," "Yes, Lord," or "Tell it." They didn't have to mean it. He glanced at the back wall as he turned, but the mocking dot hadn't reappeared.

"By a strange paradox," Grandfather charged, "Elijah religion is finally judged and ultimately defeated on the basis of its conduct, while Daniel religion is eventually persecuted because of its worship. Elijah murdered 850 Baal priests. That was his conduct breach. While Daniel prayed to a forbidden God at the wrong time. That was his worship crime. Thus, in reality worship is judged by the conduct it engenders or permits. On the other hand, right conduct can be persecuted only on the ground of trumped-up charges from another realm."

"That's right," we heard. Everyone turned in amazement toward the beige stepgrandmother, who nodded her head furiously. The front pews felt challenged and made dissenting noises with their programs.

"Jesus was criticized not because he healed the sick but because he did it on the Sabbath. Jesus was maligned not because he drove out demons but because it was possible to claim that he did it by the power of Beelzebub. Jesus was put to death not so much on account of the things he did but because his teaching was demonstrated to be in conflict with the accepted tradition. His religion far outstripped that of his enemies, who were content to tithe mint, anise, and cumin and to neglect the weightier matters of justice and mercy. Jesus was crucified not because of his conduct, which had been open and above reproach, but because of his worship, which had been private, misunderstood, and misrepresented."

"That's right," the stepgrandmother said, and thumped her cane. The sound of angry programs, the equivalent of the gnashing of teeth, increased. I wanted to say something out loud, too, but as a modern Negro youth, I was obliged to wrinkle my nose at the glad noises old darkies were supposed to make when the spirit moved them. I'd heard that Grandfather, when he had a church in Memphis in the 1940s, once interrupted the service, revived a woman, and told her if she wanted to "fall out" to do it in a juke joint, not in his church.

"Is there no hope, then, for an age in which religion has drifted so far from ethics and which has contented itself so largely with the assumption that good conduct follows automatically in the wake of an elaborated and widely exhibited worship? Is there nothing of potential value in the zeal and earnestness of the Elijah mood? And must the Christian Church go on multiplying theological Mt. Carmels in the very face of their accumulated futility? The answers to these questions are yes, yes, and no. Justice shall roll down as waters and righteousness as a mighty stream. If, then, exhortation is still a legitimate function of sermonizing, may we nourish our spirits upon the example of Daniel rather than upon that of Elijah. May we turn our footsteps toward the task at Naboth's vineyard."

The organist intervened with hemidemisemiquavers. "May we confront the new troubles in Jezreel with a greater measure of fortitude. May we courageously address ourselves to the behavior of the Ahabs of our time. Man to man shall be a brother, yet in a day such as ours when the temper of the various nations resembles that of a billy goat it becomes a crime to lean far forward. May we proclaim, after John Wesley, The world is my parish. And lest we forget, the kind of religion that gets itself expressed in conduct will bring with it its own type as well as its share of trouble for those who live it. And let us not forget, the disciple is not above his teacher nor the servant above his Lord. If they persecute me they will persecute you."

The front pews understood and were not impressed. The hymn

broke, the congregation made to rise, but Grandfather, being Grandfather, couldn't turn himself off, and we dropped heavily into our warm seats. "Augustine, the guiding star, meets the ultimate matter of the supreme power, the dispenser of values, in his prayer. Be Thou exalted, Lord Jesus, bound, scourged, crowned with thorns, hung on a tree, dead, and buried. Be Thou exalted above the heavens and Thy glory above the earth. Reign, O reign, Master Jesus, reign."

Several old-timers squirmed, as if they had to go to the bathroom or were trying to unstick themselves from the pews. Grandfather's sleeves were still catching the air like sails. "James Weldon Johnson tells of our reward so sweetly. You've borne the burden in the heat of day. You've labored long in my vineyard. Rest, take your rest, take your rest."

He would have gone on quilting the air before him, but the organist had his revenge. There was no power on earth that could prevent a black church, however annoyed and tone-deaf, from lunging into "Steal Away to Jesus." Grandfather's people snatched up the theme—"Ain't got long to stay here"—and refused to let it go until his retirement dinner some months later.

Great-grandmother said that black people had a tendency to put you out every now and then if you didn't keep a hard grip. Grandfather never mentioned his dismissal. His only defense in a series of stormy board meetings had been to repeat over and over, "The proof is in the pudding." They gave him an engraved silver tray and "peed on" the mover's bill.

It happened while I was away, off becoming convinced that everything all-Negro, separate, and tribal was a corral, and anything white a great opening-up to the general dance. The pleasant grammar school on Capitol Avenue had been an extension of our wrecked boat, nothing more. I went up the street to school and then I went home; life contrived somehow to occur in between. Westfield Junior High School, however, was, as I saw it, the Bosporus that led to the wide world.

I'd traveled far, I thought, as a Pullman porter would have, back in the days of miles of smiles, when Westfield sent the journalism club to the Midwestern Music and Art Camp in Lawrence, Kansas. I laughed into my sleeve when Grandfather said the William Allen White School of Journalism at the University of Kansas had been named for a man whose prize-winning editorials were in defense of lynch mobs.

I had a Negro roommate. He and I were the Only Ones in the dormitory. He said it was obvious why we had been assigned together. We never even said good night to each other after that. I envied his trick in the cafeteria, which was to follow a low-flying mosquito and squash it so that the blood splurted across the tiles.

He was taken up by juniors from Minnesota who dressed like Jimi Hendrix and painted psychedelic posters under something called black light. He was followed by seniors from California who had come out against Vietnam, seen Janis Joplin kick the balls of her lead singer on stage, gone to R-rated Mike Nichols films, and feigned twisted ankles so that they could get codeine prescriptions at the infirmary. He sat with a guitar on the dorm roof.

He was the Most Popular Black Kid at Camp, which didn't leave me many choices among the remaining titles. I became the Most Religious Black Kid at Camp. I was taken up by nuns. My calling included dropping in uninvited on the Sisters of Charity. They jumped out of their chairs to put on their habits and awaited my condemnation of the riots in various U.S. cities.

I'd told the whole dorm that I was a Roman Catholic, thinking my title as Most Religious Black Kid demanded that I go one better than the Most Popular Black Kid, who styled himself "a lapsed atheist" and could sing an hour's worth of hymns without a break. The Catholics at camp, even the wildest of them, went to "folk Mass" in a chapel of folding chairs. Because I assumed that Roman Catholics were different from mere Catholics, and that it was rare for us to find the proper Mass, I thought it was a safe lie. Then, in a panic, I purchased a book on the subject by Bishop Fulton J. Sheen, though it was too late to cram effectively. I entered the confessional and said "Hi."

Fortunately, Vatican II had replaced Latin with whatever. The young priest pressed me into service as an altar boy and was very patient with my blankness under pressure. He cued me, the backward, thick, terrified Negro, in a gentle, forgiving way. It happened in movies, the fugitive who has slipped into a dead doctor's identity pulls off difficult surgery. But by the time the Host was elevated, everyone from the dorms thought my performance deliberately comic, a comment of some kind on the Goody Two-shoes-ness of the abstract fish on a green felt banner, and the arts-and-crafts renditions of the Stations of the Cross. I felt almost popular. Afterward, the damp priest dared me to admit that I wasn't really Catholic and began my instruction with a highly unorthodox version of the miracle of procreation. To appease him, I said I wanted to be a priest.

"What about the sex drive?"

"I'm a Negro. I don't need one."

Our fishbowl back in Indianapolis had a guest lodger—Grandfather, the arch darky. Retirement in Pensacola had not worked out. "The Lord created Florida for the benefit of devils," he said. He was en route to San Diego, where he would or perhaps would not accept a temporary post. The stepgrandmother had stayed behind in their pink bungalow of sleep-depriving acoustics to once again pack up the houseplants.

He'd done his homework and shared with me the information

that the Portuguese explorer Juan Rodríguez Cabrillo landed at Point Loma in 1542. An Episcopalian army chaplain had gone to San Diego in 1850. The Baptists arrived in June of 1869 and the Presbyterians two days later. His Congregationalists founded their Logan Heights Church in 1886. Of course the Catholics had come first, in 1769.

He was ironing trousers. It was, I thought, just like Grandfather to call upon me to sit and have a chat with him while he hummed his way through some hopeless, darky task. I said I had embraced the Catholic faith. Grandfather gingerly laid his trousers over a hanger and said that he had to send my father to a Catholic school in Georgia because back then you couldn't trust the public schools. Places like Westfield didn't exist, not even for the whites.

He asked if I'd been confirmed out there on the plains of Kansas. He said he had never known me to have the patience to take or read instructions, which was why I had broken everything I'd ever been given. He said I knew less about the infallibility of the Holy Father than the boys from the peanut fields he used to watch over when he led a Bible camp on Kings Mountain in North Carolina.

To have a "profitable exchange," all Grandfather needed was somebody sitting there between the washing machine and the dryer—if that. He was as inclined as ever to express opinions, but the subject matter had begun to shift. The contemporary world slipped now and then from focus and the past, the cotton fields across from his house on Sunset Avenue in Augusta, reappeared. The movement of his talk was fitful, like someone dabbing with a rag at spots on a wall or plugging leaks wherever they appeared.

When he talked about preaching it was as though he was himself preaching again. I could tell from the way he threw his voice: he was projecting. He also used to run a camp that instructed preachers. "The time came for us to put theory into practice. Mr. X, will you take the pulpit today and preach exactly as you would this coming Sunday morning to the three hundred members of your church? So he did. The experience was a revelation. All the techniques of harangue were revealed. The barker selling his wares was there. The angel Gabriel suddenly appeared as an escort for the faithful up to the pearly gates. The heat of his presentation waxed warmer and warmer. He became so loud the walls could not contain his nonsense. So it thundered out. Stray dogs hastened to the windows in canine anxiety to see what the noise was all about."

The memory took him straight back to where he stood: in our basement, folding and ironing, and he fell silent. I knew it, but sympathy would have encumbered my brand-new youth. I ran away from the point, with my world unfolding and his closing down. I reached the top of the stairs first and hit the light switch.

The days grew short again. Hikers were no longer seen on the towpaths along the township's canal. Mown grass gave way to the melancholy of burning leaves. Every lawn had its crackling, acrid, black-and-orange pyre. San Diego waited. The stepgrandmother didn't know what to do with the boxes and we didn't know what to do with the suzerain among us who, in my eyes, lowered himself in order, he said, to earn his keep, and succeeded in driving even the taciturn handyman up the wall.

My interest in the Roman Church subsided along with my allergies. The distance of Westfield's teachers I accepted as professionalism. Grandfather wanted to have a talk with the zoology teacher. My parents would not miss Parents' Night, I said. For all his expertise on white schools, I didn't trust Grandfather. Westfield wasn't like the grammar school on Capitol Avenue, where the science teacher who managed to drill through the thickest heads was every parent's friend.

Grandfather himself was an escapee from that tight, closed world where every Negro was said to know every other Negro and no distinction was drawn between classroom and home. He said in his day Negro schools had good teachers because they weren't hired anywhere else. But my father hadn't discovered until graduation day at Howard that its president was an old friend of Grandfather's. Grandfather didn't stay for the commencement exercises because my uncle was to graduate the same afternoon from M.I.T., which was, to Grandfather, the better occasion. Perhaps he wanted to make an appearance at Westfield precisely because of his regard for white schools. I wanted to tell Grandfather to go out and find his own white people.

Instead, he took a newspaper and shovel to clean the dog's pen. A greater mortification was to come. It was my turn to host the meeting of the Westfield journalism club. Grandfather took over the preparations. Sandwiches wouldn't do, he said, and besides, he knew a lot about shrimp. My mother threw up her hands. She said the most I could hope for was that he would take a powder before the Saturday that was so important to my reputation. I had a new identity. I was young, which superseded my classification as a Negro.

"You know more crackers than anybody," Grandfather said.

I tried to keep the door to the den closed. Boys in crew-neck sweaters and penny loafers debated with girls in wraparound denim skirts and Weejuns. Grandfather found a reason to slip in every five minutes. The empty soda cans had to be removed, the bowl of potato chips refreshed. He was sure that he moved unnoticed, like an impeccable waiter of the old school, but he was an adult, my grandfather, and his presence, his hovering, caused an impatient hush. So closely watched, the group couldn't sparkle, and every point on the meeting's agenda lost its flirtatious quality. Grandfather's gray suit enraged me, as did his courteous smile, which could have been seen from the moon.

He reappeared with a silver tray ceremoniously balanced on the palm of his hand. I'd never seen the present his congregation had given him in recognition of his years of service, but I guessed immediately what he was carrying, though the engraved dates of his ministry in Louisville were covered for the moment by a mountainous wheel of shrimps impaled on toothpicks.

It wasn't a dream. I didn't wake up, and the tray wasn't safely packed away in Florida with the boxes of houseplants. Whether he valued it so little or thought the use of it a grand gesture, I followed the formal cargo as if it concealed a bomb. His name, which I knew swirled in the center, was still hidden. Grandfather turned and scraped here and there. I imagined that he forced the tray under the noses of my guests.

The social arbiter of the ninth grade recoiled. "Never touch the stuff," he said. "I'm kosher."

Grandfather answered the boy's light smile with his own generous, crystalline formation. "Who is the greatest Jew that ever lived: Moses or Albert Einstein?"

I took advantage of the distraction to relieve Grandfather of the unclean thing and rushed it from the room. It crossed my mind to throw it in the garbage. I ran back to rid myself calmly of the chaperon, to sweep him away like a smashed idol.

5 / Heirs of Malcolm

I was a slave in heaven. Spitballs and shouts of "Dr. Thomas," or, more familiarly, "Tom," hit my neck on the school bus. What I had heard behind my back was soon said to my face in the halls. "You must think you're white." No elegant variation, no trapdoor synonym, no you-laid-them-in-the-shade explanation occurred to me, but I learned that persecution was something you could deposit in the bank of manipulations.

Teachers stirred themselves in the direction of my betterment when they noted the price I was made to pay for my unpopularity with the black table in the cafeteria. I was the Also Chosen and withdrew large sums of indulgence from that account, even ran up an overdraft. I believed in the then often-cited genealogy of field niggers and house niggers. When I needed to blame a poor performance on something outside myself, I had only to hint that the field niggers were after me again. Supply and demand.

My fellow black classmates pulled such faces I was asked to interpret the anger. Nothing about me could make whites feel bad, as if I had been inoculated against carrying terror. It had been a short journey from tossing around paper airplanes with the Star of David inked on the wings in class at junior high school to high-school club meetings in the mute, motionless, tchotchke-free mansions of the far north side.

Our handyman broke his silence to inform us that some of our neighbors had decided we were all right because they saw a lot of white people coming in and out of our house. "Let there be a whole mess of firmament," de Lawd said in *Green Pastures*.

Then came the Revolution, that loss of the meridian, brought to the suburbs by elder siblings on Easter break. The Revolution drove up in Day-Glo vans, electric Kool-Aid Volkswagens, and souped-up convertibles. One of my sisters could be counted on to bring home the longhairs, the other sister to drag in the militants. Chrysanthemum tea and patchouli oil, bubas and dashikis were added to the ritual of waiting for the sleepy holiday meal no one knew how or wanted to know how to cook anymore.

One sister fidgeted at table next to the pacifist, the draft resister whose sunburn peeled as he held forth on the subject of humbling himself before his fellow creatures, of not wearing shoes in order to get in touch with the cosmos. The other suffered next to the soul brother, the sullen Omega whose fraternity hell week consisted of barricading the campus offices of "the white racist power structure": one or two petrified deans. My father could forbid signing up for the big peace demonstration as far as his lungs carried, my mother could cry about celebrating Kwansa instead of Christmas all she wanted, and Grandfather, when he was on the scene, could rebut until the night's sermonette vanished into a fuzzy dot. Nothing could stop the Revolution.

The Revolution was useful as a provocation. It came in handy as a face-saver in my tug of war with my parents. When I sneaked off to "the Ruins," the monument in a suburban park designed to look like a desecrated Greek temple that was off-limits because parents read more than we thought, I talked Revolution with drifters who said they had been around the psychoexistential complex. The real thing was coming along soon, which meant that we didn't have to do anything but wait to be picked up like strays at the curb and given a good home.

One morning I couldn't figure out why school seemed so eerie and reduced. I got such looks that I went into the boys' room to check the mirror. In the cafeteria, when I saw the empty table where the black students usually congregated, I remembered that it was the anniversary of Martin Luther King's death. There was no holiday, not then, but I had not stayed home, had not kept away, like the others, out of instinct. I stopped wondering if I would ever overcome.

I went over the top, "copped an attitude," which the school counselor, irritable from a diet of the CBS Evening News, took as a personal betrayal, and walked out of class rather than relive the indignities of *The Adventures of Huckleberry Finn*. Never mind that the Revolution was tardy and hollow, had come late to the suburbs, like foreign films, certain music, bell-bottoms, and pot. Revolutionary defiance was expected of me and, whites and blacks agreed in my case, long overdue. My best friend, Hans Hansen, admitted: "I used to think your people were lazy. Now I understand. It's sickle cell."

"All Power to the People." When the local chapter of the Black Panther Party, such as it was in 1971, invaded Central Meadow High School, five bad-ass dudes explained to the spellbound student council how much interest had accumulated on the promise of forty acres and two mules, and they injected into the bargain a good dose of guilt for the car keys and movie money that bulged in most pockets. "The American empire is everywhere, even in your back seat."

"You all are betraying the Jews of Warsaw," a voluptuous

woman in a black beret and a black turtleneck screamed from the back of the auditorium. "You have got to get hip to this thing. Get out of your bag. Get out of that mind-set about the feel you grabbed in the back seat of the driver's-ed car. Get out of that thing about who is or who ain't going to let you wear jeans to school. You have got to get hip to some real facts."

The head dude silenced Sister Sheryl, as he called her, arguing that they had come to us in the spirit of revolutionary discipline. She would have to restrain herself until called, although he respected the burning desire for liberation that caused her to speak out of turn.

She never got the chance to address us. Security guards, county mounties, and the sheriff's department crashed through the doors. Somebody had spread rumors of hand grenades and bazookas. The ROTC had real hardware locked up in its shed behind the football stadium, but images of Fred Hampton, Huey P. Newton, and more had come flocking. Sister Sheryl raised her big fist above the heads of her horrified escorts: "Remember the servants of the people."

I saw Sister Sheryl again some weeks later, as I was waiting on the steps of the cavernous, deserted public library. Cardinals in the bare trees looked like punctured balloons. A fringe of dirty, melting snow decorated the empty War Memorial Plaza. The dark concrete looked like a lake at night. She was carrying a sack of buffalo wings. Hundreds of tight, furious braids radiated from her scalp. She had no overcoat, no gloves.

I followed her implacable back and called out her name. She trudged on, then whirled around, ready. "Sister Sheryl?" I stumbled over myself. She breathed this way and that, shifted her package from one arm to the other, dropped a look my way now and then. I didn't know why I'd stopped her, unless it was the enthusiasm that makes you run up to a famous person in a store.

I thanked her for her righteous message to the Central Meadow student council. She said nothing.

"Sister Sheryl?"

"My name is Egba now." She sized me up, asked me what community work I had done. I left out the four-letter words with which several eight-year-olds had requested the end of my affiliation with the Inner City Tutors' Hall. She said that I might be useful to the new organization, the Heirs of Malcolm, which she had founded after her resignation from the moribund Panthers.

I didn't have a black turtleneck. I was also the only boy in the senior class without a driver's license. I didn't know how I was going to sneak into town for the meeting. There was no question that my commitment would have to be clandestine. I tried to explain my transportation difficulties to Sister Egba in what I thought of as hip, bad-corner terms. She cut me off.

"I don't give a damn where you live. I don't give a damn about wheels. Now deal, brother man." She gave me her back, reached into her sack for the company of a buffalo wing as she stalked around a corner.

Hans Hansen agreed to deliver me to my destiny. He had a motorcycle and an MG as well. He wasn't quite so sure that black people were the only people who could free the world, or that the world needed freeing, but he wasn't going to stand between me and the honor of being a fighter in the revolutionary process.

My parents thought I was at the movies. Hans Hansen waited around the corner in his MG with a glove compartment full of eclairs and the motor running. He had permission to take off and come back later in case he, an ofay parked in what we solemnly referred to as the ghetto, got scared or was cruised by "the Man" as a kid up to no good, downtown to buy weed.

I half feared a burst of gunfire when I rapped on the side of the door of a two-family dwelling as tense-seeming as if it had been blacked out for a siege. A child unlocked the door. I heard Sister Egba's voice surge from a long, dim corridor. "What did I tell you about seeing who it is before you open that damn door. What did I tell you about the pigs." The child's thumb went into his mouth. My first thought was that he should have been in bed. I identified myself and made my way toward Sister Egba's voice. She was cooking—hot dogs and baked beans. Around the red kitchen table crowded with grocery bags sat three women, each with a child in her lap or at her knee. They had a special way of snapping chewing gum. It sounded like fingernail clippers.

Sister Egba said that the first sign of a good worker was the ability to remember and follow instructions. I thought she was talking to the child. She said I had failed to knock twice on the window first, then the door, which was a serious risk in the "triangle of death" that was America. I said she hadn't told me about a code. She said she had and that she would appreciate my adhering to the security policies of the Heirs of Malcolm in the future. She did not invite me to sit down.

One of the women said something about the need to clarify and advance the struggle. I pressed myself between the wall and a refrigerator that was painted black. My knees responded to two sharp bangs on the window. Sister Egba nodded to the child. I heard men's voices. "What it am." Two of Malcolm's legatees scowled in my direction and seemed very big in their black sweaters and brown suede jackets. Sister Egba pushed them into another room and announced that the evening's meeting was closed, but she had an assignment for me if I thought I could stomach it.

The MG shadowed me and made me less afraid as I ran from porch to porch, folding leaflets into mailboxes as quietly and

quickly as I could, like a prankster soaping windows on Halloween night. Sometimes a guard dog threw itself against the other
side of a door, lights went on, and I ducked into the MG until
the noise died down. Sister Egba had instructed me not to come
back that night after I had distributed my stack, but she would
have another assignment for me at exactly the same time the
following week. I was so nervous that I neglected to read what
was printed on the coarse blue paper.

The next week three men in variations on the black turtleneck
sweater loitered about Sister Egba's kitchen table. I could hear
a child crying in a back room. "Man, he was not only rookie of
the year, but that was as close a play as you'll ever see in your
life. As far as anybody in Brooklyn in 1955 was concerned, he
was safe."

The conversation took me back to the Saturdays when the
handyman acted as bodyguard for me on my way to the barbershop on the bad corner, in case I saw something I liked. The
handyman hitched up his trousers to join the old-timers, those
still loyal witnesses of Satchel Paige, the pitching machine in
orange, those connoisseurs of big behinds and disciples of Mad
Dog 20-20, seated under the mirror along the wall. They
thumbed through back issues of *Jet* and winked every time they
thought of another sin we uncomprehending young woolly heads
ensconced in sheets ought never to avail ourselves of.

But when Sister Egba planted her black boots on the buckled
linoleum, the Heirs of Malcolm "switched up," pretended they
were in the middle of a heavy discussion about Jamming Jennys,
Armalite M-15s, M-16s that stuck because of deposits in the
barrels, and the memorable M-1s of the Korean War. The last
bullet out of the clip made a bell sound to let the soldier know
he was out of ammunition. "It did. And the Commies, too."

Sister Egba interrupted and said that what we needed to realize was that the dog power structure sent black men with shoddy weapons to fight imperialist wars against their Third World brothers and that the use of the term "Commie" was politically incorrect. The Heirs of Malcolm leaned back, as if to get out of the way of her "scientific" approach.

I could type. A heavy Underwood was produced from a grocery bag. Sister Egba and the others watched over me. She corrected my mistakes. If the notepad before me said ten had attended the rally to demand a stoplight for an inner-city playground, she inserted an extra zero; if the notes said fifty had attended the march against police brutality, she commanded the creation of another optimistic zero. There was some unpleasantness between me and another revolutionary about what sort of grammar and spelling the sleeping masses could relate to.

The strategy meeting that night was off-limits, but there were several things she needed to talk to me about. She thought I would do okay as a minister of information because I had not thrown away the previous week's leaflets and pretended that the job was done. I wondered how she knew. She shrugged and said that to integrate theory with practice she'd had me followed.

She walked with me around the corner, a "go on Shaft," all-weather trench coat wrapped tightly about her tigress thighs. She ticked on in a low, urgent voice about the necessity to begin aboveground in order to provoke the oppressor into driving the Heirs of Malcolm underground. I stalled, but she said that if I ever hoped to evolve to a higher level and one day drop my slave master's name for a "righteous handle" she would have to check out my conspicuous running buddy parked in the fast car.

Sister Egba held her beret through the driver's window. She said that the treasury needed donations. Hans Hansen swallowed and said he didn't want to do that. "I'm not asking you to, I'm allowing you to."

"Who are you again?"

"I am none of your damn business."

He fished out five dollars and gave the MG the gas.

I dressed up in my costume of revolutionary devotion and passively received the latest of Sister Egba's "executive mandates." My mother threatened to burn my new black turtleneck and flared trousers while I slept, she didn't care if they were my "movie clothes." I was careful to wear the same thing every week because Sister Egba did, ostentatiously so. She lectured the women cracking chewing gum around the kitchen table about throwing their money away in the street. One of the women suggested that they organize a clothes drive for the children. Sister Egba shouted, "Where do you see a sign in here that says GOODWILL?"

Sister Egba said she would not take castoffs from no-butt honkies or pork-chop nationalists, because she did not want to itch for the rest of her life. If they learned to make their own clothes, she said, their minds would be free for more important matters. I thought of the hours Muriel had spent, hunched over like a diamond cutter, piecing together dresses for Aunt Clara.

One woman said that at least Afros had ended the agony of the hair question. Another woman said that fixing hair relaxed her. The youngest woman around the table rested her chewing gum on a saucer to light a cigarette and said that Afros hadn't saved her any time because her hair was naturally fine and she had to sweat with a comb until her arms hurt to make it kinky. Sister Egba's look was eloquent, as if to say that the journey to a higher level of consciousness was a lonely one.

Their talk reminded me of the humiliation of having to wait inside the ladies' room when I went shopping with my mother as a child. I was never allowed to hang much with the men who slid in and out of Sister Egba's kitchen. They left, usually after a muffled conference with Sister Egba, who returned to the kitchen slamming cupboards and snorting about "foul traducers" and "avaricious individualism," ominous phrases that she deployed in a less than discriminating manner in the organization's single-sheet newspaper.

I couldn't find out from Sister Egba how many revolutionaries were moving ever onward to victory in the Heirs of Malcolm or what its long-range plans were. She repeated more than once that she would ask the questions. The little I knew about her came from ashtrays stacked next to the sink: souvenirs of restaurants, motor inns, and a large factory where telephones were made. I decided that she'd been a waitress, a hotel maid, and a telephone assembly-line worker.

Whatever her past, the future was great. It was, however, far off. Sister Egba lived, as far as I could tell, solely in her present, spoke only in the language of the moment, and did nothing but direct the servants of the Revolution. Time off did not exist for freedom fighters: even television was "the aggressor." You heard nothing on the news, she said, except propaganda and the distortions of some "flunky running off at the mouth." She said her son watched television at his grandmother's, but there was nothing she could do about that. I didn't know how old Sister Egba was. When I asked about her life, she turned from the stove and said without emotion, "Tight we ain't."

She disliked initiative. My preparation for the momentous task of harassing the oppressor to his doom was confined to unsticking the blunt keys of the Underwood and assaulting mailboxes. I was introduced at the one basement meeting of twelve I was allowed to attend, but was told not to participate, not to raise my hand. If I took notes, they had to be turned over to Sister Egba. I thought that with a pen and paper I would look busy and wouldn't have to jump up and scream "Right on" with the others. Hans Hansen was proclaimed a potential white ally and granted a seat in the back because the heater in his MG was on the blink.

What Sister Egba clearly enjoyed was the awesome responsibility of purifying the organization, delivering final warnings, and then expelling offenders from the Heirs of Malcolm for life. It thrilled me, too, to take dictation of an order that began, in imitation of the Panthers' style, "So let this be heard." Use of drugs was the most serious offense against party discipline. A comrade on drugs could not be trusted with party funds and was not a positive example in the community, because he had made himself a slave.

It was therefore essential that she know what her comrades were up to. She tolerated a sluice of gossip, "cleaning up the walls," around the kitchen table while steam rose from the soapy water in the sink and clouded the window. There was no telephone; the authorities had put too many bugs on her, so she said. It offended my vanity that she wasn't interested in the rigor of my conduct. I was only a high-school student.

One night Sister Egba informed Hans Hansen that he had to drive her to an important engagement. He said he wasn't going anywhere downtown without me. We were, I thought, moving up in the revolutionary hierarchy and there would be some liberator's equivalent of a hazing.

She had received a report about a trusted comrade that called for immediate, firm action. She arranged herself around the gear shift of the MG and managed to dominate its two seats. We were packed together so closely that my ribs could feel what I took to be a nozzle in her trench coat. She said we could talk or play music if we wanted, but she had to think. I tried to sing falsetto

through my teeth, in terrified German, that she had a gun—
Hans Hansen sat in front of me in German class—but he thought
I was making up another crazy blues tune and joined in.

We pulled into the parking lot behind Bobo's, a bar "on the
avenue" that looked more shady than it really was. No lady, no
one's mother, went there, and for that reason it was a favorite of
the big Negroes, chiefs of staff, judges, black radio station share-
holders, members of Odd Fellows, of the Boulee Club, who liked
to get nostalgic about Big Ma Bell, Jimmy Coe, the Pink Poodle,
and their many byways of "trying to make it" before they "got
over." I felt safe, knowing they did not let customers who weren't
regulars get out of hand in there.

"Move," she said. I looked around to see if I recognized any
cars from my father's bridge club. She almost tore Bobo's door
off its hinges.

It never crossed our minds to run. Perhaps we were afraid of
Sister Egba, though she did not know where we lived; perhaps
we wanted to stick around to see what would happen. She forced
her way back into the MG and yelled out an address. She
breathed heavily, like someone who had climbed stairs. Hans
Hansen asked her twice not to smoke. "Drive, blanco."

She directed us to a social club in a converted house down the
block from the pitted gothic entrance to the old cemetery. The
white steeple of a new Baptist church rose over the alley. Cars
lined the narrow street; some were parked on the grass, as if the
owners didn't want them too far out of their sight. Blinds in the
windows of the second floor opened and shut, emitting flashes
of light, as if someone were signaling ship to shore. Sister Egba
didn't move.

I didn't know how to tell her that some revolutionaries had
curfews. "It's late."

"I'm hip." Sister Egba didn't look in the direction of the house.

She waited. We also looked straight ahead at the cemetery gates. Then we heard above the party murmur someone singing bits of a Marvin Gaye hit to himself, privately, disconnectedly, in the way, years later, people on subways would sing along with Walkmans, unable to hear how spacy or off-key they sounded because of the earphones on their heads. I turned and saw a slim man in a black beret grope toward the edge of the porch, lose his balance on the first step, and roll slowly and happily downward. "Yes, Willy my silly, your ass is surely grass."

Sister Egba shoved me out of the car, stepped over me, and advanced toward the porch in a boneless, fluid motion. I looked through the rear window as Hans Hansen swerved the MG around the corner. She was standing with one foot on the giggling pile of clothes at the bottom of the porch and her right hand was deep inside her trench coat.

We studied murder stories in the newspaper for days and skipped two Fridays after Hans Hansen confessed that he preferred going to Laura Nyro concerts to parking on spooky streets and watching his hair turn gray.

We cleansed ourselves at football games, and at meetings of New Life, a group popular with jocks led by a middle-aged man in gym shoes and sweat pants who would not act his age. Women with stiff permanents and rhinestone butterfly glasses gave away suspect editions of the New Testament and glowing cheerleaders flew to greet us with the question "Do you know Our Lord Savior, Jesus Christ?" A screen was set up in front of the lodge fireplace. Simon and Garfunkel's "Bridge over Troubled Water" swelled as each slide projected more oozing red, the blood of the Son of Man. The women in butterfly glasses hugged us and sobbed.

When I finally showed up, Sister Egba barred the door with

a harpoon look. She said she was in the process of writing out the executive mandate that expelled me from the Heirs of Malcolm for life. She had proclaimed that the "correct approach" would be to buy a bus for the relatives of prisoners held at the state penitentiary. I was in charge of the fund-raiser; she didn't care where it was held so long as it was deep in the suburbs among my honky darlings and their checkbooks. I'd hoped she'd forgotten.

"You been wrong for too long." Sister Egba was in my face. I smelled hot sauce. I'd been purged, tried in absentia for bourgeois thought, infantile Marxism, revolutionary decadence, and flunkyism. "Let me break it down for you: this shit is too serious for your shit." I couldn't argue, I was so relieved to have been "included out."

Hans Hansen said that if I was an enemy of the people he'd be an enemy of the people, too. We drove around, searched up and down the barren avenues for the place funky enough for Baby Huey. A cool English teacher—it's always an English teacher—once played us a warbly tape of Baby Huey singing, "There are three kinds of people in this world: white people, black people, and my people."

We'd asked the English teacher questions about Baby Huey. He didn't say much and we figured someone had given him the tape or he had stolen it, that he had never seen Baby Huey in person or made a pirate recording at all. It didn't matter. The English teacher tired of the school board sending people around to listen to what he was saying and the winters made him cranky, so he moved to Tampa without saying goodbye. But we were desperate to hear that song again. If we could only hear that song again everything would be all right. Then Hans Hansen said he didn't want to feel guilty for being white anymore. He just wanted to save himself.

———

"Europe," Grandfather said, "is disastrous to the patriotism of colored Americans." We were taking a turn around the barbed-wire fence of the golf course. The sky walked along with us, or just a little ahead. Maples closed ranks behind us. I knew this was to be a duel between large and small minds because Grandfather had removed his olive-green jacket.

He was outside in his shirtsleeves, in spite of what the neighbors might think, the better to "relate" to me—an expression he could not use without an involuntary pinch around the nostrils. Grandfather was going to save me from myself. High-school commencement exercises were over, and I knew that I'd be across the state line before the farmers again mounted their collateral tractors.

In a moment of weakness, I, then at the peak of my Ernest Pontifex phase, slipped and admitted to my parents that I had no intention of returning to the U.S. from my vacation, because student deferments for the draft no longer existed. I was not planning to go to college. I was going to make a name for myself, either as a revolutionary in exile or as a star of the West End stage, I didn't care which, and the college admissions committee that had attempted to destroy me with a thin envelope would be sorry.

Back then, you couldn't easily distinguish an irritatingly persistent adolescent breakfast theme from premature self-obliteration. Flower children renounced the world and joined communes where the babies were stillborn or suffered from malnutrition. Alarmed, my parents called in Grandfather, the big gun, because it was thought that we had a special relationship, that he understood me and had influence over me, one of those family fictions that grow up unbidden, like debris in a back lot, and which are sometimes useful to accept. I'd never been to a funeral because it was said I could not stand death.

Grandfather was divided about his commission, having discovered a new respect for Wanderlust. San Diego had not worked
out for him, and in the five years since he'd left Louisville, Phoe-
nix, Arizona, and two towns in northern Michigan also had
proved wanting. The Oldsmobile, the old shoe, had given out;
his furniture had ended up in a barn in New Jersey; his books
were deposited with relatives in Boston; and his wife, the beige
stepgrandmother, was also in storage, with her sister, either in
the Bronx or in Brooklyn, he seemed grateful not to be sure
where. The world was near and savage, he was homeless, but
nevertheless he was more at ease than I had ever seen him.

He was pleased that for once his help had been asked for.
Usually he just turned up in a phone booth at the bus station.
He'd appeared so often that he no longer tried to justify his
intrusions. My father said that our having busted into a white
neighborhood probably accounted for Grandfather's willingness
to come to see us so often in his wanderings from sea to sea.

Grandfather walked with a cane, swung lightly at pebbles,
golf balls, and the armor of my revolt. He may have been older,
"shipwrecked and dismasted," but he was still fearless, comfortable with his I-call-you-old-men-because-you-know-the-way
posture.

I suspected that a part of him was also delighted that I had
not made the grade, that I had been turned down by his alma
mater, that I was not, after all, as good as he, in the forefront of
Negro Firsterism. "Providence, Rhode Island, is the costume-
jewelry capital of the world."

He had to remind himself to keep his mask of disappointment
pulled down, but I simply refused to see myself through his eyes.
He had not a clue as to how free and complex I thought I was
about to become that leafy June afternoon and how much a
prisoner of the predetermined forces in black history I considered
him to be.

"We have done our best to train you up in the way you should go, so that when you are a man you'll not depart from it." He said that I would be the first in four generations not to earn a college degree and how I was hoping to live with that knowledge he couldn't say. I said that Uncle Castor had dropped out of the conservatory.

"You take my point. Now we have room for debate." He said Uncle Castor had ended up dying alone in an infested house with telephone operators his only companions, operators who ran his life for him, told him when to wake up, when to go to bed, told him not to refreeze the fish. I wanted to say that at least Uncle Castor had a home, but the idea of property was offensive to what I then called my system of belief.

Some mechanical form of me kept pace with Grandfather, halted when he paused to make a tip-of-the-hat gesture to the back of a reckless station wagon that pushed wind over the blank pavement, but my real self was elsewhere, already united with the vibrations of the Hungerford Bridge and the screeching of Waterloo Station. "You've been hornswoggled," Grandfather said to the uninhabited manifestation of the far away, bounding me.

It was barbershop wisdom all over again, the cult of the Bible and of education, with a lone razor scraping on a strop in the interval between tall tales as thoughts loped happily back to the way whole stadiums shook under the weight of excited fans, except, in Grandfather's case, "The Scholar Gypsy" was likely to be appended to the homilies about getting involved in something you wouldn't ever want to have to explain to yourself.

Grandfather said, "Let me ask you this: did I ever tell you about the Phyllis Wheatley Hotel? Have you ever heard your father speak of Harlem?"

Who hadn't heard of James Baldwin? I'd even driven down 125th Street once.

"I had to haul him out of there after he got out of the army. Before he was born, his mother almost had to come and snatch me out of there. Marcus Garvey had captured my imagination through his Back to Africa movement." I'd never heard of Marcus Garvey, and addressing a black man as the Duke of Uganda struck me as lèse-majesté. "That was the cleanest hotel I had ever seen." But he thought that the President of Africa was, like him, a student of Thomas Nixon Carver's thesis that workers would own corporations. He said Garvey's people had fingers smarter than flypaper. "Riches have wings and sober thought soon ruled out that speculative venture."

Grandfather was speaking off the record, drawing aside the curtain, but he was also suckering me down a trail mined with sympathy. Once he sensed that my real self had been lured back from the Imperial War Museum, once I had slipped back into my body and it began to give off the warmth of human curiosity, he turned on me as he had always done, right there before two evergreen bushes at the edge of a stranger's driveway.

"You talk so big and so much about needing your own life. I just want you to remember how often your own life has put nothing but heartache and misery into the lives of your mother and father."

He knew he had scored a direct hit. He didn't have to spell out which crimes he was referring to. The true bill I returned against myself included grand theft auto, reckless endangerment, and perjury. I went soggy inside at the memory of the tears and the smashed metal and squad-car lights, the tow trucks and the lettering on the lawyer's door. Luckily, my two joy rides and destruction of three automobiles had not ended in jail or in terrible injury either to myself or to others.

Grandfather studied me, his look uncomfortable, somewhere between the disgust and pity you have for specimens. I told myself that I could fall apart over my career as a car rustler later.

Laying aside guile, he touched my arm. The weather and the road reminded him of the day when he had to have his trusty Oldsmobile put down. It had begun to fail just outside Flint. It was, he said, a sign of how low he'd fallen that when God talked to him that afternoon He said he'd get a flat tire and he thought that if God didn't have anything more pregnant than that to say he'd go ahead and ignore Him.

We turned a corner, into a shady lane where I had done a great deal of hiding throughout high school. I told Grandfather that the cul-de-sac was private. He said he didn't see any signs about trespassing. Grandfather, always the first Negro to be respectable, to knock on a door to point out that he alone had, indeed, kept off the grass.

Grandfather said I looked tired and sat. The ledge of the bridge was over a deep creek bed. He even shut his eyes. Steel-colored water splashed on the rocks below; tree limbs, heavy with early summer, bent and straightened. Odors from a septic tank reached us.

I'd waited so often on that bridge, the meeting place between me and the ghost of a future me, had invested the secret spot with such an occult power that it didn't seem right that it was, in the end, just a lane where people had laid out grandiose gardens, arbors, and goldfish ponds because they had more lawn than they knew what to do with.

Grandfather came to. "Tell me what I was talking about. And don't tell me you know anything about the railroads."

No matter what he said, I was only prepared to hear an old darky telling a young buck to be reasonable and practical, which, to me, were code words for envy and frustration that the thaw and the masculine exhibitionism of Black Power had come too late for him.

I was talking to give him a wall to bounce his thoughts against, in the way we had answered school counselors who advised us not to worry and to have a good time, not because they worried that we worried, but to shut us up. REMAIN CHEERFUL TO THE END, signs in the high-school nurse's station said of nuclear attack. I said I wanted to join the Peace Corps.

"You'd look ridiculous sitting in a ditch."

I was not going to be shaken by Grandfather's darky pessimism. The sun reached its climax of cadmium yellow, accompanied by the boom of country-club air conditioners as large as trailers. "It is easy to live with the idea of life," Grandfather said out of the blue, "and when you lose it, you will think of the time when you had it, green and gold."

I regretted the age of ocean liners and felt the injustice of the *Queen Mary* being ogled at a California amusement park. I was not grateful to the designers of the 747, the size of which was such that to fill the cabin the price of tickets fell within my reach. The jet was so big that for most of the flight I thought the wing out in space was the shore of Greenland.

As far as I was concerned I was flying home. My bedroom door may have been guarded by posters of radical heroes, but behind that giant silkscreen of the once-fugitive professor of philosophy, the then-captive gap-toothed beauty with an Afro like the lunar corona, I had inscribed my "Stanzas—Written in Dejection near Indianapolis."

Sometimes my parents came home and, instead of finding me mowing the lawn, saw me loafing in front of the house with a secondhand Edwardian treasure, lolling in a shopping mall and hippie-boutique version of Byronic drag: frilly prom shirt, shoes and belts with big buckles, and a knock-off of an Inverness cape. Jim was ruined as a servant because he got stuck up on account of having seen the devil, Huck said.

A young couple on the plane that I played Hearts with was confused by the accent I had worked hard to perfect. It sounded to them like a blend of Katharine Hepburn and Godfrey Cambridge. I told them what tube station they had to look for on the way in from Heathrow. "Have you lived in London before?"

"Sort of."

Messages in bottles had floated toward me: in England's green and pleasant land. I had retrained my handwriting so that it resembled the script on the dust jacket of my edition of Lord Hervey's memoirs. In those rare moments when I thought about the problems of black Britons, I, the born-butler type, made up an argument in my head that began and ended with how much Dr. Johnson had liked his spendthrift servant.

Nothing had prepared me for the desolation of eating furry peaches in the drizzle in St. George's Park, the soot marks on the carpet in my transients' hotel, the discomfort of being a catfish blowing in the silt while schools of angelfish glided overhead. To be among the young, I hung around the Round House, then a rock-and-roll venue. So much hippie hair that smelled of avocado shampoo.

Some days the only words I spoke were at the counter of a Wimpy Bar. He who hopes for his reward in heaven because he pledged so much to the church deserves what he gets. I circled Notting Hill and Earl's Court like a moth. Blacks exchanged greetings of solidarity in the snack bars. I looked away from fists raised in salute. I studied cocktail menus in restaurants and discos I could not afford. Blacking out under theatergoers' feet during intervals was not the best position from which to strike up conversation. To top it all off, Her Majesty was out of town.

An advertisement for a friendship society took me not to old boys drinking whiskey neat but into a run-down loft of shy Asians in paisley shirts. A clerkly man given to deep blushes controlled how many cups of watery pink punch I could have and eyed me suspiciously, as if I were competition. I did not need English lessons, but I claimed a place around a beaten-up table and took my turn reading from Agatha Christie's *Ten Little Niggers*.

Mile End was part of the East End of London and the declining Cockney world. One stop beyond Whitechapel was my working-class film set, updated by extras speaking Urdu. Still following up leads in the newspapers, I wandered into a political meeting where, as a black, I generated considerable but suppressed excitement. I'd caused a similar stir at meetings of Unitarians and Young Republicans back home. I saw it as a chance to be catered to, like the black speaker at a Soledad meeting who wanted a cigarette, was inundated with every brand of the international white left—Marlboros, filterless Camels—and then asked, "Does anyone have a Kool?"

The unkempt, neglected, upstairs room of the Plasterer's Arms was spacious, bigger than the pub's business would justify, and felt cold, though it was summer. Buffalo horns jutted from a wooden plaque on the wall. The Buffalo Club, whatever that was, along with various rotary groups, shared the meeting space with the Revolution. A smattering of believers gathered to discuss "Productivity Deals and How to Fight Them." My other choice that evening had been a public meeting on "Troops Out of Ireland."

Strong-willed, bosomy girls and women thin as rakes with equally powerful personalities wrangled over how best to convince the working class that established practices and day rates were being undermined by the promises of piecework. The Trotskyite style had something to do with sneering. "We are under no illusions," the women repeated.

The few men present looked as if each had one pair of shoes

and trousers to his name. Though they supported the struggle against productivity deals, they seemed in an awful hurry to get downstairs to the bar during the break. Their freedom in debate as they waited for their drinks came from not having to defend a Trotksyite state, because none existed. They could be as rude about Cuba and Vietnam as they wanted.

I gathered that the assholes among them called one another "comrade" all the time, even in private. Behind their backs, their comrades in turn called them Stakhanovites, a term referring to people who thought of themselves as doing more for the Revolution than their colleagues, digging more coal out of the mine in one day than most could in a year.

The introduction to sectarian politics made me think I had penetrated the skin of the tough city. London was about to redeem the faith I had in the books and films about it. I was having a romantic, literary experience, even if it was an Orwellian down-and-out one. I didn't know whether to think of congenial, self-abnegating Trots as the hobos or the church group that ran the relief house.

A pint of mild was a very proletarian drink. Three of them cleared my head sufficiently for me to see that the man whose assignment it was to draw out newcomers was Ernest Pontifex, a gentleman intellectual who had had hard things happen to him in his escape from his church family but would never concede that he had had a hard life. People matched characters in books, I thought, just as everyone said you could see Old Master portraits in faces in the streets.

The Ernest Pontifex who took me under his wing had nothing to prove and regarded his membership in the group as absurdly difficult work, like the shoveling he had done in the mud of a glove factory in Florence after the flood. He was in his twenties and had already lost his hair. In a matter of months it had gone into the sinks of Poland, he said. The only thing that stopped his forehead were his eyebrows, which cordoned off his half-ironical, half-in-the-movement expression.

I noticed that the publican was hostile to a group of young whites. Ernest explained that they were medical students who worked nearby. They didn't know how to behave. When one of them came in and asked if he could get a pack of cigarettes, the publican said yes, but he wasn't a tobacconist. The thing, Ernest said, was to have a pint of bitters and then buy cigarettes. The pub was white, but it was also working-class. Yet he wouldn't sell a socialist paper in the pub. He wanted to merge with the local builders' teams.

"England is divided into counties of the saved and counties of the damned. My landlord got me prosecuted for creating a multiple occupancy dwelling when I gave refuge to a couple of Pakistanis. I won the case, but I got charged costs. England is like that. They say, 'This is the conservatory,' when it is obviously a piece of ill-fitting, corrugated plastic over the joined sitting room and bathroom."

I put on my solemn face, the one that said there was a lot of racism in this world, not just in the anti-Paki East End. I mentioned the schoolchildren who pulled my hair without my permission. Ernest said people were more kind to strangers than they used to be. During the Napoleonic Wars a ship put in at a place called West Hartlepool. There was a pet monkey on board. It escaped. The townspeople had never seen the enemy. They mistook the monkey for a Frenchman and lynched it.

I slept through the second half of the meeting. When I woke I got censorious looks from the women. To make up for my Stalinist boorishness, I swore to Ernest that I wanted to sell newspapers at the dock gates at six in the morning, nourished only by reserves of caffeine. I hoped that my blackness would be more prestigious than my politics.

"This is not Oakland," he said over the next round of pints. He didn't believe blacks were automatically the spearhead of the Revolution. "What we have to do is organize the working class."

I said the question was, Could the working class in Africa organize and control its destiny, and found myself smiling idiotically, the way I did when my mother begged me to tell the truth.

I tried to imagine Ernest making the rounds with his socialist newspaper at street markets and tower block estates, his mouth disclosing an accent very different from that of the people he asked to be more working class. While at Magdalen College, Oxford, he had knocked on a door, looked across a great swath of carpet, and told Prince Tomohito that he was collecting for the Black Panthers, only to be asked, "It is an animal?"

Encouraged by yet another pint, I confessed that I was feeling relaxed and at home at last. Ernest said that if I needed ancestors, it was quite reasonable to borrow anyone's. It was a spiritual need, not a historic one. He offered to lend me his. "My grandmother, as she grew older, became devoted to her ancestors until in the end she wouldn't see the vicar. I wondered if she would end up worshipping rocks and trees and wells. She had been a snob. She became an ancestor-worshipper, like the Chinese, or a Thai friend of mine who can remember forty-four generations."

The dialectic of Negro Firsterism boiled down to the old Marx Brothers joke, "I don't want to join any club that would take me." A place couldn't be any good if blacks were admitted, which led to a view of life that the best was always eluding you. For Grandfather, Harvard had been really Harvard in the days of Henry Adams, but had gone downhill just before he arrived in New England.

I commended my feelings to the night, sent them on their journey. The streets of London were as empty and oppressive as downtown Indianapolis. I lost the way back to my room. Far from the rattling lines of night buses, two policemen interrupted the contact of extremes, me debating whether to relieve myself like a free spirit against a Nash terrace, and screamed that I had no business in that part of town, which I took as a hint that I had to catch the earliest train that would take me to the dock at Southampton. I made it to the bathroom on my floor, where I spent a sweaty night pleading with the proletarian liquids I'd sampled. Someone bashed on the door in the early morning, but I slept on in my hiding place.

6 / Valley of the Shines

"Ah, masqueraded Harlem," Lorca cried, "your rumor reaches me." On an autumn day 125th street offered its "poem of display"—carts of bargain clothes, false gold laid out on squares of fake velvet, "freedom wigs" mounted on poles, and plenty of bad corners with phonograph speakers hoisted above record shops from which funky anthems blared. The crowd flowed, a Niagara of traffic that never ceased, not even at the corners where domestic dramas were acted out. Langston Hughes once gazed with longing on those analeptic streets from his Columbia University dormitory, but since his time Morningside Park had become a DMZ and new students rode the subways in terror of emerging at the wrong 116th Street. Take the A train?

The Negro Capital of the World, the old-timers' Seventh Avenue, which boasted "fifty-two Easters a year," I knew had moved, long before, to the rare-books desk of the Schomburg library. The Hotel Theresa was dead, the Apollo was in a coma, and the lush exchanges between neighbors in the pretty town houses of Stanford White had to wait in a nourishing obscurity, like a piece of music whose neglect makes its revival all the more rapturous. The voyeuristic possibilities of the remains, the bad corners, were more animating to me than that dissertation-giving ardor for the ruins of melanophilia.

The legends of the high life didn't tempt me as much as the worn-out ones of danger. I went to Harlem, "Valley of the Shines," Grandfather called it, for the sake of having been there, as if the adventures I planned to enter into and then embellish at a comfortable remove had entertainment value. If I couldn't have an encounter of the Harlem kind, perhaps a quick immersion in the scene itself would yield a horror recognizable from the newspapers, an accusatory contrast to the euphoric idleness of life as it was lived in the dormitories, in Central Park West apartments when parents were out of town. Having been on the Harlem scene would enable me to extort from my unsuspecting classmates—the expression "get over yourself" hadn't caught on yet—something of the awe that attends a chief mourner. My people.

The Muslim bakery did not stop for me. I submitted the way you pause near a concession stand to listen to the hawker and catch the gaiety of the carnival. I was teased by two young men laden with bales of *Muhammad Speaks*, drawn into being a part of their performance. They wore white shirts and their hair was conspicuously neat. Their formality said that the Nation of Islam was not so terrifying. They reminded me of the eager scouts who once gratefully and gracefully collected for UNICEF, of the manners that were taken for granted before the thaw, when a stranger was someone not from the neighborhood, but even so not the enemy.

They were talking about the "Original Man." The earth, they said, was about to move and Babylon would soon be taken. The planet was in battle array. They wondered if I knew Chapter

30:41 of the Holy Koran. They asked if I knew that I had been kidnapped by the white race. I said I knew that. This tactic sometimes worked with Jehovah's Witnesses. If one of them asked if I read the Bible, I'd say that I opened it every night. The Witness would stand there with an armload of *Watchtowers*, confused and temporarily at a loss, long enough for me to make my escape.

These were not Jehovah's Witnesses. They said that I did not know the Holy Koran. They said I didn't sound like I knew what they were talking about. I began to think of bear-baiting but did not move on. They said that if I was one of the Negroes, I was opposed to the truth. Their politeness, I realized, was a kind of parody. They said that if I became a black man I would be the truth. Two girls with rollers in their hair stopped to watch us. A woman asked us not to hog the whole sidewalk, please. The followers of the Messenger of Allah said that I smelled like cigarettes. The two girls moved on. Perhaps they'd seen that show before.

I remembered the young inmates I once saw on a fifth-grade field trip to a reform school. We were invited to inspect several classrooms, stood at the doors as if stopping before various explanatory signs at a zoo. The cagelings pointed and laughed at us, the outsiders. The halls rang with the shrieks and whistles and curses of hundreds of embittered boys as we shuffled from doorway to doorway. The trusties and counselors kept up a patter about training programs, indifferent to the noise and our fear.

I was not sure which man, black or white, they said had invented which race in a test tube. They said that white people were devils. I argued with the confidence of being two steps ahead of their next attack. Their primitive weapons and defenses, their slings, stones, and breastplates, were no match, I thought, for the shining mail and Excalibur of my Popular Front mentality.

They said that I smelled lonely. I hadn't counted on that. They smiled at each other like gentlemen vaudevillians at the crest of their routine. The audience had been set up for the punch line.

"We know him," one said of me.

"We do." His partner nodded. "Black on the outside, white on the inside."

Con men, ready and agile in broad daylight, added themselves to the path of pretended friends, like the swift nothing of brown paper and tawny leaves hanging and dropping into the sidewalk's grate. The arithmetic of chance and need put me in the sphere of operations.

"Please help me." I first saw a piece of paper with a smeared address and then a long sleeve of stove gray. Attached to that was a face as sable and glossy as the desk organizers marked down 30 percent in the window behind us. "Please help me." He got out that he had been looking for this address all day, but no one would help him and those who said they would were not very honest. "My daddy said don't never be scared of nothing. But I don't know where I am. My mama's counting on me." He called me sir.

I asked him not to call me sir. He said they called him Tunk back home in South Carolina. He'd come up by Greyhound all night long, directly after his father's funeral, to collect the insurance money. I believed him. Tunk said he had been hunting for his father's people. I watched him remove a large flowing red handkerchief from his back pocket. He dabbed at his smooth, childish face. "My mama gave me it." He lovingly wrapped it back into his trousers and looked around, lost, alone.

"Please help me, sir." Tunk accosted a wiry man in a hat as wide as a tire. I didn't move on. Beneath the brim the dandy stroked his goatee and bore down on Tunk's mauled piece of paper, as if the address had been written in a hieroglyphic the secret of which would be revealed if we only had patience. Tunk raced through his story, loud and desperate. The Samaritan in the plum leather coat said that Tunk was on the right street, but a study of the buildings, their windows like the sockets of skulls, showed that the address did not exist.

The frightened farm boy said he couldn't get a bus back to South Carolina until the following day. He had to find his cousins, his father's people. He had heard bad things about hotels. Besides, his mama needed every cent of the insurance money. I'd seen the film of *A Raisin in the Sun*. I'd read the play and worried when Tunk pulled out a clump of cash as thick as a biscuit. The Good Samaritan and I agreed that a stranger to the city as naïve and trusting as Tunk had to be careful about whom he showed so much money to.

"We got to find you a bank," the Good Samaritan said. He turned about wildly, as if he meant to hail the first emergency vehicle.

Tunk said he didn't believe in the white man's money house. Man is more complicated than his thoughts, they say. The Good Samaritan was appalled. I believed in Tunk's backwardness as thoroughly as I did his distress, precisely because both were played so broadly, laid on so thick. I believed in the existence of young men like Tunk, up from the tobacco fields, careful not to let their Sunday best make contact with the dirt, slow-witted and abandoned in the coursing streets. We must help him, I thought.

In the urgency to make Tunk believe in the white man's money house right then and there, that very afternoon, in the struggle to pierce the country boy's obstinacy that so aggrieved and astonished the complicitous Good Samaritan, I didn't reason very far, not to the illogic of why someone leaving town the next morning had to be persuaded that banks did not steal your dollars, at least not in that way. Tunk cried out that we were just like everybody else, that we wished him evil. The Good Samaritan was on the verge of throwing up his hands.

Tunk said that if I proved to him that the white man's money house was safe he would regain a little of his faith and courage, enough to go on. I remembered a check from home still in my back pocket. Some mystical force had preserved it there for that purpose. I volunteered to step into the Freedom National Bank, open an account, and make a withdrawal. Tunk said that such a thing could not be done. I hastily produced the check and waved it at Tunk. I didn't think about the sudden silence in our uproar until later. Tunk had stopped complaining and the Samaritan had left off beseeching. They had looked at each other. It was a brief moment that betrayed a resemblance around the eyes. We are one family, I thought, as I hurried into the bank. Later the rapid look that had passed between them I interpreted as amazement that they had hooked such a stupid fish.

I wanted Tunk to see that some money houses were black men's money houses, but he wouldn't come inside with me. He had a change of heart and pleaded with me not to go in there, as if a bank were a burning house. I saw through the window the Good Samaritan comforting Tunk, who looked up now and then at me from his wet hands to make sure that I was still alive, wriggling on the line.

The manager was kind. She asked me what I studied. "Smirnoff's," I said, the good deed I was about to do had enlivened me so. I told her about Tunk. I pointed at the window. I told her that I needed to bring money to Tunk, to show him that I had told the truth, to make him believe.

"Tell me you're kidding, honey." She called to a colleague. "Those flimflams are at the Drop again." The aim of the scam was to switch their fake bankroll for your real money, or steal your money outright, if they thought you couldn't run fast enough. Tunk and the Samaritan were gone when I looked back at the window, when I ran out to the street to beg them to come inside and clear up the misunderstanding for the manager.

By dusk garage doors were pulled down over the shops, revealing murals painted in a sort of local Zhdanovism. The fast-food joints were open and so were the bars where what went on went on softly behind the clarity of pink, blue, green neon. "Positively no guns. Positively no loitering in the restroom. Positively everyone will be searched." The armada of churches was quiet, the storefront dwellings of the Holy Spirit as well as the flagships guarding the Haussman-like boulevards. Eighth Avenue and the tenements leaning toward St. Nicholas Avenue were nervous bazaars for heroin, with brand names like Circle B, Sure Shot, Three Hearts Ready to Kill, and Blue Magic. Glassine packets were passed through peepholes by children too young to be prosecuted.

Every stray encounter was decisive. Every evening held magical promises of renewal. I was going to walk out the door and reinvent myself. I was going to turn a corner and there in the configurations would stand the agents of my conversion. I was going to step out of a taxi and the life in which I existed without inward definitions or external categories would finally come.

Everything was possible because this life continued to be something that stood outside myself, a little way off, in a diner maybe. This life hadn't recognized me yet, like love or history, both of which always seemed to be walking on the other side of the street from where I was. I never noticed as the days took on a similarity to a neurotic pattern: doing the same thing again and again, and each time thinking the result different, significant. Sometimes I misplaced that dream, which is what dreams are for, found it again, and once more departed from the world of facts.

Nevertheless, what a miracle it was to climb the twisting monumental stairs of Morningside Park, frightened by the shadow of a falling leaf, to return unscathed, to take the day out of my pocket, to lay it on the desk along with keys, coins, and folded lunatic leaflets from a group more paranoid about the reasons the comet Kohoutek had disappeared than they had been about its collision course with the earth.

After one of my feeble excursions to test the hypothesis that the sum of Harlem was greater than its parts, I tried to fit my imagined hurt to the balm of being with acquaintances who, having enchanted their brain pans with LSD, talked so much I couldn't see where I was going. They blocked traffic with their heads and assured me that there were some black people whom they thought of as "just normal people. I forget that you're black." It was, as the song goes, nobody's fault but mine, and I didn't want to hear myself say that I forgot some white people were white.

"God has put into my hands a whip to flog your back," Grandfather said straight off whenever he called. He quizzed me about my reading—"Yes, but can you bend over and tie your shoes without your glasses falling off"—my Columbia classmates— "Their parents don't mind their children growing up with poor people"—and predicted that I would come to no good among the no-accounts, burrheads, shines, smokes, charcoals, dinges, coons, monkeys, jungle bunnies, jigaboos, spagingy-spagades, moleskins, California rollers, Murphy dogs, and diamond switchers. He liked to be shocking. Perverse opinions were among the few pleasures of his old age.

The more Grandfather threatened to descend on me with

meals, the greater my paralysis became, but when he picked up the telephone in a different mood, asking me to reserve a room for him at the Hotel Olga, long defunct, as it turned out, or offering to send a consignment of Spam, the more insultingly transparent were my excuses. But I had to be careful. A phone call from Grandfather was sometimes followed by an interrogation from my parents, upset that my rudeness had brought them a fierce dressing-down on the subject of what I had not been taught about how to speak to my elders.

Sometimes Grandfather was in town, but mostly he was not. The complications of his own life had almost simplified mine. His scandalous separation from the beige stepgrandmother— "I'm going to ride until I can't hear them call her name"—limited his invasions, his surprise visits to the dean that he called keeping an eye on me and which I thought of as spiritual scavenging. As long as the stepgrandmother and her equally hateful sister were in their matching pigeon coops for senior citizens on upper, upper Third Avenue that Grandfather had had "no head chief's say" in the purchase of, he kept away.

Perhaps his snobbery made him unable to consider anything less than the sacred groves of the Talented Tenth—massive apartment buildings on Sugar Hill, like the Dunbar Court. Having crusaded throughout his ministry against the wasteland of low-income housing, the projects were to be his destiny. He described the pigeon coop as being near Harlem, above Harlem, on the edge of Harlem, or "sleeping against Harlem's backside," anything not to admit that it was in what could be spoken of as Harlem. He had seen Harlem in its glory, but back then he had just been passing through.

Not to be outdone, Grandfather had established himself, as he liked to say, unmindful of his reduced, improvised circumstances, in Cambridge, Massachusetts, within pestering distance of family. "There the wicked will cease from troubling; and the weary will be at rest." He maintained parity of forces with the step-grandmother: if she had her sister, he had his brother, Uncle Ulysses, though he had little contact with him, except when he needed something.

He was strangely, suddenly inhibited toward the rest of us, as if some embarrassment had caught up with him. In his time he had had an exalted social vision, which rested on what could be done for the next generation, a cabalistic idea of one soul born again and again on the tormented journey toward final purity. "I remember Cassius Clay as a boy," he once said. "The Golden Gloves. Some joker pinched his brother's bicycle and he wanted to win the money to buy him a new one." Grandfather, my father and aunts and uncle said without rancor, believed in doing everything for the children—except his own.

I'd never conceived of my dealings with my grandfather as a relationship: the term implied choice. His having come with the territory precluded thinking about him that way. Family didn't require the considerations that went with voluntary association. Then Grandfather one-upped me and gave me what I thought I wanted: he stopped calling, boycotted me altogether.

For a while I stewed that the possessive old darky who had nearly made a colony of my mind was trying to manipulate me into feeling that I had somehow let him down. Like those people who you think reciprocate your feelings, not understanding that what truly interests them about you is your interest in them, I had come to depend on his pursuit. No one had ever given me the power to reject. Once given, this power is almost impossible to take back. Grandfather had retrieved the advantage, and as much as I told myself that I was well rid of him, I was uncomfortable and not unmoved.

I heard that Grandfather sent cheerful, solicitous notes to my sisters. I admitted that I sort of needed him, like people who look outside but don't trust their sense of the weather until they see what other people are wearing. Then I heard that he blamed me for the interregnum of coolness and I was back in the driver's seat of negatives.

He wanted to see me, I was told, but was too proud to beg. It wasn't like him to take a position and not hold to it. I was sure he would begin to tie up the campus phone again and complained to myself about family obligations. I made plans, but was told that Grandfather didn't want to see me after all. He'd got me, as when a machine that has been silent long enough for you to forget it suddenly starts up again and fills every cavity in your head.

I went to him anyway, telling myself that at his age I had to pay the price of just showing up at his door, of sitting for hours noting the feline sounds a fly could make on a wall, of patiently watching as Grandfather rocked gently, kept time with his slippers as an old, abused song crept into him and carried him, nearly asleep, head bowed, in a terry-cloth-covered chair, from his borrowed, musty living room in Cambridge, back to the wide, hot fields where men and women cut and pulled their way through the furrows.

The sound of a car horn called Grandfather from his reverie. Surprise wrinkled his face, angular and sharp, like a tribal mask. He remembered that he was in retirement in a brown wood frame house on Dana Street, not squinting at the sun that baked the red clay. The passage Grandfather had made through life from Dublin, Georgia, was something—of that he was certain. But he wanted to know more about what he had come to. Where from, that he knew.

Grandfather was no longer so tall, but he was still ascetically thin. The cap of granite-colored hair had liberated itself into crumpled stalks that shot out over his ears in an alfalfa-like way. He moved in quick, small steps, stopping to support himself against the unsteady gateleg table, pausing to ask for strength to get to the stained stove or the almost empty bookcase. There was something valiant in the way he stumbled about, kept moving and fending for himself, pushing through his daily routine, as if his body were not betraying his will hour by hour.

Students lived above Grandfather, and also next door, in the left half of the splintered wood house. I was jealous of his interest in them, of his love for Harvard students in particular. In his mind Grandfather followed them down Boylston Street and into Widener Library. It was impossible to know how many lived there at any given time. Grandfather was disappointed that they remained strangers, that the faces of the occupants changed so frequently, that he had not formed a kind of pedagogical rapport with them.

He longed to advise the students who shared his back yard how to tend their tomatoes and peppers. Once, catching them at work, he stunned them with lyrical remembrances of the plush, full vegetables that grew down home. They stopped their dog-like digging and looked up at him, an old black man leaning with his cane against the puckered screen door as he traced images of cabbages on the clouds.

Grandfather retreated, a little confused and embarrassed. He latched the door and mumbled something about what Paul had written to the Philippians about good works. The students watched him shrink into the dark house, pulled at the red bandannas over their heads, rubbed their hands on faded dungarees, and exchanged smiles. But one of them, the one who had just returned from a hitchhiking tour of the country, defended my grandfather, asserting that every "Pops" he had met was very heavy, close to the earth, wise in the way of herbs. Grandfather had yet to identify the marijuana plants they were trying to grow near the fence.

His fondness for the ebb and flow around him came from the

perplexing contradiction of his somewhat worldly Old Country tolerance. He liked students, partly because he believed that, unlike children or the middle-aged, they were not impatient with old-timers. He carried their remarks away, and examined them, like a shoplifter who doesn't dare to pull out the booty until well away from the detectives and alarms. Though he was a good man, incorruptible, in his way, he loved sinners and had never experienced a dearth of supply.

Grandfather really enjoyed his part-time helper, Red, a reliable old sinner who lost vast sums, as he told it, playing the numbers and sending healing dollars in to radio preachers. Red lied about his age, claiming any year between fifty and sixty. Red had told so many whoppers he believed most of them.

Among Red's other businesses was a car service. I doubted he had a license, but he taped a livery sign on the windshield when he took Grandfather for a thrilling ride. Usually, a thin green bottle of wine slid around under the seat. Red talked about how quickly a fistful of Jacksons could unstable you, while Grandfather tipped through the revolving doors to pay his bills on time.

Grandfather didn't trust Red unsupervised around the house. He complained that Red's irresponsibility upset his own schedule. Red was sometimes detained elsewhere by the consequences of "flea-collar" crime. He banged around trash cans to announce his arrival and went to the back door, massaging his shoulder, explaining how he'd had to start another job at six that morning and hadn't finished sanding the floors until noon.

Red had a long list of projects to see to around Grandfather's retreat, including putting up storm windows, but there wasn't much to do really, and mostly they argued back and forth about "the race thing," the screen door between them like a net. "Let me culminate what you're saying, Reverend."

Content with his solitary chores, Grandfather watered the lemon plant that was placed like an altarpiece on the bright blue

TV tray. The one pale yellow lemon was the size of a grapefruit and the whole thing threatened to topple over under its weight. I was made to pay homage to it. Grandfather was a little superstitious about his lemon plant: if it remained healthy, so would he, more or less. I saw him wink at it from the kitchen. It did not, like the beige stepgrandmother, talk back. He wet his cracked lips and whistled melodiously "O How Glorious, Full of Wonder" as the kettle hissed, calling the world to reveille.

His presentation of himself—setting himself apart from Dorchester, from Roxbury, from the unhappiness of the Rutherford Street projects—still mattered to him. Always the limp dress shirt, somewhat baked around the collar, the cuffed trousers smooth with age, whether he was bouncing to the market, list and pencil in his breast pocket, or clawing his way across the Charles River to try the patience of a teller at his savings bank. He lived in terror of anyone mistaking him for a welfare client and got around the shame of a Medicare card by treating it as a charge plate.

"Come to the speaking blood," a lanky boy brayed in the street, his long hair pulled in a ponytail held together with a strand of beads. "Today is the day of your salvation. One drop will melt the mountain of your sins. Would you like to make a contribution to Jesus?"

"I certainly will. If He shows."

"You're going to be holy one day for sure."

"Lord, if you love anybody, love me."

His cane a divining rod, Grandfather extended himself down Massachusetts Avenue past the "Soul-Saving Station" toward the Red Line. He was dressed in his brushed brown Borsalino and olive-green overcoat slick from so many seasons of cold rain. He enjoyed the atmosphere of Harvard Square, the youthful chatter in front of the Brattle, the aroma of cider drifting from the doors of the Pewter Pot so early in the autumn term.

His errands: the bank, the grocer, the cleaner, the newsstand, Keezer's Men's Store, a peek at the Salvation Army Thrift Store, and then happily to Goodspeed's to inhale the sweetness of pipe tobacco and to spend his ration of conversation, if anyone was willing to accept it. "Good books are a man's best friend," Grandfather had written inside Giovanni Papini's *Life of Christ* in 1925, a present to his first wife, my grandmother. "They are companions silent, consoling, understanding. For silence read them and they will give you rest. Will fill you with heavenly peace." It was one of the few volumes of his library that he had not sold in a much-regretted punitive fit.

Grandfather's excursions ended in daydreams in Boston Common, where spots of earth showed through the hard grass like skin. He began each visit with a silent prayer before Martin Milmore's monument to the men of Boston who died in the Civil War for slavery and the Constitution, "that their example may speak to coming generations." Crispus Attucks continued his solitary vigil. Grandfather had seen so many statues in his time that history itself seemed to have taken on the greenish color of weathered bronze.

He did his part on these walks, devoting a few minutes to picking up, with more than a little effort, the litter of cigarette butts, cans, plastic. Around the elms and rodents he went, tapping through the mash of leaves. He sat alone, far from the couples and the old men waiting with folded newspapers in their laps, another broken Brahmin brooding in the oil of the pensioned life.

Under the brag scat and hum of the venerable city the tennis court was silent, the baseball diamond abandoned. He surveyed the new buildings that got lost in the Milk of Magnesia fog. A hunchbacked woman complained to herself in Polish. Rooted in mismatched shoes, she searched the garbage with the skill of habit. The smell of urine blew our way. Grandfather pulled himself up, a little saddened. Predictably, someone had sprayed WAR IS HELL over KOSCIUSZKO.

You cannot grow up with a city; it grows away from you, a speeding landscape that veers off to present itself to someone new. Grandfather had no feeling for his first home on Mill Street somewhere deep in Boston. He had no urge to see it, as if it belonged to a history as remote as the days of "Nigger Hill" when Irish gangs lay in wait to attack free blacks out walking with their wives. He found being himself a protection of sorts, but he was not a man to rummage as if the optimism of the 1920s were like a memento at the bottom of a forgotten suitcase behind the door.

A burned-out church that resembled the hull of a sunken ship was a milepost. Grandfather loved to discipline himself, and so rode into town and walked back, counting the steps, impressed by his own moxie. The bridge was near and soon he would cross the expressionless Charles, joggers and gulls flying by; soon he would be on Massachusetts Avenue again, back with the falafel trucks parked in front of M.I.T. Boston was an agreeable refuge for a man who had been an exile all his life.

"One of the Adams girls lives in the dormitory next to mine."

"The Quincy Adamses?"

The stately Philco radio in its burnished cabinet was a great comfort, though the vintage tubes had long since given out. He had the address of a shop where he could buy them, but he put off calling from day to day. Grandfather thought most radio commentators were idiots anyway and those with a little sense were liars. Mostly, we watched television.

My aunt had given him a large television set equipped with

a battery-operated remote control. He said it reminded him of a motorcycle. Grandfather didn't like to admit how entertained he was by it. He pretended that he let the television run, as if he were humoring the faces on the screen. But he looked forward to evenings of new situation comedies, as the magazines called them, "recorded live on tape before a studio audience"—a phrase he very much liked because of its jingle quality.

These shows were quite marvelous to him, especially the ones aimed at the "minority audience." No more yes, Mr. Benny, no, Mr. Benny. It was the dawn of *Sanford and Son*, starring Redd Foxx, a clever sinner whose "party records," Grandfather said, more than one fool had wasted his time preaching against. He also watched *The Jeffersons* and his wonderful pulpit tenor sang along as the credits rolled up the screen. "We finally got a piece of the pie!"

He reminded me of students who enrolled in that most notorious of "gut classes," the History of Television. They'd tell their parents to shut up, they were doing their homework, and turn up the sound of *Star Trek*, which they were very serious about decoding, in the French tradition. As a student of the "higher biblical scholarship," Grandfather examined the premises of these popular television shows about blacks as if they were mistranslations from the original Greek.

"George Jefferson has made more money dry-cleaning skirts and jackets than the Chrysler Corporation has made building sedans. That, as we say, confounds historical truth."

Grandfather also liked documentaries—Vietnam, the pollution of Lake Erie, the problems of juvenile offenders, the life cycle of sea horses. He had an insatiable appetite for filmed moments of historical importance and never tired of seeing Haile Selassie address the League of Nations, Jesse Owens cross the finish line, or the motorcade pass on its way to the Texas School Book Depository.

Some stretching, hazy days must have been spent nodding over interpretations of the Psalms, browsing through *Masterpieces of Religious Verse*, underlining Homer Smith, or copying out passages from Volume X of Buttrick's *The Interpreter's Bible*. Index cards were covered with his graceful script and neatly arranged across the scratched table according to category. These cards were destined to join stacks of others in boxes under his bed. His research.

Sometimes Grandfather came upon a forgotten book such as Georgia Douglas Johnson's *Bronze* and a geyser of remembered scenes erupted into the quiet evening—Memorial Hall, Holden Chapel, the black All-American halfback Fritz Pollard, the beloved English teacher Benjamin Crocker Clough, the hated campus humor magazine, *The Brown Jug*. But Cambridge and Providence were more and more confused in his voyages into the past. Thayer Hall was transplanted to the ice above Narragansett Bay. These lapses startled him, made him trust himself less, made me think about what was bearing down on him with the irreversible movement of a glacier. He penned reflective letters to alumni magazines that were never printed.

"Is your memory infallible?" he used to demand of me.

"Of course not."

"Well, mine is."

Age, more than anyone or anyplace, had humbled him. He was where I always picture him, not in church, but at the sink, carefully rolling up the blue sleeves of a tattered dressing gown, a birthday present, but from whom or when he couldn't say anymore, a man who against the tide of things unsaid could only lower his head and notice his hands' conspiracies. He sang as his trembling fingers reddened in the hot water. Dusk spread over the window, orange and gray.

———

"I can't find your great-granddaddy's pocket watch. Good one, too. I thought it was in this drawer. I wanted to give it to you."

"You keep it, you may need it."

"No, I won't. Where I'm going all I'll need is a skillet."

Grandfather was writing his memoirs. Perhaps that was why he had tried to bring my visit to a close with a meaningful, departing gift. The working title was "Looking for Home." The stories crawled forth from the marriage of two dark lips. He had written most of these memoirs and yet they scarcely amounted to one hundred pages, even with a generous number of quotes from Browning, Cowper, Ezekiel. His long life was making for a short book.

He treasured his own life of profound circumspection, dignity, repression, and disappointment, but the chapter he planned to call "Retirement and Reflections" interrupted the work. He could not write it. He meant his chronicle to be instructive, uplifting. It was a sermon, much like any other he had prepared during his half-century as a minister. Those thoughts that would make his gentle audience, his parishioners, himself uncomfortable were suppressed, evaded, and here, the redeeming power of the heavens was unsatisfactory.

"I am a traveling man, trying to make heaven my home." So, God's in His heaven—all's right with the world? Grandfather had never offered "all's right." He knew the real story and loved the imagined one. That was the wilderness in him, which kept the monotone from setting in. He had no intention of "catching misery."

He talked about the scalding effort of "writing up life." Another generation was out there, busily piling up stones. He, too, was preoccupied. "Good things come to those who wait. The Lord works in mysterious ways. Therefore, allow six to eight weeks for delivery." His pride was like that of a man who, dismissed by friends because of his predictability, his regularity of habit, has a reckless affair, as if to say, "Look at me, I'm up to something."

At the table, rolling a pencil in his palms, switching on a lamp, untying the string that held a folder of brown sermons, yellow notes, and a reconciliation of voices—he was, then, most like a man put out to pasture, fighting the wish to travel and be known.

In the night a battered satchel waited, filled with canceled checks, stamped telephone bills, unused subscription forms, torn receipts, irrelevant bank statements, prescriptions, and old deeds of sale. Grandfather got up from the sheets that had soaked up years of restlessness. Barefoot, he felt his way and took the key to the satchel from its hiding place under an oval rug. He spread the grainy pieces of paper over the kitchen table, added and added again the columns of acres and dollars, rubbed the stubble on his chin, inspected signatures until dawn entered like a nurse.

Sometime later, Uncle Ulysses died. One moment he was trying to pump new insulation into his basement walls and the next he had fallen. I hurried up to Boston—not for the funeral, but to be on the scene—with the same coarse expectations of racial spectacle that first drove me down to 125th Street, as if an assembly of old-timers, of elderly relatives at a wake, would stand as a substitute for Harlem, as if their tongues could do what its bad corners had not—lead backward, either into history or into a sense of belonging.

I looked forward to the wake in Uncle Ulysses's house, which smelled perpetually of the dry cleaner's carbon tetrachloride and stood high on a hill with a view of bus stops in one of the satellite towns around Boston. I'd never been to a wake. I imagined men worn out by bluster, women keeping themselves together by concentrating on pulp swimming in the lemonade, youngsters with ears sticking out of new haircuts like sugar-bowl handles. Cousin Aszerine, Cousin Airedale, Cousin Salonia—the weird names were like countries I used to make lists of. "This is Pooky." And Pooky would turn out to be a huge man in his sixties.

Upstairs, around the table of condoling hams, I thought the old women, whose authority smoothly canceled that of my mother and father, would gossip, tell another version of that funeral in 1962 in Philadelphia when Uncle Dirt's brother and sister missed the burial because neither trusted the other not to make off with the non-existent stash of Confederate gold pieces. They'd torn up the dead sibling's yard and house in their treasure hunt, and drunken Aunt Bunny had searched everywhere, including the laundry chute, in which she'd got stuck until the fire department came.

Downstairs, something of that generation-bonding barbershop camaraderie would circulate among the men in the remodeled basement. "Our father who sits in Washington, whatever be thy name. You took me off Chesterfields and put me on Golden Grain." As a boy, when I wandered among my father's friends, I heard, between talk about the cornucopia of FHA loans, voter registration, and relaxed credit terms, about Foggy Bottom in Atlanta, Chicago, Paddy's Bottom in my hometown. Every town had a Bottom, every Negro had a story with a Bottom in it.

Men and women would meet again in the living room, under the dispensation of a shared "sadidiness"—an Old Country expression for narcissism—as if they constituted an endangered genus. The line would go something like: She may cheat at cards, but she's family; he may be a crook, but he's family; she may be in the CIA, but she's family, he may be a drunk, but he's our drunk. My elderly relatives could call their New Orleans connections a bunch of French-speaking niggers. I, however, hadn't earned the privilege. And yet for all the tear-ful, laughing embraces what this woman had hated about this man in 1925 would never change. She would never forget his refusal to pay the five-cent fare to have a tooth extracted.

I hadn't known Uncle Ulysses, except as Grandfather's congruent hypothesis, so to speak. I couldn't even say what he looked like. His most distinguishing feature was his stomach. It cast his shoes in shadow, a symbol of well-being from the days when blacks didn't think any more than anyone else about high blood pressure.

Uncle Ulysses gave the impression of concentric circles, a brown snowman. His head was very large, a fact that made him sensitive about Grandfather's passion for hats. Perhaps he had suffered as a student when the cephalic index was taken seriously. I was told that when the medics attempted to resuscitate him, his stomach grew monstrous with air, and Aunt Odetta, remembering his girlish vigilance about keeping himself covered at all times, interfered with the wires and pads to pull his shirt over his bloated paunch.

He called me "Cotton Chopper," which I never liked. It sounded, to my ten-year-old ears, too Southern, that is to say, too Negro. He knew that I didn't like it, but that never stopped him. Though Uncle Ulysses was known as parsimonious with words, reserved, given to elaborate sentence structures to avoid the overly assertive pronoun I, he was a bully. He used to demonstrate pressure points and judo holds on me. He talked about chickens eating the weak among them, asked if I meant seriously to imply that I had never enjoyed wringing a chicken's neck.

He imposed an insane frugality on Aunt Odetta. The first time I ever saw a lock on a telephone was in their house. It was as odd a sight as women who diet by having their mouths wired shut. He doled out his coiled, aggressive, bullying facts to his forever-assenting, grown-up son, while Aunt Odetta cooked and cooked: "Did you know onions were first grown in Mongolia?" He was fussy, down to the toothpicks he liked—the minty kind.

The family had a theory. Uncle Ulysses worked all his life at a paper company. He entered as a stock boy in the 1920s and was retired some fifty years later, at not much higher than a stock boy's salary, though he was spoken of as practically running the whole company. Some said he hadn't been "right" since the trenches. Others disagreed, saying he'd been well behind the lines with the rolling kitchens. That's the way it was with the past: live long enough and you could massage the facts.

I remembered his fragile glass cabinet, which held intriguing French coins, a bolo knife, a copy of Moss's *Private's Manual*, and two intensely cherished German pike helmets. I had some idea that it was a memorial to an earlier version of himself, before his entombment in the back office of the paper company. Classroom editions of books like Storm's *Immensee* with his name thickly written in black ink along with the forgivably pompous "Universitas Bostoniensis" had the poignancy of faded snapshots of total strangers.

It was possible to connect Uncle Ulysses with the vulnerability of colored regiments that marched with broomsticks, which made people laugh. There weren't enough uniforms, so most of them had to wear clothes that blended in. His father, Old Esau, didn't think much of the army because the ranks of officers were closed.

Old Esau didn't think much of Woodrow Wilson either. Just as Uncle Ulysses had remained a Baptist, as firmly in place as one of the decayed concrete lions on the steps of the Holy Zion Fired Baptist Church, he also had stayed with the GOP. I held over from my childhood the notion that Negroes, even rich, light-skinned ones, were supposed to be Democrats. Uncle Ulysses was suspicious of Negro magazines, Model Cities programs, quotas, Harlem, James Brown. He never "bought black" in his life.

Once, when they were both in Indianapolis, Grandfather, in one of his moods, said that we all knew that "Ulyss" had spent most of World War I sitting on his duff in Hoboken and that he bought his pike helmets off someone later. Calling someone dishonest was Grandfather's method of deep fishing. Usually the person fell into the trap and, to prove that he wasn't a liar, said more than he meant to.

Uncle Ulysses had his defensive details about the transport and the convoy from Sandy Hook, how the men sang "Rock of Ages" to calm themselves, how the ropes tore gloves and the cold at sea burned hands. He went on at Grandfather about the officers who kept the regiment uninformed about its movements, partly from disrespect and partly because of their uncertain relations with their French superiors.

I couldn't believe that Grandfather hadn't heard Uncle Ulysses's stories before; they were over fifty years old by that time. Uncle Ulysses recalled Senegalese drivers at Maffrecourt and women atop the rubble of buildings. He said they would have made anyone think of the refugees down South after they were burned out of their homes.

The rats of Fortin and Ravin des Pins—it wasn't as though Grandfather hadn't known his own brother back then, where he had or had not been. But I wasn't sure. They were a feuding bunch. It was puzzling to me how people lost sight of one another, how siblings fell out of touch. I thought perhaps it was a function of age, or a regrettable outcome of an era when people didn't have the means or the time to visit. I couldn't imagine life without my parents or my sisters.

Grandfather smiled at Uncle Ulysses's standard information about whizbangs and whuzzes, how they sailed in at a very low ordinate and a soldier in their way became a very sorry fellow. Shells dug craters, blood dyed pools red. Wooded ravines and high hills afforded the best protection, Uncle Ulysses said. Then he noticed something in Grandfather's face. His own puffy cheeks flushed with fury and embarrassment, as if his younger brother had tricked him again into saying something personal or showing emotion.

Not every busybody is a moral primitive. I was both, and alone in Grandfather's house. There was no wake. No ancient relatives had come from deep pockets of the Old Country and Uncle Ulysses had not had much of a knack for cronyism. Crowded, exciting, singing wakes only happened in the movies, in the folklore of continuity where people were allotted one town from cradle to coffin. The family, when I thought about its gatherings over the years, had been more territorial and less adhesive than customers in a self-service laundry.

They were either ailing or dead themselves anyway, those weird names from my childhood when I couldn't understand why my mother's relatives didn't know my father's. Grandfather struck me as being one of the last of his period. He was "collectible." I sat at his desk, eased out his drawer à la *I Spy*, co-starring Bill Cosby, and put my paws on his manuscript. He didn't belong to himself; he had no right to privacy. The old darky was mine.

Convention led me to expect an attempt to evoke the sweet milk, the raw turnips, the thunder, sandflies, and linguistic isolation of the Old Country. Talk de ole African talk? Grandfather had some understanding of irony. From the memoirs: "To our astonishment, as we discovered much later, the little church which our father pastored consisted for the most part of the lineal descendants of the once prosperous slave owners." It was 1905 in that sentence. Madison, Georgia. Grandfather was the third of five boys and had three sisters whom he neglected to mention, which was perhaps what he meant when he used to talk about the strength not to languish where there were no constraints. "There were white churches also, but no one said that a person could not worship there if he wanted to."

The starched jackets, straight-legged knee pants, scrubbed brick church, the Christmas barrels and separate but adequate school of the happy colored childhood. However: "Life's romance is never a high road of complete sweetness. There were months of tenseness that touched the nerve center of our being." This was an incident in Madison. A lynch mob had formed in town. The mayor was quickly ushered into the study of the parsonage. "A horse and carriage stood waiting at my father's disposal, in which he might ride hastily around the town and advise all the colored people to get off the streets immediately and stay indoors until morning," Esau, the leader, riding off into the night.

Another happening from Grandfather's record: Madison's liberal white superintendent of education found himself in danger with some "underprivileged Nordics." He was escorted out of town under heavy guard, having agreed that if the party was overtaken he would be left on his own. "Here again my father was brought to the table to share and give advice. Oh, how he understood: he that leadeth into captivity shall go into captivity; he that killeth with the sword must be killed with the sword. Here is the patience and faith of the saints."

All Grandfather had left that had been his father's were a few books. *A Catechism of Scripture and Doctrine Practice for the Familial and Sabbath Schools, Designed Also for the Oral Instruction of Colored Persons*, Benjamin Tucker Tanner's *Theological Lectures*, an almanac entitled *Progress of a Race*, and Booker T. Washington's *The Story of My Life*—worn volumes upright like Pilgrims, wedged between a rose-colored lamp and a pot of coins and buttons. There was also an old edition of Milton's poems. Esau's initials were inscribed on the title page, along with the price. There were serpents in relief on the cover, the pages flaked at every turn. Included were texts in Latin and Greek which, in Grandfather's jealousy, he did not believe his father could read.

Not surprisingly Old Esau, in Grandfather's version, never got out of the wagon, returned from church business. The chapter on Madison was brief. Grandfather blessed the boys Grady and

Paul, who'd brought him milk when he was ill as a child. He recalled the Stovalls, the Atkinses, the Shaws. "There was neither bitterness nor fear in the little blue-eyed lassies who showed me how to 'play store' with chests of Confederate currency." Then it was over, his seven years in Madison giving way to boisterous Augusta, Georgia.

Grandfather lived without photographs. His house was bare, like a bunker. No shoebox, no leather album with which to beguile the hours, none of his first wife. He was more than a bit vain, but he didn't even have pictures of himself on the job, signing a wedding certificate or standing among the well-met at the conclusion of some interdenominational conference. Perhaps the beige stepgrandmother was holding hostage the images from his past.

A light rain began. Through the dirty curtains clouds trapped the city's illumination and threw it back to earth in silver strands. The air grew cooler and cooler in the way friends write to one another less and less and finally vanish. Modern life roared over the rooftops a few blocks away, but Dana Street was so quiet it seemed to belong to a backwater where you couldn't tell if the population was aware of what it lacked.

The telephone rang. I froze like a burglar caught with a sack of silverware on his back. I rearranged Grandfather's manuscript, shut the drawer, wiped away my fingerprints. The phone rang and rang, like a recrimination. I'd heard a man in the club car of a train brag that he had hopped up in the middle of the night and lied to the receiver that he was sleeping, alone. I watched a woman eavesdrop. Her expression into her plastic cup said that the telephone always sides with the injured party; but it's the victim who throws out the verdict.

The telephone wanted to know if Grandfather had turned up.

Evidently he had run away from the funeral. He was last seen moving ahead of his brother's body. He was down the steps and around the corner before anyone spoke. The hearse waited, gave up, and went to the cemetery. My instructions were to call Uncle Ulysses's house the moment Grandfather showed.

The rain increased, the wind moved the spray like particles in a dust storm. Under the streetlamps the rain took on the character of smoke. It came through the window that I had opened to let air into the overheated room and to let out my sneakiness. Drops as fine as salt mingled with the punctuation marks of Grandfather's church bulletins. "Nothing like a good storm to scour the sky," he used to say. Those wise sayings he was forever coming up with—some satire in them after all, some laughing at himself, at old darkies everywhere, and at all of us who only wanted them to talk in the language of buildings that done gone to leaking.

Several telephone consultations later it was clear that Grandfather was off, maybe boarding a Greyhound in the rain without a stitch of luggage. He had moved on, severed himself from pleasant and unpleasant situations in that way more than once. Rise, take up thy bed, and walk. I thought of him on the road, like Uncle Castor in the weakest days of the big band era: at the Municipal Auditorium in Cleveland, at South Parkway in Chicago, trying to get hot in Omaha.

Before I thought about the worry his disappearance had caused my parents, aunts, uncles, sisters, about the calls to hospitals and the missing persons bureau, before we found out that he had gone to the last place we thought to look for him—to the beige stepgrandmother's table overlooking Harlem—I admired him for still gambling, after so many years, on the fresh start.

7 / Soul

It was over. Firecrackers and sparklers went off all over campus, from South Field to the law school terrace. Around the Sundial, the setting of many historic harangues, up and down College Walk, on the steps in front of the notorious administration building known as Low Library, the twang of guitars, the crackle of radios, the putter of three-wheeled security vans, the eruptions of voices, and the flags of the NLF said it again and again. Even the jocks were out drinking, throwing footballs in the twilight, crashing into hedges, showing off for the Ophelias of the peace movement, who straddled the windowsills of the Student Mobilization Committee.

I squinted from my dormitory's entrance across the nappy lawn to the Quad, the courtyard on the other side of campus, where student-leader types were trying to hook a pair of Harpo Marx glasses on the statue of the young Alexander Hamilton, so available to militant decoration after his shoes were painted red in the golden days of '68. No matter that since then demonstrations and sit-ins degenerated into farce; "living theater" we called it. I remained in the doorway for some time, afraid to take a step. It was the end of spring according to our psychological calendars, study period, the week before final exams, after which you would have either blown it or not blown it, but in the joyous and idle meantime Saigon had fallen.

I backed up the steps into Furnald Hall. The lobby was busy and unexpectedly cool, like a church on a travel itinerary. The guard, Jesse, union member, moonlighter, and taker of beer bribes, already snored at his post. His head rolled against the back of the chair. His bald spot matched the leather, like expensive luggage. "You ain't holdin' no air," he said, if he was awake, when I flashed my ID card in the small hours of the night. "Mess with me, boy, and I'll have to jump down your throat and swing on your liver." He was conspiratorial with black students who flouted the rules, such as they were, and distanced the white ones with a grunt, hardly condescending to hear them out. White students who knew how to give a driver the Black Power salute, or who had raised their consciousness, as the expression went, to the point where they said more than thank you to the doorman back home were intimidated by the political correctness in Jesse's glance. He was nicer to the jocks who didn't care to know even his name.

"Boy, does your daddy know you're up here running the streets?" That was the night I passed out on the subway, bolted at the 116th Street stop so as not to end up in Harlem, and turned to see the graffiti of the doors close on my glasses left rattling in the seat. But Jesse had got it right. It was as necessary to self-conscious living as the Fourteenth Amendment: your parents sent you out into the world; that is, they sadly waved you off with a cashier's check and had no idea what you were up to, apart from the information that could be extrapolated from computer printouts at the bottom of the semester or from how often you called home to beg.

My mother called every Sunday. If I had to, I would have

taken a plane or an all-night train from the scene of the crime, experience, to be in my room in time to get my script together. Once she called in the middle of the week. "Are you still in school? The FBI was here to question you about Patty Hearst." Two of the heiress snatchers were from my home state, Indiana, and had lurked about the local Committee to Free Angela Davis. I rushed all over the place with the news that the FBI was looking for me, careful to wipe the smile off my face before I knocked.

My parents were not reconciled to my being in New York, so far away. One learned things in Indiana, too, they argued. From time to time I received clippings about the harm marijuana and LSD could do to chromosomes. But jurisdiction was precisely the point. What I wanted was the veil of miles, the freedom to stay up all night, to waste my time, their money, you name it. In those days, when months were like years, when students thought of themselves as bravely parasitic and "I miss you" wasn't just another lie—in those days when we had more appetite than good sense, the punishment for mistaking white clouds for distant mountains was not loss of life.

I saw a Frisbee bang through a chandelier. I saw Jesse straighten up. "You look like you about to throw up a Buick again," he said, and closed his filmy right eye, one of his many disconcerting tricks. "Don't cry Hughie 'round me." The left eye shut like a ticket window.

Upstairs was the ragged, dicey atmosphere of an inner-city bus station. People I had never seen before, many elites of one, came out of the plaster to mass in the lounge in front of the television, which was a 26-inch color job, as a result of a Cox Commission recommendation, so the rumor went, that the quality of everyday life be improved to appease some of the discontent that had helped to make all-male Columbia the most unattractive, volatile, and abandoned member of the Ivy League.

Girls—students at Barnard across the street—descended on armrests. They made O's with their mouths around bottles of Tab or Miller Lite. Coed floors were also a post-'68 improvement, but my floor, Furnald 6, was not officially one of them. "Holy shit" was the general comment as we watched, with the sound turned off, replays of film that showed people in a melee twelve time zones away. They scrambled over rooftops, clung to helicopters, accomplished gravity-defying feats of locomotion.

Was it possible, was it so? A young girl, an escapee from small-town New Hampshire, a sort of mascot to the hippies on the floor, started to hum "Kumbaya." She rocked on her haunches, a beer between her sandals, and fixed her watery, puppy stare on the Jim Morrison cultists, who snickered, and then on the bra-less Barnard women, who declined to acknowledge her. Someone handed her a joint to shut her up. She turned it over, threaded it through her grubby fingers. "Are you going to worship it or smoke it?" her old-man-of-the-week barked. The lounge was thick with the aroma of Acapulco Gold, Thai sticks, patchouli oil, leftover anchovies, squashed Marlboros, Budweiser breath, and slept-in Grateful Dead T-shirts. Through our 26-inch color window on the world we saw a Marine ball his fist. It went up and down on the mob. His brow was knitted but calm, like St. George having his vision.

Boredom is not out of the question even when worlds collapse. The party broke apart. Each to his quarters, his ardent nonchalance. I had no more connection with my fellow cellmates on Furnald 6 than spectators do after the ambulance has turned the corner. They took me for a black separatist. I knew no one on that floor, an isolation which, at that moment, was no longer as hip as I had thought. All day I had been calling people without success. I worried that my friends were hiding from me. However, loneliness was swept aside by another big emotion, one maybe common to seniors who have not begun their term papers and who have no marketable skills: some awful mix of love and pity for mankind.

I stood in the dim corridor dumb and, so I believed, invisible in a seizure of oneness. An overweight girl, so important in radical circles that she always wore a shroud-of-Leningrad expression, pounded on the wall near the elevator to affix a leaflet crammed with fine print that announced a demonstration against—she was never not in the vanguard—the Shah. Her faded corduroy trousers dragged on the carpet, drooped so that they revealed to the comprador-bourgeois onlookers the crack of her rear end. I was with her and with the onlookers. I was at one with the floor's would-be dealer on his water bed, a longhair from Arizona whom no one trusted, whose door stood wide open hour after futile hour, and who seemed forever stuck on the same brown page of an old paperback edition of Kerouac.

I was also with the congressman's son in whom philosophy had gotten the upper hand, with the pompous slogans on his door like "Relinquish no part of me to the state" or "Hell is badly done." I was at one with the stoop-shouldered souls on what was called Grind Row, where no posters or stickers of any kind distinguished their cheders, where there was only the sickening smell of a can of Chef Boyardee heating up on a hot plate. In my mind's eye I was at one with the stupidities scrawled above the urinals and, with the Magic Marker that was made to write yet again "Eat the Rich," I was there. The lichen on the ledge, Jesse in his dream of Jones Beach, the shadows on the Ho Chi Minh Trail—I was with it all, at every festival, until someone passed by and handed me a look like a traffic violation. "Man, everybody's stoned out of their gourds today." Down as a result of contact, as they say in football.

My room was one of the coveted singles, which meant that I

was spared a stranger's socks and nightmares. The sink, the chest of drawers, the cot with the plastic hospital mattress, and the desk that was unusable because of the number of black candles I had melted on it left a bit of floor space the size of an aisle in tourist class. I heard a blast of music—Suicidio!—from a monster stereo system, the property of my neighbors, two guys who had grown up drinking from the same glass but who had lately come to the fork that led one downstairs to sleep in study hall, the Grub Room, and the other to lavish on the walls of their room his masterpiece in oil, an endeavor encouraged by the speed and peyote he swallowed in lieu of macaroni in the cafeteria. At any hour he shouted to himself of his inspiration: "Well, all right now." In everyone's face except your own a map was visible.

My inner composure depended on the lone window in my room. It looked out on Broadway, on Chock Full o'Nuts, trucks, taxis, delis, abused chestnut trees, panhandlers with fringed cowboy jackets slung over their shoulders, tables of textbooks and SWAPO pamphlets at the college gates. I saw two dedicated teachers, one huge, one thin, both in the throes of tenure battles, scrape gum or shit from their soles. "Don't they know I'm the greatest poet since Dante?" Mr. Huge once demanded of a seminar. "Trotsky, who was in love with my grandmother," Mr. Thin had begun a lecture. Furious student petitions were circulated in their behalf. The pair headed toward the West End Café, the hangout of the unappreciated, the persecuted, and the fired.

Broadway was so crowded with vegetable buyers and buildings streaked with weather that I hadn't noticed the dark. Of all the things to witness in the street—flyers and newspapers that tumbled waist-high above the pavement in warm gusts; blue, lemon, red, and green lights in a diaphanous blur of gases; grit that miraculously retained the day's heat as it flew to my teeth—

nothing was more consoling than the sight of people caught by nightfall in their shorts, their muscular tank tops and bobbing stripes.

Summer was coming in as fast as what we thought was the liberation of the people of Indochina. Summer, that season of disappointed travel plans and joke reading lists, that slowing down into which your classmates disappeared and from which they returned russet and altered, made the hairs of my Afro stand on end, as if life itself had been invented by my generation the day before yesterday.

The time had come. Summer had always meant no school, but it had not meant, until then, with the tanks rolling down Tu Do Street, with the Chekhovian solution imminent—either hand in those term papers or shoot yourself—no school ever again. I saw summer whistling in over the water towers of Broadway as a great postponement of the Next Move, a beautiful ellipsis limited only by my cowardice, by insufficient wantonness of mind.

My parents had never allowed me to spend the summer in New York. Their policy against dancing in the street began the August before my freshman career, when I zoomed back from my first solo moon flight with one dime. I used it to call collect, to wonder how I was going to get from JFK to the Hoosier-bound plane at LaGuardia, and then I plugged the coin into a pay toilet. After that my parents enforced between semesters the uplift principle, which I interpreted as surveillance, wing clipping, Indiana arrest.

How I'd spent my summer vacations: the uplift principle put me to work as a counselor at a "student leadership" camp where the teenagers believed down to their tan lines in nonsmoking, Our Lord Jesus Christ, "role-playing," Karen Carpenter, and the war on apathy. The uplift principle also permitted me to haunt my room back home or, sulker that I was, to teach my wounded parents that nine-dollar scoops of chicken salad and debates about busing at NAACP conventions were not fun. But all of that was over. Go ahead, the lights in the wild air said, throw your heart over the fence.

New York City was going bankrupt that summer, unraveling toward its high noon. I found what back then could be described with sarcasm as a studio near the cathedral alumni called St. John the Unfinished. My belongings smelled funny when they dried, having been transported down Broadway in a stolen cart during a BB-gun rain. I coated every surface of the room with a glue that sort of killed roaches. The guy who rented me the place—I was the subletee of an illegal subletee—generously showed me how to construct an exploding trap that involved a 12-volt transformer, pieces of magnesium, and peanut butter.

The walls vibrated with hypnotic anthems like "Negrito Bibón" by Ismael Rivera, the Spanish Elvis. Children screamed, bananas fried; something scooted about in the walls themselves. The window faced an airshaft down which came boxes, bottles, plates, arguments, and that was difficult because I needed the nearness of a street to be at rest. I was usually on the stoop among the old men studying dominoes, the young men haggling over stripped cars, the mothers braiding daughters' hair.

I discovered that Morningside Heights, when cleared of students, was a black and Hispanic neighborhood. Just when I was learning to act normal in the barrio, trusting that exchanges in the bodega late at night were not about how to mug me, my father decided that I would sail away with myself unless he intervened. He gave me the last thing I wanted as a housewarming present: a job.

Through the sad Negro imitation of the Indiana contingent of Good Old Boys, the very reason I could not refuse his assistance, this is what my father came up with: his accountant, with the blessing or wink of some minority-business program, maintained an office in Manhattan that audited federally funded community projects. I was to be an auditor's trainee. One majestic Monday, when odd vapors enveloped my fellow workers as they made for the holes of public transportation, this job, this violation of my personal liberty act, had me sneaking upstairs on a wrong stretch of Broadway in the uninspected vicinity of the Flatiron Building.

I entertained dreamy feelings about dereliction. Granite that long ago had been stained by fumes of coal, vacant lots, junctions of shattered glass—these pockets, when depopulated, silent, were to me, at night, the height of romance. Run-down, bricked-up blocks were cozy, and when a building was fixed up, which seldom happened back then, I resented it, as if it had been taken from me or a friend had kicked cigarettes and left me puffing. I'd not reckoned with having to be a working part of the land-scape of marginal stores and squalid businesses, as if my job would force on me a clarification of social status. But the ac-counting office didn't take my presence seriously. I was one of the absentee boss's whims, a favor he was doing a client.

It was a skeleton of an office. The Filipino manager and his wife were not around much. In a room of army-green file cabinets the secretary, the third runner-up in the 1969 Miss Afro America Contest, swiveled in her house slippers. I sat in a back room at a blank metal desk with an adding machine and a manual. Whether I read it or not was of no consequence to my supervisor, a corpulent Argentinian who spent much of the day bawling out his rabbi. He was after a religious divorce. He dealt out handsome documents in Hebrew on his desk while his wife obstructed justice from Buenos Aires. He talked to the ceiling fan about her, about the trouble that had started when he confessed that he wanted to become a U.S. citizen. He'd met a woman in New Jersey and the ceiling fan told him not to lose hope.

Meanwhile, if you can't have it all, you can get away with something. My lunch hours got longer, I came back reeking of mouthwash. The secretary painted her nails tequila-sunrise orange. I'd ask how she was and invariably came the reply "Trying to be better." I settled into a boogaloo of come late, leave early; became as adept as my supervisor at inventing errands that required my immediate attention around 3:30. This summer rhythm suited the secretary, whose duty it was to lock up. I departed in a mood of perfect blamelessness, a cog in cream or sky-blue three-piece suits, costumes no pimp would suffer near his skin. Along my noisy block the fire hydrants ran on and on, just like in the movies.

Then my supervisor announced that I was ready to go into the field. Issued a plastic briefcase, tablets of giant graph paper, and bundles of virgin pencils, I followed his stomach into the subway. He asked the driver-education ads why God had sent his wife to torment him, and somewhere in Brooklyn he beseeched God Himself in different languages. At the door of a day-care center my supervisor pulled out the name tag of his charm, tossed his thick mane, which he must have thought was still fragrant with the morning's shampoo, cocked his head in boundless sympathy. I thought of the flesh of his handshake, soft like pads of butter in a humid restaurant. The director of the day-care center fluttered and showed us to a corner room where ledgers and cartons of receipts were layered on a table. It was like putting yourself in a jar and screwing on the lid.

My supervisor fell to, as if it were a meal. I copied whatever he told me to, filled columns with numbers, and in the sweat surrendered to something like a Carthusian's serenity, though I did not know what FICA stood for or why I had to retrieve this information by such slow means. This was before portable computers, but Xerox machines were not unheard of. The audit consumed several days. We munched lunches that tasted like shredded telephone book. I switched to my supervisor's brand of cologne. He revived himself with Hostess cupcakes. Outside, the children rioted, and then I laid down my pencil nub and taped together sheets to make a chart the size of a tablecloth.

I was sent out in my drenched paisley tie, shirt, and vest to audit books on my own. I was given Bedford-Stuyvesant, the part of Brooklyn where theft was known as the five-finger discount and sneakers as getaway shoes. I got lost and everyone I asked directions of either ignored me, tried to sell me diamond rings, or ran from me. Even the pigeons were fierce. Day-care centers in converted warehouses, in basements, in mere sheds compressed by too much sun; in streets depleted of cars, empty of shop life; streets overrun with small people skipping rope, playing jacks in the potholes, jumping on tar patches—"God will give you back the days the locusts have eaten," Grandfather liked to say—and I could not hear those children without the fear that I was heading home, guided by their cries, to my own childhood, my early summers, when I suspected there might be something shameful about my crowd of little baseball players and lagged behind so that white motorists wouldn't think I was one of them.

I was treated at some day-care centers as a lackey for the revenue man, and at other places, holding pens for children, the wardens were amused that I fit right in, watched soap operas with them straight through the blazing afternoon. I had no idea what those numbers, forms, and vouchers were supposed to amount to, and proudly faked findings, made up sums, jotted down any combination of integers in order to complete the intricate grid of those green sheets. It never occurred to me that I might slander a scrupulous staff or acquit a dishonest one by tinkering with the figures. I didn't care if someone skimmed from the milk money so long as my head was free to wander. I thought the deep-eyed Black Muslim women in flawless white that made them look like nurses in photo histories of World War I were sending out the murderous vibe that they had figured me out, when they were, like me, just waiting on the subway platform.

The best thing about working was not showing up. I called to tell the secretary at which day-care center I'd be—and who was to check that I was not in a stupor in front of my fan? Sunday conversations with my parents I padded with talk-show-level sincerity about how much I was learning about Black America through my job, yarns that had the self-sabotage of the patient in analysis who gets nowhere because he thinks he has to keep the therapist entertained. Then the con man got conned: my paycheck bounced.

The secretary said the boss had forgotten to put the money in payroll, don't worry about it until Monday, and continued to file her nails. A week later the yellow rectangle bounced again. The secretary said that was why she had a second job as a salesclerk, the manager and his wife as teachers of English, and my supervisor as an instructor at a business institute near Macy's, and to come back that afternoon. I saw HELP WANTED notices at Dianetics centers in my sleep. The third time it bounced, the secretary turned down the voice reeling off baseball scores and said that the first lesson of Black Capitalism was faith, faith that the money withdrawn to dig metaphorical ditches out there in the great somewhere would one day make it back to behave again as payroll.

My connection with the office trailed off, much like those other relationships you forget because they were made out of having had nothing better to do. Then I called home to play injured.

The boss had taken the secretary on a Caribbean cruise. I was never so happy to have been associated with a crook.

I didn't have to roam the Village, the meat-packing district, or the Lower East Side. Summer loitered in boxing gloves on Broadway, close to my front door. I met Jesse, the security guard, barrel-chested between shifts. His personality changed with his uniform. "You look ready to Freddy," he said. To reaffirm our kinship as soul brothers he introduced me to Betty, a redhead of indeterminate age with sharks in her eyes whose name was on the liquor license of a dive called the Melody Coast. "He's good people," he told her. Betty smoked cigars.

To Jesse I was a college boy, and Betty, I learned, did not like students. *Absolutely No Pot*, a banner in the men's room read. When students, the few around for the summer session, happened into the Melody Coast, they received a lesson in discrimination: waitresses vanished into the clatter of the kitchen; Betty became hard-of-hearing when sophomores yelled for pitchers of beer. "Their politics stop at the cap and gown," she said. Black students were not above suspicion. "You're not one of those brain-washed gray boys, are you?" She didn't want her place to become an "in" spot, which is what made it so "in" to me. The jukebox offered no rock, just the Philadelphia Sound and some throwback favorites like "Fine Fat Daddy, Please Don't Reduce."

Cats prowled the shelves. Most students looked in and went away. The Melody Coast presented too much of an exclusive scene: concrete floors, red booths that recalled the interiors of gas-guzzling cars with tail fins; mirrors; low yellow lights; an enormous pool table in the back cave; and at the long, dark bar mottled with polished burn marks the murky regulars, the "working people" to whom Betty catered. Some of them were between jobs or waiting for the right thing, but it was against the code of the Melody Coast to ask too many questions. Everyone understood how hard it was out there.

Betty was in sympathy with their struggle, with all struggles, with Union 65, the Palestinians, the Khmer Rouge, women, women of color—as if a person could be discolored, Thoreau said—Puerto Rican nationalists, the Tupamaros, the June 2 Movement in Germany, even the Molly Maguires, the secret society of miners in nineteenth-century anthracite country. A prole or a member of an oppressed minority never left the Melody Coast without the support of a free drink. "No sleeping in my bar," Betty repeated several times a night.

Jesse said that for a white woman Betty was more than right on. "The lady's down with it," he said. She had poured drinks and expressed solidarity for years, but I wondered if any of her best customers could say where she lived in the hours between last call and the unlocking of the gate over the door the next day. Betty hired only women—many off the books—but not even those single mothers and former topless dancers who swore they'd be up the creek without her seemed to know much about her beyond why she did not believe in voting. "We go way back," Jesse said when she cashed his checks.

She fueled discussions about batting averages, and the "links" between Vesco's private army and the Freemasons, and gave advice. "He wants an apartment near his wife to be near the dog? Tell him the dog can take a taxi." Mostly she called as little attention to herself as possible. She kept watch from her post at the till, a smooth hostess—that is what I and the other comboozelated flies told one another, happy with the summer lightning over the dark brick façades because it gave us a reason to stay a little longer. What we whispered to ourselves when we came to well after noon was something else.

The idea of going someplace my friends from school

couldn't—or wouldn't—gave me a feeling of sophistication. I could have it both ways. "You're with us now," Jesse said. "I'm watching your back." I belonged and he was looking out for me. When the telephone rang I could show Betty that I, too, was down with it by joining in the chorus of "I'm not here." When an old-timer wavered in the doorway and called out to the assembly, "If you see my wife, you ain't seen me," I could join in the ritual response of "I hear you." No one had to know that I set myself apart. We all thought ourselves the exception to the rule, the one elect among the lost.

Sometimes I checked the newspaper to see what day it was. My parents had every sympathy for how hard it was out there. By the time my neighbors came home from work, by the time their wet children tromped in, by the time the airshaft reverberated with sheer living, I was ready to take up my position in the bar, my back to the window, ready to shake my head with Betty over the "heightening contradictions" in the political situation, ready for the consolation in the way she said, "Your usual? First one's on the house."

I looked forward to meeting Jesse on his dinner break, on his way home, the hair around his bald spot tame with Afro-Sheen, his shirtsleeves somehow crisp when everyone else on the street dripped like a rag. "I'm as broke as the ten commanders." It was my business to be there to greet the twinkle in his left eye when he performed his pirate-patch gag with the other. I appreciated his eloquence during uneventful innings of a baseball game when the whole bar seemed to be engaged in an effort to get to the essence of things. "What we're saying to you young folk"—I adored the distinction—"is come on out of the fog. It's time to put something on the table. You got the contacts. Now what are you going to put on the table." Usually another Jack Daniel's for Jesse.

"Who's backing Jesse up?" Betty polled before she flipped the bottle upside down.

I looked forward to his brotherly confidences, often on the dangers of whipping "it" out. "Don't do like I did. You break it, you buy it. Got four kids and two jobs. And they act like they don't want to be bothered with me." His children were in North Carolina with his mother. "But you're good people. My main man. Cheers." My brain floated in my drink and said that Jesse was a man of parts as numerous as the valid and invalid laminated employee ID cards that swelled the gills of his wallet. "Fass-ism. It means the world's living too fast."

When Jesse wasn't around I went undercover. Nurses, tellers, and social workers flopped into the red booths, tucked soggy shopping bags between their ankles, slipped off shoes, wiggled feet. "Same old same old, girl." A group of retired gentlemen, among whom bets were on and off as swiftly as transactions downtown, claimed the area around the pool table to remember who of their number had been "funeralized." Stray misanthropes frowned over their chins at crossword puzzles. The configurations changed according to who was on—every waitress had her following—and then the evening let loose over the regulars, the hard core, the bangtails and double clutchers like something that had been wound tight and suddenly released.

A fraternity of flamboyant players had the cue sticks, their quarters and shot glasses on the rim of the table as they took aim in an expansion of goldlike watches and rings, and their good time was ruled over by a group Jesse called the Five Bottoms, though there could be anywhere from three to nine of them in a booth. They wore makeup that lightened or darkened the anticipation in their faces, sculpted Afros or hairpieces in terraces that fell here and there like hopes. They checked their reflections in the mirrors, displayed fancy cigarette cases and bejeweled lighters, were themselves accessories to the ear loops and arm rolls of bracelets that chimed when they squirmed.

Jesse said their purpose in life was to "get up in somebody's face, smell under somebody's dress, and generally get into everybody's business." I admired his ease with the Five Bottoms. They shot contemptuous looks of appraisal in my path, raised their glasses almost in unison, like musicians preparing to attack the same note. They latched on to gossip, ravished it, and slumped against the ersatz Naugahyde of the booths. They went to the ladies' room in pairs, rearranged blouses, skirts, switched in tight denim by the pool table. I thought of the girls back in my grade school who said to a new girl, "Let me see your purse." They dumped the contents of the new girl's bag on a desk, sifted, studied, dropped the items back in one by one, and returned the purse without comment to its humiliated owner.

An outbreak of some kind was never far from the surface. Old scores were settled and resettled, but every musty night the verdicts were overturned, and the same misfortunes, bad breaks, had to be gone over and dispatched again. Spouses, Presidents, New York City, white people—the world had a lot to answer for until ice watered down the bliss of analysis. Sometimes the boredom alienated best friends. People succumbed to unknown reveries, groped down steep, unlit alleys in their minds. Jesse was rare in that his cheerfulness never failed him. He was always ready to rally anyone with a slap on the back. "I just came through to holler at you."

But we enjoyed someone "going off." The Five Bottoms liked to scream. "No fighting in my bar. Outside, 86." Once Betty threw you out, Jesse said, she didn't let you back in. She could count on the muscle of her regulars. We demonstrated our loyalty by not deserting the Melody Coast when the air conditioner went on the blink, by hauling garbage sacks from its door to the door of some other establishment when the sanitation workers went on strike. Betty repaid our devotion by flipping bottles upside down, her bun of red hair flecked with ash from the cigar clenched between her tiny teeth.

A new face was an irresistible adventure. "Baby, I went to California for the weekend two years ago and I just got back," I heard at the front door one night. I saw a squat tumbler of a woman remove space-age sunglasses to unleash eyes as startled as a doe's. Her honey face described a beautiful oval thickly powdered, like a cake. A huge mouth raced ahead of her under a shield of bright red lip gloss. To look at this woman for the first time was to feel yourself about to get run over at an intersection.

Jesse helped her onto a bar stool as if it were a throne and hovered around the artificial rose that heaved in her cleavage. Burgundy-brown curls peeked out from under a black sombrero, paused on her forehead shiny with excitement, and came to rest around black saucer earrings. "I told the woman straight up, 'If you don't do my head right I'm taking you out.' Well, she messed up and now I have to see some friends uptown to cancel her jive behind." It came out at top volume and wiped out the roar of the National League fans on the television overhead.

Jeanette accepted the homage of the regulars and a vodka gimlet from Betty, who was not otherwise inclined to make a fuss over her return. She did, however, allow the homecoming party to spill over after she locked the doors for the night. I was in with the in crowd, Jesse's grin said. Jeanette said she kissed off L.A. because she got sick of nothing but promises from record companies. Jesse said Jeanette had worked as a backup singer all over the globe. Jeanette said she hoped to get hooked up with a tour like the one she made to Australia in 1966 or the one to

Amsterdam in 1968. We drank a toast to the absence of racism among the Dutch, to Jeanette's future, and one to Jesse and all good people. "We go way back," Jesse said. "She's one dynamite lady." I bought Jeanette a vodka gimlet and she said that black clothes solved her laundry problems. We hit it off immediately.

It was like a party whenever Jeanette came. Phantoms from her past, men with unclear faces, like those in a group photograph, cropped, sliced by the margin, somehow got word to attend. Jeanette never made her moist and out-of-breath entrance before eleven o'clock. We saw her sombrero and space shades in the streetlight, navigating around boxes and Hefty trash bags that multiplied at the curbs, reproduced on the sidewalks, heaps of waste that took on the aspect of barricades. Jeanette brought in the perfume of one who had seen something of the great world. The pool players and even the surly Five Bottoms crammed into her corner to listen to scurrilous tales about the real "Miss Diane," to get "the truth" about Tammy Terrell's brain tumor. "Baby, give me a drink first. This is a good one."

On the third night after Jeanette's return Betty refused at four o'clock on the dot to mix another drink. "She'll be back," Betty said when I protested, the way you tell a child that the circus has gone. Maybe that's why she laughed when she heard Jeanette count for me the clubs where she'd been held over. The curtain fell on Jeanette's act, on the microphones that had loved her blister of a mouth. Outside her fans forgot her, went home talking about the play-offs. I found out from Jesse that Jeanette had been back in New York for some months, slowly working her way down Broadway, but in the Melody Coast absence was a kind of victory, and everyone had his story. It was a breach of manners to doubt these covers, not to respect them in the fabricator's presence.

The next day at sundown Jeanette was on her perch in the

window, right next to mine. She wore unflattering jeans and a baseball cap with the bill turned backward. I ordered a vodka gimlet; "clear and green," she called it. "Baby, you take your vodka, gargle with vermouth, and say 'Hello' right over the vodka," she said. She knew many things. "To make brown rice you just take it easy. You check the clock and then you check your pot about three albums later." She admitted that she was not feeling quite her old self, maybe was a little down.

Men had been through Jeanette as through a canal. This one didn't come back, this one never phoned again, this one stuck her with the bill on Lake Pontchartrain. "Imagine trusting somebody like that? Like having rats for lunch. If it was just about stepping, he'd step, quit you like nothing." She'd never learn, she said. She needed to be in love in order to work. She looked for the handsomest man in the club and sang to him. I said she should have more confidence. She said I was probably right, but it was a tough, lonely business, and yes, thank you, baby, she wouldn't mind another vodka gimlet. It was, she said, one of those days. I said I believed in her talent and she said she believed in me.

We came in entitled, as if we'd been on the job all day. We left bushed, as if we'd run all night, though we hadn't moved for hours. I told myself I was just getting away from my dreary studio and Jeanette said she was just waiting for a call from her agent. Big emotions sprang full grown in the Melody Coast and Jeanette told Jesse that she had the super feeling that she and I went back a long ways, that she had always known me, that we probably knew each other in one of our past lives, maybe in ancient Egypt. She said she'd show me the real Harlem, the Harlem that could still jump, but the evening I put on my glad suit the excursion was indefinitely delayed by one more vodka gimlet for the road.

Talk was Jeanette's only capital and I was, she said, her last friend. I knew how to treat a lady, how to listen, and whom to listen to. I knew what she should say to her agent, who was giving her the runaround, and what she should say to the desk at the private hotel, as she called it, that threatened to lock her out. I was her kind of people, she said, not like the pool players who couldn't see their paunches, the dudes who arrived in white hats and a state of almost insane confidence. I was not like the Five Bottoms, who twisted their bangles and belts in the red seats and handed her attitude because, she said, men preferred her company. I was more dependable than Betty. "I don't want to tell you how many white women I was silly enough to trust." Night swirled against our window, ran across the jealous street, and air like that from the back of a furnace tried to steal through the door when someone hesitated over which way to go. "Stick with the winners," Jeanette said.

She held a seat for me every day. "Baby, I hate to ask you for another cigarette." If Jeanette had had one of those days, with a flick of Betty's wrist she was her old self again, revving up behind tinted glass, her lips accelerating, soaring from left to right. I'd picked up the shell of a crustacean just to take it for a stroll, but it turned out to be a living thing, a giant clam that left pink half-moons on several glasses. With a flick of Betty's wrist I was swallowed up, pulled through sewers of Jeanette's repetitive reminiscences until Jesse's shadow made her cough me up.

It was only because Jesse inserted himself between us to holler at his number-one lady and saw my change on the bar that he got the ten dollars I owed him. Jeanette said he shouldn't take money from children. Jesse said he wasn't taking anything. Jeanette said if he was so flush why had he told her he couldn't lend her five dollars. Jesse said people fell into two categories:

those you loved and those you loved and lent money to. Jeanette said after what they'd been through she belonged on both sides. Jesse said she was all over his list. Jeanette said she didn't understand how he could talk that way after the ribs she had cooked for him. Jesse said he didn't eat ribs. Jeanette said she had never met a nigger who wouldn't eat ribs and then lie about it. Jesse said if she started something he'd have to teach her how to play the Dozens. Jeanette said she didn't use language like that.

The precious little in my pocket wasn't going very far and Jeanette said I should have kept my ten dollars. I said the money wasn't mine and Jesse was good people. "He sure enough is good people. Come a long way for a man who's done time," Jeanette said, as though Jesse weren't standing there. "You know what I'm saying? Work with it." I asked what prison was like before I could stop myself.

"No big thing." He walked away.

Summer was almost over. Already leaves in the parks I never visited were beginning to turn. Express mail from my parents was my only rope to the real world. My friends had thrown away my whereabouts and I had misplaced theirs. Often when I held my telephone I heard nothing. Not even a wrong number could get to me. Water as dark as tea bubbled out of my faucet, hit movies had come and gone without me, but dusk still wallowed in a red lion sun. My street beamed with hubcaps, discarded refrigerators, exploded sofas. Black bags made fences and didn't know whether the sanitation strike had been called off or not. Children on safari beat the creatures that stalked the industrial-strength jungles with vacuum hoses and table legs.

Day was sneaking off, going home to make a salad, to try out a new contraceptive, to watch reruns of situation comedies, or to get gussied up. I stood in a bodega deciding between potato chips and corn chips. I thought I saw my former self zip by on roller skates, a large radio on my shoulder, but it wasn't me. I never skated. I didn't wear loafers without socks like preppies just back from Shelter Island. I wore a jacket so threadbare it was comfortable. It had belonged to Grandfather, but I had made it mine, had made it sour with the poisons I had to sweat out. I bought marshmallows. A smoked bank window showed me what I looked like eating something like Styrofoam. Behind me Broadway was spacious. The rush from work was over, but a nebulous light reigned, and that was the mischief about summer that still made me marvel: how the planet rotated to turn wayward side up.

A group of students joshed on a traffic island. Soon it would be time for freshman orientation. It was starting again, but I was separated from that identity by a muddy river. I thought of the doors in Furnald Hall that flew open and shut on the slightest pretext, the sound of Grace Slick, the incense and psychobabble that went with the music, even the list of classes. The students kicked up dust, milkweed, and I obeyed my steps until they delivered me to the feeble wires over the Melody Coast, refuge of the down with it.

I saw Jeanette's silhouette in the window and turned away. A man in suspenders sold gloomy meat from the trunk of his car. A few women swatted the air, searched through the stacks of coagulated plastic. A streetwalker hurried by with her breakfast of Chinese-Cuban takeout. I saw a boy launch record after record from his window. Maybe he was weeding his collection in preparation for the upcoming parties. Black discs spun against the deepening sky, nested in awnings, broke under tires. Lights in a pharmacy went out, others went on. The M4 bus glowed and swam on to mount the darkness. Passengers were reading, talking, or looking straight ahead. They had someplace to go. "Where you been?" I saw Jeanette's mouth grand and teeming in the pit of the door. Her eyes scanned the street like headlights, as if someone might be after her.

All the good people were in the bar, and on their backs their pet ghosts egged them on. Betty said nothing about my absence. I looked for Jesse. He returned my wave but stayed where he was, adjudicating, jabbing with his index finger. Jeanette said that she, too, had been away, to Long Beach, the Long Beach in Queens, to her new hairdresser's patio, where she ate barbecue and counted the golf carts that rolled by on the other side of a ravine. Her talk advanced, but I interrupted, said I'd been to Montauk, where I square danced, drank champagne on a dune at midnight, and threw myself into the surf with all my clothes on. Maybe, like me, she had been holed up in a room, pacing, waiting for the relief check. Maybe not.

Jeanette said it did a body a world of good to get away, to hang back and get a good look at things. She licked the remnants of a vodka gimlet, sprinkled my face with talk. I thought of the vending machine in the basement of Furnald Hall that had taken all my quarters and agreed with her that the world was, indeed, in chaos, but I didn't respond to the suggestion in her face that because of the way things were going we might as well have another. She had attached thick, lustrous brushes to her eyelids that made a scratching sound when she looked down to see how far along I was with my drink. She said she had had a day of bullshit from her agent and was tuckered out with all the trying to keep up with herself. Her chatter was muffled by her empty glass. She put on her space goggles and sighed that she could do no more that night. I said it was nice to see her. "What's wrong, baby? You're only as sick as your secrets."

Jeanette didn't leave. She was afraid to go home. The doctor might have called. She folded her arms on the bar. I started to retreat and she said she hadn't wanted anyone to worry, that's why she hadn't mentioned the tests before, she was used to dealing with bad news on her own. She took a cigarette from my pack and waited for a light. She said she had had an operation for her condition three years before and was pretty sure that she was strong enough should a second procedure be necessary.

I watched her from a great distance, amazed, vengeful, and righteous, the way you are when crossing out a name. I said that we all had our problems, bar talk for "So what, get lost, you're bothering me" and, emancipated by rudeness, flaunted that sometimes scarce medium of exchange, a drink. I was a regular. I'd heard it all. I didn't even pay attention to my own rap. But Jeanette was made of nails. She laughed, as if I'd told her a funny story, dried her eyes, and said a vodka gimlet would do her friendly. I said I had no money. Jeanette leaned over, as if to clue me in on something big. "Ask Betty for credit."

I knew not to look at the mirror behind the altar of bottles. I roamed among the regulars, fell into conversations as into foxholes, even into the red booth of the Five Bottoms. "That's right, I told him, don't pack, just get out. Can we help you or something?" I forced my way into a circle of bloods, Vietnam veterans, and asked them to tell me about lurpers and door gunners. I scribbled my name on the chalk board, though I had never played pool, and would have asked Jesse to let me buy him a top-shelf Jack Daniel's had he not departed in a cry of Hi-yo, Silver.

The moment had come, that super feeling we waited out the decent hours for, stared down the disapproval in the clock to get. As if a bell had sounded, everyone was feeling fine out of nowhere and flying around the bar, broad, unreserved. The Five Bottoms blossomed like the last best hope of men, and the pool players slapped five and forgave those who had trespassed against them. The Melody Coast, on these special nights, was complicated with tight places, hidden squares. I thought I would need a map to get from one corner to another.

When the regulars got tired of dancing to throwback favorites, they made Betty turn on the radio. I saw Jeanette rumba in my direction and buried myself in a debate on who was the greatest heavyweight champion of all time. When the good people became impatient with the radio, the oldies on the jukebox came back to glory. I saw Jeanette pachanga over to the pool table to lift some unclaimed dollars. Her hips said, "Fine by me: if you don't know me I don't know you neither." When the good people tired of the Bump and the Camel Walk, they fanned themselves and called out for more.

I surfaced near a woman in gold lamé and a man with a gold-tipped cane, two oscillating charges impressed by the binding energy between them. The man scraped me away with his cane. I saw Jesse hug a white boy in a tie-dyed T-shirt. I saw Jeanette peer over a fat man's shoulder, as if she were hunting for someone more important at a party. I smiled recklessly on delicate ne-gotiations near the bathroom. I saw Betty rinse towels and forget to hang up the telephone. I saw Jesse in the racket arch like a dentist over the white boy who looked passed out. I was thinking of the stories I'd heard about cabinloads of sinners going crazy on the flights to the Mardi Gras in Rio when Betty pulled the plug on the jukebox.

The selection lights disappeared, "Hey Juanita" by the Five Stars slurred to a halt, but the good time went on. Then the news rippled from the crowd around the bar to the good people in the red booths, to the clusters of tables in puddles of light, on to the recess behind the pool table and back again, each time gaining speed, accumulating detail. Someone had been cut. Someone had been cut on the street. A kid had been cut with a razor by assailants unknown, right on Broadway, just outside the door, and Jesse had carried him in. Word got around and everything ceased for ten years. No one wanted to be seen taking the first sip.

The lights went up on the smoke. I saw the Five Bottoms put their hands to ruined mascara, make the sign of the cross. I saw good people pour out some of their drinks on the floor as a token of respect. Everyone who had ever been to a doctor was suddenly a medical expert. I heard some say that they knew something was going to happen. It was more than anyone had bargained for. The crowd moved back. I had to look.

"Go on, boy, wipe your ass with your morals," Jesse said.

I saw him embowered by bar stools, laid out on the floor. His mustache wasn't more than two weeks old. His T-shirt was not tie-dyed, that was something else. He was completely pink, his arms, his lids. What I saw when I shut my eyes was a thin, raised, red line that went from behind his left ear across his throat and entered his pale green T-shirt just below his right shoulder.

"What the hell are you doing?" A policeman shoved me into the unsteady others who wanted to get out. Policemen were everywhere with walkie-talkies, with midriffs of guns, nightsticks, handcuffs. They locked the doors, cleared out the bathroom and the kitchen, interviewed Jesse, Betty, and Jesse again. Another ten years passed. Word got around that the police were going to take every name in the place. Good people fed on this bulletin, became hysterical, unreasonable, important, insisted that they could not get tangled up with the cops, that they had more than a few answers but due to mysterious policies could not be questioned. The boy was encompassed by a sheet as pure as the Alps. I wondered where they had found something so clean.

"I sure need a drink now," I heard Jeanette say in line behind me. The law of the binge is that the binge comes first. People gave the policemen plausible names and phone numbers. "The Double Purchase is open," Jeanette said. Murder was the best excuse of all to get loaded. Her hand slipped into mine. I gave up my name to a policeman's clipboard. "Moved. Left no forwarding address," my eyes said. A summer night waited to take me firmly by the other arm. I wish I could say I was thinking about him, stopped, subtracted, about his parents asleep, unprepared for the anniversary that had entered their lives.

8 / *Summertime*

Manhattan was burning up that Bicentennial summer, and those without air conditioners, those who could not buy refuge in the cinemas or bars, were driven into the streets. Far into the spangled night, welling up from the muggy cross streets and streaming avenues, came the noise of tapedeck anthems, revving motorcycles, breaking bottles, dogs, horns, cats in heat, bag ladies getting holy, and children going off the deep end.

I was, as the expression goes, beginning a new life. I was still on the Upper West Side, but every change of address within the twenty-two square miles of Manhattan was, back then, before I knew better, a hymn to starting over. So, two rooms with splintered softwood floors and walls the dingy, off-white color of a boy's Jockey shorts after scout camp; two rooms at 2— West Ninety-fifth Street in a small, shaggy building of only two apartments, rooms sanctified by rent stabilization.

The old brick held the mean heat, sun streaked through the windows and lit up the smoky dust that hung in the air. The pipes leaked, the doors were warped, spiderwebs formed intricate designs in the corners. The oven and refrigerator refused to work on days that were not prime numbers. In the mornings paint dropped from the ceiling like debris idly flung into traffic from an overpass. The bathroom tiles had buckled and the cracks in the plaster resembled outlines of fjords on a map of Norway. Roaches?—Yes, the totemic guerrillas of urban homesteading were there.

None of this mattered. I was unpacking boxes of secondhand and overdue library books, fondling dirty envelopes of tattered letters, hitting my shins on milk crates of blackened pots, tarnished flatware, and chipped Limoges plates. In the new, ascetic life I imagined I would not need much. I was not made for keeping up the perfect kitchen for the right sort of dinner party, not equal to the task of digging up that intriguing print for the gleaming, glossy-white vestibule. I was through with telephone madness at 5 p.m.—that calling and calling to find someone home while a tray of ice melts on the thrift store table. And the nights of the wide bed, of the mattress large enough to hold the combat of two, were definitely over. The seediness into which I had slid held the promise of a cleansing, monastic routine.

My rear window looked out on a mews, on Pomander Walk, a strand of two-story row houses done in mock-Tudor style. The shutters and doors were painted blue, green, or red. The hedges were prim and tidy. Boxes of morning glories completed the scene. An odd sight, unexpected, anachronistic. I thought of it as a pocket of subversion against the tyranny of the grid and the tower. But Pomander Walk's claims were modest, as were its proportions—a mere sideshow of a lane that ran north and south, from Ninety-fifth Street to Ninety-fourth. Its survival probably had something to do with its being in the middle of the block, not taking up too much room, and that it was family property.

A little street in the London suburb of Chiswick was celebrated in the play *Pomander Walk*, first produced in 1911. I was told that an Irish-American restaurateur was so charmed by it that he brought a designer over to help build a replica of the set. That is what he got—a set. It was built in 1921, a rather late, unhistorical-sounding date. When Pomander Walk was finished, the land immediately west of it was virginal, undeveloped. Residents had a clear view of thick treetops down to the Hudson River. Perhaps then it was close in mood to the ideals of the City Beautiful period, to the harmony of Hampstead Way or Bedford Park. Perhaps not. This was a mirage inspired by haphazard Chiswick, not by an architect's vision of a utopian commuter village.

I was disappointed to learn that Pomander Walk had always been apartments. I thought each structure had originally been a house and, like those of Belgravia, had only later been violated, cut up, humbled by the high cost of living well. Pomander Walk harbored high-ceilinged efficiencies "intended for and first occupied by theatrical people," the *WPA Guide to New York City* reported in 1939. In the twenties, so the lore went, it was a pied-à-terre for the likes of the Gish sisters, Katharine Hepburn, and Dutch Schultz. Bootleggers threw scandalous parties at which guests refused to remove their homburgs.

Pomander Walk had seen better days. The sentry boxes were empty. The caretaking staff had been reduced to two elusive Albanians, the apartments themselves were in various stages of decay, and behind the valiant façades, in the passageways between the tombs of West End Avenue and the cheap clothing stores of Broadway, were fire escapes grim as scaffolds and mounds of garbage through which chalk-white rats scurried. These were the days before gentrification—where is the gentry?—before the ruthless renovations that would turn entire neighborhoods into a maze of glass, chrome, exposed brick, polished blond oak, and greedy ferns.

Pomander Walk had become a kind of fortress, as it had to be, surrounded as it was, like the enclaves of early Christian merchants in the Muslim ports of the Levant. Pomander Walk struggled against the tone of the blocks swarming around it. High gates at either end of the lane, at the steps that led down to the streets, spoke of a different order. DO NOT ENTER. PRIVATE PROPERTY. A peeling red rooster kept vigil over the main entrance. The fields sloping down to the Hudson were long gone. Sandwiched between dour, conventional buildings, Pomander Walk seemed an insertion of incredible whimsy and brought to mind Rem Koolhaas's phrase in *Delirious New York*—"Reality Shortage."

During my vacant hours I fed my curiosity about the inhabitants of that pastoral, pretentious, Anglophile fantasy. The tenants were mostly women. I imagined that they were widows surviving on pensions or on what their husbands had managed to put aside, and that there were a few divorcées sprinkled among them, the sort not anxious to define themselves by respectable jobs with obscure galleries. Their custom, on those hot afternoons, before, as I supposed, trips to married sons at the Jersey Shore, was to leave their electric fans and gather on the stoops. They sat on newspapers, pillows, or lawn chairs for cocktails. Sometimes large, festive deck umbrellas appeared.

The women got along well with the blond or near-blond actors and dancers who lived in warring pairs in some of the smaller apartments. The artists, when they came out in tight shorts for a little sun, joined with the women in discouraging intruders from looking around. No, they said, there were no flats available and the waiting list was as long as your arm. Defenders of the faith. I kept the frayed curtains over my rear window drawn after some tourists, as non-leaseholders were called, stepped up to the bars and, seeing me, a black fellow struggling with a can of tuna fish, asked, "Are you the super?"

———

Once upon a time I was morbidly sensitive about the impertinence born of sociology. Taxi drivers would not stop for me after dark, white girls jogged to keep ahead of my shadow thrown at their heels by the amber streetlamps. Part of me didn't blame them, but most of me was hurt. I carried props into the subway—the latest *Semiotext(e)*, a hefty volume of the Frankfurt School—so that the employed would not get the wrong idea or, more to the point, the usual idea about me. I did not want them to take me for yet another young black prole, though I was exactly that, one in need of a haircut and patches for my jeans. That Bicentennial summer I got over it. I remembered a gentleman of the old school who, after Johns Hopkins and Columbia, said his only ambition was to sink into the lower classes. By the time I knew him he had succeeded, and this gentle antique lived out his last days among harmless drunkards at a railroad yard in Norfolk, Virginia. I resolved to do the same, as if, away from my mother and father, I had been anywhere else.

As a matter of fact, I had been sinking for some time since my job as an auditor's trainee. Next stop downward: a bookshop. Not the supermarket variety where women phoned in orders for two yards of books, repeating specifications of height and color, completely indifferent to title. Not one of the new boutiques where edgy Parisian slang skipped over the routine murmur. But a "used" bookshop, one of those holes-in-the-wall where solitude and dust took a toll on the ancient proprietor's mental well-being, much like the health risks veins of coal pose to miners. That summer, unable to pay the rising rent, the owner gave up, wept openly at the auction of his stock. Next stop: office temp (let go). Waiter (fired). Telephone salesman (mission impossible). Then I found my calling—handyman. The anonymity of domestic service went well with the paranoid vanity of having a new and unlisted phone number.

I should have advertised my services in *The Westsider*. Even so, I lucked into a few appointments. Among my clients was an exalted bohemian on the upper reaches of Riverside Drive. I spent most of the day cleaning up after her impromptu séances. Two mornings a week I worked for a feminist psychologist who lived in one of the hives overlooking Lincoln Center. I walked her nasty Afghan hound, which was often woozy from pet tranquilizers; stripped the huge rolltop desk she hauled in not from the country but from Amsterdam Avenue. I was not allowed to play the radio and, in retaliation, I did not touch the lunch of tofu and carrot juice she left for me on the Formica counter. Then to Chelsea, where I picked up dry cleaning for a furtive youngish businessman. His mail consisted mostly of final notices from Con Ed, Ma Bell, and collection agencies in other states. I was certain that I was being tailed whenever I delivered one of his packages to the questionable factory outlets with which he had dealings. I made him pay me in cash.

One glaring morning someone I knew in publishing called to say that she knew of a woman who was getting on in years and in need of some help. The only thing Djuna Barnes required of her helper was that he not have a beard. I shaved, cut my hair, and fished out jacket and tie in spite of the heat, having been brought up to believe that I was not properly dressed unless I was extremely uncomfortable. I was so distracted that my socks did not match.

Miss Barnes lived in the West Village, just north of the old Women's House of Detention, in a blind alley called Patchin Place. Shaded by ailanthus, a city tree first grown in India that in the days of the pestilence was believed to absorb "bad air," the lime-green dwellings of Patchin Place had once been home to Dreiser, John Reed, E. E. Cummings, and Jane Bowles.

Through the intercom at #5 came a deep, melodious voice, and after an anxiety-producing interrogation, I was buzzed in. I found the chartreuse door with its DO NOT DISTURB sign, and after another interrogation, it slowly opened.

The home of this "genius with little talent," as T. S. Eliot said of Miss Barnes, was brutally cramped—one tiny, robin's egg–blue room with white molding. The kitchen was such a closet that the refrigerator hummed behind French doors in a little pantry packed with ironing board, vacuum, boxes of faded *cartes d'identité*, linen, and, so my covetousness led me to think, hoarded Tchelitchew costume sketches. Great adventures, I was sure, awaited me in the clutter—bibelots on the mantels and side tables, picture frames on the floor turned toward the wall, shoe-boxes under the fat wing chair. On either side of the fireplace were bookcases. Her low, narrow bed was flush against one of them. Two plain wooden desks dominated the dark room. Stacks of letters and papers had accumulated on them like stalagmites. Meticulously labeled envelopes warning "Notes on Mr. Eliot," "Notes on Mr. Joyce" rested near a portable typewriter. The blank page in the Olivetti manual had browned.

The booming voice was deceptive. Miss Barnes was bent, frail. The lazy Susan of medicines on the night table was so large that there was scarcely room for the radio, spectacles, and telephone. Her introductory remarks were brief. She came down hard on the point of my being there. "See that you don't grow old. The longer you're around the more trouble you're in." Miss Barnes had been old for so long that she looked upon herself as a cautionary tale. The first day of my employ I was told to see to it that I never married, never went blind, was never operated on, never found myself forbidden salt, sugar, tea, or sherry, and above all, that I was never such a fool as to write a book.

Yet there was a hypnotic liveliness to her, moments when the embers of flirtatiousness flared. The thin white hair was swept back and held together by two delicate combs. She wore a Moroccan robe trimmed in gold, white opaque stockings, and red patent-leather heels. Her eyes glistened like opals in a shallow pond and her skin was pale as moonlight. Her mouth was painted a moist pink, her jaw jutted forward; her bearing was defiant, angrily inquisitive. The tall, stylish eccentric of the Bernice Abbott and Man Ray photographs lived on somewhere inside the proud recluse who cursed her magnifying glass, her swollen ankles, overworked lungs, hardened arteries, and faulty short-term memory. "Damn, damn, damn," she said.

My inaugural chore was to refill the humidifier. Under her scrutiny this task was far from simple. Her hands flew to her ears. "That's too much water. We can't have that." Next Miss Barnes wanted me to excavate an unmarked copy of "Creatures in an Alphabet." Stray pages were tucked here and there, none clean enough for her. She settled on one version of the poem, retreated to the bed, and set about crossing out the dedication. "Can't have that. He ruined my picture." The explanation of how some well-meaning soul had smudged a portrait when he tried to wash it gave way abruptly to a denunciation of modern pens, how they were made not to last. I gave her my Bic, told her to keep it. "Why, thank you. Would you like to support me?" She sank into the pillows and laughed, dryly, ruefully, as you would at a private joke.

By some sorcery the laugh became a racking cough. She clutched a wad of tissues and coughed, coughed. I tried to help—water? A pill? She held up her hand for silence. The barking subsided. She sat for some time with head lowered, fists in her lap. Then she looked around, as if disappointed to find herself still in the same place. Fearing dizziness, she asked me to fetch her black handbag. She found a leather coin purse, from which she slowly extracted five one-dollar bills. She laid them on the bed in a fan shape and commanded me to "run along." She pushed the pages of "Creatures in an Alphabet" away, like a patient trying to shove a tray of Jell-O and thin sandwiches from view. Miss Barnes was tired. Asking for a fresh copy of that poem was a symbolic gesture—she was no longer a writer at work. At least she had an air conditioner, I thought, as I closed the warm gate to the street and put a match to the cigarette I was not permitted to smoke in her presence.

I learned not to call and volunteer: Miss Barnes turned me aside with mandarin courtesy. I went when summoned, which was not often. If I arrived early she implied that the zeal of the young was inelegant, and if I came late, panting, she stated flatly that the young were hopelessly self-absorbed. Miss Barnes thought my given name, with its contemporary Dixie-cup quality, ridiculous, and my surname, with its antebellum echo, only barely acceptable. I had to admit that it had the goofiness of a made-up name. Delmore Schwartz, what a beautiful name! Delmore Schwartz is said to have exclaimed.

I went to the market—"What's an old woman to eat, I ask you"—for bananas, ginger ale, coffee ice cream, hard rolls, and plums. "Not the red ones, the black ones. When they're good, they've white specks on them." I rushed out to the hardware store for pesticide and back again to exchange it for a brand to which she was not allergic. I went to the shoe repair and back again to have her black heels stretched even more. "I forgot. You're young. Don't mind running up and down the steps, do you?" And, of course, I stood on line at the pharmacy.

"I haven't been out of this room in five years. You'd think I'd be climbing the walls, wouldn't you?"

"Yes."

"I am."

Miss Barnes was not above a little drama and I believed she exaggerated the extent of her isolation. She had a brother in Pennsylvania, a nephew or some such in Hoboken. Regularly, her devoted "boy," a Pole in his sixties, came to wash the floors and walls. I had heard that two elderly gentlemen, her doctor and her lawyer, still climbed the stairs to pay their respects. There were romantic rumors—one had it that an heiress to the company that supplied paper to the U.S. Mint sometimes stepped from a great car to call on the friend of her expatriate youth. I hoped the radio was a comfort, that it filled her room with music, voices, but it was never on in my presence, during business hours, as it were.

She was reasonably informed about large events, seemed up on literary gossip. The *TLS* was stored in a basket like kindling, the light blue wrapper unbroken. If she did not have much to say about the outside world, well, she had lived a long time. The ways in which most of us burned up daily life were, to her, pure folly. "What fools are the young." I am sure Miss Barnes managed to do a great deal of wrangling by telephone. She had a combative, litigious streak, an outgrowth, perhaps, of the yearning to take hold, to fend for herself. Rights and permissions had become an obsession that filled the place once occupied by composition. She dismissed me before she dialed the number of some unsuspecting publisher.

It was bad manners to be too curious. Many had been banished. She spoke of one former helper as being "stupid as a telephone pole." She fumed against one enterprising character who had insinuated himself into her confidence, gotten into her will "with both feet," and then packed up cartons of treasure. She claimed to have been relentlessly ripped off, down to the monogrammed spoons, but I wondered about that, since, evidently, she regarded the sale of her papers as a kind of theft.

As for admirers, those pilgrims and would-be biographers who brought her "one bent rose from somebody's grave," she declared that they wanted her on Forty-second Street standing on her head with her underwear showing. Some acolytes, she said, had taken advantage of her failing eyesight to smuggle out a souvenir or two. She complained that a bookstore in the vicinity had, without her consent, used the name her father had conjured up for her, and that when she called to protest the manager hung up on her.

Pessimism Miss Barnes wore as regally as a tweed suit, and perhaps an early career as a reporter had taught her not to expect too much of the "hard, capricious star." Everything and everyone came down to the lowest common denominator in the end. "Love is the first lie; wisdom the last." The one time I was foolish enough to quote from her work she looked at me as if I had lost my mind. "Am I hard-of-hearing," she screamed, "or do you mumble?" That was a break, the possibility that she hadn't heard. "You're shy, aren't you? Pretend that you aren't." I wanted to be different, to be one who did not ask about the cafés, the parties, Peggy Guggenheim, or her portrait of Alice Rohrer over the fireplace.

Her seclusion was a form of self-protection as much as it was a consequence of age. Even if she had been temperamentally capable of going off, like Mina Loy, and leaving everything to scavengers, it was too late. When Miss Barnes was on a roll, off on a tirade, her tiny figure seemed to expand and take up the whole room. The bold voice forced me into a corner, words came like darts. I had the feeling that the locksmith's clumsy work stood for something larger, that it was simply an occasion for the release of fury. I nodded and nodded as she pointed to the scratches around the new cylinder in the door. "You mustn't say 'Oh really' again." Then the inevitable deflation, that rasping cough. I stood very still, like an animal waiting for a hunter to pass.

The temper had its source in the underground fire of physical pain. Once I was sent away minutes after slipping through the door because clearly she was having a rough day. Though Miss Barnes, like most old people, talked of her ailments—"I can't breathe and I'm going blind. Damn"—she did not want a stranger to witness her private struggles. She arranged five dollars on the bed and apologized for having ruined my Sunday.

I told her that I admired her work, that coming to see her was one of my few joys. "You're mad. You're absolutely mad. Well, there's nothing we can do about that." I refused the money. Miss Barnes did not part with cash easily. In her life she had been broke and stranded more than once. My wage she regarded as wildly generous, a gift to, say, the United Negro College Fund, because she thought of dollars in terms of a prewar exchange rate.

She insisted, gave me a bill to mail so that I would feel I had earned my pay. "I used to be like you. Not taking the money. It didn't matter." She wagged an index finger. "Make money. Stuff it in your boots, as Shakespeare said." Behind me I heard the bolts slide across her door.

The summer unfolded like a soggy sheet, and except for Miss Barnes, my clients casually drifted away. I lived on an early birthday present from home, but somehow I managed to get behind in the rent. I assured my parents that I was knocking on doors, sending out résumés, proving once again that if you nag your children they will lie to you. Days evaporated like spilled water on sizzling pavement. Rock bottom was not so bad, and if sinking had not turned out to be as liberating as I had hoped, it was not without some consolations. The afternoons I traveled in humid subway cars from Pomander Walk to Patchin Place lifted me out of my torpor. The chance to see Miss Barnes struck me as an omen—but of what?

Fame was not much of a consolation to her. She was not rich, could not trade her name for much, and so reputation she treated as a joke—on herself mostly. "You may like the book but not the old girl." Being a character, a survivor, made her one who had evacuated a large portion of her life, mindful of the clues carelessly left behind for detectives. "Would you believe I lived in Paris nine years and never learned a word of French?" Her memories, those she shared, had the quality of set pieces. Even when she talked of intimate matters there was something impersonal about it, and I wondered how many visitors had heard her say that she was never a lesbian, could never abide "those wet muscles" you had to love to love women; or that she was too much of a coward to take her own life.

A joke, yes, but not entirely. "No, don't move those. I'm a vain woman. I want them near me." Miss Barnes meant the translations, the various editions of *Nightwood* and *Ryder*. I was putting the bookshelf in order, not that it was needed. She was resistant to change: an autographed copy of Dag Hammarskjold's *Markings* had to remain where it had been for ages, a red pocket edition of Dante was also happy where it was. "Mr. Eliot learned Italian just to read this poem. He must have liked it, don't you think?"

I extracted a paperback, a biography of Natalie Barney, from under the bed. "Let me see that. Remy de Gourmont called her 'the Amazon of love' and she never got over it. That's what you get, that's what you end up looking like," she, peering through her magnifying glass, told a photograph showing Barney in later life. I broke my promise to myself and asked about Colette. "Yes, I knew that silly, blue-haired lady."

I got carried away and told Miss Barnes about a night at the opera when I, an undergraduate, just off the boat, was introduced to Janet Flanner. I mentioned to Miss Flanner that I, too, was from Indiana and she, taking in my tan polyester suit, red, shiny tie, and platform shoes, said, "I haven't been back since 1921— and I would advise you to do the same."

Miss Barnes didn't crack a smile. "Often she knew whereof she spoke." I found yet another copy of *Nightwood*. "Sometimes I wonder, Did I write this? How did I do it? Do it while you're young. Put all of your passion into it." She smiled.

But that was enough, not a syllable more. The shelves had to be scrubbed down, and then the windows. So there I was, clinging to the fire escape, with Miss Barnes telling me over and over what a mess I was making. She leaned on the windowsill, handed out bouquets of paper towels, pointed to the lint and suds left in the corners. She absolutely refused to hear my thoughts on investing in a sponge. "Don't tumble into that Judas tree." She groped her way back to the bed to prepare for another onslaught of coughing.

In the shelves of the bookcase were mysterious little phials solemn as votive candles. She said that they contained oxygen. They looked like cloudy empty bottles to me. I had to wash them, all twenty-four of them. One lid got trapped in the drain. "Now you've done it." I worked with a pair of scissors to pull it out. "Oh, you've done it now," she repeated, swaying against the bathroom door, fretting with the collar of a pink, satin-like dressing gown. "Take down the trash and you may go." The sad thing was realizing that there was really nothing I could do for her.

When I got the bright idea of devising a chart for her flotilla of pills—often she had complained of headaches, of not knowing what to take when—she was offended. I argued that many of the prescriptions had been voided, that some of the tubes were empty, that it was amazing she could find anything in the jumble. We had a tug-of-war over a box of opium suppositories on which she depended for whatever peace she had. I made a little speech on obstruction, in the way you sometimes talk down to the elderly, on not being able to help if she didn't let me. "I know what I'm about, thank you very much, Mr. D."

Miss Barnes ordered me to wash out a silk blouse in the sink. I said no. She started to say that she didn't understand why blacks had become so touchy, caught herself, and said she didn't know why young men had such silly notions about what they considered women's work. But I knew what she meant, knew it from the way she swallowed the "knee" of "Negroes," that despised word of recent generations, knew it from the soft blush that spread like ink across the folds of her face. I don't remember what I said, but I can still see the five dollars on the blue coverlet, Miss Barnes hunched over, her dressing gown slightly hitched up, she hitting her palms together slowly. I paused at the door —for an apology?—but she was too old to take anything back. She met my gaze with a look of her own, a flicker of bewilderment, then hard as a stone tablet. I walked out.

I went back to living in steerage at the edge of Pomander Walk. Families were staking out territory along the masculine river to watch ships, couples were hiking with blankets and beer to fireworks, but I had other things on my mind. By nightfall, when bagpipes started up within Pomander Walk to commemorate the Queen's walk down Wall Street to Trinity Church, the misunderstanding with Miss Barnes had assumed, to me, the magnitude of an incident.

In a punitive, self-righteous mood, I decided to "get" them all, to expose, as I termed it, the sins of Western literature. I set out the pens dipped in venom, the crisp, militant index cards. I turned up the flame under the pot of bitter Bustelo and started off, like a vigilante or a bounty hunter, in search of them. I was going to make Hemingway pay for the nigger boxer in Vienna in *The Sun Also Rises*, for the nigger this and the nigger that of *To Have and Have Not*. Fitzgerald was going to be called out for the Cadillac of niggers who rolled their eyes when they pulled up on the highway next to Gatsby.

I was going to get Dashiell Hammett for "darkie town," and Evelyn Waugh, Ronald Firbank, even Carl Van Vechten. This was serious—no Julia Peterkin, Fannie Hurst, or Dubose Heyward. I was going to stick to the Dilseys and Joe Christmases. If Conrad had to go, so be it, Céline too, for his scenes in Little Togo. Lady Chatterley's lover conceded that a black woman might be able to have an orgasm, but that would be like sleeping with mud. Sweat dripped from my nose onto the index cards. The laughter boiling in the streets added to my sense of lonely mission.

I woke in my clothes determined to beat up Stephen Crane, and poor Hart Crane for "Black Tambourine." Not even Berryman or William Carlos Williams was going to get off easy. The jig was up for Rimbaud's sham niggers. Sins were everywhere. Poe, Defoe. Katherine Mansfield in a letter spoke of one woman as "the sort to go with negroes." I was going to let Shaw and Genet have it, show Sartre a thing or two about the aura of the text of *Black Orpheus*. How dare Daniel Deronda condescend to defend Caliban.

But, by noon, thanks to hypoglycemia, I wasn't sure it mattered that in 1925 Virginia Woolf had come across a black man, spiffy in swallowtail and bowler, whose hand reminded her of a monkey's. How to bring down Whittier? Or Katherine Anne Porter's "Uncle Jimbilly" and Kate Chopin's "Aunt Peggy"? And to what purpose? How far back would I have to go, to Pushkin's Ibrahim or to the black ram tupping the white ewe? Roussel's *Impressions d'Afrique* didn't even take place on earth, not really. Dinesen's farm was real, but so what? What was done was done, though most of the "gothic horror" was far from over. "Let them talk. You know your name," Grandfather had said. I threw out the cards. The motive for my pedantic note-taking was pretty sorry: after leaving Miss Barnes I had fallen into the pit of trying to prove that there was more to me than she thought.

There was more to sinking, to being a handyman, to becoming a part of the streets around me, than I had thought. I had only to approach the surface of things, like a child coming too near the heat of a kitchen range, to discover that. Being in arrears made me afraid to meet anyone from Pomander Walk. I didn't have the nerve to ask the caretakers to examine a faucet. I sold off some big books to keep the lights on. The curtain over my rear window stayed down. What companionship of the outside I had was provided by the view of Ninety-fifth Street from my front windows.

It was there that I sat on those penniless summer nights, watching the elderly across the street scrutinize me from their bolted prisons. There was a parking lot belonging to a nursing home. Daily the employees dragged themselves to their horrible duties, and in the evenings they exchanged gossip with the night shift before hurrying away. Sometimes, on Sundays, guilty families came to wheel their begetters into sleek sedans for useless outings.

It was a street on which anything could happen, and a lot did happen. Sometimes the angry voices after midnight terrified me, as if a wife or a whore were being beaten at the foot of my bed. I gave up calling the police and got used to it. That accounted for Pomander Walk's general fear of invasion. Between Riverside Drive and Central Park West, Ninety-fifth Street was a no-man's-land, a zone of welfare tenements. There were enough stories of ivy being torn from the walls by vandals, of someone who had had her purse ripped from her arm by a fleet-footed phantom who could not have been more than fifteen. The chilling cry of "Motherfuckers! All y'all motherfuckers is gonna die!" was enough to send every light on Pomander Walk blazing, as if a whistle had been blown to alert the local militia.

The building directly across from me had the most unsavory of reputations. It was an SRO, a very dark, benighted affair embedded in a slope. I noticed that pedestrians crossed the street to my side rather than risk the building's contagions that waited in ambush. A check-cashing joint occupied one of the rooms on the first floor, and from the number of men coming in and out in their undershirts with soiled paper bags from which the tops of wine bottles were visible, I guessed that there was also a bookie joint somewhere inside. These men with missing teeth who paced back and forth on the street, discussing their chances in snapping, high-wire Spanish, made a strange tableau with the drag queens who also congregated outside the SRO.

The drag queens were impossible to miss, impossible not to hear. Hour on hour they milled around the entrance, dancing complicated steps to snatches of music that came from automobile radios. Most of them were in "low drag"—cutoffs, clogs, improvised halter tops, hair slicked straight back. Some appeared in wigs, curlers, black bathrobes, gold house slippers. They held cigarettes, long brown More menthols or Kools, which they rationed scrupulously. They gossiped, waited, and played whist, "nigger bridge." They taunted young mothers who pushed baby carriages and balanced Zabar bags and balloons; they hissed at broad-backed boys who sauntered up the street in school T-shirts. "Honey, you need to go home and take off that outfit. That green gon' make yo' husband run away from you." Or: "Come over here, sugar, and let me show you something."

Sometimes, for no apparent reason, just standing there, one of them would let out a long, loud, high scream—"Owwwwwww"—and then look around with everyone else on the street. This was particularly unnerving to the people who lined up with ice-cream cones in front of the film revival house to see Fassbinder or Fellini. Equally unsettling to the neighborhood was their booby-trapped friendliness: "How ya doin', baby? Okay. Be that way. Don't speak, Miss Thing. You ain't getting none no way."

I watched the people of the SRO every day as the buds on the ginkgo that grew at a slant toward my window failed one by one and the pigeons pushed through the litter of frankfurter buns, hamburger wrappers, and pizza crusts. I recognized some of the SRO inmates in the Cuban tobacconist, the Puerto Rican laundromat, the Korean deli, the Yemenite bodega, at the hippie pot store, the Sikh newsstand. I watched them with a kind of envy. I loitered on the corner one night, but everyone stayed clear of me. Perhaps they took me for a narc. But it was perfectly natural to cross the street to get the instant replay after a checker had slammed into a station wagon or a fire had been put out three blocks away.

Of course I did not find friendship, no matter how swiftly some of the drag queens and youths stepped off into the personal. Raps about the doings on Broadway or in the park inevitably shifted to breathless, coercive pleas for loans, though I told them I had had to break open my Snoopy bank for cigarettes. The soft-spoken owner of Pomander Bookshop took me aside to give me a warning. More than one innocent had fled that SRO without watch, wallet, or trousers. Three "bloods" invited me up to discuss a deal. An alarm went off in my head. I remembered how, as a child, three classmates had invited me to join their club. They escorted me to a garage and kicked the shit out of me. Remembering that, I got as far as the lobby, made some excuse, and split.

It is hard to recall the murky, inchoate thinking that led me to make those inept gestures toward infiltrating what I saw as the underside of life, hard to camouflage the fatuity of my cautious hoverings. One illuminated night, late, a young woman was attacked by two kids. I heard her scream, saw her throw herself to the ground and thrash about. The kids couldn't get to her purse. By the time I got across the street others had come running. That was it, she moaned, she was going home to Nebraska.

One grinding dawn I stumbled into the haze with loose change for a doughnut. The intersection of Broadway and Ninety-fifth Street was clogged with squad cars. Flashing lights whipped over the faces of the somber onlookers. There had been a shooting. A handsome Hispanic man in handcuffs was pulled over to the ambulance, presumably to be identified by the victim. His shirttails flapped like signal flags. A policeman cupped the "perpetrator's" head as he pushed him into the rear of a squad car at the curb. The man's head sagged on his smooth chest and shook slowly, rhythmically. Who was it that said the man who committed the crime is not the same man as the one in the witness box?

The violence was arbitrary. I was in the crowd that watched

in horror as the policemen who had been summoned to defuse a fight beat a black teenager until coils of dark blood gushed from his head, his mouth, and drenched his shantung shirt. To my shame it was a black cop who used his stick with the most abandon. We were ordered to disperse, didn't, were rushed, and the voltage of fear that seized us was nothing like that of the political demonstrations of another time.

Shortly afterward, I called home. It seemed that I packed more than clothes. I carried to the corner all the baggage of my youth. I thought, as the taxi driver slowed to look me over, that I could leave that weight behind, like a tagless piece chugging round and round on a conveyor belt. Pollution made the sunset arresting, peach and mauve, like the melancholy seascapes of The Hague School. On the way to LaGuardia, stalled somewhere near the tollbooth, I, looking forward to my prepaid ticket, to the balm of the attendants' professional civility, felt a wind. It came like forgiveness, that sweet, evening breeze, the first promissory caress of the high summer. The storm that followed delayed the departure of my flight.

9 / Equal Opportunities

The little branch library on the Upper East Side, its shelves as depleted as those of the nearby store selling painted Catholic statuary, was Grandfather's equivalent of the laundromat, that haven where the elderly wander in their noon dreams and, warmed by dryers and the lush scent of detergent, count with either satisfaction or regret the number of stoplights they have obeyed. At a desk with a Rosetta Stone density of carved hearts and obscenities, he relived the promises, the seduction, of instruction. You cannot learn unless you fall in love with the source of learning.

History books for young readers that Grandfather checked out and dutifully returned at the end of the day, helping the woman at the desk with her coat, had become substitutes for stories about himself. He said that what fascinated him most about the "back years" was the story of how young Frederick Douglass, driven by the sound of his master reading from the Book of Job, stole a primer and copied the letters on pieces of pine plank.

Grandfather couldn't get over it. As he retold the historic episode that had for him, as a fact forgotten and relearned, the excitement of an excavation, ignorance had been more intolerable to Douglass than the overseer's beatings. Grandfather couldn't stop smiling. Perhaps he wasn't used to his new teeth. Douglass made impudent progress in secret, he said, and, lo, one day literacy, like the fleet waters of the earth, swept him to freedom.

Neither of us mentioned his memoirs. I maintained a guilty silence. Boston was taboo as a subject with Grandfather as well. We sat with it unspoken between us, like two people after a failed assignation. One of them, the one who had the change of mind and traveled alone, hopes the canceled party has enough pride not to beg for an explanation, but to be on the safe side injects into the conversation a preemptive civility.

Grandfather described how Booker T. Washington learned the alphabet in secret from marked pork barrels at a loading dock and deepened little Booker's cunning until it rivaled the kickback schemes of the president of Standard Oil. By the time I was to understand that to Grandfather the education of such men was his Borodino it was too late. Meanwhile, he, a "friend of goodness," wanted me to enjoy myself, to find him worth talking to, though his sovereign insights had become a little hard to fathom.

I would have let his eightieth birthday come and go without comment. My parents added my name to family cards. Since Grandfather's surrender to his portion, the beige stepgrandmother, four or five years earlier, I had seen him a half dozen times. It was too easy to blame the stepgrandmother, triumphant, balky, rude, accusing. I put off visits, crosstown trips to the pigeon coop for senior citizens and low-income families on upper, upper Third Avenue, the way sweethearts postpone the bus ride to the Wyoming Correctional Facility, the minimum security prison near Attica. I fought like hell to be excused from meals with him in salty restaurants when my parents and sisters came to town.

Sometimes I looked up through my windows that I cleaned under pressure from my neighbors and imagined that the pigeons in rapid transit—it was hard to follow them, the sky itself was often so pigeon-gray in winter—were carrying messages on their legs to Grandfather, but I couldn't think what the messages would be.

Along the Harlem River that helped to wall him in, the Circle Line tour guides fell silent and cameras were given a rest. People went below for refreshments until the boat had gotten by the oil drums and irrelevant crates on the eddies. The tour boats navigated toward the strait with the Dutch name where the microphones would come alive again.

Grandfather didn't ask what I was up to anymore, and something in his bright manner made it unnecessary to wonder what was going on in his world. Three plain rooms: first hers, with the television the size of a motorcycle; then his, with a prominent shoe rack; and in the main room at the end of the narrow, unadorned hall the old, mute Philco. Seeing it there in that greenhouse, bravely presiding over the stepgrandmother's maze of savage houseplants, made me think of those "white telephone" films of the thirties in which heedless revelers in top hats are astounded to discover a corpulent Russian nobleman handling the nightclub door.

Below Grandfather's windows, as hypnotic as the ocean, the song of the FDR Drive. He'd dressed up for me, put on a jacket. The beige stepgrandmother adjusted her hairnet. We heard her double the sighs that were the most important part of her preparations for lunch. She saw every chore from the viewpoint of someone who had no one to count on. She sidewinded to the table with a plate of bread and, to break up the fun, told me to get ice, to fill the pitcher. She was agitated by Grandfather's devotion to the library and said again that sooner or later someone was going to crack open his head and lay him out because he never looked where he was going.

Only two places had been set. *TV Guide* rested on the stepgrandmother's plate on the kitchen counter. She groaned and fished out a pair of tweezers to operate the broken horizontal control knob on the portable television crouched between two toasters. I said we could manage if she wanted to watch television in the comfort of the easy chair in her room. She remained on her bar stool, behind Grandfather's chair, one eye on the game show and the other on his conversation.

"In my day," Grandfather said, "Negroes understood everything. They didn't have time to talk. They were in school eight hours a day. None of this 'Let Aunt Mary Anne take care of it.' " He meant the American Missionary Association. "Now they are totally isolated. They are cut off like the poor." He didn't eat. He smiled at his fingers, at the colors playing on the rim of his wet glass, then at me. "And they bear children behind the mill." He turned over his fork to read what was written there.

I left soon after offering to wash the dishes. Grandfather said that was his favorite part of any meal. I had the feeling that the beige stepgrandmother wanted to search my pockets. The elevator took several minutes to come in their building, one of five bleak concrete towers on what had been the casual intentions of a landscape artist. I knew she was watching me through the little hole in the door. Designed for people with walkers or in wheelchairs, the elevator opened and closed very slowly, enough time for the stepgrandmother to phone her sister and have her cover my exit from the other side, to see if I met any shady characters and tried to fence the silver soap dish she said was missing.

My expedition had not been a success. I'd needed a small loan. That was the reason I called and went by in the first place. Grandfather hadn't referred to my request and I hadn't had the nerve to bring it up in person. Lord, plant my feet on higher ground. Almost instantly a check from my father fell through the slot in my door with a note saying not to embarrass Grandfather anymore. Light can break in upon you only by degrees, Douglass said.

My father always said that breakfast was the most important meal of the day. I was late to my first real job. A cold torrent swept through Central Park like a pack of unruly teens after a rock concert. I invested in a four-dollar umbrella at the subway exit on Seventh Avenue. It had blown inside out and gone its own way by the time I reached Fifth Avenue. The company occupied four floors and sundry pockets in a sleek tower of black syenite on a fashionable midtown corner. I hadn't seen the bus that created an enormous wake and my shoes squished on the marble-like tiles in front of the security desk under the gold lettering.

The chairman came out to welcome me aboard, a custom from his father's day. His head fit snugly into his collar like a shell into a canister. A part began far down on one side of his head, from which his gray was combed over to the other ear so that he looked as though he had his full head of hair. He wore the dirty glasses of old money. His pupils were small, but the whites around them were exaggerated, as if he were in a constant state of surprise.

"Wet out there?" He released my hand. "The good stuff is back this way, Maurice." I mumbled my correct name. He walked inside the memory of Princeton football injuries. Let's go, Tigers.

My new boss wasn't in yet. The chairman left me to get acquainted with my desk, to which I had been introduced several times by my distrustful predecessor. He would have presented me to the other secretaries—editorial assistants, the union called them—had he remembered their names. The effect of a long marriage to the *Late Late Show* was that I looked at my new job as a rerun. I expected a first day like that in the opening scenes of those 1950s Technicolor movies about office life when the old hands gather about the newcomer and quickly give the lowdown. My new co-workers didn't budge and I didn't peek over the pattern of plywood partitions at them.

Those partitions were at once territorial and neighborly—the white picket fence effect. They gave to the otherwise claustrophobic space and narcoleptic lighting of the department a kind of *Saturday Evening Post* domesticity. The aisle was the street, on either side of the street the white fences marked off small yards for the secretaries. Each yard was followed by an office with a door. I had the urge to run a stick along the white partitions to see which of the secretaries would run up and bark.

I removed my predecessor's fussy plants, switched folders around, and scribbled my name on the stenographer's pad, just to make the area mine. It had been unbalancing to want to move into the neighborhood, to want the desk, the gigantic IBM typewriter, the passport for union dues, the pension plan. During my interview I'd gone down on my knees and reminded my boss-to-be, Stanford, Class of '62, of the Bakke decision, in case he had also seen through my appreciative reference to his unremembered book of poems that called out after the Beats like the lonely cry of a bittern to its mate. Fortunately, he was amused. "I know where you're coming from." He probably hadn't been able to use phrases like that in a while.

I'd wanted him to think of me as a grownup. That hoax was much like the deception I'd heard people who had more self-knowledge than self-regard condemn themselves for when they were forced to shift gears in their love stories. They faulted themselves for misleading their Others into thinking that they were sensible, solvent, and sober. Without warning they reverted. They couldn't help it, they said, they didn't feel like tidying up or being cheerful anymore. The Others discovered that they dedicated all of Sunday to reading last Sunday's newspaper. Sometimes you land the job anyway.

"On deck already? Let's do it." Which meant picking up my new boss's raincoat. He would not ask me to make coffee, he said. He brought his own, when he wasn't on an herbal tea regimen. He felt silly giving dictation and hoped that I wouldn't mind coping with his handwritten notes in the "out" box. I was not to clean up the avalanche on his desk for any reason. Nor was I to do the twist around the towers of papers, boxes, page proofs, books.

A glance at the walls of chaotic bulletin boards, charts, notes, disorderly shelves, snapshots, and children's drawings made me think of some noisy migratory species conglomerating on a cliff. I was expected to make myself familiar with his buried projects and yet to keep in mind that what was a mess to the uninitiated spoke to him and his "authors" of the labor for self-transcendence. He was developing a line of self-help books for the New Man.

What he really wanted me to do was shield him—from unwanted telephone calls, hectoring mail, and nuisance manuscripts. No problem, I told him. I might have flunked the typing test, but dissembling was a skill I trusted. He liked that. He closed the door and pulled out a chair. He said it had hurt at first, but he found out very quickly that you couldn't work in an office without lying. It was impossible to get from 9:30 to 5:45 without telling a lie.

He said several of his colleagues were dangerous. Only the Big Boss, the chairman, could afford to indulge in Christmas speeches about everyone pulling for the team. He said the company was pretty laid back as far as companies went. The basement was on a first-name basis with the executive suite, but the bottom line was that it was a business. Even Bob Dylan was a brand name when you got down to it. "We're not changing your life. We're just paying scale. Now go out there and find me a winner."

I was sorry for my boss. He dreaded the life he had made: the commute from the horse country of New Jersey, the school fees, the cookbooks that sold well, the Hollywood agents with expense accounts twice his salary, the mocking, jazzy memos from the art department downstairs, the belittling, intrusive summonses from a vice president upstairs. Slabs of unsolicited manuscripts caused his step to falter in the mornings.

Most of the manuscripts arrived festooned with gimmicks to draw a reader's attention, pleas for special consideration like contestants in a studio audience: "Pick me." My boss was conscientious and wanted a written report on every manuscript. I tried to sneak these tomes, so hopefully dispatched, into the slush pile housed in a room called the Morgue, but my boss retrieved those addressed to him personally. I poured what I thought was kindness into the rejection letters that I sent out over his name.

That the letters were not supposed to be from me stayed my fingers when I was tempted to add some ameliorating touch, a question about how many children were still at home or did the "author" also keep a garden. To sound interested involved the risk of being encouraging. Addressing rejection letters to tollbooth attendants who wrote lacy blockbusters between shifts or insurance agents who produced spy thrillers at night made me feel that I was in correspondence with convicts about to be paroled who might turn up at my boss's door if I made him sound like an easy mark.

When my boss forgot to close his door and I saw him rub the bridge of his nose over disappointing sales figures, look out the filmy window that offered a close, troubling view of a vacant office in another building, I thought maybe he was wishing for those drunken, turbulent readings at City Lights, the candid hills over the bay, and wanted him to know that I was on his side. I went to the coffee station and made him a cup with just the right amount of honey that I had brought myself, knowing that he considered refined sugar the enemy.

Someone had to take care of him, the unreconstructed hippie playing hardball with what he called power bitches. He said no matter how long he'd been in the business he went into conferences with the Big Boss ready to shit his pants and when he got home he sobbed because his kids were healthy and adored school. He said he cried some more after supper because his working wife was scared that he was going nuts on her. He thanked me for knowing when to talk him down after a meeting with the salesmen and when to leave him alone, to hold all calls.

Who wouldn't prefer to make coffee than to type a letter? I was frightened of his quick confidence in me because the hand that raises you up always tires and flings you down. Because my boss trusted and perhaps also liked me, I decided that there was something wrong with him, that I had hitched my wagon to a lame one. "See you on the bevel," the nice guy said when he left early to panic on the train about what sort of statement he was making of his career.

I'd never seen five o'clock, not the five o'clock of vendors with steaming black chestnuts and pretzels, of ennobling panhandlers, stinking back doors of fine midtown restaurants, the lunatic with a can in front of Carnegie Hall singing the weeping clown from *I Pagliacci*, the five o'clock of jamming through turnstiles. Underground, with the smell of wet wool, foreheads crept up to high, unbearable temperatures. Strangers glued to one another's stomachs were on the verge of disgrace. Briefcases and shopping bags took the place of chastity belts. Who ate garlic, who had answered too heartily the clarion of Johnnie Walker, why did she use that hair cream, and why could we not stop breathing it in?

It was a job my parents could tell their friends about without the usual psychological gloss. That was progress. I censured them for asking how many blacks worked for the company. I didn't see why their Negro problem and mine always had to come into things, but then I had not grown up in the days when a position in the post office was a prime civil service occupation.

I could fend off Grandfather's wise sayings, the kind from a remote, never-to-return history, the lessons I used to think of as plentiful and therefore missable in the Afro-American Culture class that met too early for me to roll out from under the covers for. It was chastising to speculate about your parents as people who had had another life—that life—and had been through more than a few texts. I used to meet my parents' friends in line at ticket counters, people whose embraces said that they had seen and cared for me at my worst. They always asked how was school and left me with advice: "Remember: they have to take us now, but they don't have to keep us."

Life-preserving decrees from Negro Section of the Keep Walking Union that had become life-constraining returned, passed through me, as if I were a medium. They took me by surprise. You are shaving and stare at a discoloration you hadn't noticed before. The ledger of how to be simultaneously yourself and everyone else who might observe you, the captain's log of travel in the dual consciousness, the white world as the deceptive sea and the black world as the armed galley, gave me the comic feeling that I was living alongside myself, that there was a me and a ventriloquist's replica of me on my lap, and that both of us awaited the intervention of a third me, the disembodied me, before we could begin the charade of dialogue.

My parents, the wide thumbs, took turns warning me that though they laughed about local black banks, black radio stations, and black country clubs as weedy as disused airplane hangars, I had not known adults who were not self-employed. Even the teachers in my life had seemed above school boards and trustees, and Grandfather, as we knew, answered only to God. That was Mom-and-Pop corner-store stuff compared to the real world. I admitted that I didn't know how many blacks worked at the company. They told me to behave, to watch my step, and, above all, to remain a child of Brooks Brothers, not to show up in the prejudicial club hopper's garb that made them slow to claim me.

I also had not really been on the good side of nine o'clock before. It was pleasing to be a part of the herd, not to have the feeling that the rest of the world was headed in the opposite direction, not to be subject to the criticism in the clear morning eyes of dogwalkers suspicious of after-hours Charlies who slipped from unmarked doors, sour-mouthed, oversmoked, and overspent, after a shoving match on the stairs between heroes of the unsteady like Sid Vicious and the girl known as Banana Daiquiri.

The competing ideology, the oldest message of the moon, was that the night was color-blind. In those embryonic New Wave days access to your feelings, expressiveness of any kind, views, opinions, were social liabilities downtown. Conversation required no practice if you dismissed everything and everyone, including yourself. By day the people of whom you approved waited by telephones and planned what to wear; by night the people from whom you wanted approval waited for drummers, dealers, DJs, divas of 5 a.m., free rides. The question of you had to stay home, and home was a place to sit and remember what it was like to cry, how good it felt, while the invisible you cast no shadow in the Molotov Cocktail Lounge, Tier 3, the

Eskimo, Reggae Palace, The Nickel Bag, Save the Robot, A–7, Dave's Luncheonette.

A job couldn't be just a job, a source of "chump change" that passed for income, at least not for very long. Heritage had a way of catching up with you in the office cafeteria. It tapped you on the shoulder and made you feel bad about the thoughtlessness of your desires and actions. It made you feel as bad as when you didn't get up to give your seat to an old-timer, or when you ran ahead to the playground and forced the babysitter with the rheumatoid hip to try to keep up. I found myself looking around for a black table in the office cafeteria.

I had always courted the quick signals that said you were tolerated, put up with. The blacks at the cafeteria tables in high school, in college, handed back your solidarity, as if they were returning your bug collection, which was mostly paraffin anyway. One try, and after that you didn't have to ask how was metal shop class, how were the med boards going, how was the family, and they didn't have to waste their time saying fine, fine, and fine all afternoon, scratching purple knit caps, the emblems of fraternity, wondering what you were trying to prove, what had come over you.

If for some reason you didn't feel comfortable among them, that was your problem, but their body language said don't turn around and put yourself through changes and come on all friendly like a black alderman out for the vote. They knew your heart was in the right place, because your heart didn't belong to you. They kept it in a vault someplace, like an indiscreet letter or a forged bill of exchange in an old-fashioned blackmail scheme. Where your head was at was another story, but they'd vote for you anyway, because there was no one else to vote for.

All of this was communicated to me by the way six black men

in the office cafeteria blinked and made room for my tray. Guilt is a wonderfully stimulating condition, like certain forms of incarceration. They said they were from maintenance, Xerox, mail services, production; carried themselves with an air that said they had been through battles, shared a common bond, that I couldn't just walk in and be part of it. I chose to be reminded of the army films at the beautiful drive-in during which as a child I had fallen asleep. In the unit there was always one who was vehemently detached. By the time I woke and the canopy of stars had thickened the loner had put his life on the line for the squad.

The assistant managing editor held himself like the isolated soldier in the bunk. He held a "roosty" position in the hierarchy, though he was younger than the other men, and that, I thought, accounted for the aggression in the way they referred to him as St. Maurice. He looked the part. The gravity, the sort quickly read at a distance, made his companions want to tease him. They treated one another to little goodies, traded cookies, like kids with lunch boxes, but did not include him. Maurice sat, coiled about himself, his basketball-player's limbs so folded, negated, that he mimicked the design of a paper clip.

I asked to see the book Maurice had with him. He removed it from the table and sat on it. I knew something about the ecstasy of suspicion. "I got a crown in that kingdom." As an icebreaker I related with disbelieving shakes of the head what had happened to me when I had dared to go to the men's room on the executive floor. A white security guard stopped by my desk and asked if I had been on the eighth floor recently. I had. Puzzle solved. The chairman's secretary had alerted security that there was a black prowler in the building. Some people can demonstrate intractability through the simple act of eating soup. Maurice was one of them.

We were joined by two women in similar business suits. They

delighted in shopping together, except at the jewelry store. The woman with too many gold chains said she liked to meet the new unmarried faces on the block. She knew already that I worked in the trade department and said that she'd been trying for two years to transfer up to that main cabin from the juvenile books division. I shrugged. It was boring, sharecropper's work. Maurice laughed, either appreciatively or derisively. I couldn't tell which.

The woman with the better watch said that I was another wedge. I said everyone knew that the trade department lost more money than any other in the publishing company and that without the lucrative textbook line the whole place would have gone bankrupt. She said the prestige was with the trade people. Maurice said she talked like a stockholder. She said she was sick of negativity every time he opened his mouth.

"If I'm lying I'm flying. I'm getting depressed by your resistance. If you don't like something, well then, get up and change it. We're here and it's on us to do what has to be done." Virtea was head of the company's Black Caucus.

Maurice grimaced, as if to say he could tell us the worth of that obstructing, petitioning lobby, that blockade to escape into employment's immensity. Virtea eyed him. "I haven't even did my nails yet." She continued her catechism of blackness—we're here, we're keeping on—and watched for another chance to squash Maurice, who one moment was looking hard between the bread of his sandwich and the next was up and gone.

Virtea said Maurice was bitter because he had run against her for chair of the caucus and lost. One man who hadn't opened his mouth since I sat down said St. Maurice would make a good union rep because he was so mean. The problem was that he changed his faces so much no one knew who to vote for. Another man said the cat's real problem was that he was wrapped too tight. He said cats that uptight deserved to keel over from heart atttacks.

My boss said that the assistant managing editor's job was the unhappiest in the company because he was obliged to spy on employees in the name of cost efficiency. Maurice sat between the elevators and the stairs. The open design of the floor lobbies gave his office a view of the floors above and below. Everyone had to go by Maurice's door, which was always open since a cabal of disgruntled editors had been caught trying to smuggle out equipment in big straw baskets. Someone had also made off with the Big Boss's antique long glass clock. Not only could Maurice see the comings and goings, he was theoretically visible every hour of the working day, the unpopular, baleful extension of management's monitoring eye. The Big Boss's argument was that even the Rolodexes of names and telephone numbers were company property.

My boss said that Maurice had changed since he first joined the company five years before. It used to be a joy to go down to production services and have a chat with St. Maurice while pages of manuscript flipped through high-powered copying machines. Maurice relished discussions about grades of paper, styles of type, anything that had to do with the nuts and bolts of print culture. He even knew antiquated techniques of book binding.

Then one day management went on a rampage of panic buying. Shaken by the Black Caucus's threat of a suit, my boss said, the Big Boss ran through the office, accosted Maurice, the first black he saw who had a college degree, and promoted him. Many promotions were handed out that day and the gentlemen from the watchdog agency that had agreed to help the Black Caucus read the riot act to the company that had thought of itself as a family departed entirely satisfied. The Revolution fell, like Agrippina, under the blows of her own children, Herzen said.

At first Maurice took his new job very seriously, but the managing editor wasn't interested in his "return on investment" projections and vetoed his suggestions. Any attempt at problem-solving on Maurice's part the managing editor, Little Boss, took as a usurpation of his authority. Little Boss was backed up, even ruled, by his secretary, who maintained a regent's jealous guard. She, the Power Bitch, wouldn't give up control of a single flow chart.

When Maurice went upstairs with his grievances he was told to work them out on his own. Little Boss had been with the company many years. My boss said he would have taken Maurice's side, but he couldn't afford to alienate a man who so completely enjoyed the Big Boss's friendship. He said the Big Boss didn't trust anyone after his favorite clock was stolen.

It became apparent to Maurice that his work didn't truly exist. He sniped at his superior in secret memos when the phone bills, messenger bills, temporary help bills, and production schedules got out of hand. He meant to protect his flank and contest Little Boss's turf by ingratiating himself with the Big Boss, who liked to see pockets of waste stamped out. Instead, he got stuck in a petty function that lay outside the job description.

A large cost-saver would have been the elimination of Maurice's superfluous position. He even asked to be demoted, but there was no way back to the anonymity and autonomy of downstairs, and once you earn more money, my boss said, you spend more, find that you need every new penny, as if you are worse off than before the increase, not to mention the vanity of the whore or the lapse of the rebel who said his master would not part with him for even a thousand doubloons.

Then Maurice had an inspiration: the company wanted him

to quit, to perish in a fever of frustration. He saw it as his moral duty to stay on as the sandbag, to beat them at their own game. "Window dressing," the tactic was called. He sat under his thatched roof of hair, on display, mechanical, like the figures that appear in the Christmas windows on Fifth Avenue.

My boss said that at first it upset everyone to see Maurice so miserable. That was what Maurice wanted them to see. After a while everyone got used to it. This wasn't family; it was business. My boss revived at the thought that one day Little Boss would retire, one day Maurice would draw up contracts and advertising budgets. One day he would have "input." Meanwhile, Maurice was marooned on an island of resentment, surrounded by the buzz of the office.

My boss always stopped before Maurice's door, in memory of their morning chats in a simpler, more innocent time. He spoke over the threshold, the barrier, as if Maurice had flayed himself and hung his fiery skin on a clothesline like a tattered rug that cordoned off an oily corner in a welfare hotel room. My boss stood there, scraped one dissenting Hush Puppy against the other.

He couldn't think of what to say, except to ask Maurice what he was reading. Maurice was never without books. They were, like his skin, a form of privacy, his screen. The weight of the books that accompanied him through his hours was also a rebuke to the company. Maimonides, Saint-Simonians. "Ricardo's analysis of rent," he answered one morning.

I learned, indirectly, at the black table, where we dealt in false impressions with the aplomb of black marketeers, that Maurice had had some serious problems as a teen trying to find himself in East St. Louis and later as an athletic superstar at college in Baton Rouge. From him, we heard almost every day that he would one day work in television. That's where the influence on culture really was.

Meanwhile, he had a complicated relationship with other blacks who crashed the perimeters of his cultural preserve. Unfortunately, that took in so much, he was argumentative about almost everything, from *Soul Train*, the black version of *American Bandstand*, to Aesop, "the great black moralist." Maurice thought of this as rigor. He'd start off on how fantastic realism had long been a part of African culture but the white critical establishment pulled a fast one by letting the South Americans take credit for it.

"Mother, this is too lovely," Virtea told him. "You are a scream."

He withdrew, saying that it was time for him to make a dash. An old hand from maintenance reminded Virtea that Maurice was, in fact, painfully shy, and she should be sympathetic when he tried to come out of his shell to them. Virtea said the strands of long hair on his nasty sweaters proved that the caped crusader wasn't too shy to do the Mess Around.

The company Christmas party was held in our floor lobby, between the banks of elevators and the coffee station. There were plates of morose Santa cookies on the receptionist's hastily cleared desk, a poinsettia brown around the edges, and a string of taped-up lights. The lethal Christmas punch that put us in mind of English pond life was a tradition. *Aqua celestis*, the old hands called it. The ingredients were a secret. The brew peeled the wax from the sides of cups. Theories about the recipe were disgusting and, after one swallow, absolutely convincing. Morale worsened by the glass.

Bonuses were small, sales poor, and projections so laughable that many employees didn't put in an appearance until after the

Big Boss's seasonal toast. By this drink it grieves me to tell you that we spent it all. My boss, whose list of holiday books, which included one on how to dress to enhance fertility, was having a spectacular flop, chugged three cups and went to wage war in toy stores.

Our honeymoon was long over, but he would not yell at me for my idiotic mistakes like a real boss. I saw the wisdom of the secretary's motto: Not only did I not do it, but you made me do it. The milder his reproaches, the more keenly I felt his disappointment. Whenever he came up to me, from behind, to ask a question to which I never had an answer, I was, invariably, eating a second lunch at my desk, and not only was I covered with crumbs, I was in the middle of a personal call, long distance.

It was the Christmas cease-fire, but the white partitions did not come down. The clusters formed according to rank: editors remained with editors; publicity people with publicity people; and evidently the Black Caucus had gone fishing. I began to experience the reality of the phrase "social death" and missed my boss, as when the only person you know at a party has fled to another room, leaving you to pretend that you are fascinated by the barometric pressure gauge on the wall.

"So this Knut Hamsun, is he in town?" Little Boss asked the Power Bitch.

Some of the employees took advantage of the occasion to stuff their book bags with office supplies. The most that I had been able to decide about them was that they suspected that interoffice mail transmitted germs and that they went to shrinks. Insurance forms often fell into the aisles. My fellow secretaries and I seemed to have taken our work habits from the CIA's *Freedom Fighter's Manual of Sabotage Techniques*: Come late to work; delay completing tasks; call in sick so as not to work; telephone to make false hotel reservations; damage books; break light bulbs and windows; cut down trees; drop typewriters; spill liquids; leave lights on; telephone giving false alarms of fires and crimes; threaten the boss by telephone.

A lithe, dewy secretary, the office beauty, floated toward the elevators with a cord, possibly that of an answering machine, wagging from the bottom of her Annie Hall coat. Delfina was the department's balletomane. Her neck lengthened and the bun on her head tightened week by week. A biochemical salt tablet was forever dissolving on her tongue. She had a slightly affected Foxcroft drawl when she spoke, which wasn't often, since she let a perpetually ironic gaze say everything.

Delfina was so aloof that Little Boss, who thought of the lowest form of love, the office romance, as another corporate perk, went so far as to intercept her getaway with "I nearly did a triple soutenu turn after that last glass of heaven." She paused to blow away the come-on he had laid before her like a dried rose. "Looks like a dick, only smaller," she was known to have said to a flasher. The cord was plainly visible between her white stockings. Little Boss's leer was bound to slide in that direction.

Maurice announced an international call for the managing editor. He called out again, like the Philip Morris bellhop. Little Boss grumbled about his secretary as he tried one after another of the dead buttons on a nearby phone, which gave Maurice enough time to signal Delfina that her tail was showing. It had retracted into her coat by the time she turned in the elevator, and she bestowed on her prince a smile of mischievous luminosity.

Little Boss spooned out punch for the troupers, those who understood the season's spirit and hadn't taken advantage of it just to have a half day. Loyal copy editors were made to guess the day's temperature in various cities of the Southern Hemisphere. A wrong answer brought another cup of punch. The

Power Bitch placed herself discreetly in a referee posture and discussed with the publicity director the pressure she had been under to get her house in Amagansett ready for the holidays.

Once the punch bowls were empty people sneaked away. They tottered off in tight affinity groups. I heard the Power Bitch invite Maurice along for eggnog. Maybe she was feeling the strain of always maintaining combat readiness. Go out into the highway and hedges and compel them to come in. He didn't answer.

By the time I got off the telephone, a security guard was making his rounds, the cleaning lady in her blue smock was dumping ashtrays in the garbage. Soon she would run a dust cloth over the enormous wall cases in the main hall, which made me think of ducal bonnets and red gowns in glass caskets. The cases contained mostly the new titles of the season, sure shots that were not helping the company out of its hole. Discountenanced already, the books would be piled all too soon on remainder tables in big bookstores like damaged altinelle bricks on a wharf. My boss once said he knew the company was in trouble because the employees didn't steal its books.

The sky was a scrim of creeping mists, but the papal bubble car and its detractors had been visible from our office windows. Demonstrations at Rockefeller Center were audible. Feminists in chador or in the attire of the Peacock Throne's generals, and students in ski masks or in the chains of the SAVAK's prisoners, raised the symbols of another misread revolution. The company's employees stepped over it all. They knifed through picket lines, squeezed around police barricades, argued with badges, ignored bullhorns. They did what they had to do to cross the street and get to the office.

The New Year had begun with a round of layoffs. The corridors were quiet except for the sounds of flu symptoms. A muzzled quality was palpable on every floor. Telephones were snatched up on the first ring, as if to shut them up. Employees were afraid to wander too far from their desks or to be too conspicuous. An unattended desk might be jotted down or the Big Boss might come along and lop off the loudest heads, even the editorial director's.

No matter what was happening outside, inside the office affairs had compressed around a single point: survival. Secretaries no longer gathered at the coffee station to savor the fall of a snotty higher-up type. Press clips that ridiculed the Big Boss's high-handed, inept rule appeared on the departmental bulletin board above the premature softball sign-up sheet. Maurice didn't bother to hide that he was the culprit.

Maurice seemed to fatten on the company's bad luck. Natty herringbone suits replaced his usual formless sweaters. His breast pocket overflowed with silky colors. My boss discovered him showing his teeth into the telephone in the mornings, his weighty books set aside.

He unlocked his jaw and ate up every discouraging report, which earned him the distrust neighbors in hard times are said to show toward someone they suspect is feeding on a secret stash while they go without. There was something taunting in his demeanor, the strut of a man who has no intention of revealing the whereabouts of his hoard.

Maurice straightened up to his true height. Little Boss put a stop to the funkadelics of Maurice's new radio, but he was powerless to prevent his whistling as he walked about at a smart clip. He saw red when Maurice cleaned his office, made room for Delfina, who paraded across the threshold that no one else had thought to breach. She perched on the edge of Maurice's desk, swung her long legs, laughed in a throaty way at the mirror of her compact, and waited with him for five o'clock.

The secretaries said Delfina was making Maurice as happy as a Rasta. Little Boss made scenes. "That message was for me. It was not for my assistant. If you take a message for me, please be so kind as to put it on my desk. Do not put it on her desk. If you can't do that, I'll thank you not to take messages for me."

"Well, we all commit crimes against humanity, don't we," Maurice said over his padded shoulder.

Maurice began to stay away from work for days on end. We never knew where he went, but go places he did, because he would return with stories that were a little revolting. He had a brutal picture of the city. We watched Delfina to see if there was any change in her ironic expression, but she hardly seemed to notice his absences. She sailed out of the elevators as usual, intent upon the mystic book of the dance and nothing else.

Little Boss turned on her one afternoon. "Why do you have an electric pencil sharpener and I don't?"

"Because she's a terrible person," the Power Bitch said.

Little Boss followed his scarlet ears back to his office. The Power Bitch went also and shut the door, but not before she had fixed Delfina with a look through her thick makeup that made it clear that it was for his sake alone that she had spoken up.

I got the impression that my boss felt challenged by Maurice's disaffection. He stopped throwing the I Ching when he had to make decisions. He discarded his Hush Puppies and cut his hair. He said he knew I was paid enough to invest in a tie, apologized, and promised to take me to lunch if his latest deal worked out well, if I owned a tie by then. He began to talk of "product."

One morning I thought that everyone had gone out the night before and splurged on new hairdos, facial massages, contact lenses, acupuncture, résumé-writing classes, and tennis rackets. The company rallied. Executives congratulated one another, like scientists after a successful rocket test. My boss had a surprise hit on his hands, a sleeper from the slush pile. In the aisles, among the white picket fences, the sales figures made him hearty. "Look at me. All grown up and having lunch with a television producer." Privately, he was afraid of success and called home to make certain that his children were still breathing. He also began to ask me to dial numbers for him, like a secretary should.

Enthusiasm for the profession was everywhere. The Power Bitch made overtures to Maurice under the sudden spell of peace and prosperity. "We haven't seen your beautiful face around here in a coon's age," she said after one of his mysterious absences. My boss was alarmed that Maurice hadn't reacted to having been treated like a jockey on a lawn, the sort his parents, after a stern lecture, had rushed out to paint the first non-referential color they could think of. The integrity of St. Maurice might be betrayed for the spoils of tokenism.

But Maurice took the activity around him as a short-term remission. He told Delfina that he wasn't signing up for softball because he had bigger plans for the spring season. The Power Bitch hadn't listened. She was too busy showing photographs of Christmas at her new country house that a guest had sent her in the mail. She had three white trees last year, she said. She was especially pleased with the batch of shots that showed her nephew in his naval cadet's uniform. She cornered Maurice at the coffee station and urged him to take a look because she thought he'd been in the service.

"Cold busted," Maurice said to himself. I saw him slip one of the Power Bitch's snapshots into his pocket and take the stairs three at a time up to the executive suite. In less than an hour the Power Bitch was choking on tears and packing up eleven years of office life. She'd been fired.

Usually, when word went around that someone had gotten the sack, the neighborhood of white picket fences vibrated; ed-

itors and secretaries running around with the news collided at
the coffee station. But the Power Bitch's demise shocked her
fellow employees into under-the-desk conferences. My boss heard
that Maurice had pushed into a meeting. The Big Boss had no
trouble identifying his antique long glass clock in the Power
Bitch's photograph, though its distinctive face was almost blurred
in the background, behind her nephew's epaulets.

Her humiliation was total. The details of what the Big Boss
had said to her got around as she sobbed and pried her framed
posters from the wall. Some who didn't want to believe it arranged to leave early for lunch. Little Boss took his devastation
to the men's room. My boss said that he was sorry for her, though
she was crazy to have pinched or received something so hot, so
personal. Delfina alone entered the Power Bitch's office to give
her a hug.

My boss said he wished Maurice wasn't so happy about his
revenge. It was true that he positively sat on the receptionist's
desk and crowed. Didn't Madame Du Barry's page turn her in?
Little Boss was called upstairs, to be told that he had to turn
over the Power Bitch's work to Maurice, with a generous raise.
The white picket fences got another shock. Maurice resigned.
Promptly at five o'clock he stretched a leg over the cartons maintenance had brought up for the Power Bitch. He took nothing
with him. He left his desk as it was, like a man called away on
an emergency.

On one of those bracing days when manic radio voices forecast
diminishing winds, Grandfather called from a corner. I was surprised that he had found a phone booth in working order and
that he knew where to find me. I was afraid he had run away
again. I put him on hold and contacted the beige stepgrandmother. She wasn't worried. He'd signed out properly. Grand-

father said, "The companions of the Messiah could forget how to work. Real people can't think that way."

He wasn't on the corner where he said he would be. I ran around the blocks. I saw him examining an array of mass-produced statues and ersatz Navajo blankets in front of a crafts museum. He said he had been thinking of how Uncle Ulysses's wife used to warn my sisters and me about sticking out our lips; that if we weren't careful our mouths would get stuck.

I didn't remember his being around when Aunt Odetta made my sisters walk with books on their heads or took a ruler between our spines and the backs of her dining room chairs. She used to say that thought began in the mouth, that we should practice comporting our lips so that the lower one did not protrude too much, because eversion was fine for the masks of the Dan people but it made American Negroes look "deficient."

"Whenever I enter the Public Library I have to go to the bathroom," Grandfather said. He'd lost a glove and had been retracing his steps. I noticed the seam beginning to come apart on the shoulder of his cashmere coat. Appearances, Jesus said, are deceptive. He slapped away my attendant arm. I guided him toward a cozy Russian deli where the small, voluble couple didn't mind if customers sat for hours with only coffee and newspapers.

Grandfather rested his showy stick. He wouldn't let the Russian couple bother about his coat. He moved it from floor to chair, fingered the rip in the shoulder. I'd heard that he'd had to find a new laundry because he'd frightened the Cantonese proprietor. He'd taken one of his vintage jackets to be cleaned, and when the laundryman pointed to the lining and tried to explain that he could not be held responsible for a garment that had been brought to him in such a state, Grandfather ripped apart the man's racing forms.

He said he hadn't been able to rest of late because "the rum element" in his building went to Barbados every night. "Been to Barbados" was slave slang for drunkenness, he explained. Grandfather's research in the reading room. "Who filled with lust and violence the house of God?" he said sharply when I asked him to tell me about Nat Turner.

He blew at his tea, moved the salt and pepper to new positions, found his reading glasses, and scanned the iconostasis of Kodak pictures and framed city health ordinances on the wall. He said that he would like to see my office. I said I didn't have an office and things up there were too chaotic that day for visitors. He said it was good that something was keeping me out of trouble.

"I feel as though I'm wasting my life."

"Yes, but what life isn't wasted?"

Already there was a little dessert in the corner of his mouth. I'd expected the old story of his first job, at a ladies' ready-to-wear store back in Augusta, which I'd heard many times since the day I had refused a paper route. His father didn't like that sort of independence, but the owners were happy to hire a boy who could "make time," clean the sidewalks. He was also to deliver COD packages.

One Saturday he delivered a package. The black girl who answered the door said she would take it because the lady of the house was out. He reminded her that it was a COD order and took it back to the store. Shortly thereafter he was picked up in spite of the store owner's protest and taken to police headquarters, where he was tried for having spirited away both the money and the package. One man served as prosecutor and judge. The bailiff acted as witness. They said they made three dollars a day and didn't dress as well as he. They said he dressed and spoke too well not to be a thief. He said he didn't have to steal to get the clothes he wore. They wanted to know if he meant to call a white man a liar. Two years in the county reformatory. He wasn't allowed to call his mother; his father was out of town. Grandfather was sent away on the supply wagon. When his parents got him out two weeks later, they were told they were lucky.

Grandfather said again that he wanted to visit my office. "What's the matter? Don't you want them to find out your grandfather is a Negro?"

I didn't want to say that while I was collating pages that morning the emanations from the file cabinets had persuaded me to type up my resignation and drop it on my boss's desk. Grandfather refused to let me pay for lunch. His wallet came from deep within his clothing. I waved, but he, the embarrassment to my act, didn't look back.

I watched him go, sinking in the architecture of signs, layer upon layer, and even now when I imagine that I have felt his presence among the souls who ponder discount chicken wings, stand apart at bus stops, brood over damp chess boards in the park, or lean on windowsills above deserted uptown streets, the consequence of my self-loathing fills me with the sadness that comes from squandered intimacy.

10 / The Handbook of Interracial Dating

Bargetta was the only black friend I had in college. Blessed be the tie that binds. The Black Student Union, and even some whites, lamps without lights, denounced us as Uncle Toms, but we knew the truth: we were just messed up. "You can't borrow your oil from somebody else," Bargetta said. We were the Also Chosen and loved our people—the dead ones, the many thousands gone. We were rather hard, I must admit, on the living.

Bargetta and I didn't talk much about that, it was so much a part of the atmosphere of our friendship, of being stranded together, that we didn't have to. Besides, false guilt would have been too much of an obstruction. She lived for pleasure and to give pleasure to others. Life was one big Lenten sale. "Jesus paid for everything so we shouldn't have to." She came to college out of nowhere—Memphis, actually, where her father had run her grandfather's funeral home into the ground, but we used to say that she had been born in Poise, Tennessee. A financial aid officer inquired about the Sony Trinitron she somehow charged to the school. "How do you expect me to compete with whites?" Bargetta had only to open a door to make her presence felt.

She was striking, tall as Muhammad Ali, with a head that seemed modeled after those on Ptolemaic coins. Each term she would experiment with her thick black hair, as if to announce a new theme. One fall it was shorn, which set off her perfect copper skull. That winter it became a riot of coils. By spring it had been conquered, braided on the right side into a stiff tail that hid one of her watchful eyes. Most often it was wrapped in one of the fantastic scarves that became her trademark.

Her family was religious in that sprawling, devout, Baptist manner. "I came to God before I came to Barnard." Bargetta laughed about the ashtray and cigar with which her father had started his Martin Luther King, Jr., museum, but a deep worry about what Jesus and her mother would say had kept her walking the narrow way—after a fashion. She represented to many boys a dangerous opportunity, as the Chinese say. Bargetta's popularity, her caressing trustfulness, brought her to the attention of the Soul Sisters of Barnard, a consciousness-raising group that smeared her name at the least provocation. What the Sisters could not abide was Bargetta's refusal to be answerable to them.

One spring, word went around that Bargetta was going out with the one Jewish guy at Columbia who was not pre-med. "He's in the Hasidic wing of Black September," Bargetta said. He was big, blond, with, she confided, "Sargasso eyes. Thank God for those Cossacks." From their lounge a cadre of Sisters spotted Bargetta alone and in a fit of offended sisterhood dropped egg bombs. Bargetta glided on and was immediately surrounded by gallants who wiped the yolk from her turban.

That night, a little drunk, she interrupted the Sisters' session on Obote and Amin with her loud contralto:

> There were three niggers of Chiceraboo—
> Pacifico, Bang-bang, Popchop—who

Exclaimed one terribly sultry day
"Oh, let's be kings in a humble way."

We had to make a run for it, but Bargetta was pleased that she had controlled her vibrato. A high-school choir director once told her to cut it out. "You're not in church," she said he'd said.

The black dean told Bargetta she could easily get into graduate school, but for a reason she probably wouldn't like.

"What's that?"

"Because you're black. Someone had to tell you, dear."

"I couldn't do your job. I couldn't go around telling people what they already know. I'd freak out."

"You're from the South, right?"

"Born and raised like a chicken."

"I know your type. One of those girls with her little finger out. From what I've seen and heard, you don't identify much with other blacks."

"Are you going to tell me that my being a black woman can only be as valuable to me as my being one is to you?"

Bargetta wouldn't divulge what more she had said to send the dean hurrying from her own office. Bargetta gave the strong impression that she was someone who knew very well who she was but she wasn't going to tell you.

It did seem that Bargetta took "the black experience," as it applied to her, as just so much light opera, which struck me at the time as unbelievably brave. She nourished her reputation as the queen of that joke about C.P.T.—Colored People's Time. If she said nine o'clock, she'd show at eleven dash twelve. She was known all over campus as an amazing student who was subject to complicated distractions en route to exams. Once, she explained her tardiness by saying that she was experimenting with brewing her own perfume. "I'm calling it Aujourd'hui. 'When you want the morning after to smell like the night before.' "

Bargetta was outrageous, but not unconventional. She was far from being a free spirit, ready to accept any price for giving up the world. She didn't think of herself as independent of her family until she figured out that she had replaced it with a more powerful institution: school. From the moment of her arrival on campus, she was already thinking beyond the cap and gown to another kind of protection.

She said she knew why she liked men, but she didn't know why she hated to go out with them. She was not, back then in the heady time of patriarchy bashing, what a coed would have called a feminist, but she instinctively resented men for what they could get just because they were men. I wanted to talk about her father, but she said her family life had been too normal. She said her irritation had more to do with what she had learned about the natural arrogance of boys, one of life's lessons that transcend color.

We usually met in the library, like spies, when Bargetta was in between boyfriends and in a philosophical mood. One evening in the main hall, after the ritual awkwardness of my having reached for Bargetta's hand, which she withdrew to tie and tie again her bandanna, I asked if she only went out with white boys. She thought a moment. She knew what had happened in the way back when, and what the Sisters had to say about militants who said that going out with white girls was a form of revenge, and the lanker their hair the better. She also didn't pretend that her taste had anything to do with progress. "Does that make me a bad person?" She said she wasn't sure what the reason was, or if she needed one, but whatever the cause, she owed her choice to Jack and Jill. "To me, that was like my mother making me go to Hitler Youth."

Jack and Jill of America was a national organization that forced the right sort of black children together with other nice children of the "upper shadies." It had been founded "with tax forgiveness" in 1938. You didn't join, your mother did. No city chapter could be larger than seventy-five women, so to your classmates who didn't rate in the opinion of mothers who believed in blackballings you either had a secret life or were a stuck-up in high-water pants. There was a rule that said that members should abstain from whatever is unkind and mischievous, and could not knowingly undermine the policies of the organization.

Once your mother had signed up, you were drafted into the appropriate age group and you faced what seemed like a lifetime subscription to the club magazines, *Up the Hill* and *Scope*. There were nightmare weekends of recreation and concerts of spirituals. Your mother learned more about children through "careful study," contributed to research in rheumatic fever, and held polio drives.

It was a bargain—for your mother. She paid dues, and you were out of her hair, hauled off to transportation exhibits, to keelboats and copies of Ohio River side-wheelers. Enough lunch was funneled into you to make you drowsy, and then you found yourself packed off to sketch prairie schooners, to wrestle with chiefs' trumpets, firemen's hats, and man-drawn engines. A designated mother had you by the elbow, and you were on the verge of tears in the Prehistoric Gallery with minerals, dinosaurs, and mounted birds. By the time you were handed back, like the laundry, to your own mother you were too worn out to argue about what was on television after bedtime. The rules further stated that if a child missed three consecutive group meetings or activities without the chairman's being notified, the family was automatically dropped.

In Indianapolis, at least, Jack and Jill was harmless, like hellish family vacations that are pleasant to recall, maybe even laudable, a word Old Guard black-sorority types liked to use when you opened the door for one of them or stood when they came, corsage first, into a room. The worst thing that ever happened to me at a club function was when my sisters tried to drown me as I bobbed for apples, and on my last field trip to Lockerbie Street, home of the Hoosier Poet, in downtown Indianapolis, a spooky caretaker said that when the beloved children's poet was locked in hotel rooms so he wouldn't drink before readings he bribed bellhops and received what he needed through keyholes with straws. But Bargetta wouldn't grant that Jack and Jill, in Memphis, was just a part of growing up Negro. "Who can live with the thought of having been a child?" she said.

Real toads in an imaginary garden, the members of Bargetta's teen chapter of Jack and Jill liked to sit around and say, "Your Mama." If she asked someone to pass the mustard, she got "Your Mama." No elaborate "soundings" or insult contests, just "Your Mama"—for years, so she said. Her mother didn't believe her and made her go to the mixers, the dances. It was hard to fit clothes on a miserable girl, Bargetta said, and because of her height, she was snubbed by the boys, even the ones who could convert from Celsius, and, because of her unreliable wave of ideas, cut by the girls with heated patios and pretty hair.

I understood too well the reticence that overcame her among her black peers, which had an element of shame, the source of most rebellion. But not fitting in was also flattering. You were different, not like the others, not one of them. The fix was in, and the world arranged things so that you could act black with whites your own age, which had something to do with what it was like to show off as a child in front of strangers, but with blacks you shut down—became, as it were, as uptight as a slumming white, which had something to do with the spanking you were going to get for having shown off.

Fashions for Freedom was the main Jack and Jill event on the Memphis calendar. Some of the mothers had banded together to launch Jack Be Quick, a training program "intended to alleviate the dilemma of young black males in a matriarchal society," as Bargetta remembered the language of its publicity brochure. The year Fashions for Freedom planned to donate its proceeds to the "underachieving Negro male," Bargetta was in the banquet room, in a Peter Pan collar from Peck and Peck, resigned, not asked to dance by the street-quick scholarship winners, and feeling, as a girl, unimportant to the race.

"I didn't want to go," Bargetta said. "Our Cadillac was so dirty. I felt so sorry for everybody. I mean, here we were sitting with these stringbeans amandine and mess bourguignon shucking about what we were doing for the ghetto, and the hotel wasn't even in a black neighborhood. Chuckie Beauchamp's mother made him sit with me. I had to give him my Supreme of Fresh Fruit Fantasie. He clapped for the strapless stuff, and the moderator thought it was such a big professional deal, kept saying that the models were professionals, like it was a big serious professional deal just because some of them were white." As she told me this, Bargetta glanced around the reading room, missing the spidery smile of the senior monitor, who was admiring her from his post at the nearby information desk.

"Anyway, I was peeling a Hershey's Kiss when this guy with a big Dick Tracy face came down the runway. The escort was supposed to grin when his partner styled. He wasn't real fine or anything, he just looked like he didn't dig her personally and would punch out the first biddy who asked him to be more, you know, interracial," Bargetta said when we were outside. She changed her mind about the stack of books she'd checked out, and shoveled them into a campus mailbox. "But he looked at me, I swear. I switched tables three times. I wish I had gone backstage. It was wild. A look that could break night. I gagged. No one had ever looked at me like that, you know what I mean?"

An elderly cousin, Aunt Bollie Lucia, my family called her, took out of storage and wielded, at the close of her long incarceration in an old maid's body, the doubtful memory of the Scottsboro trial, in 1933, when she nearly fell from grace and ran away with a white man from up North.

She: "You're a Communist, aren't you?"

He: "Yes, I am. Are you?"

She: "Why, no. I've never even been out of Georgia."

Somewhere along the line it turned into a status symbol: going out with a white became like having a foreign car. "This girl's mother used to carry a fat wedding album to every open house," Bargetta said. "She almost sat on my head to catch my expression when she showed me a photograph of the groom. She was so proud her daughter had married a white dude."

In time, Bargetta's mother bore her daughter's romantic misadventures, of which Bargetta spared her not enough of the throbbing details, as part of the higher life into which education had launched her. Bargetta, the misbeliever, discovered that she intimidated her family, those followers of the double-duty dollar. She did a wicked imitation of the Kelly Girl and enjoyed arriving more or less on time for job interviews and being told that she hadn't sounded black on the telephone.

But after the Ashkenazi heartthrob, the Finnish news stringer with the telephone in the refrigerator, and the Irish video-maker with the greasy railroad flat, Bargetta moved her duffelbag of scarves to Paris, to Pierre-Yves, a lethargic artist with whom she had collided during her junior year abroad. She managed to acquire a vague position with a New York record company's office in Neuilly—"I'm part of the overhead"—and because its phone bill was not, as they say, itemized, I heard from her often.

My flight to Paris was a flight to Bargetta. I sneaked out of Leiden without leaving a note. I had gone to Holland to find peace in the way I imagined burned-out souls lugged their mad hopes to ashrams. As it turned out, the old university town was anything but soothing. My high-school pen pal had taken to Rudolf Steiner, and his five cats loathed me with the vehemence of stepchildren. Everywhere some kind of construction or renovation was under way and for weeks I had stumbled over the cobblestones in search of soundproof corners.

I made it to the rendezvous on the far side of the outer canal. I saw one of the New Zealand street performers I had met in a pub the night before. He, too, must have had a lot to drink because he didn't remember me or the promises he had flung like millet. His companions had no recollection of their rowdy offer of a ride to France, but gas was expensive and they found room for one more in the battered Volvo, where I remained hidden until we were well out of Leiden. My parents had drilled into me that to hitch a ride with strangers was to tempt fate and I worried that the New Zealanders weren't street performers at all. Dikes and low pastures flashed in the sunlight, herons strafed the lakes. I willed the arrival of the lumbering tub that was to ferry us to the border.

Once across it, the New Zealanders frequently pulled over to inspect herbs and mysterious weeds, to buy overpriced fruit from big-boned farmers' daughters. They complained that my chain-smoking was making them sick, and indeed, two packs lay crumpled between my feet by the time we finished with the stench of Belgian towns of historical interest. Their tales of how they almost got busted at various frontiers hadn't helped. A quarter-moon monitored our passage across France, through valleys of bundled hay. I was thrilled that I had disproved my parents' theory of brigands on every highway when the New Zealanders dropped me off, in one piece, in a confusion of yellow lights.

Bargetta loved to be "contactable." Therefore, I had several telephone numbers for her in Paris. After I had played roulette with them at a café phone, the sound of her deep, smoky voice came to me like rescue. I had to walk outside to see where I was, Les Petits Nègres, because I just could not speak again to the bad teeth and lopsided toupee that belonged to the man behind the bar. Bargetta told me to chill out and she'd be right over. I settled at a table outside and prepared for a long wait, but she wasn't on C.P.T.

Through my glass I saw Bargetta stride toward me. I could not look at her without thinking of a poster by Zig or of a leopard cruising in a diamond collar. We stood cheek to cheek in the silver honky-tonk light for several minutes before speaking. Bargetta was, as she liked to say, dressed to the nines: black top, black miniskirt, which caught the beams of passing headlights, black fishnet stockings, black flat shoes, a black rayon scarf, which wound its way around her head and rediscovered itself at her waist, and the black leather jacket she wore when she stood in need of luck.

"You look serious, preacher man, but kill the shoes," Bargetta said. Then: "He's at another party, in another part of the country." I hadn't asked about Pierre-Yves. Love me, love my three-legged dog. Her mascara was thicker than it had been Stateside. She said that what I smelled was the eucalyptus she put on her temples to cure headaches. Across the street, in front of the dim Hôtel d'Angleterre, perched on little scooters, pink-haired boys and girls with severe buzz cuts passed a bottle and "chased the dragon"—snorted lines of brown heroin. "My mother told me to be careful because she heard there were a lot of drugs and blacks in Paris," Bargetta said.

All that night I followed Bargetta through the dizzy streets. Though the weight of the bag on my back made me want to cry, I had long ago learned to go along with Bargetta's program without question. Her talent for sussing out the hideaway where, for instance, Keith Richards might be sucking on a Guinness made her a coveted companion. We rolled from café to café, moved whenever a song on the jukebox did not meet with Bargetta's approval. "I'd rather shoot myself than sit through that shit."

Holland seemed far away, but in between stops, on the streets, Bargetta was pensive and remembered her duties as guide with one-liners such as "Quasimodo hung out here." If I hadn't known that she slept all day, I would have thought her stamina miraculous. In Bargetta's code it was okay to throw up in a club—so long as she wasn't doing it—but it was definitely uncool to be seen taking a sudden dip with the sandman. She once said her greatest fear of Manhattan was that she might fall asleep in a taxi and wake up in another girl's clothes.

For the first time since I'd known her, Bargetta seemed to be stalling, to be waiting for an idea. Though I'd dropped in on her without warning, I never thought of Bargetta as someone you could take by surprise. She had always seemed so effortlessly inventive, two steps ahead of the dawn. She hoisted herself up and directed us toward the Champs-Elysées. I thought we were going to a party until Bargetta put a finger to her lips. I crept behind her up several flights of polished stairs. She smuggled me into an apartment, around the proper mixture of squeaks and moans, and into a pantry where there was a mat among mops and boxes.

"Happy birthday," Bargetta said.

"You remembered."

It was pitch dark in the pantry when Bargetta shook me awake. She led me by the hand, Harriet Tubman taking a runaway to free territory. I heard snores and the mutter of someone in the throes of a terrible dream. A pale blue rose behind the blur of trees. We walked in a trance up the yellow-and-cream streets. At a café near the river a youth whose shirtsleeves smelled of smoke brought warm red beers.

Bargetta said we had been in the apartment of a Brit from the record company, who was letting her stay for a while, but the Brit was on simmer, rising to a boil about the number of people crashing on her floors and the rings left in her swank bath. One more guest, Bargetta feared, would send the poor thing over the top. Bargetta made apologies for getting me up, but she wanted to escape before the woman started on her body count. We watched the barges on the Seine. "A girl can end up with nothing if she knows how to work it right," Bargetta said.

"If you come from a close family, you can feel lost without them," Bargetta said. "But what's my excuse?" We were on our way back to the apartment, to pretend I had just dropped by, and then to test the possibilities of taking a nap. Bargetta talked more to the stone dressing over the streets than she did to me. "I used to feel sorry for him," she was saying, "but he's just another rich kid in disguise. I think he should paint on velvet, get in touch with his real level."

Pierre-Yves had inherited his mother's devious looks and one of his father's apartments, Bargetta said. His parents were *pieds-noirs*, French who had made good in Algeria, and had his father been alive Bargetta probably would not have moved in. What Bargetta liked about Pierre-Yves was that he had gone to a slick school like Saint-Martin-de-Pontoise and forever afterward was unable to get himself together. "The cold thing about it is that I spent all this time building him up, and the next thing I knew he believed me."

Bargetta said that Pierre-Yves began to talk a worrying amount about his style, his career, and that when he got analytical about himself it meant trouble. "I should have known after our first night. I'd set him up. Made him feel he was one of nature's rapists. And me thinking the cracks in his ceiling were the most beautiful thing I'd ever seen. I slept with his glasses before that. I stole them. I should have stopped there."

Pierre-Yves got out of taking Bargetta to the country this time by saying that he hadn't been able to work, implying that she was the cause. His holiday coincided with the disappearance of a girl who hung around the apartment too much for Bargetta's taste. "You know, one of those girls in ankle socks who's into Zen and sleep therapy and macro diets. I warned her not to work me, but she kept coming over with all that brown rice."

A sinner needs a witness or else something is missing. Pierre-Yves flaunted Bargetta in front of his mother. "It killed her to have me to dinner. She watched me the way crowds do when somebody's out on a ledge, just waiting for me to pick up the wrong fork." His mother, that amanita, decided to surprise him and have his apartment redone while he was away. Bargetta was in the shower when she brought over the crew. To finish off what could not be defended, she refrained from inviting Bargetta to stay with her.

Back in the Brit's apartment, Bargetta had emptied the contents of her bag on the pantry's mat—shades, tortoiseshell combs, Borghese lip gloss, Chloé, Motrin, Efferalgan, valerian root, Aspro effervescent, Xanax downs, Zomax downs, Halcion sleeping pills, Coedetheline Houde, dagger letter opener, joint, address book, and a quantity of black cotton headgear—when screams and household articles flew by the crack in the pantry door. All explanations end at some point. The Brit had snapped. Her Carr's biscuits and hearts of palm had vanished, as had the caviar and the tin of cassis stashed behind the floor wax. She found two couples on her futon, one of which she didn't even know. "The domino theory of eviction," Bargetta said on our way out, looking wistfully up through the bannister. "She had that ten-little-Indians look in her eyes."

Along Boulevard Saint-Michel, near Cluny, guys with guitars—in 1980—lined the curbs. I saw some flower children who rivaled the holdouts of Amsterdam, and Bargetta grabbed me. A fight had broken out in McDonald's, an old-fashioned rumble complete with everything not bolted to the floor going upside down. People ran out and ran back to watch. We heard metal twisting loose, and scattered as the huge window of the restaurant jumped down from its hinges to challenge the mob. It shattered into a thousand pieces, glimmered for an instant, like a summer swarm of mayflies, and then crashed to the pavement.

Bargetta took off when she heard *les flics*. She was fast in her kid slippers—was, in fact, yards ahead of me. I stopped and watched her race on, her lucky black leather jacket aloft in her fist.

"Am I having a good time?"

"The baddest."

She said that the movements of street-sweepers in the Gare du Nord had the eloquence of people committed to survival, and that Barbès, the African-Arab quarter north of the peepshows, was the headquarters of those determined to hang in there. Migrant widows waited near the equator for paychecks as the sources of their mail, black and brown men, distressed the streets around us. We entered a couscous den and extinguished its conversations. Goat and the music of Nass el-Ghiwan cooked behind a moldy partition. Molecules heated up, closed in, and Bargetta breathed through her mock-debutante smile.

"One thing about money, if you have it you can tell certain people where to go," she said. Pierre-Yves had taken Bargetta —at gunpoint, but he took her—to the Grand Véfour, one of the most elegant restaurants in town. She phoned ahead to make sure the kitchen knew a vegetarian was on his way. The waiter presented the most beautiful omelette the world had ever seen. "I do not eat eggs," Pierre-Yves said. She liked losers.

I was no help, dragging our bags around town, riding the bus with used or no tickets, feeling more freakish and fifth-wheelish than usual while Bargetta fended off gypsy kids and made change for the phone booth. On the steps of Sacré-Coeur, she distributed cigarettes like the Red Cross. We missed the Mass for St. Rose of Lima, who, though prudent, had failed to be martyred and was therefore only second-string. Bargetta had no need of intermediaries, being on the direct-dialing system with the Lord. "Now somebody up there slap me. Hard."

A hotel would have been our last resort. We ended up on the rue des Trois-Frères, in the rump of an ash-colored dwelling with a rancid charcuterie downstairs. The torn and divided rooms, which reeked of sulphur and vintage kitty litter, belonged to Gilles, a boy Bargetta had known in Memphis, where his absenteeism got his mother kicked out of Jack and Jill. "Did I say friends, ha, are my aces high?" Bargetta said as we made our way to his flat.

He had visited Bargetta in New York frequently before he lived there, selecting the longest butts from the hubcap she used as an ashtray, and it annoyed me that everyone said what a handsome couple they made. Not only was he the first black at Harvard to be asked to join the Fly Club, he was the first to turn them down. I offered myself the dubious consolation that Gilles never wanted me around because I could read his mind. I divined that he liked to be the only "shine" in the room and resented the presence of other black men.

When I was in the fourth grade, a new boy in my class became the most popular. He had wavy hair—"good hair," it was called—and he wasn't dumb. He wore black bow ties, white shirts, and red mohair sweaters. The girls sang "Ooh-wa-ooh-wa-ooh-wa-diddy, tell us 'bout the boy from New York City," and oohed when he got up on Savings Bond Day to buy fifty stamps instead of the decent twelve. I bullied my mother until she let me dress like him. Then we moved, and I didn't need him anymore. There were real whites at my new school. When happiness comes it brings less joy than we expected, Cavafy said.

It was pretentious for someone whose real name was Luther to call himself Gilles, I told Bargetta. I didn't believe his stories about Fès and St. Bart's, about the grams he had consumed in a producer's town house, about how his mother, a sex therapist, had been overly married, four or five times. I didn't even believe he went to a shrink. I couldn't touch his will to cool. Bargetta said I had nothing to worry about, because Gilles only liked white boys.

We didn't shake hands. Mine was cramped from the straps of Bargetta's bags. I was being unfriendly, Bargetta's glare said. After all, he was giving shelter to strays. "You look as though the world is too much with you," Gilles said. He was supposed to have been away. Bargetta had called him on a hunch. He didn't say where he'd been or why he'd come back, but a bruise was waking up under his right eye. We'd interrupted him in the middle of a brick of Mujahideen hash. He was busy cutting out pictures of young workers with mustaches who were barricaded inside the Lenin shipyards.

"If Cheetah could talk, she'd tell my story," Bargetta said, brandishing a Marlboro. "I'm afraid of going cold turkey."

"I hear you, Sister Girlfriend," Gilles said. "My heart resembles an Etruscan vase. Broken and mended, broken and mended."

There were shutters that looked out on other Montmartre shutters and empty flower pots, bedbugs, and fleas, but Gilles didn't care, he was just passing through. He made enough money as a model in Milan to do nothing for months. Passive, with air-brushed magazine-cover looks, Gilles was, I had to admit, completely without vanity. He had the melancholy that never goes away, of someone who has lost a parent at an early age.

Gilles got by the door at the Safari, cadged Veuve Cliquot at the Privilege, avoided the tab at Le Drug Store, and another at the Bains-Douches. When he was having fun, he reminded me of guys in New York who picked fights with the Hell's Angels after having silicone implanted in their cheekbones and called themselves neo-romantics.

"Cut the herbivore loose. Forget him," Gilles said.

"I can't. Your phone?" Gilles shrugged. Bargetta dialed her mother's number in Memphis. "Maybe I should let her know my new number. No, I should wait until I need serious money. Mad money." Bargetta dropped the receiver. "I'll skip town. I'll just book. I was once on Corfu in a heat wave. On cobblestones. It was like stepping into a pizza oven. I had to go every day to the fortress where the national guard took their swim breaks. I had errands. There was this policeman named Lazarus. He didn't shower after the beach. He was salty. He would come to the hotel on official business and interrogate mercilessly. Am I horrible? Do I deserve to die? I can't remember the Greek word for it. He removed the photograph of his wife from his wallet. That's where we should go. You would be worshippéd as a god. They would carry you through the streets."

Bargetta said Pierre-Yves was a crucial investment. She said she was tired of being alone, tired of the loneliness that was like a mortgage she could not kill off. I couldn't think of a time when Bargetta had ever been by herself, but she insisted that Pierre-Yves was her last stop. "If things don't work out, I can always sell my lingerie and retire. I can take up where Miss Beane left off, right?"

"She had so much fun it killed her," Gilles said.

Bargetta was comparing herself to the mascot of Manhattan, Dee Dee Beane. It was one of their big themes and I'd remembered lunches picking at my plate while they went over and over poor Miss Beane's career.

"Self-destructive people can make their point only if they can take a few people with them," Gilles said.

Bargetta said it was not a good sign that she had dreamed about her three nights running. Dee Dee Beane was, for Bargetta, the outer limits. They had pretended to great indifference to each other when they both did a short stint at the same black woman's fashion magazine in New York. Miss Beane, as Bargetta called her, to draw attention to the unmarried state of the older black woman, got the boot when she tried to put Andy Warhol in blackface on the magazine's cover.

Miss Beane intrigued Bargetta because she was beyond disillusionment. "There she was, thinking she could inhabit her skin like a litter, raised above the mob, and she rode herself out of town on a rail." Bargetta heard that Miss Beane had been in love, but—who would not sleep with the brave—the heir's family hired detectives who broke up the wedding. They paid Miss Beane to take a hike. She came back when the money ran out and they threatened her. Bargetta had every sympathy for the wound that never heals.

Miss Beane's history frightened Bargetta more than her temperament. Back when no one knew anything, Miss Beane let people think she was the first black ever to have gone to Radcliffe. Miss Beane had a first-rate, logical mind, Bargetta said, which she wasted in dissecting the faults of others. She could tear people asunder. "You had to be a man to think she was amusing," Bargetta said. "But I had dates; she had walkers."

Miss Beane had no respect for anyone, except for an art history professor or two back at Harvard. Nevertheless, she was cared for and watched over by the Class of '59, who remembered her as a brilliant amanuensis, a born schoolmarm. She typed many papers for others and improved them. But her standards were so high and what white people thought of as her self-esteem was so great that she inevitably fought with everyone. She had burned her way through many careers, from the Fogg to being a bouncer at Max's Kansas City.

Scorn was Miss Beane's empire, but she ruled over a territory depopulated by drunken scenes. Bargetta said that Miss Beane took a neutron bomb or Khmer Rouge attitude toward life in the city: empty it out, leave the buildings standing, and start over. She purged everyone she had ever known and threw away every chance she had ever had. She refused to acknowledge her own sister on the street. When she was mugged by two black men, she was elated, as if her part of a cruel bargain had been canceled.

"We were on the same party circuit," Gilles said. "One night she noticed that I wasn't white. She called me a two-bit whore. I got up, crossed the room, slapped her, said 'Sorry, Sister,' and sat back down. What could she do? She ordered another drink. Hard stuff. None of this fine-wine business for her."

But Bargetta was attracted to her antisocial stance. A vituperative, vitriolic, Indian-looking black woman small enough to fit into snappy children's clothes, Miss Beane drove parties into the kitchen and when she walked into the kitchen people escaped back into the living room. At one party in the Village the host stumbled onto the terrace where Miss Beane sat alone and fell over the railing into his garden. "He left," Miss Beane was said to have answered when his guests finally missed him.

Every party with her, Gilles said, ended with her passing out and falling off a chair. She liked being in the swing of things so much that she became a vehement example of that celebrant of metropolitan life since Juvenal—the fag hag. She called herself "the spade of queens." The lofts, town houses, and Southampton decks Miss Beane haunted she called the Fruit Stands. Gilles said that her sackcloth was that she tried to seduce young men who had no interest in her. The photographers, painters, museum workers, architects, lawyers, and parasites with whom she fell in love were the Forbidden Fruit and she was the Fruit Fly. She drew the line at airline stewards. She never had a crush on an airline steward, much like a drug addict who doesn't consider himself a junkie because he doesn't touch needles.

"There was a white faggot trapped inside her black woman's body," Gilles said. "She hung in all the sawdust bars. She felt she had been cheated. She envied the freedom."

"The farther you are from something," Bargetta said, "the more wonderful it seems. You're walking down a street in a foreign country and spot one light in a dark house and wish you could have that life. But if the window were yours you'd be plotting to break out of it."

Gilles said booze had made Miss Beane's generation too Freudian. The more peculiar the behavior, the more fascinating it was to them, and rather than not know or be the last to know something, they jumped to malicious conclusions about everyone.

Bargetta said she hated people who called only when they knew something or wanted to know something.

"They forgot that sex is comic and love is tragic," Gilles said.

"Dee Dee Beane didn't," Bargetta said. She usually felt better after a deep-dish session about Miss Beane, but the therapy wasn't working anymore.

I was homesick for the anxious gullibility on the other end of the wire. Meanwhile, Bargetta slid into something like ego disintegration. "This life isn't mine. I'm only squatting in it." In front of a hotel she asked some black women from Abidjan who admired her diadem if they knew of any work cleaning up.

Every generation is an enemy of its father's and a friend of its grandfather's, and maybe that was why, when I pontificated to myself about Bargetta, her spirit of contradiction, so famous on campus, seemed, in the middle of unfazed Paris, suddenly old-fashioned, like nostalgia for Philistine terror about nigger-lovers and honky-lovers, for the days when the sight of her on Pierre-Yves's arm would have been a provocation. As a black who had grown up in a small, mean American city, and in a secure, protective, claustrophobic family as well, I had always looked to Bargetta for clues, for lessons about how to be a modern Negro in the great world. I began to wonder just where what I had always called her sophistication had taken her—whether she had anything to teach me about how to be free after all. I felt disloyal when I thought this way about her.

"He owes you," I said.

"Only when he gives," she said.

Elderly animals patrolled the lanes of Père-Lachaise, silent women washed the panes of Gothic-revival sepulchers. Initials sprayed inside hearts guided the way to Jim Morrison. A dozen figures with acoustic guitars or yellow ribbons for the hostages stared at unmarked squares of earth. Bottles poked through the hallowed ground. A girl began to sob, a man crouched. Incoherent poems in English adorned the surrounding stones.

Gilles went to pay his respects to "C.3.3." Bees chased me from one sector to another. I heard the rolling vowels of the Antilles. Festively clad black women walked the road; ahead of them, matrons added more blossoms to a mound of floral tributes. A large bust stood at the center. It was the grave of Allan Kardec, the mystic and healer who succored women from the beyond. Housewives wept like Ceres and entreated his thorax of marble. I found Bargetta, her head swathed in a blazing scarf. She towered above the profusion and raised a tentative hand.

"Masochists are the proudest people on earth," she once told me. I knew that meant she would never demand anything of Pierre-Yves, or of anyone else, for that matter. I knew also that she had no deep policy. She wasn't interested in making Pierre-Yves feel guilty, which is what people who find themselves at a disadvantage in a relationship tend to do to get some leverage. Never, with her, the beatific glow of the injured, just as she never referred to the helpful things she had done for others. Another kind of girl might have enjoyed behaving better than Pierre-Yves. It would have confirmed a sense of moral superiority. But she refused to make Pierre-Yves responsible for her feelings. That was her pride, her integrity.

Unfortunately, the masochist also risks making a gift of himself, and the beneficiary is obliged to lug this gift wherever he goes, much like the old woman in the story about the dead dog in the suitcase. Consequently, Bargetta knew what she did not want: for her beneficiary to regard her fine feelings as a burden. That was her sadness. She was left alone with her emotion.

Bargetta could have been the star at many tables; instead, she waited for Pierre-Yves's crumbs of affection. For some reason, this time, with him, she had lost that ability to go on to the next thing, to imagine replacing one situation with another. Perhaps it is true that you fall for someone from the inside, and that when you do, you see what your friends can't and let them think you've lost your mind. Like many superior girls, Bargetta had a talent for getting the man she asked for instead of the one she needed. "What others missed or messed up I found."

"Get off the stage," a roadie once said to Bargetta at an invitation-only sound check in a lower-Bowery rock club.

"She's with me," the star of the band said. He, her charismatic deliverer, looked down and smiled in a confident way that made a dozen girls in Bargetta's immediate vicinity want to throttle her. But Bargetta saw the pink slip in his eyes.

"The hell I am," she said. In those days, when she knew her own worth, Bargetta had been elusive as an eel.

"I can't let this man dance on my last nerve. You get the pitcher's mound down," Bargetta said, "and they go and juice up the ball. If they give you hesitation, then they're throwing heat." She never could drink. Her speech began to get puréed. "You don't see it, you hear it. You hit what you think you hear. You get your front foot out, get your weight balanced, follow through, and hope it's not a gooseball."

"Have you ever thought of going home?"

"Right? Niggers and flies, always hovering around some shit." Bargetta sprang up and barely looked back over her jacket. A fabulous murkiness obscured the tips of landmarks, and I half hoped she would keep walking. I let go and surfed until I saw Bargetta as I first knew her, when she looked up from a book as if she'd alighted from a calèche that had just flown over the steppes.

Bargetta had never been driven into the ground before, but she lay around as if Gilles's place were a preparatory tomb. She was superstitious about going out, leaving the telephone unattended, though she traced her nausea to the slanting floors of the apartment. She chose carefully from her duffelbag of scents. "I made this one myself," she said. "It's called La Mort. 'When death need no longer be an excuse.'" She painted her mouth, allowed Gilles to move discussion to her hair, but wouldn't report to the record company or to any of the piss-chic parties Gilles always knew about and avoided mention of to me. I didn't know *verlan*, the "in" slang of the moment. I could only smile in French.

Gilles lectured on the military strategy of love, saying that the minute you told the Other how to treat you, the battle was lost. "But your manners won't matter if you're dull." He helped Bargetta to tape note cards on the wall beside the mountain of dirty sheets so that she could write down her dreams without spilling a drop. She was desperate for a sign.

Charlotte Forten came to Bargetta in her rocky sleep. Forten had left her prominent black family in Philadelphia to teach the freedmen in South Carolina after Appomattox. Dr. Rogers, a New England gentleman, read Emerson to her under the magnolias; Colonel Higginson took her riding in the lunar bloom. She was tempted to take their civility as something more than that, and could barely disguise the yearning in her diaries. But these soldiers for equality moved on. With her heart out of danger, she went back home, a woman who had come to her senses. Strangely enough, Bargetta believed in Forten as the patron saint of interracial dating.

"I was walking around with my dry cleaning when the streets

vanished and I fell into this big hole," Bargetta said. "I was buried up to my neck. The wind howled, all this old newspaper was hitting me in the face, but I couldn't move. I saw these headlights. They were coming right at me. Then Charlotte got out of a jeep. I heard her skirts in the dust."

Gilles played with the jewel in his left earlobe. "What was she wearing? How do you know it was her?"

"Because she said, 'You've had it rather easy, my dear, and that ain't good.'"

Gilles, a "sexual realist," chatted up the postman, and Bargetta abandoned herself to her impasse. "You could get the idea that I think not being unhappy is boring," she said. She muted the television, used it as a night lamp, draped scarves on light fixtures until they threatened to burn, aligned her shoes with the radiator, counted the packs of Marlboros she had tucked around the apartment. "My mother would pray up away out of this feeling. 'Guide my feet while I run this race.'"

Bargetta made unanswered calls she would not admit to. The thought of Pierre-Yves's fresh paint made her reach for Gilles's pipe. "The smart thing would be to keep my mouth shut and live with it. Maybe he didn't ask me to come to Paris, but he'll beg me to stay. I want to do my mother proud." She struggled with the latch of the gray bathroom. Gilles inched to the door and raised an eyebrow above one of his green contact lenses.

Sometimes I hardly recognized her and couldn't understand how the former Bargetta, with all her merry ferocity, had been swallowed up by the obsessive girl slamming things around in the bathroom. She said that when Pierre-Yves first left she kept his toothbrush in a glass, consciously in the spirit of the candle the sailor's wife places in the window. "I can't find the next righteous move." She explained things to the ruined parquet.

She said no one was more ruthless than a guy trying to get out of a relationship. "Adulthood has no gender, but you get to it one way as a boy and another way as a girl."

I waited for the real Bargetta to emerge and make war on the world, but nothing could penetrate her indifference to the weather outside. She covered pages with her argument to herself, tore up what she had written, rewound the B-52s cassette with a pen, wrote again, shredded once more. She hugged her shoulders, a piston at the end of its cycle: intake, compression, power, exhaust.

She said she used to keep a list of the return addresses on his mail. She said she could pick up one of his books, not that he was much of a reader, and just by sniffing the pages tell where he had given up. Was the problem, she asked, what she had given or what Pierre-Yves had taken away? "What can happen can be so bizarre. He maintained a berserk posture toward me for days. His expression didn't change. This wild, unenlightened look. I thought he was going to kick down the door. Instead, he opened it quietly and left."

Not long after I had gone back to Holland to wipe away some of the protection I thought I had acquired from my distasteful, true self that may yet turn out to be merely provisional, when wind carried inland the scent of peat, I received an unsigned, antique postcard. It showed one of those scenes of a bygone, music-hall Paris. The original message from some stranger had been painted over. I recognized Bargetta's handwriting, lovely as an anchorite's:

> Rule #1: Don't think he's better than you are
>   and don't think he doesn't think he is.
> Rule #2: Eat first—then storm out.

11 / *Minority Business*

The beige stepgrandmother gave up the ghost in her sleep. Her sister was furious. Their plans had depended on Grandfather, who was many years older than his wife, being the first to die.

The funeral home, a brownstone on Lenox Avenue, looked too cut-rate to advertise. A sign claimed that it had been serving the community for thirty years, but something about it was so provisional that I doubted it had ever known Harlem's golden age of three-day wakes, marching bands, and corteges followed by lines of mourners that stretched around the corner. It was the kind of place that said, "This won't take long."

The ground floor of the house was bare except for potted trees that added to the anxious silence. The place was wildly humid, as if the basement were flooded and the furnace going full blast. How much the bereaved paid did not appear to influence the set. I had the impression that the staff recycled its props in order to hang on to something like a profit margin.

When I arrived for the "viewing" a man was pushing a trolley of flowers across the hall. Another man in a shiny black suit carefully packed away folding chairs. I expected him to reappear as the presiding minister. Grandfather used to command $2.50 per funeral during the Depression. A woman in a frilly blouse laid a mop against the banister, tucked her apron behind a curtain, and asked whom I had come to see. She preceded me and shut doors as she went.

I hung back by the door she left open. The stepgrandmother's sister had my aunt by the arm. My aunt, a teacher who wore her skirts well below her knees, called the sister "the Judge" because she talked continually about using a gun to clear the nasty teenagers from the playgrounds. The Judge led her to the casket. "Don't you think she looks like herself?"

"No."

She hadn't reckoned on my aunt's Episcopalian control of Old Country emotion. I hurried away while the Judge insisted that the stepgrandmother had been that light as a girl, that everyone knew black people got darker as they grew older. My aunt said the stepgrandmother looked artificially brightened, like black singers who have their skin peeled for the video mass market. "Those blue lips," Tsvetayeva instructed Rilke. "Negroes' lips are not red."

The brownstone was surrounded by small storefronts, few of which were open for business; nevertheless just having gotten away felt like life. Though the days of militant graffiti on the brick walls had given way to the art of senseless nicknames inside fancy designs, vendors tried to keep warm before the usual pile of knitted goods in the three colors of Pan-African unity. The proprietor of a liberation-books table wheezed, stacked Van Der Zee postcards, and complained about the uninterruptible plot to keep the ghetto quiet with drugs. Since the assassination attempt Angel Dust had been known on the streets as "Hinckley."

The cold pressed into my clothes. I ducked into a fast-food restaurant on 133rd Street. The huge steel oven sent out gusts of heat mixed with the odor of fried chicken. People seated at the counter passed the napkin dispenser and a city marshal said without preamble to the woman on his left that what wouldn't change was white people thinking he had his rights only because they decided to let him have them, and they were the rights nobody cared about anymore anyway.

The woman said, "If you've been around the Afro-American community for any length of time you know things change. I always knew things would change up."

The city marshal polished off a bucket of extra crispy and said white people were always trying to do something on black people. More sad than Europe paying to dump its garbage off the coast of Africa, he said, was West Africa taking the money.

The woman, a private nurse whose three sons were in the army, said he should go live in Russia. The KGB would dig him. The KGB was desperate. The Soviet police resorted to psychics and, because of Afghanistan, doused the drinking water with a chemical that induced docility.

He said he wanted her to be able to identify disinformation when she was exposed to it, to "get" the connection between the eye in the pyramid on the dollar bill and the Trilateral Commission before it was too late.

The nurse said she didn't have to get anything, but he ought to quit using the seat of his pants as a soap box. The rest of us became intensely interested in our chicken.

He said with an eloquence I had not expected that all he knew was that he was not patriotic about any one country. He didn't know how to answer where he came from when he filled out a form. There were substitute countries, but prior to them his parents had been his homeland.

I knew it was the beginning of the end for Grandfather because though he was present we referred to him in the third person.

We threw together some of his clothes without consulting him. He paced the hall, smiling on the deliberations around him.

Perhaps the thing he feared had come. His son, my father, the boy he used to accuse of either hanging out or wanting to hang out in pool halls was about to pull the plug. Lots of parents would like to give up their children and there are many socially acceptable ways to do it, about which Grandfather knew a thing or two. The converse was another matter. My father said that when it came time for us to put him in a nursing home to shoot him instead.

The first thing the Judge had wanted to know after the lovely ceremony was who was going to reimburse her for the funeral and what say she could have over the savings account. The sum involved was pitiably small, which probably made her all the more determined. Job's comforter was the beneficiary of her sister's life insurance policy and a Christmas account. She was so efficient at cleaning out the stepgrandmother's closets she had to send one of the teens who lurked about the basement incinerator to steal another grocery cart. My aunt said that her scheming proved she did not believe in an afterlife.

The Judge had not forgiven Grandfather for his impetuous changes of scenery and hunts for new stimulation in the past. It was the thought of Grandfather sitting on the purse strings she had wanted to be rid of. She had dreamed of bank books resting and accruing where they belonged, in sisterly possession. The dream had vanished with the coroner's van.

Grandfather could neither feel nor answer her questions. Having done his duty, he was gliding out of his mind. When he discovered his wife lifeless in her bed he had remained sufficiently conscious to make the necessary calls, ever a gentleman when talking officially, enunciating carefully and too loudly, the way a rural person not accustomed to telephones would be portrayed on television. His sense of honor would not permit him to abandon even the enemy dead. But after the family had been notified and the body removed, he graciously spaced out.

He set out to water the plants and in his eagerness to make up for having forgotten to do it, to do it because the stepgrandmother did it, he got water over everything. The Philco radio was suddenly a measure of time. I could see how much smaller he had become when he stood next to it and apologetically dabbed with his tie at the spills. He obeyed when anyone suggested that he take a seat. Watching him follow orders was disorienting. He used to descend on us like a stage director who worked on the principle that to get the best work out of his cast he had to maintain a high level of terror. The Judge said he was as lamblike as if a white person had been in the room.

She worried because that morning he'd been distracted enough to burn the stepgrandmother's best pan. She said to me in the corridor by the elevator that Grandfather was a fire waiting to happen. Balancing boxes of monogrammed handkerchiefs, the sort found unopened in every old woman's drawers, she wanted to evacuate the Spode before the china cabinet went up in smoke. I said a fire provided motivation for finding a new home.

I told her about the time I was living near campus, boiled an egg, passed out, and woke in time to say goodbye to the firemen. The following month my ashtray sent flames up a pair of jeans that hung on the door. The fire spread so fast my neighbors had to flee to the roof. The inferno and the building's inoperable sprinklers were more than my business student roommate had wanted to experience in New York and he went back to Japan. The Judge said I was as disrespectful as the rest of my family.

In her nest across the playground, the Judge was waiting to swoop down on the carcass of an uninhabited apartment. Had my aunt not had to catch the shuttle back to Boston, she would have changed the locks just for fun. The wicked sister wanted Grandfather out so that the apartment could be sold—not that it was worth anything. I didn't see Grandfather's lucky lemon plant anywhere and grabbed the nearest clay pot of leaves. I had never grown anything. Already I was engaged with the Judge in a contest over the spoils.

I was killing the roots of my prize with an overdose of plant food when my father called. They hadn't left for Indianapolis. Grandfather had set up such a racket that the airline wouldn't let him on board. He screamed that he was being kidnapped. Grandfather saw the next plane at the ramp and jumped over the wheelchair. Security agents chased him up and down the LaGuardia terminal, astonished that a man his age could move so fast in so many directions.

My father brought Grandfather back to the pigeon coop. When I got there Grandfather was very quiet and it was my father's turn to pace. He reasoned and begged. Grandfather simply said he had some papers to go over, which was to make me hope, long after it had ceased to be possible, that there was some method to his alternating periods of catatonia and excitement. We heard him in his room. He sounded like a burglar and then like a mouse. I struggled not to interfere, not to get up and ask what he was doing. Worry can be the worst form of control. I was afraid he was destroying his shoeboxes and folders of Right Opinions.

There was an argument with my mother in Indianapolis on the wisdom of renting a car. The time not so long before when Grandfather inexplicably leaped into Washington traffic was fresh in our minds. My father said Grandfather got away from him in Washington by trickery. He'd pointed to a character standing under a heated hotel awning, sworn that he knew the man, urged my father to stop the car, and bolted. My father said he should have known better: Grandfather didn't have any friends.

It was true that, apart from family, Grandfather hadn't had anyone to call. Though he had long been at the age where his peers would have begun to die, I'd never heard Grandfather speak of any. It was impossible to think how many days or months he had passed at a stretch within his wheat-colored walls with no company other than that of his wife. He struck me as being very much like a jailhouse scholar. "I have something on the inside that the world can't take away. I'm going to let it shine."

Once I paid a surprise visit. The stepgrandmother was in the middle of an unstoppable complaint. Grandfather said she was wasting her time. The stepgrandmother said she could cook for her sister if she wanted to. Grandfather said she would have to do her cooking at her sister's because he would not have them eat his food. She said he didn't like anybody and nobody liked him, not even his own children had any use for him.

I said I liked him. "He that fears shall find friends." I was pleased with myself. I'd come up with something at least atmospherically biblical to show that I had sympathy for Grandfather in his line of work. The stepgrandmother said I wouldn't like Grandfather if I knew what he really thought of me.

Grandfather passed over my offering and said to his wife that peace on earth was predicated on never telling one man what another man has said about him. I was stunned that he had not risen and roundly contradicted her. It had never occurred to me that he didn't dote on me or that, if he did, his feelings could change. An old man's loyalties were, I assumed, like a fixed income: barely enough for necessities, a definite amount that didn't stretch very far, but something to count on.

I'd gone so far as to think of my showing up with a sack of

desiccated fruit as a big sacrifice, and the dripping flowers plucked from buckets at the Korean deli as an addition to his life, like the sighting of a comet. She who had once stood behind Grandfather like a rock formation, his immovable support and foundation, said he just liked to hear himself talk and smell his upper lip.

Maybe she carried on every day between morning talk shows and the news. There was a time for lunch, a time for puzzles, and a block of hours left over for trying to get a rise out of Grandfather. She wasn't going to let my presence throw her off. What I couldn't tell was how much Grandfather's restraint was due to me. He was quietly incandescent, saving it up, with traces of a smile playing about lidded eyes.

The stepgrandmother never raised her voice. She kept it to a growl, like the motor of their old refrigerator. She said she was worse off than a woman busting suds. She even had to go out in the rain for light bulbs. Were it not for her he'd be sitting in pitch-dark and not doing a thing about it. Grandfather calmly took her gibes and handed back a guffaw, as if he were passing the salt. She snapped a pencil. Grandfather, she said, was of no use to anyone.

To save the day, I asked what Atlanta had been like in the time of his early mentor, Hugh Proctor, then an important black Congregational minister. The past was Grandfather's high ground. But he'd long since stopped talking about his past, as if, to live with the stepgrandmother, he had given up memory.

The stepgrandmother said he could fool a little boy but he couldn't fool her. I said I liked it when Grandfather talked and I was not a little boy. He had not been able to fool the people in Atlanta, she said. They were too up-to-date, that's why he didn't like them.

Grandfather laughed—sheepishly, I thought with a contraction of my heart—and said she didn't know anything about Atlanta, but if she wanted to talk he'd be glad to help her to remember her mother's dirt floor. She said at least her mother hadn't been a debtor. She said he left Savannah owing everybody in sight, and if he wanted to name-drop he should mention the IOUs he skipped out on when he made her leave Memphis in the dead of night.

Grandfather said he'd walk me to the corner. Was I to believe her? Rectitude is not always a nice quality; we think of it as going with a kind of spiritual pride. He had to get his mind around quite a lot of things, like everyone else, and I had never heard him say, "I'm sorry." But many had been taught by him, helped by him through difficult periods, and for them he had been a real figure. They knew there was this problem called his wife.

I couldn't know what had passed between them all those years. Sometimes what you hear is what there is. Usually, Grandfather and the stepgrandmother sat in different rooms, pointedly not speaking to each other. They nearly answered the question, Which is more painful: the incapacity to live with anyone or the inability to be alone? Perhaps Grandfather had gotten something in the bargain: punishment, expiation, daily confirmation of his other opinion of himself.

Manhattan, that far uptown, in the copse of plain towers, did not exist after dark. No sirens, gangs kicking over trash cans, teens making harmonies on the playground, or stoops for people to crowd. The international depressed style, the concrete hives of the working poor, could have been in any city: Pittsburgh, East Berlin, Mexico City. Periodically the elevator responded to someone either finished with or preparing to report to a late shift. The heady smell of a complicated thing like gumbo came through the vents.

We couldn't get Grandfather to go to bed. If he was staying

awake, so were we. I could feel the coffee clicking through the vessels in the back of my head, then causing what I was convinced were palpitations, ventricular fibrillation. I picked up the prescription form on Riverside Drive and shot across town to an all-night pharmacy on Lexington Avenue. Black men, instant premonitory signs, sat on benches along the road through the park, as if it were afternoon.

I looked through the window of the pharmacy before I entered. In Manhattan, in front of an all-night drugstore, you were sure to meet the weirdest in improvised attire. The man who opened the door for me and thrust out his paper cup emerged from a blanket held together by a wide leather belt with pictures of cowboys. His shoes were wrapped in plastic and he wore a headband made of bent table forks. The clerks inside yelled at him to scram. He saluted and continued his work.

My scanning of the pharmacy made the guys in the plexiglass cage extremely nervous and rude. I switched automatically into the demeanor of reassurance: I was not one of the bad ones. They did not relent. One almost threw my change on the floor. It was insulting to hold out my hand and to have a clerk bang the money on the counter. I'd "tommed" again for nothing.

The taxi I'd paid to wait while I dashed into the pharmacy had gone. I shivered with a displaced anger that turned outward against Grandfather. It was his fault that I was on Lexington Avenue under the seething lights, never mind that in my self-manipulated, blurred escapades around Manhattan it was just luck that nothing bad had ever happened. A black driver said he'd cut short his break because he'd watched too many other black drivers pass me by.

Grandfather used to talk about the time he took my aunts shopping in Louisville. Girls home from college, they were told in one store they could buy dresses but couldn't try them on.

Manners were morality, he said. He made them leave the store without the dresses. In his way he got it right. I do not believe he believed in his reward—definition everlasting.

His career as a mesmerist of the color line—in the old days it was called "the Veil"—had worn him out long before the morning my father and I spiked his coffee with tranquillizers in order to get him on the plane and into the nursing home. His last wish, he said, was to be left alone. We won and he let us dress him, thick in his Valium trance, radiant with despair. I walked him onto the plane and to his seat. Trembling, he shook my hand and thanked me. He'd forgotten who I was.

The slippery manager of Grandfather's project said that because of the numerous subsidies and regulations involved, the premises couldn't be sold unless they passed inspection. He reminded me of stories Hispanics told about immigration officers —La Migra—who'd failed to extract baksheesh. I overlooked his hints and thereafter he ignored my requests for cooperation.

It was left to me to do something with the things that without occupants around to blow life into them had become a ton of junk. I called a mover, a tai chi chu'an instructor widely respected for his hillbilly truck, mule's back, bohemian working hours, and amateur's rates. The climax of the evening was spitefully dumping the sofa in a parking space at Yankee Stadium.

The Judge greeted the news that I'd claimed the Philco, the television, the silver, and the caned chairs for myself with a rapid blinking of her eyes. She'd been to the hairdresser's and in a new copper pants suit looked more like the stepgrandmother's daughter than her sister. She dragged herself through the empty rooms, stooped and fondled what I had not had time to pack for the Salvation Army. A closet of towels and shower caps was something like paydirt. She said she knew someone who could use the box of screwdrivers and said the same thing about the ancient tins of cocoa and tea.

When I admitted that I'd thrown out an old-fashioned washboard she could no longer contain herself. She accepted the tax-deductible receipt from the Salvation Army with a soundless weeping that made it hard for her to breathe. I asked her to take over the disposal of the apartment, which was too complex for me. There was nothing else to offer other than a broom and dustpan.

The day after I handed over the keys to the Judge the cold spell broke and the People's Park of shaggy annuals and borders of aluminum cans at Ninety-sixth Street and Broadway lost its zoning battle.

Radio-station activists and schoolchildren pelted the bulldozers, but over the months a yellow condominium that, incredibly, resembled a giant cash register rose steadily and, as predicted, swallowed up my field of blue skies. That you could hear your neighbor brushing his teeth through the flimsy walls did not prevent the terraces stacked like aboveground mausoleum slots from selling out before the building was completed.

The Cuban drugstore at Ninety-fifth Street became a gelato shop, which in turn quickly reopened as a sports-shoe boutique and then as a video rental center. A dive popular among short-order cooks was transformed into a restaurant splayed with Art Deco mirrors. When an indifferent coffee shop was born again as a spartan fish store run by obsequious Asians of unspecified nationality, the lady who drew bangs on her forehead with a red Magic Marker was out of luck. To shut her up, the coffee shop always gave her the Blue Plate Special for the price of whatever she had in her purse. She took her profession seriously, wailing in all kinds of weather to the accompaniment of a tape recorder hidden under her pavement-length lime-green chiffon.

Fences went up, deep loamy holes were dug, ineffective POST
NO BILL stencils decorated the building sites. The change in the
West Side was like having a tooth pulled: once the gaps in a
block were filled, you couldn't remember what had been there
before. The police broke up the ring that sold subway slugs.
Instead of the bells of store alarms, you were more likely to
encounter the deadpan of a new automobile's voice alarm: "Intruder, intruder."

My supermarket was still as drab and sparsely populated as
the neighborhood churches. Efforts had failed to upgrade its
appeal, to push it in the direction of the upscale food emporiums
that were wiping out rows of cheesy driving schools, hardware
stores, and travel agencies that specialized in flights to San Juan.
The supermarket inaugurated an imported cheese bin and the
deli wasn't so deli anymore. There were croissants and baguettes
made with too much sugar. One woman said she was waiting
for them to feature chocolate-chip Brie.

"I'm ready any time you are," the checkout girl said. She was
beautiful and wore two long gold earrings in her lobeless left
ear.

"What?" a man too old for his blond Prince Valiant haircut
answered from the manager's raised booth.

"I said I'm ready when you are. You can check me out. I'm
leaving early tonight. Remember?"

"Nope." He kicked cartons out of his booth. The kid from
produce sloped by, cut his eyes at the falling cartons, and kept
moving.

"I'm leaving at seven."

"You leave when someone gets here."

The pedal at her foot that moved the counter belt was broken.
To be helpful, I shoved my purchases toward her. I put on my
best it-be's-that-way-sometime smile.

"What you grinning at? I have to work here and you have to

shop here." She scratched at the expiration date on the milk carton with a bright cherry fingernail. "That so funny?"

I had to walk far to find services like the old tailor or the little cobbler. I must have been asleep for a long time. One morning I noticed that the SRO across the street was boarded up. The mailman said he didn't care where the tenants had gone. They'd become so brazen in their addictions he saw a streetwalker pick her nose and try to free-base what she'd found there.

The night belonged to the young and their admirers, and as long as the automatic cash machines cooperated, the night went on forever. They said every bartender was a dealer, along with every messenger, and many of the waitresses felt glamorous enough to act as go-betweens for the men who'd lost their brief-cases of recruitment brochures and those who read *Easy Rider*, the magazine of choice among bikers who'd done time. These were the days before crackheads turned Amsterdam Avenue into a river of appliances as they rushed to the pawnbrokers with the last of their—and anyone else's—worldly goods before closing time.

I got into a snit about new neighbors on Pomander Walk. Legs dangled over plant boxes, champagne watered the hedges. I didn't think their parties would ever end and wished bats would fly into their hair. The noise disturbed my neighbor upstairs, an elderly woman who was afraid to go out at night or when there was ice on the sidewalks. Sometimes I heard her fall. She explained that now and then her legs just gave out. The impact of person on wood floor sounded like a gun report. She'd tap on the pipes to signal she was okay.

We could always tell when the saxophone player was at home. The flash of what neon there was in the marquee of the movie house was reflected in the blackened windows of buildings awaiting renovation. Also cinematically correct, bald, in plus fours, the musician stood in his window and blew at the steps. He started again in the afternoon, when the mailman sat to listen to a few bars. The mailman said the music reminded him of the days when there was a fountain in Times Square.

He said these days if he dropped a quarter between Seventy-second Street and Ninety-sixth Street he'd kick it to the post office before he'd bend over to pick it up, there were so many queer bars. The saxophone player told him not only were The Boys part of the Great Old Sacrament, "ha-has" had been in the vanguard of the inimical pastel look of gentrification. The boundaries of Sparta were on the tips of their spears, he said. Sometime afterward, the brightness began to fall from many heads.

While I was finding room for the loot from Grandfather's apartment, co-op fever struck my dilapidated home. Mr. Chips, as Pomander Walk called the former headmaster who defended himself against the safety committee from his campanile of flammable newspaper, became a hero when he hosed down shingles during a fire that started next door, deep inside a closed-up paint shop. The grapevine attributed it to the arson of a landlord anxious to see the property turn over.

The women once happy to plant begonias and tipple in the sun discovered the property was cute and worthy of shareholder maintenance payments. They who had regarded it as quaint that their Albanian caretaker owned two buildings in the Bronx suddenly marched around together in splenic black book committees. "Feeding pigeons, birds, or other animals from the windowsills, sidewalks, and yards is not allowed." My air conditioner came in for criticism because it was secondhand and disrupted the uniformity of the façade.

A grounds committee circulated memos about preparing the

property for conversion. This seemed to include discouraging loiterers. Every tactic short of driving spikes into the pavement and ripping out the steps was tried. We were charged with telling anyone we saw who didn't belong to please move on.

The same woman was on my steps every day. She left whenever I came home or went out, no matter how often I asked her not to disturb herself. I tried to tell her the steps weren't mine to give. She sat in her clothes like a bird in its covert. The first time, I surprised her. In a swift lowering of her eyelids, she shielded some precious memory as she rose. Her voice recalled the Old Country. "Beg pardon. Didn't mean to bother your privateness."

She refused any gesture I made toward her, but once she asked if I smoked. Only poor people, fat people, black people, and alcoholics were still smoking. Some people went to Europe just to smoke. It was the one day I wasn't, but I also didn't want to let the chance go.

She was way ahead of me, already pointing to the failing Palestinian deli at the top of the hill. Her words collapsed on top of mine, pushed them down. She moved across my hint as if I had placed a cape over a puddle. She said she was on her way to get some supplies: cigarettes, coffee, and doughnuts. She'd just had to rest first, take a breath from walking up the hill to the Muslims, as she called them.

Once, in a cloudburst, I saw her going to wherever she lived. I ran after her with an umbrella. She wouldn't let me cross the street with her and indicated by the way she stood that she wasn't going to budge until I turned back. My standing there in the rain would just make her get wetter. "Tell me your name so I can respect you the next time I see you." But she never called me anything as she plied back and forth for her supplies, slow and soundless as a cypress canoe.

One night I skulked around the velveteen rope at the entrance to a disco on Fourteenth Street, a club where the music reached painful decibels, pounded the walls, traveled over the parking lot, and bounced off other buildings. It was a social clearinghouse where those going down in Manhattan tried to grab on to those on the rise. I made as much as $40 there selling the VIP passes sent to me in the mail by mistake, unloading them on Manny-Hanny types unwilling to risk the humiliation of not being acknowledged by the moody doormen.

New Age coolies—punks, students of free subjectivity, youths from immigrant families that had never participated in the census—intimidated the well-dressed and scrambled for the final edition of two yippie-like Xeroxes: one gave the telephone credit card numbers of major corporations, the other explained how to reverse electricity meters. And I ran into the very person who could make me feel my circumstances most acutely.

Trip stepped off the curb to avoid the throng and continued in my direction. His friendliness, honed in the anecdotal brotherhood of business pressure, had a quality of getting the other guy first. Brisk, extroverted, insensible—Trip, the black preppie, was so comfortably mainstream and having such a good time being casual there was no suggestion in him that integration was a kind of infiltration. The only chink in his armor as an insider I'd ever detected came from a story he told about arriving for the first day of school and being told that his fees were in arrears. His chic parents whipped him across Philadelphia and enrolled him in another elite academy.

I assured Trip that I didn't hassle with queues either. He didn't introduce me to the woman with him. She waved to a doorman, smiled on the general public, on the caravan of "stretches," and told Trip she never noticed when people recognized her. I placed her face: the actress who played the new black doctor in town on my favorite soap. They were on their way to the back door of the club that took the gorgeous, famous, and ultra-hip straight upstairs to private rooms. Trip said he was planning an informal "Easy Street Brunch." I asked if he'd won the lottery.

"Life is brilliant, dude." He pronounced "dude" like a surfer. Whites had made the word their own. Black guys didn't use "dude" anymore; they said "homeboy."

I said I would check my date book, though I had nothing on in the near future except a menu advertising the opening of an MSG-free Szechuan restaurant.

We'd met a few years before, when he selected a number of expensive works on architecture in the antiquarian bookshop where I got away with costly thefts and doing as little as possible. The shop owner muttered that if that black kid bought any of those books he'd eat his hat: he didn't trust Trip's khaki and flannel. Trip produced an array of credit cards for identification and told the owner he could hold the books until the check cleared. The owner sucked up to Trip when he returned to fetch his purchases and make others.

An analyst in a brokerage department that composed ecologically sound portfolios for careful pension fund managers, Trip browsed regularly in the bookshop with his girlfriend, Ellen, who collected books about sparrows. Trip's grandfather had been the first black to sit on the Keystone State's appellate bench, and his father, a banker, was tapped for political office but turned out to have questionable golf partners. Trip, however, was thoroughly contemporary. He amused himself by reading up on medical patent applications. He had a passion for jazz, but it was a Frenchman's love, not a homeboy's. Before Wall Street his work experience had been as a loose rider on a horse farm in Chester County.

He lived completely free of the entanglements of racial identity.

When he discussed South Africa, it was from the standpoint that apartheid was too antiquated for the demands of capital-raising mechanisms. His insularity had none of the revealing snobbery of the light-skinned, "Blue Vein" world. He was as dark as the Ethiopians Pepys heard turned white at death. If there was any hesitation in Trip's pursuit of happiness, it came from the fat boy who lived on inside the dynamo who hit the gym at least three times a week.

Ellen had an income and therefore time to schmooze. Her history of getting caught up in causes began with joining the picket line at Woolworth's as a pre-teen. She and Trip were introduced at an anti-apartheid demonstration outside the English-Speaking Union. But he was not a cause. The shadow over their living together came from Trip's parents, not her widowed mother. Their disapproval noted that Ellen was Wrong School and six years older than Trip.

At a Main Line dinner she complained to a Hungarian diplomat that a Filipino friend had been denied a visa to Budapest. The Hungarian was not surprised: the applicant was "colored." Trip's parents were enraged, as if Ellen had called attention to a man's handicap.

After Trip took a job at a conventional Wall Street firm, he spent his weekends playing squash and elaborate computer war games, and came less to the bookshop. Trip's secretary took to putting me on hold and then announcing he wasn't at his desk in a way that made me think of myself as a drag. He'd never let me pick up a check. As often happens with couples, the attitudes of one are adopted by the other, and after the bookshop folded I was not surprised that I lost touch with them both.

Trip's name was still linked with Ellen's on the code board below the camera, and their building on Riverside Drive hadn't lost the smells of stuffed cabbage and gefilte fish. Puffy creatures darted from Trip's door. Ellen excused herself and caught one cat she said was a Blue Cream. Its eyes were as noncommittal as hers. Another Ellen identified as a naughty Shaded Cameo whined around her Mao slippers. She softly scolded the cat when its paws tangled her black hair, which showed luxurious ribbons of premature gray.

An Angora shook itself on the edge of a bookcase in the cavernous room where Trip sat in mussed painter's trousers with two guests. Cat hair settled on avocado plants, on his collections of first editions and stamp albums ruined by pesticide, and in his ceiling-high, alphabetical library of rare jazz dust covers. Bright tropical fish flitted through Disney sets inside several tanks. Trip said the glass enclosure of lettuce and brown smears was home to Ellen's accumulation of forty snails, which began with her discovery of two stowaways in a box of strawberries from Japan.

Trip said he had been drinking to his reincarnation as vice president for research for a "wholly black-owned" firm of corporate troubleshooters. They had just won their first big contract selling "computer solutions"—whatever they were—to Nigeria. I wouldn't have been more surprised if he had become a trapeze artist. He asked that I do him the courtesy of never mentioning his former brokerage firm in his presence again. "I developed a destination problem."

"I'm going to get mine. If that means taking yours, I will. Am I right?" Rayburn, the vice president for marketing and development for the meteoric black company, asked me if I knew that the future was in inductive computers. "Better move fast. The drawbridge is going up. You don't need a weatherman, you need a probability theorist. Forget the Wagadus and get real. What's the point of having a tank full of gas if you've no place to go?"

It flashed through my mind that Trip was doing a little window dressing of his own, scrounging up "homes"; that he had asked

me over after not having seen me in such a long time to show
Rayburn that he had black friends. From the number of plates
and forks stacked on the table, I suspected that he had dug out
a lot of old telephone numbers.

Trip said they were going to get to the Pacific century early.
Their ultimate objective was to penetrate the Korean markets.
Ellen brought a tray and said she hoped their goals would be
considerate of dissidents. Trip said she was asking for a black
eye that would prevent her going to his new firm's networking
bash.

Rayburn, a big cuff-links type, said Ellen reminded him of a
girlfriend he'd had to set free because she dragged him to church
meetings and demanded that the Polish harmonium player, the
Refusenik, or the Native American pro-incorporation advocate
speak directly into the microphone.

Trip said Ellen was a liberal and, like typewriters, her days
were numbered. "She tells me she can't feel what I need her to,
but I'm going to work with her on this." She wouldn't permit
a television, let alone cable, in the house and wanted to cancel
their many subscriptions. She retained the radio to listen for the
lot numbers of products being recalled.

"I'm not a vegetarian," Ellen said. "I'm a hysteric." She dodged
Rayburn's jolly tap on the bottom and went back to the kitchen.
Rayburn's wife, who looked very pregnant in her red dress, finally
spoke up. She said she perfected her English by tuning into
American breakfast television. She came from Rumania. Pleased
with her contribution, she settled the grape leaves on her stomach
and eye-beamed her husband, handsome in the O. J. Simpson
mode, through wispy bangs of platinum-blond hair. I imagined
she was not above telling her struggling countrymen as she
tipped them, "You should have married me when you had the
chance."

Rayburn said one day soon he would have a computer in his home that automatically transcribed Radio Free Europe, Radio Moscow, and Radio Peking. "I believe in communication." He said that being computer illiterate was like not being a part of the gene pool. The bottles Trip poured lubricated Rayburn's ego. His wife commandeered the bowls of chick-peas and leaned, intent on his every word, like a child on the alert in case a single part of her favorite tale is left out.

The cats nibbled the African violets as Rayburn recalled his days growing up in Los Angeles's Baldwin Hills. The fish swam back and forth to his beach antics. The snails and I lost sight of Trip as Rayburn hacked through Yale, torts at N.Y.U. Law School, and an MBA. Trip came back into the saga the happy day Rayburn, stung at not having been made a partner, convinced Trip, disquieted at the prospect of being forever low on the arbitrage pole, that his fledgling black company was the fast lane to cooking the mark. I waited for him to fling open a window and roar, "Ali, boom ale-yay."

"We're coming on top," Rayburn concluded. He varied his style of speaking: Eli one minute, street the next. Squeamish women in light-skinned social clubs like the Northeasterners would call it trying to sound black. He jived in the almost-Thonet rocker as he talked, in an I-don't-need-no-chiropractor fashion. "No half stepping. You got to be down with me." He high-fived Trip.

"I'm down."

"Bhani ghani," Rayburn said.

"Abari gari," Trip said.

"What's new," they said in unison. Rayburn's wife said their big noise was sweet. She pushed herself out of her chair to help Ellen. Trip looked bashful, which I hadn't thought him capable of.

"This one bitch said to me when I got accepted at N.Y.U. and her silly ass boyfriend didn't, 'If anyone had to take his place I'm glad it was you.' Let's show some Jews how to shimmy." We heard Ellen's exclamation in the hall. "I meant Jew boys, not Jew girls." Rayburn said he forgot Ellen was Jewish because her family came from Canada. "Man, this wine has been corked."

Division of labor: the women looked at fish in the kitchen, and Rayburn held forth, mostly about his stick dipped in gold. "I put myself through law school by making deposits at the sperm bank. No lie. Good money." He recommended pumpkin seeds to combat testicular exhaustion. He was a dog, he admitted. "Foreplay is for idealists," his wife caught him saying. "I wasn't in prison before you met me, baby."

"Don't 'baby.' "

"You love it, Malibu style, wicked and wild." Rayburn had something to say at all times: the salmon steaks reminded him of Bonnard nudes; Dutchess County, not Connecticut, was the place to buy; and a black nationalist's Letter to the Editor attacking a black professor began, "Laid up at Yale with a white woman," which, to him, had the grandeur of "Sequestered at Troy." He wasn't sure Ellen's Mickey Mouse T-shirt would do for an executive's lady. Ellen said she had a black Mickey Mouse T-shirt for evening wear. Rayburn's money clip came from Paul Stuart. I changed position to hide the sheen of Grandfather's hand-me-down trousers. I was too ashamed to ask for an ashtray.

Rayburn made me think of the time a roomful of black girls in Indianapolis joked about the exploits of their maids and the girls whose mothers had in fact been maids laughed the loudest. I watched to see if Trip answered Ellen's look at the way Rayburn patronized him. Rayburn found an opportunity to say free blacks had had it as bad as slaves, a dig at Trip's ancestors, cabinet-makers in Pennsylvania before 1830.

I didn't believe they had been as friendly at Yale as Rayburn said. Trip was a novice to the "wholly black-owned" style. Compared with Rayburn, he was a Quaker. I waited for the outburst against the white world that had let him go only so far, which was like hoping for an answer to the question: Does the white of an egg have a taste? Trip's pores exuded encouraging statistics, among them that there were over 300,000 black companies in the United States.

Rayburn's wife had the gift of total recall for the fifty soap-opera episodes I'd missed, until a shoeless, equally pretty neighbor arrived. A personal exercise coach, she'd just come off the back swing and limbered up all over the room, giving Rayburn the best view of her spandex crotch.

"You have purple hair."

"It's fuchsia."

Rayburn's wife took sick because of the cat hair and pouted until he found her scarf with the sardine-can-size Cartier logo on it. Rayburn said pregnant or not, there was a thin line between psycho and intense.

The neighbor glanced at the empties and crossed her legs at the ankles, as if to say she wouldn't ask much of the conversation. She patted her gateau with a fork and rubbed her lips with orange slices. "I haven't been hugged enough today," she said, as if she were monitoring her vitamin intake. She said she was tired of running from the crazies on the streets.

Trip said he was tired of hearing about what he could learn from the poor. "I think it's as sad as the next guy, but asking society to change its value system is a very heavy-duty thing." He relaxed, faked dunk shots that made me wince for the floorboards, and swung an invisible bat at his future of data base spec systems battling computer terrorists.

"I don't take our bottles back to the store," he said. "My woman believes in recycling. I make the elevator man leave them outside because I know the bottles will be rescued by someone who needs the money." I ceased to doubt the company's acumen in its choice of vice president for research. Trip said he thought a lot about the contractual compulsions in human relationships. Ellen said she thanked God he actually cared more about dust on the turntable.

He said the neatest thing about his new job was the possibility of relocating to someplace sunny. When the Japanese talked of investing in the Northeast, they meant Washington State. Ellen said Northern California was a retirement community for people in their thirties. Trip said at least in California he wouldn't be threatened by the people he gave spare change to. There'd been an incident when they went shopping that morning. Ellen said Trip hurt the man's pride. Trip said he'd tried to tell the man that if he cleaned himself up, maybe he could look for work.

What had been mysterious shapes in the dark of the afternoon, things I couldn't examine under the pressure of Rayburn's need for attention, became, when Ellen turned on the lights, a player piano, an easel, a harpsichord Ellen said they had erected from a kit, and a loom Trip had assembled for her. The one other time I'd been to their place, it was practically empty. Evidently Trip had not been able to withstand Ellen's tendency to accumulate, that mysterious feminine ability to contrive a world of whispering things.

In his study he defended his style, a certain pride in discipline and self-denial. The studied bareness of the room said he was a young man in no hurry to put on the extra pounds that got in the way of enjoying the good life. The objects were few and, like the dramatic view of New Jersey, expensive. Trip had a special chair with phonograph speakers built in. Ellen said it took ten years off his face when he sat in his chair because there was room for only one inside.

"See that SOB there?" Trip pointed to the ancient Angora. "It took a swipe at me. I smacked it and it took a hunk out of my hand. I tried to hit it again and the sucker drew blood. It flooded my mustache. I could taste it. It was humiliating to get beaten up by this cat. So I stood up like a primate and grabbed it by the neck. I hung it out the window and thought how weird it would be to see this cat sail, like in a cartoon, but Ellen grabbed my belt, so it wasn't a cartoon. She screamed and the cat freaked. Clawed my arm. I buttoned up and that cat knew its time had come. I could hear it panting in the dark. It took Ellen an hour to coax it from under the sofa. She fed it with her own hands and told me to get the fuck out."

Ellen parted the Algerian ivy over the kitchen window. A man on the next rooftop swung a rabbit on a chain in a full circle. She was speechless with outrage. The rabbit squirmed pitifully. Ellen pounded the ledge. She compared his method of torture to that of the DINA, and said that Puerto Ricans were incapable of anything but barbarism.

She had once volunteered at a Catholic shelter for unwed mothers. She liked some of the names they gave their newborns: Toyota, Yashica, the twins Celanese and Dacron. She said her sympathy was for the women and perhaps the children, but the fifteen-year-old fathers were bastards. Though she was very fond of her super and her mother's super, who prattled on about the immortality of the soul as he botched the plumbing, she regretted that Latin men were a menace. Charities called it "compassion fatigue."

What the eye doesn't see the heart doesn't grieve over, they say. I would have gone on a retreat but my check to the religious order bounced.

12 / *Going Home*

I wasn't heartless, but I was the next best thing: almost heartless. You've said goodbye to the house. You want someone else to take responsibility for it before it explodes or has squatters in it. Sometimes you go back to check the attic and the basement, but even then you don't always get every piece of the china.

I cultivated an indifference that would be so big not even I would see it, but I didn't know what to do with that funny feeling. I bumped against television images and wet newsprint, against people in the street, spotted myself, and couldn't suppress that funny feeling.

I saw a black man asleep on the subway, an entire row of seats to himself. He turned over, reached into his trousers, and scratched. He was wearing a ragged shearling coat, a relic of better days or one of fashion's castoffs. I wish I could say my reaction was one of pity. Instead, I felt embarrassment, the sort I would rather not submit to analysis. He opened his eyes, which compromised his fellow passengers, myself included: I'd been looking at him and he caught me. It had been easier to look at him when he was asleep. He got up and staggered into the next car. Those of us standing did not make a move toward the seats he vacated.

Some days when the streets were filled, I wondered where all the people were going. I picked out the blacks in the fancy restaurant windows, the way my elderly relatives used to examine the television screen and count the number of black faces in the chorus. It was as though I went around the city conducting my own informal survey, "Blacks I Have Seen." In a West Side church, what united the convicted Brinks robber who rested behind Polo sunglasses and broke into cars for a living with the television producer who shopped at Agnes B. and chased her daughter around the pews as the simmel cakes were blessed? The priest didn't mind either of them because he thought of his as an inner-city church.

In the end, the bone has to come out of the soup. I was noticed myself by a woman in a small group of the homeless who had made a stretch of St. Mark's Place in front of Cooper Union their living room. I'd been milling around flea-market tables until I happened onto the makeshift encampment. It had fallen on her, as the only woman in the group, to be busy with household chores, to sweep the sidewalk around the ramshackle chairs on which the men sat as they listened to a radio. I was close enough for her to appreciate my aftershave. She said she had a slogan for me, free of charge: "If you want to make God laugh, tell Him your plans, and if you really want to make Him laugh, tell Him your plans for somebody else."

The cult of Prester John was still going strong in 1985. A man would rise up with the sacred jewel of kingship around his neck and restore Mother Africa to her glory. Contenders were everywhere; they rushed to keep up with every controversy, like a flock of rooks, crying in the air currents, trailing gulls to a dump site. If you fired a bullet into space, you'd bring down a black leader.

I went to the Felt Forum, where the Pretender was to speak. Toward Thirty-third Street the crowd thickened and I had the dizzy sensation of being a child again, lost among legs. Surprisingly, there were few representatives from the lunatic fringe: lonely figures in quasi-military gear holding up charts showing the twelve tribes of Israel. The police shouted instructions— "Keep them off the barricades"—and their anger added to the crowd's excitement.

Scalping began in earnest. More wanted to buy than to sell. One guy hugged his ticket and said he just had to hang on to this one. Filing into the arena, I saw the lines split up: men were directed to one side, women to the other, and for a crazy moment I thought some Islamic segregation of the sexes was to be imposed.

Instead, we were searched. Young men dressed in tight-fitting suits and bow ties, like middleweight champions at press conferences, told us to raise our arms and keep moving. Hands tapped lightly up and down every body. The mass frisking demonstrated the scale and discipline of the organization and announced to everyone that we had been transferred from police jurisdiction.

Supermarket music came over loudspeakers. I worried that my fake press pass would be challenged during a scene between one of the Pretender's security guards and two white journalists who had settled on the steps. The guard told them they were a fire hazard and would have to move. They pretended they hadn't heard. He made a show of getting angry, but that could not disguise his pleasure in telling them what to do. His stance said it was his turn to do some bossing around.

The two journalists gestured helplessly at the press section.

All the seats were claimed. The guard told them to look for seats in the balcony. They said it was important that they be able to see. He told them it would go hard on them if he had to tell them twice. "Would you talk that way if a white man asked you to move?"

They picked up their cameras and surveyed the rows. The concrete walls were streaked with rust. One of the journalists suggested that they forget the assignment. A black woman testing her tape recorder said, "Stick around. This could be as much fun as Purim." She obviously liked the looks on their faces. "Not to worry. I'm not halakahically Jewish."

At 7:20 p.m. it was announced that there were 25,000 people waiting outside. "All brothers seated anywhere in the auditorium who know how to check please come to the rostrum immediately. They must be checked immediately. You know the atmosphere that's been created here."

Applause for the numbers waiting outside, applause for the volunteers, applause for the tense atmosphere, applause for the further announcement that the organization had its own film equipment and high-speed duplicating machines, and still more applause that videotapes of the evening's ritual would be available immediately.

"I just got a whiff of something disrespectful. I smell that reefer right here on this rostrum and will not tolerate this. If someone is sitting near you, tell him to put that reefer out. You can't understand better high." That, too, was applauded.

The members of the audience also gave themselves a big hand. They were impressed by the scene they made, the threat of potential energy that they as a body conveyed to onlookers. A large proportion of the curious and the believers probably came to experience again the surge of power they once felt at protest rallies in churches, halls, and public squares.

A similar astonishment must have greeted such mass demonstrations in the past, when the marauding voices and scattered blacks came together outside their usual precincts. Marcus Garvey, they said, had done it, had shown them what they really looked like, and though he had been forgotten by the time Malcolm X was selling sandwiches on trains, having his hair straightened in the best place in Boston, and laying them out in the Savoy Ballroom the next night, he did it, and because it was impossible to imagine Malcolm X at sixty, new "buccaneers of the street," "dim-descended, superbly destined," were doing it again.

Some identities were like fires in old houses. There was no grate; just a big pile of ashes smoldering away. Maybe there was a hound snoozing nearby. You put on another log. The thing was to create a hotbed of ash and the fire would look after itself, though the applewood was neither as dry nor as old as it should have been. English had become a term of abuse, even when used by the English. People would rather have gone on about their Welsh identity. Only minorities could have an identity. It was too jingoistic in others.

But the links with Africa had fallen away, though there were plenty of people who would try to convince you otherwise. What survived was true. Some things remained, but that in its way was as wild as saying, "I come from Kentish men," or, "That's the Angle in me showing."

A formerly despised people also once despised themselves, the theory went, and so there was no way to value the expressiveness of "sweating like a coon trying to write a letter" or "busy as a jump cable at a nigger funeral" when a white person said it. If you laughed, you would go to the other extreme once you'd stopped laughing, and a dog could have told you that.

"Welcome to the oppressed," one of the night's many warm-up acts said. "There's a ticket for every seat. We don't like to charge to tell the truth God has blessed us with, but we don't charge much. When Michael was here it cost thirty dollars. Some of you have never been here because the tickets are too expensive."

Another warm-up act: "Let's lay some truth on the FBI agents planted in the audience so they'll work for us. We are not poor, we are poorly organized. We don't need talk, we need guns. I love the spirit here. I'm a born-again primitive. Your leadership told you not to come here. Either you're not listening or they're not your leaders. We're going to take a bite out of this apple and spit it back at the mayor." An exclusive invitation to the vernacular pie.

The Pretender appeared late, like a rock star. Flashbulbs exploded and made him poppy bright. He arrived onstage with his mouth working, coming in the name of Allah, who alone would give them victory over their enemies. "Who knocked Henry Ford out of the ring? The International Jew." This was the main event: leftovers; an hour of peelings, bones, onionskins, fat.

"You may wonder why I'm smiling. I know something." The Pretender had his work cut out for him, converting mundane ingredients into a high-caloric meal of sound bites. "The politicians call me ugly names. They are trying to undercut my magnetic attraction in my own people. They are trying to destroy my influence among you and ultimately murder me. They think they are doing God a favor and seek my death. Now, isn't that something?" He held up both hands in an attempt to calm the storm of applause.

I remembered the thrill of a slippery kitchen floor during the lunch rush. I washed dishes. I hadn't the time to properly scrape the plates. I flipped them at the bins. Most of the food went on the floor, and skating across the mixture of water and slops I elevated to a skill.

"What do you think will happen to America if anything happens to me?" the Pretender asked. "They say I am divisive. It has to be that way. You can't mix Satan and God. Am I from Satan or God? If I were from Satan, this world would love me because this is Satan's world."

I saw stacks and stacks of dirty dishes, Mount Rushmores of crockery, as the Pretender talked on. "The wicked are surprised and angry. Jews are going through America trying to line up blacks against me. Your excuses are ending. I am your last chance. God makes me pleasant for you to look at. This little black boy is your last chance. You can't frighten black people the way you used to." The cheers were furious. They had licked every pot. Somewhere a watermelon was weeping.

A journalist with snowy hair like Mark Twain's bit down on his pipe and said, "Begin life as a con and your character can improve; begin as a prophet and you can only go downhill."

The Crooked Creek Retirement Home in Indianapolis asked Grandfather to help out at its Sunday services. Sometimes he smiled. The companions of his swift decline liked to "get happy." He sat apart, infirm but correct, with his Borsalino in his lap. The staff didn't press him. Participation optional. They had other preachers under their care, men willing to stand until needed, though they tired in their ushers' poses, hands neatly behind their backs. Confusion overtook a few faces, as if they were afraid their patience might fall in the category of what the mild staff termed "something uncalled for."

Never finding Grandfather in his room, we'd wander apologetically through the television room, nervous about what we'd catch him doing. I once saw a nurse pry a telephone from his hand. "That man's in a home. He don't know what's he doing." She hung up and asked, "Now, was that called for?"

And always the shuffling of slippers and the smell I thought

I'd grow accustomed to. I tried to get my face ready by thinking of the experiments in which young macaque monkeys were force-fed in order to induce aging, but certain kinds of sympathy can't be faked.

This for the man who used to tell me that the world was not made for equality. Grandfather used to say, "One morning Martin Luther and Erasmus were riding by the dead on a battlefield. Martin Luther said, 'They died in a just cause.' Erasmus said, 'They were men and had something better to do today.' The hope is with Erasmus."

I brought a map of South Carolina to the nursing home and asked him where the old plantation had been. Grandfther confirmed that the tobacco-producing area was shaded lavender, that the soybean region was gray, exactly as the legend to the map indicated. Together we read that clay and mica were the major mineral occurrences. Sassafras Mountain stood 3,560 feet above sea level and Grandfather said to the air, "No good ever came out of Galilee."

Then we got a call that he was missing. My brother-in-law searched the laundromats and hamburger restaurants along the highway. Grandfather was found in the back lot of the nursing home, standing in the toolshed with the lucid shovels, and ever afterward he sat in his chair disenthralled, silent, inscrutable.

We, my father and mother, my sisters and I, went armed with magazines in the hope of tricking his vanity into speech. He used to read aloud from these "wheels of life"—*Newsweek, The Crisis*—for hours on end, in his stirring pulpit tenor, without comprehension, the volunteer social worker insisted, until his fellow inmates were wet with tears of exasperation. Our ploy didn't work. He refused to speak to us, we who had conspired to finish him off.

He declined to say another word to bird, child, or bored nurse's assistant in the days that were left to him. He betrayed no interest in the news items we dangled before him and breathed in answer to such questions as who raked the gravel drive to the nursing home, or why did he want to hide and miss that delicious black bottom pie. Grandfather looked at us and our glossies as if from a great height, enveloped in the stillness mountain climbers are said to discover once the summit is gained.

I gave up hope of the heirlooms, the stories of how, in the old days, the poor boiled dirt to recover the salt that fell from meat as it cured. Grandfather checked his vest pocket to make sure that during the one-way hug I hadn't lifted his valuable, handed-down tale of hooded night riders advancing under an ashen moon.

Grandfather was moved from the nursing home into the hospital and died after a lengthy rehearsal period in the form of a diabetic coma. His death in 1985 came to me in New York in the shape of a yellow envelope, a terrifying telegram lying on the floor. I hadn't paid several telephone bills. I knew it was bad news. I opened it, lying on my back so that I had the telegram's view of the mail slot in the door. I was relieved that it was Grandfather and not someone I was not then and am not now reconciled to losing.

I didn't go to Grandfather's funeral and never visited his grave. In the end, I went to Georgia to say goodbye to him, because, in spite of myself, I believed that if he was anywhere, he would be there, wandering along the banks of the Ogeechee River.

"Be careful of crackers," Grandfather once said to me. We were talking about the farm he used to have. Many blacks were forced off their land. Grandfather wasn't one of them, though it sometimes suited his mood to think of himself as such. In fact, he'd been anxious to get away after my father's mother died.

I reminded him of what he'd always said about good whites.

He was peeling an orange. His hands shook. "I know. It just seems like I ran into so many bad ones."

"What do you make of all that now?"

"That it's typical."

"Painful?"

"No. Well, if it is I don't believe I have much right to the pain."

"Why not?"

"Because I haven't earned it."

The farm had long since been turned into a motel, but Grandfather made pilgrimages to see the trees he'd planted. Everyone thought these sudden trips of his dangerous, at his age, but once he had made up his mind no one could turn him left or right. He had begun to show signs that he could remember in detail things that happened years ago, yet what had occurred the day before was a blur to him, like an interval at sea.

I was told that on his final journey to Georgia, sometime in the late 1970s, Grandfather had been very jumpy and often rushed to the window to follow the sound of a distant train. He landed in a small town in South Carolina. A black woman found him. He had no clothes, no money, no idea of who he was, where he was, or how he had traveled so far. She took Grandfather to the sheriff, who put him in jail for his own safety.

The sheriff's wife cooked when there were prisoners. They enjoyed talking to him, somehow discovered his name, where he had family, and called around. After that he was kept under the close guard of old age. No more uprisings against himself. He'd been on his way to his ancestral home at Sugar Creek.

I had not been South since my childhood and still believed in the hurry-sundown Dixie of movieland. The New South was a surprise. Augusta, the last of the Fall Line cities, had treated itself to a facelift. Along the Savannah River, dwellings once "segregated in place, but integrated in sin," as Grandfather remembered them, had been turned into a historic development. The bordellos and their world of paydays had given way to crab-cake parlors done in a sort of minstrel-era decor.

New businesses had taken over the old mansions; shopping centers had conquered the cotton fields. In the cafeterias, small families made room for larger parties, who in turn gave up corners to youngsters on dates. Not everyone was either black or white anymore, but people apparently hadn't caught on yet to the multi-racial shoving of "up North." Even the fundamentalist churches in what had been butcher's shops appeared to go out of business cheerfully. I was taken to praise the new addition to the medical center. The president of a black college told me he was trying to persuade his daughter to transfer from her predominantly white school to his because he found out she didn't know who Joe Louis was.

The graveyards were the last remnants of the Old Country. I was shown the way across the park through which Grandfather and his brothers had hurried when they were late to church. The house where he grew up wasn't there anymore, but beyond the cedar branches was a cemetery. The plots flooded in heavy rain, including one topped by a large pink stone.

Grandfather's sisters were lined up behind his mother, as they had been in life. One of them, I was told, ended her days in a web of superstitions, which included a time-consuming dislike of blacks darker than herself and putting a bowl of water with a fork in it under her bed in order to trap the hostile spirits that might get her while she slept.

Another sister was reported to have said, "Such a pity about Eustace, getting one of those nasty men's diseases."

"How did you work that out?"

"Just like Waldo. When he went bald Mother wouldn't let him in the house. She said he had one of those nasty men's diseases."

The youngest sister, the first to die, had had an almost punishing interest in the cause of convicts. In those days, hangings in the yard of the city jail drew crowds that watched from across the street. Men on chain gangs were starved, put in stocks, hogtied, flogged. It was said that the desperate letters from some prisoners almost tempted her to burn down a warden's house. In 1932 an eighteen-year-old on the Chatham County chain gang, suffering from tuberculosis, killed himself. He had been laughed at when he asked for medicine. It was a famous story that spread quickly around the state. They said Grandfather's mother, fearing what revenge his sister had in mind, locked her in the cellar until she cooled down.

Grandfather's mother hadn't liked his first wife because she was too light. She didn't like blacks much either. That was enough, his wife said, she was through trying to please a woman so active in the church. They were buried within yards of one another, in competing family plots, so to speak. Grandfather once told me that long ago he had overheard his mother talking to his first wife.

"How did you get up here?"

"By that road."

"Don't be arrogant, child."

"I walked."

"I suppose you think you're sitting pretty now."

"No, I'm talking to you."

What frightened him, Grandfather said, was that the conversation had taken place in the cemetery, his mother in her grave and his wife in hers.

———

The feeling of the Old Country also survived in some of the churches. Visitors to the Thankful Baptist Church were given paper shamrocks to pin to their lapels. Old Esau was remembered as a fine, upstanding churchman in a semicircle of white glass above the main door, mostly, it seemed, because he'd brought central heating to the church.

People who didn't know me at all opened their doors and hearts, just because I was family. "Root hog or die," they called hospitality. I was moved by the elderly who spoke of Grandfather as one who had been born in this church, who had grown up in this church. They were very proud and thought of themselves as contemporaries of the church. The immense vault of brown brick they called home was built in 1893, in the "cathedral style," they said. True, there was a nave, a rose window, a tower, and the big bell rang lustily at eleven o'clock.

The entire church was light green carpet, from the street door, up the first few steps, through more white doors, all the way to the pulpit and the back wall. The old panels had been replaced by a perhaps accidentally primitive painting, a copy of a copy. John had his hand casually on the Lord's shoulder. They had hippie rather than biblical hair and beards and were half submerged in aquamarine blue, posed for a snapshot taken on a freshwater fishing trip. The halo around Christ waited to turn into a cartoon bubble. People pointed out to me the newness of the windows along the walls and the freshness of the white clapboard ceiling.

The Gospel Choir sang "I feel like going home," with someone, somewhere, letting out a long, low, dry "Yes," and the emotion I'd been looking for all those years finally came. Beaten armies learn well, they say.

———

Perhaps the old-timers were right to insist that we, the Also Chosen, live wholly in the future and, like early Christians, preserve only detached sayings and a wagonful of miracles from the past. The facts were many, too many. If I'd sat where they'd sat, my trousers would still be burning.

As in the game where the word selected at the start of the row changes as it is whispered from ear to ear, it was their faith that being black would not mean what it did twenty years before, or back when the larder always had to be filled, when the woodpile could never go down, when the dairy had to furnish butter and cream, and the pickaninnies had to have molasses and gungers. They could not foresee that anyone would want to revise the story or renegotiate the terms of belonging after them.

Their understanding of what it meant to be colored, Negro, black, Afro-American, their experience of the life because of it and the life in spite of it haunted me much like a religion you are born into and struggle to either reject or accept. I looked to my elderly relatives as revealed texts, guides to a great landslide that would tell me what to feel about this ode in a shell called blackness when the time came. Meanwhile, there was a big hole in the middle of my heart that needed filling up.

I had taken a utilitarian view of Grandfather. What else were old blacks for, except to be repositories of racial lore? Beautiful, maligned, obsolete Negroes, discussing themselves, "this race thing," and feeling like philosophers—I used to sit back and wonder how they managed to be all-inclusive. It never occurred to me that they might be making it up as they went along and sometimes backing down.

My piety and resentment toward the tales of what I had missed before the thaw, what had been gone through for my sake, turned out to be like a camouflage maneuver, a prolongation of the adolescent lament that I wasn't real but everyone else was, a comfortable resignation of the self that was also useful as a sort of certificate of exemption. But one thing about the real world, if you aren't careful it will tell you what you are and just how low you stand.

I had the most dramatic conclusion in mind for my visit to the Old Country. I would walk over the bridge from Augusta into South Carolina, as a kind of humbling of myself before history. My fossilized picture of a rustling, pregnant landscape had me in the sweet myrtle, the dagger-pointed leaves of Spanish bayonet, and then in the great swamp of the Congaree. I'd make noises, the way a child alone in a creaking room adds his own sounds just to scare himself more.

The span over the river was much longer and higher than it had looked from my hotel window. The water below ran with red suds and the way ahead promised only more highway unfriendly to someone on foot. A hydraulic whine blotted out the sounds of my steps. I simply turned back. Even Grandfather's memories were lost to me, like the Book of Jashar was to the Israelites, as he himself would have said.

Someone bequeathed to me the "fifty miles of elbow room" I took for granted. It was a luxury to believe that better days were being kept in layaway just for me or that the elderly held my consciousness in trust and I could take up the burden of knowing later, after my youth was no longer renewable and my second chances had all been spent.

The future in my early youth was a wide sea of aloneness and my catalogue of adventurers read: children of calamity, offspring of sin, outlaws, isolatoes, Negroes, and me. Two slaves ran away from the Dutch trading station during the Tokugawa period when Japan was closed to foreigners. They dressed in geisha clothes, made their way into Nagasaki, and were hacked to bits. I didn't get to a place that far out.

I never could explain or admit to myself what I was fleeing

from and what I was escaping to. I assumed that either time or defeat would fill in the blank spaces. However, escape I did, the accidents of opportunity or sloth I interpreted as divine corroboration, and getting away was easy, like skipping school, avoiding the job, slipping out of the theater—a kind of gigantic, trivial something.

The sociological heat in which I grew up said you could live by yourself, but not for yourself. The community's pastor shared everything, but he didn't share the problems unless he came from the community. That was the difference between the war correspondent and the soldier. The former was not under orders. The situation would not change. You would always be pursued by it, and by your being who you were. If you had your ticket out, then you were under an obligation to allow your imagination to tell you what it was like for others.

Then the psychological terrain shifted violently, an entire history lay exposed, right there under our sandals and tennis shoes, as profound as a lost city. Appreciation of it called for initiation, a degree of worthiness, as in the practice of certain mystical sects, and you had to defer to those people who had known the worst, what seemed more true. I didn't like the togetherness that expressed itself as suspicion; now I miss those whom injury made gracious and also those who simply uglied up and died.

I minded the strict rules of conduct and the tribal code that said that I, as a black, had a responsibility to help my people, to honor the race. Now I am sorry that I went to such lengths not to be of much use to myself just so no one would be able to ask anything of me. To have nothing to offer was not, after all, the best way to have nothing to lose.

It doesn't always begin with a suitcase. Sometimes it starts with the wrong book. Back in the days when books were deeds and every situation was, I thought, polemical, the language of

being black stressed "summers of dreadful speculations and dis-
coveries" and "going behind the white man's definitions," as if
American reality were an illusionist's trick that could be exposed
by a peek through the correct hole. We, the Also Chosen, a
unique creation, meaning more soulful than white people, had
to understand history to be released from it.

Those "dreadful speculations" are much like train stations that
were once important but are now passed over by commuter lines.
The stations disappear in a rush; you whiz by faded arches,
fanciful embellishments. Other things have grown up around
them, overtaken them, and, in some cases, embarrassed them.
To pick up one of these books is to find yourself on a platform
in a country of arrested development.

As the day winds down, you begin to panic that there is no
way out. No comfortable sleeper has pulled in; the ticket window
is closed anyway. The signs are in an alphabet you cannot de-
cipher, the coffee is bitter, the cigarettes stink, the cafeteria has
sold its last potato. Everyone else seems to know where he's
going, why he's waiting, and can't help you, though clearly he
wants to explain the departure schedule to you.

You give in, put on your adventurer's cap, assure yourself that
you will bed down in the sorrel patch if it comes to that. You
read on and find that the streetlamps are more subdued than
they are in most cities today. The moon enchants the sky and
prevents the night from darkening completely. Stars are visible.
They throb and shine down on those Freedom Summers of not
so long ago. Until death or distance do us part.

You take away phrases as if they were souvenirs to add to
your collection of abolitionist ha'pennies, Wedgwood medallions,
Aunt Jemima saltshakers, blues records from a Heritage Tour
or a cousin's basement. You want to retain the past, as if through

preservation its sufferings will have meaning, but sometimes suffering has no meaning; it's just suffering.

The past gets longer and longer. Yet it has also gotten closer. It's sitting in a plastic bag by the front door, awaiting collection. The bag might even be punctured. Bits of stuff are blowing across the yard, spiraling into the lovely, reborn, neutral blossoms.

My parents remind me that my last NAACP convention was a while ago. Miami Beach. Yes, I recall the bar bill I stuck them with. At the Fontainebleau Hotel, which, like the rest of the nation, had seen better days, the smoke from the riot in Liberty City across the bay was visible. "When are you going to run for President?" I asked every famous face. "When I get your check," every famous face answered. My father has been known to sell NAACP memberships from stall to stall in public toilets; volunteer work has my mother so harried she leaves mailing lists in the freezer; and my sisters know they are losing hope. Occupy till I come again?

When you go back, things look smaller. You almost go back just to see how big you've become, how much has been diminished, how much you've grown away from the mattress that sags in the middle and the door where the concrete was painted with yogurt and water in a final attempt to grow moss over it. My parents fall asleep over their reading; my television burbles through the night; a raccoon or an opossum sacrifices a rabbit in the attic at dawn; and the department-store box of photographs at the bottom of the linen closet has split under its memorial load of faces that stuck by traditional remedies, preferring feverfew from the back garden to aspirin.

> _My aspens dear, whose airy cages quelled,_
> _Quelled or quenched in leaves the leaping sun,_
> _Are felled, felled, are all felled._

One day—if it comes—I may be someone's old darky, exercising my fictitious cultural birthright to run off at the mouth, telling someone who may insist on being called a Senufo-American how in my day so many—black, white, and other—were afraid of black teenagers in big sneakers with the laces untied, and three o'clock, when the high schools let out, was considered the most perilous hour for subway riders.

I will be on my feet and the Senufo-American will be suicidal to get away from me, as I sometimes felt in the presence of Grandfather, whose fear of forgetfulness I mistook as a wish to muddy my choices. I may elect myself a witness and undertake to remember when something more important than black, white, and other was lost. Even now I grieve for what has been betrayed. I see the splendor of the mornings and hear how glad the songs were, back in the days when the Supreme Court was my Lourdes, and am beyond consolation. The spirit didn't lie down and die, but it's been here and gone, been here and gone.

FOR THE BEST IN PAPERBACKS, LOOK FOR THE

In every corner of the world, on every subject under the sun, Penguin represents quality and variety—the very best in publishing today.

For complete information about books available from Penguin—including Pelicans, Puffins, Peregrines, and Penguin Classics—and how to order them, write to us at the appropriate address below. Please note that for copyright reasons the selection of books varies from country to country.

In the United Kingdom: For a complete list of books available from Penguin in the U.K., please write to *Dept E.P., Penguin Books Ltd, Harmondsworth, Middlesex, UB7 0DA.*

In the United States: For a complete list of books available from Penguin in the U.S., please write to *Dept BA, Penguin*, Box 120, Bergenfield, New Jersey 07621-0120.

In Canada: For a complete list of books available from Penguin in Canada, please write to *Penguin Books Canada Ltd, 10 Alcorn Avenue, Suite 300, Toronto, Ontario, Canada M4V 3B2.*

In Australia: For a complete list of books available from Penguin in Australia, please write to the *Marketing Department, Penguin Books Ltd, P.O. Box 257, Ringwood, Victoria 3134.*

In New Zealand: For a complete list of books available from Penguin in New Zealand, please write to the *Marketing Department, Penguin Books (NZ) Ltd, Private Bag, Takapuna, Auckland 9.*

In India: For a complete list of books available from Penguin, please write to *Penguin Overseas Ltd, 706 Eros Apartments, 56 Nehru Place, New Delhi, 110019.*

In Holland: For a complete list of books available from Penguin in Holland, please write to *Penguin Books Nederland B.V., Postbus 195, NL-1380AD Weesp, Netherlands.*

In Germany: For a complete list of books available from Penguin, please write to *Penguin Books Ltd, Friedrichstrasse 10-12, D-6000 Frankfurt Main I, Federal Republic of Germany.*

In Spain: For a complete list of books available from Penguin in Spain, please write to *Longman, Penguin España, Calle San Nicolas 15, E-28013 Madrid, Spain.*

In Japan: For a complete list of books available from Penguin in Japan, please write to *Longman Penguin Japan Co Ltd, Yamaguchi Building, 2-12-9 Kanda Jimbocho, Chiyoda-Ku, Tokyo 101, Japan.*